Laura,

Love is often unexpected!

KIM KARR

BLOW

Kim Karr
xoxo
2015

SHE'S ON THE EDGE.
ONE BREATH IS ALL IT WILL TAKE.
BLOW.

D1495344

Editor:
Mary-Theresa Hussey, Good Stories Told Well

Interior design and formatting:
Christine Borgford, Perfectly Publishable

Cover designer:
Hang Le, By Hang Le

Photographer:
Brice Hardelin, Brice Hardelin Photography

Cover model:
Cyril Mourali

PROLOGUE

FOUR MONTHS BEFORE

LOGAN

MILE AFTER MILE, I ran. Faster, feet pounding against the broken asphalt, breath crystalizing in the air. I'd been fleeing along the edge of the road for what seemed like eternity. Trucks zoomed past me, taillights fading in the distance, and still there were no sirens.

The moon slipped behind a cloud and left me moving blindly. Finally, a whistle filled the darkness. It was what I'd been waiting for.

Let's see how bad they want this.

I spun in the opposite direction and spotted the familiar red and blue lights. With a quick jump, I vaulted over the damaged guardrail and found myself tumbling down a steep ravine.

Landing on my stomach, blood dripped from my nose, and the taste of rust flooded my mouth. I didn't take the time to wipe it away. I had to keep moving. I'd started this game and I was going to finish it.

Quickly, I leapt to my feet and began to run again. When a sharp burning and throbbing pulsated in my right ankle, I knew my speed would be impaired. I must have twisted it in the fall. With everything I had, I tried to ignore the pain.

Adrenaline pumped through my bloodstream, making my heart race and giving me the strength I needed. I was no longer on the pavement and my terrain was harder to navigate. Trees, broken branches, and the sickening smell of the stagnant river surrounded me. I pushed onward.

It could have been worse—at least there wasn't any ice.

Still, it was fucking freezing out here. Snow fell around me. Chilled to the bone, I tugged my hat farther down over my ears.

I didn't stop, though—I had to keep going.

When my eyes were streaming from the cold and my leg muscles began to seize up, I knew my body needed a break. I'd find cover and play the wait-and-see game.

The dilapidated abandoned warehouse a few yards away seemed like my best choice. The hinges were rusted and appeared broken, but when I yanked on the door, it wouldn't open.

With a sigh, I stomped my salt-stained shoes in the slush I was standing in and looked around.

No sign of them, yet.

They'd be here soon enough.

My lungs burned as I bent over with my hands on my thighs in an attempt to catch my breath.

Poised to move in any direction, I thought about my decision to bait them.

Smart?

Stupid?

I couldn't believe the game of cat and mouse I had entered into—with the Boston Police Department nonetheless.

But I'd had enough. They'd been following me around for almost a week. Their more-than-obvious tail was bordering on harassment. Pushed to the limit, today I'd decided it was time to find out what it was all about. I was going to force their move. I left my vehicle and took off. They were tracking me, but what they were waiting for to approach me, I had no idea. At this point I had two choices—approach them or keep going. Since I didn't want to make it easy, I kept running.

Time seemed to be at a standstill as I looked around again. I knew they were close. Yet, as I searched my surroundings, there were no signs of life; everything around me was dark except for the golden glow from the cables of the Zakim Bridge.

The bridge.

I couldn't believe I'd ended up on the West End. That was more than a slight hike from the tip of the South End, where I'd started all this.

What time was it anyway?

Before I could look at my watch—the one my grandfather had given me, the one worth more than most of the houses in the surrounding area, the pretentious Patek Philippe with an authentic enamel dial and custom-made rubber watchband, the one almost a match for his own—a yellow beam of light shined down on me.

I guess the BPD finally decided to make their move.

A heavily Boston-accented voice carried through the wind. "Put your hands in the air where we can see them."

"Fuck me. Really? You're going to arrest me? For what?" My gaze scoured the area until they came into sight.

There were three of them and one of me. I didn't plan to keep running. I didn't need to, but even if I wanted to, there was nowhere to go. The riverbank was on one side and they were on the other. The trio moved closer and drew their weapons. I responded with equanimity and raised my palms. Still, not a single one of them lowered a gun. Step by step, they moved toward me. When they were about five feet away, I decided to help them out and face them, but before I could, the tallest figure lunged for me.

He pinned me to the wall. "I just wanted to talk. I wasn't going to arrest you until you assaulted me. But thanks for giving me a reason."

"I was putting my hands behind my back, asshole," I grunted.

"Right," he snickered.

Nostrils flaring, the fatter one grabbed me by my collar and yanked me to him. "Stop resisting."

What the fuck?

A quick punch to the gut and a kick to my leg had me belly down in a matter of seconds.

Most men would have been scared shitless, but not me. I grew up living in two very different worlds, the only similarity being power and greed. To look at me, you wouldn't believe I was capable of doing the things I had done. Born with a silver spoon in my mouth, I was the grandson of one of the wealthiest men in New York City.

It wasn't my trust fund background that anyone had to worry about, though. I was also the grandson of the former head of Boston's Blue Hill Gang—a piece of me I had tried to renounce. That I wanted to escape. But my family ties kept me bound. The Irish Mob might have changed since my father's father ran things, but there were some things that never changed.

I'd been raised in both worlds and these cops knew it. They were counting on the Blue Hill Gang part of me to greet them. That's not what they were going to get. "What exactly do you want with me?" I asked calmly, exuding that civility I'd been reared in. When no one answered, I pressed on. "Why have you been following me?" Although I knew my heavy breathing was starting to betray my calm façade, I didn't care. And besides, in the mood they were in, I doubted they noticed my breathing at all.

When one of them ground my face into the icy concrete, I knew he was more than aware of my forced calmness, and he didn't like it. He was trying to rattle me. Which cop it was, I couldn't tell. But then he muttered, "Did I tell you to talk?" with that thick accent of his and I knew who it was.

The reserve I'd been holding on to faded as soon as the coppery taste of blood seeped into my mouth for the second time tonight. Unable to restrain myself, my jaw tightened and I spoke through my teeth. "Do you know who I am?"

His laugh was cold, mirthless. "Do you think I give a shit?"

A large boot stepped forward and a voice of authority drew their attention. "Not here, not now."

Spit landed near my head as cuffs were slapped on me.

The cuffs were clenched good and tight around my wrists and I winced. There was no hiding the fact that I felt pain. My skin scraped mercilessly against the metal when I was yanked to my feet and I knew my wrists were already raw. Regaining my stability, it no longer seemed so dark. The neon green of the TD Garden billboards lit up their faces. And the sight wasn't pretty.

Anger.

Hatred.

Disgust.

The fatter one glowered at me with narrowed eyes. "Wearing a five-thousand-dollar suit doesn't make you any less of a piece of shit."

"Fuck you."

A shot to the jaw—my head swung and my face ached.

A jab or three to the stomach—it felt like every fist in the world was punching me.

The sock to my gut had my lungs swinging from my rib cage.

A club to the back of my knees took me to the ground like a pussy.

But it was the swift kick in the ribs that had me swallowing hard and gasping for air. "Fuckkk."

I looked up.

There was one.

Two.

Or all three of them on me—I wasn't sure.

"Get up," one of the men barked.

Blood was still dripping from my mouth, but this time I couldn't wipe it off even if I wanted to. One of them attempted to pull me up, but I shrugged off his help. I could get myself up.

Fuck you very much.

When I was on my feet again, I squared my shoulders and looked each of them in the eye, memorizing their faces should our paths ever cross again.

"Who's putting that shit on our streets?" one of them asked from the shadows.

The fatter one took a step closer. "Who's running the operation? Who's involved?"

I stared at him blankly and said nothing.

He moved even closer and barked, "When's the next shipment arriving? Who's it coming from? Where's it landing?" I could smell coffee on his breath.

A tirade of questions I couldn't answer.

Trying to tame my emotions, I lowered my eyes to study the ground. "I don't have a fucking clue what you're talking about."

Hissing loudly, he lurched forward, drew his gun, and pointed it in my face.

Shock arrested me.

What the fuck was this?

What was obviously the more sensible cop pushed the guy's arm down and muttered, "Follow procedure. Eyes are on us. We aren't even supposed to be the ones asking the questions."

Abruptly, the one with the gun still in his hand moved back, but his dark, cold eyes never left mine as he holstered his weapon and zipped up his police-issued brown leather jacket. "Just bring him to the car."

At his words, the flashlight shined again. "With the trouble you caused me tonight, you're fucking lucky someone else wants you."

"Who wants me?"

My only answer was three smiles.

"Wants me for what?" I pressed.

The yellow glow of his flashlight pointed toward an unmarked car with the back door swung wide open. Someone was waiting inside. Not just someone. A woman. Long red hair, long legs, and red high heels that matched the color of her lipstick.

"Who the fuck is she?"

"Blanchet," one of them mumbled under his breath with a snicker.

Another of the pricks shoved me her way. "You have the right to remain silent. Anything you say or do may be used against you in a court of law. You have the right to consult an attorney before speaking to the police and to have an attorney present during questioning now or in the future. If you cannot afford an attorney, one will be appointed for you before any questioning, if you wish. If you decide to answer any questions now, without an attorney present, you will still have the right to stop answering at any time until you talk to an attorney."

I turned to face the cop before getting into the back of the car. "I know my rights. I *am* a fucking attorney."

chapter
ONE

Elle

IMPRINTING, ACCORDING TO FOLKLORE, begins when you are gravitationally pulled toward another. When this occurs, your connections to everyone else become secondary. You'll do whatever it takes to protect the one you love. Keeping that person safe is the only thing that matters.

Imprinting doesn't only apply to romantic love interests. I imprinted on Clementine the moment I laid eyes on her.

At first sight, she took my heart.

Her lips were so pink.

Her skin was so soft.

Her big blue eyes so beautiful.

And her heart-shaped face was perfect.

The minute I saw her, I knew I loved her—that I'd do anything for her.

Now, her little hands patted my cheeks as she babbled on. I took one of them and kissed it. "Ready to see Daddy?"

Clementine's legs started kicking against my hips and her entire body quaked with glee.

She loved her daddy.

It was the first day of spring and I might have been a little too anxious for the warm weather. I attempted to take

Clementine to the small playground around the corner from Michael's office to watch the kids play, but the wind was too much for her.

Due to our early departure, it was closer to five o'clock than six when we entered the reception area of the Michael O'Shea Law Firm. Michael had fired his secretary this past Monday, and he had yet to replace her. And the paralegals left promptly at four thirty every Friday. So as I'd expected, the office was empty.

Michael's door was closed as usual. I removed our jackets and hung them on the iron coat tree before knocking lightly.

"Come in," he called.

I opened the old wooden door and it creaked loudly enough to make me cringe.

Michael looked different than usual. His dark hair was sticking up everywhere and when he raised his gaze from the yellow legal pad beside the stack of papers on his desk, I could see how tired he was.

"I hope you don't mind that we're a little early?" I asked.

He glanced at his watch. "I'm expecting a call from someone anytime now. Can you just bring her home and I'll meet you there?"

He seemed more distracted than usual, too.

Clementine held her tiny arms out and cooed, "Daddy."

"How's my girl?" he beamed as he stood. His suit was neatly pressed, his tie in place, his shoes shined. But his thirty-five years were showing. Lines creased his brow and there were bags under his eyes. For the first time, I could see the toll the past three months had taken on him.

"Sure," I answered him, and then I set Clementine down. "Just let her say hi and we'll go."

Clementine turned one last month, and took her first step shortly after that. Ever since, she doesn't like to be restrained. She toddled toward Michael in her hot-pink patent leather shoes and I couldn't help but smile.

Suddenly, the front door burst open. The echoing sound

of the doorknob slamming against the wall made me whip around. A man stood in the doorway, anger and hatred shooting through his eyes, looking like whatever he wanted was personal. Michael's office was located in an old brownstone in Boston's South End, and I considered the neighborhood relatively safe.

Until then.

Instantly, fear flowed through my veins. Horrified, I froze. My purse. My purse was all the way on the other side of the room. Clementine. All the air seeped from my lungs as terror ripped through me. I had to get to her. My head spun back around to calculate just how far away from me she was.

Not that far. My rubbery legs inched backward. She was between Michael and me.

The crazed man didn't seem to notice me, though. His eyes were on Michael, who was standing in the doorway to his office beside me. As soon as their stares locked, his voice boomed. "O'Shea, what kind of game do you think you're playing?"

His Boston accent was thick like Michael's, but his words were crystal clear. My heart stopped at the malice in his tone.

Fury covered Michael's face. "Sean, I'm not playing any game."

Michael knew the man?

The man's face screwed into a different position and his stance remained dominating, although his demeanor seemed to ease slightly.

Pitter-patter.

No, Clementine, stay in Daddy's office, I thought.

Pitter-patter.

The two men continued to stare at each other.

Taking the opportunity, I twisted and bent to scoop up Clementine, but Michael had beaten me to it. He enfolded her in his arms.

Thank God.

Thinking more clearly than me, he turned her away from the madman.

Voice gruff, the man asked, "Then what exactly are you up to?"

This had to be about *her*.

"We talked about this earlier. I told you everything I knew. There's no need for an outburst." Michael spoke curtly, somehow managing to keep his composure even in the face of potential danger.

Had he done this before?

Even though the man's anger seemed to have dissipated, my terror wasn't pacified in the least. The only thing I could think of was getting Clementine out of here and into safety. I began to assess the situation. My purse was with my coat on the rack over near the stairs, right next to Sean. That was out. I knew Michael kept a gun in his desk drawer, but as soon as I left the doorway, it would alert Sean. That was out too.

When Sean's gaze shifted from Michael to Clementine, then to me, his features softened and his demeanor changed.

I think he was noticing Clementine and me for the first time.

With deliberate focus, he stared at me for more than a beat, and a shiver ran down my spine. His stare lingered and then he blinked rapidly, as if he were seeing a ghost. Almost as if he were snapping out of a trance, his eyes became remorseful and he stepped inside. "We need to talk."

I flinched, bewildered as I slowed my breathing. I took a moment to study him. If he hadn't come in here all guns blazing, I would have thought him harmless. He appeared to be in his mid-fifties. Dressed in a dark suit, crisp white shirt, smooth silk tie, and wingtips, he looked nothing like the madman he'd seemed to be.

My heart finally started beating in time with my breathing, as Michael looked over at me, and with a nod, indicated I should follow him. He then slowly started walking toward the waiting area, the farthest point in the room from *this* Sean. I trailed behind. As soon as we reached the waiting area, he handed me Clementine. "Don't be worried. I won't be long."

"Should I take her home?" I asked.

He shook his head. "No. Just wait for me. Everything's fine."

I nodded, looking for evidence in his face that he wanted me to do something else. It wasn't there. I knew better than to ask if he wanted me to call the police.

Clementine squealed, not at all happy with the change-off as Michael hurried back into his office and the well-dressed man followed behind him. As soon as the door closed, shouting erupted. I couldn't make out what they were arguing about, but I would have bet it wasn't over a case.

I tried to harness my heavy breathing so my concern wasn't obvious to the baby. Clementine, however, was oblivious to the danger and wiggled in my arms. I took a few deep, calming breaths before I set her down. I knew Michael would never do anything that would endanger her, and that knowledge helped push me through the uncertainty.

Walking toward the foyer, I retrieved my bag and pulled out a package of animal crackers. "Are you hungry?"

She toddled over to me and reached for them.

"Hang on, let me open them, silly girl."

The bag didn't seem to want to tear. Michael's former secretary's desk was a few feet away and I crossed them quickly to find a pair of scissors. I opened the middle drawer. It was empty. I opened the one above it. It was filled with Michael's yellow legal pads. When I pulled out the center drawer, I hit gold. His former secretary had left her scissors. I grabbed them and cut open the bag.

"Mine, mine." Clementine was reaching for it.

I handed it to her and put the scissors away. When I did, a small, tented piece of legal paper fluttered out of the shallow drawer. I shouldn't have opened it when I picked it up, but curiosity got the best of me. It read, "Pick one."

Okay.

The bottom half was torn off so I didn't get to see the list to choose from.

"Juice," Clementine asked.

I put the note back and shoved the drawer closed.

While I searched in my bag for her juice cup, Clementine quickly darted for the stairs. I dropped the bag on the first step and let her crawl up them, hovering above her. "One, two, buckle my shoe. Three, four . . ." I sang to her as she took each step.

My heart had just stopped beating wildly in my chest when I felt the weight of someone's stare prickle my neck. I quickly whipped around and let out a small gasp. There was a man, younger than the one who'd just stormed in, standing in the entranceway. I should have been afraid after what just occurred, but I wasn't.

He didn't look like he wanted to hurt us.

As I took him in, the air was once again ripped from my lungs, but for an entirely different reason. I drew in a breath and wasn't sure if my reaction was the adrenaline high I was still on or if it was because he was utterly, unquestionably perfect from head to toe. Handsome face. Strong jaw. Sensuous lips. Beautiful eyes. Broad shoulders. Flat stomach. Narrow hips. And long legs.

He stared at me just as the other man had, and concern began to stir in my belly. I picked up Clementine and remained where I was for a moment, trying to decide whether I should leave or stay.

I couldn't read him at all.

His voice was soft yet husky when he finally spoke. "I didn't mean to startle you. The sign said to come in."

Despite my inability to read him, I felt secure enough to walk down the stairs. "It's fine. I just didn't hear the door."

His smirk threw me for a loop. "You were busy . . . singing."

Exhaling, I ignored the slow flush I felt spreading all over me. "I guess I was."

The handsome man's eyes swept over me as he said, "You carry quite a tune."

Warmth radiated all the way to the tips of my toes. That voice did something to my insides. Something that made my stomach dip. Not knowing what else to do, I laughed.

I sounded ridiculous.

And I needed to focus.

To snap out of it.

His chuckle in response was soft. I found myself staring at him again.

"Down, down," Clementine demanded, forcing me to pull my gaze away.

"In a moment, silly girl," I reassured her, and then once I handed her the cup I'd taken out of my bag earlier, I glanced back at the handsome stranger. "Are you looking for Michael?"

The heat in his eyes was undeniable.

"Actually, my father."

There was a strange feeling coursing through my body from head to foot. It had my head spinning. Finally, his words registered and I refocused.

Was he looking for the madman?

"Sean?" I asked in a surprisingly calm tone.

His slight nod told me I was right. My eyes studied him, as if my body somehow wasn't in sync with my mind. I couldn't help myself. He had a small jagged scar just under the inside corner of his left eye, but it didn't detract from his incredibly good looks. As I stared, I could see the similarity between him and the older man. Same square jaw, chiseled nose, same face shape.

But his hair wasn't peppered with gray. Instead it was the color of the most delicious chocolate. Brushed forward on his forehead, feathered toward his cheeks, and shaped perfectly around his ears, in such a way that he looked professional yet hip at the same time. But more than his hair, it was his eyes I noticed. They were the most vibrant hazel eyes I'd ever seen.

And they were still looking back at me. "So he is here?" he asked.

With a nod, I gestured toward Michael's office. "He seemed . . . upset."

Long lashes fluttered as his eyelids shut and then quickly reopened. "I hope he didn't do anything stupid."

"I hope you understand, there are no second chances." Sean said sharply.

The door had creaked open, and a heated conversation floated toward us.

"I do," was Michael's short but tense response.

The handsome stranger strode toward his father, his face now a picture of restrained anger. Sean spotted his son and narrowed his eyes. "I told you to wait in the car."

His son squared his broad shoulders. "And I told you to wait for me to park."

Clementine, still on my hip, was oblivious to the bitter exchange as she reached forward toward the handsome stranger. He was closer now, and the playful grin he gave her made my stomach flutter.

His eyes went from her to me, and I could feel the weight of his stare. I shivered under its intensity.

The moment was broken when Sean huffed and shot Michael one last glance. "I'll deliver your message and be in touch." He then rushed by me, glaring at his son. "Let's go," he ordered.

His son nodded toward Michael, and then he cut his gaze back to me. He was staring again.

I found myself staring back.

And I studied him further. His brows were slightly darker than his hair color. His skin was smooth. There were faint, very faint, freckles on his nose that perfectly matched mine. And his slight beard was scruffy in a way that looked like he shaved daily, just not close, or maybe it was a five o'clock shadow.

Looking at him made my body feel like it was made of Jell-O.

"Good night," he said. And then just like that, he turned and walked away.

My heart stilled. "Good night," I whispered.

I couldn't help but watch him. He had a slight swagger that made him fit right in on the streets of Boston. That walk had my eyes still glued on him as he strode out the door. On his neck and the way his short, wispy hair exposed his nape. On his pants and the way they hung low. On his tight ass. On his long and lean body.

I very rarely found anyone even mildly attractive, but I found him extremely so. I wondered how old he was. Not that it mattered. Still, even after the door closed, I couldn't get the picture of him out of my head.

I tried to turn my mind off.

To focus on what mattered.

But it was extremely difficult to do.

The gravitational pull I felt toward him was just undeniable.

chapter
TWO

LOGAN

"**W**HAT THE FUCK?" I barked.

My father kept walking and ignored me.

Furious, I grabbed his arm. "I said, what the fuck was that?"

Of all the things I'd helped him do for the Blue Hill Gang over the years, we'd always steered clear of women and children; they were off limits.

My father turned and glared at me. "Don't ever challenge my authority in public like that again."

Remorseful, I dropped my grip. "You're right. I shouldn't have done that in front of them, but you crossed the line."

He started to pace. "I thought he'd be alone."

At least he was rattled. "Maybe the next time you go off half-cocked, you'll make sure you know what you're walking into."

The sunlight was fading but I could still see the lines on my father's face. This kind of shit was wearing him down. He stopped and looked at me. "Look, Logan, I appreciate your help, but I told you on the way over here, I want you to stay out of this."

The anger I had just managed to suppress flared up.

With a step toward him, I pushed my finger into his chest. "You don't get to decide when I'm in and when I'm out."

"I saw the way you looked at her," he said, his voice more even now.

I shoved him, still pissed as fuck that he went in there. As soon as he saw the woman and child, he should have bolted. "I didn't look at her in any way. You don't know what you're talking about. All I want is for you to slow down and think before you involve people who don't need to be involved."

Maybe I had looked at that woman in a certain way, but it didn't mean shit. I might have grown up in two very different worlds—one where wealth bred cordiality and one where violence led the way—but somehow there was a part of me that wasn't divided, and that part would never fuck another man's wife.

My father's laugh was dry. "Slowing down isn't an option and you know it. Just stay away from her," he warned.

With an uneasy feeling, I said, "Promise me she will be left out of whatever Patrick has planned."

He shook his head. "That's not my call. He already thinks O'Shea needs a little motivation, which is why he sent me. Besides, Logan, chances are good that with what's on the line, Patrick has already looked at different ways to solve this problem."

I got right in his face. "I mean it. Make sure she's not one of them."

Visions flashed before me. Kidnapping. Rape. Torture.

My father looked around as if someone might be watching. "You know I can't. That's not my place. Besides, my visit today was strictly social."

"Right," I muttered under my breath.

He pointed his finger at me. "You need to calm down."

Irate, I balled my fists at my sides. "Don't tell me what I need."

If that horrible gut feeling wasn't worrisome enough, my father looked equally as troubled. "Go cool off. I'm going to see Patrick and I don't think it's a good idea for you to be anywhere even in his vicinity. I'll catch a cab."

I didn't argue. "Fucking best idea you've had in a while."

My cell started to ring and without a second thought, I walked past him and left his ass.

chapter
THREE

Elle

"WHO WAS THAT?"
As the thought escaped my lips, I cringed that I'd spoken it out loud. Michael wasn't paying attention to me, though; he was already putting his coat on, and his aloof demeanor snapped me out of my daze.

Either he hadn't heard me or he was ignoring my question. I waited patiently for an explanation but as the moments passed, I knew one wasn't coming. Especially when he reached over and took Clementine from me.

Once she was fully in his arms, icy blue eyes darted to mine. "You shouldn't have brought her here early."

I peered at him. "Excuse me?"

"You heard me," he responded tersely.

"Were you expecting him?"

"No," he snapped. "He called earlier and told me he'd call me back later, or I would never have had you meet me here."

I'd bitten back my irritation long enough. "Do you want to tell me what that was about?"

Michael grabbed Clementine's coat from the hook and put it on her. "You know what that was about."

His tone told me everything I needed to know.

This was about *her.*

He sighed and then spoke softly. "The mess she left behind is catching up with me sooner than I anticipated. I thought I had more time."

"What did he say?"

Michael closed his eyes. "He told me time's almost up."

"What are you going to do?"

He stared at me without answering.

"Who is he, anyway?" I asked as a new wave of terror overtook me.

The diaper bag was on the floor and he picked it up. "Someone you don't want to piss off. It's best if you pretend you never saw him."

"What's his full name?" I pressed as I slipped my trench coat on and then my hat.

Michael opened the front door. "Sean McPherson."

The cool wind hit my face and it blew my hat off when I stepped outside. "What does he do?"

"He's an attorney in Dorchester."

I walked down the steps and waited on the brick sidewalk. "That's not what I mean and you know it."

"It doesn't matter what he does. What matters is that you stay away from him." He sounded annoyed.

It pissed me off.

"I got that the first time you told me."

Without a second glance, he looked away.

I was exasperated but knew he wasn't going to say anything else. We'd been having the same type of conversation for the past three months.

"Where'd you park?" he asked.

"Around the corner."

Michael's Mercedes was sitting right in front of us. He nodded his head. "Get in. I'll drive you there."

I shook my head. "No, I think I'll walk."

"Are you okay?" he asked as he unlocked the doors.

"Yes, I'm fine. I just need some air."

Michael bent to buckle Clementine into her car seat and I flashed him a disgusted look. I couldn't believe he was really going to pull the "it's for your own benefit" crap.

When Clementine was secure in her seat, he turned toward me with remorse in his eyes. "I'm not purposefully keeping you in the dark."

With my brows raised, I responded emphatically, "Yes, you are."

Again, he glanced away. "Okay, you're right. I just don't want you involved."

"But I already am."

Michael shook his head and took a step toward me. "Stop saying that."

I sighed in frustration.

Michael gently put his hands on my arms. "Don't let McPherson rattle you. He went to school with my father; they're old friends. He's a hothead, but he wouldn't hurt me."

I wasn't so sure.

Having had enough, I shrugged out of his hold and stepped around him to kiss Clementine. "See you soon, baby girl," I said to her and nuzzled her nose.

I hated saying goodbye.

Michael opened his door. "You all set for tomorrow?"

"I've just got a few more things to do. I'm heading there now to finish up."

He gave me an encouraging nod. "Let me know what I can do to help."

I smiled and said, "I think I have it all under control."

"I know you do. You've done a fantastic job."

Praise wasn't what I looking for. The wind was cold and I dug into my pockets for my gloves. "Thanks."

"'Bye, Elle," he said, staring at me for a beat. When he got in the car and started it, he glanced at me before shutting his door. "I'm sorry I was short with you earlier."

"Don't worry about it," I told him.

Michael closed the door and turned back to check on

Clementine.

He was a good father.

I waved goodbye as the tires rolled forward, and then I put my gloves on and shoved my red felt hat farther down on my head.

As I walked up the sidewalk, I occupied my mind by trying to avoid getting my heels stuck in the cracks between the bricks.

It gave me something to do—I was feeling restless. I wasn't used to staying in one place for so long and it was beginning to catch up to me.

I gave up on not ruining my favorite boots when the late March drizzle began to fall and I had to move briskly to avoid getting too wet. As soon as I turned onto Tremont Street, I immediately saw that my rear tire was flat.

"Crap," I muttered as I stood there and the rain started falling harder.

I looked around for shelter. The corner bar I must have passed at least a dozen times was only a few feet away. I decided to go in and call AAA from there.

I didn't want to bother Michael about something I could take care of.

My damp, thin raincoat clung to my body and I reminded myself I should really buy a coat that was functional, not just fashionable. Shaking my head, I hurried toward the door to Molly's Pub, getting wetter and wetter with each passing moment.

As soon as I entered the vestibule, it was quiet enough for me to make the call. The operator connected me to the nearest station. "The mechanic will be at least thirty minutes," the attendant told me.

Contemplating what to do, I decided on a drink. "That's fine. I'll be at the bar at Molly's."

"Wait," she called. "What number should the mechanic call when he arrives?"

I gave her my cell but doubted I'd hear my phone. The music was already pretty loud from here. "Also, in case he has to come in, I'm wearing black—black raincoat, black pants—oh, and a red hat," I added.

She huffed and sounded annoyed. "Normally we ask that you wait by your vehicle but since it's raining, I'll let him know how to recognize you if he can't reach you."

"Thank you," I told her before hanging up.

Once I'd tucked my phone back inside my purse, I pulled open the interior door to reveal a very crowded bar. Not only was I certain I would never hear my phone, but there was also no way the mechanic was going to be able to spot me in here.

I'd have to keep my eyes peeled for him.

The large room was dimly lit, glowing with soft white light. There was a steady pulse of music. A small dance floor was filled with people. Most were standing close and talking, others were already dancing. The DJ booth was already manned and larger than the dance floor. Still, the bar was the showpiece. Glass lit shelves displayed bottle after bottle of liquor, in addition to glasses in every shape and size.

The space was eclectic. The dark paneling and old-fashioned parquet wood floors flowed into the modern space from the vestibule. I liked it.

The pub, as it was called, was more like a club, and it was jam-packed with the happy hour crowd. I considered leaving but decided against it.

It had been a long week, and one drink was deserved.

As if moving in slow motion, I tried to push through the crowd.

I wasn't dressed like the other women. Wearing leggings, boots, and a simple long-sleeved cream-colored blouse that buttoned up the front, I was dressed for winter even though it was spring. Most of these women had stripped out of their work jackets and sweaters to reveal sexy camisoles or sheer tops. They had planned for their night out.

The large bar was so crowded that I had to squeeze my

way through to it. A shove, a push, another shove, and I'd been turned around. That's when I saw another room that was also dimly lit, but seemed a lot calmer.

Unbuttoning my coat, I made a beeline for the space, ignoring the men who stared and women who leered. Booths lined the walls and there was a smaller bar with dozens of beer taps behind it. Still crowded, but nothing like the other side; I could at least move without being jostled. Luckily, a space opened up at the bar, and as I walked toward it, the female bartender glanced up from the person she was talking with.

It wasn't her I was looking at, though; instead my eyes landed on the patron sitting at the bar. I knew who it was immediately. I'd studied his backside no more than thirty minutes ago. It was the younger McPherson. He appeared to be sitting alone, chatting with the bartender.

My heart skipped a beat and I automatically slowed my approach.

Obviously curious, he twisted his head around when the bartender's eyes lingered on me a little too long. And when he saw me, he gave me a small smile.

That smile.

Wild, gorgeous, sexy.

Heart-stopping.

The current I felt surging between us earlier now reappeared with a jolt. It was unsettling. It made me think I should turn around, but I couldn't.

The magnetic pull was too strong to ignore. This was a dangerous situation. Uncharted waters. In the past, I'd never felt a strong enough attraction toward anyone to worry what it might mean. There had never been sexual chemistry for me with anyone else.

I never really cared.

It was better that way.

If there had been, I would have fought it.

But, right now, I couldn't.

Ignoring my intuition, I took off my hat. I immediately

regretted it. The bottom half of my hair hung sodden against my partially unbuttoned flimsy raincoat while the top half sprang to life. I was certain my normally ginger-colored locks looked tangerine.

The younger McPherson didn't seem to care. He stood and pulled out the empty bar stool next to his, motioning me toward him.

While my body urged me forward, my mind fought it every step of the way.

"What are you doing here?" he asked, and the sound of his voice made my spine tingle.

I wanted to be offended, but his tone wasn't in the least bit harsh. "Following you." I tried to sound nonchalant but I think my voice was more raspy than matter-of-fact, and I let out a slight laugh.

He didn't seem to notice that I was joking and I saw his jaw tense.

I sat down. "Relax. I'm kidding, just kidding."

Relief softened his features and he offered me his hand. "We haven't officially met. I'm Logan."

Logan. The young McPherson had a nice name. It suited him. He seemed formal in his choice of words but informal in his dress. And the hard lines of his body contradicted the softness of his voice.

I shook his hand. "Elle."

"So, Elle, where are O'Shea and the baby?"

Odd question, I thought, but answered anyway. "They went home."

With a raised brow, he asked, "What brings you into Molly's?" He paused for a second and the corners of his mouth quirked. "Besides following me," he said with a slight laugh of his own.

I withheld my laughter and frowned instead. "Flat tire." I pointed out the wall of glass to the pretentious white Mercedes SUV parked out front that I had yet to get used to and noticed a second door. Interesting—what I'd thought was a remodel might actually have been an addition.

Logan looked out the window and then glanced around. When he noticed I was watching him he said, "That really sucks."

"Yes, it does."

"I can change it for you," he offered.

I looked at him. His face was as breathtaking as he was charming. "Thank you, but that's not necessary. I already called Triple-A."

Logan glanced around again and finally leaned against the bar. "Then I'll buy you a drink while you wait."

His confidence turned me on.

My eyes slid down his body. I shivered—cold to the bone and more aware of his movements than I should have been.

In what seemed like a lifetime ago, when the rare urge for male companionship would strike, I'd simply go into a bar and pick up a man. It was easy. An art learned over years—lipstick bold, skirt short, heels high. Men liked women who looked sexy. They flirted with me. Bought me a drink. Complimented me on my eyes, my hair, my body. They didn't know they didn't have to—that was why I was there, after all. To have sex. No questions. No repeats. And even better, on my terms, which meant little conversation and no phone numbers. Relationships just weren't in the cards for me.

I wasn't certain Logan McPherson met those no-strings-attached criteria, but then again, my life was different now. And that's why I needed to leave. My resolve wasn't as strong as it had once been. My emotional blockade had been slowly crumbling since Clementine entered my life. I had to leave. Yet, I didn't.

He continued to gaze at me, waiting for me to respond to his offer.

I knew I shouldn't give in, but I didn't have the will-power to turn him down. Words eased out of my mouth that shouldn't have. "Sure. Something to warm me up," I answered, rubbing my hands together.

With a single nod of his chin, he looked down at me for a beat or maybe two. Then he scanned the bar again. Even distracted, he was mesmerizing. After a few moments, he turned around and motioned for the female bartender he had been chatting with when I first arrived.

Although the other side of the bar was packed, this side wasn't quite so crazy. However, the tables were completely occupied. As soon as she slid two plates of burgers and fries to a waitress, she hurried toward him. "What can I get you?"

I swiveled around in my seat and noticed a cup of coffee in front of him and another in front of me with a red lipstick stain on it. I wondered if that was why he was searching the bar.

Was the person who had been sitting here returning?

A girlfriend perhaps?

"Two shots of Jameson," he said.

"Coming up." The bartender's smile was wide when she looked at Logan, like she thought she might just hit the jackpot later. It irritated me. She stretched and her flat belly visibly reflected in the mirror in front of her. I caught Logan's gaze tracing the lines of her body as she reached higher, exposing more skin, and that irritated me more. But then I realized it was my gaze he was watching.

Our connection wasn't broken as the bartender set two shot glasses between us and slowly began to pour the amber-colored liquid.

When she finished, I broke our gaze with a laugh. "You're staring."

He didn't seem to mind that he'd gotten caught. "How about you take your coat off."

Again, not a question.

"No, I'm fine. I won't be staying long."

The music seemed to be getting louder and he edged a little closer. "Uh-huh. The garage told you they'd be here in about thirty minutes, didn't they?"

"They tell everyone that," the bartender blurted out.

My eyes darted to her in annoyance and then back to him. The young McPherson didn't find her intrusive behavior funny either. Then again, other than the cute wave he gave Clementine earlier, he seemed so serious. "Thanks for the drinks," he said dismissively.

She took the hint and returned to the other end of the bar.

His gaze traced the lines on my face and I couldn't help but wonder if he was trying to guess how old I was. "She was right—all the garages around here tell you it will take much less time than it actually does."

"Why would they do that?"

He raised a brow. "Why does anyone do anything—for money. The economy is suffering in South Boston. All the small businesses are hurting for cash and want to make sure they secure your business."

"Well, I guess I'd better take my coat off, then."

The raincoat had soaked through, so ridding myself of it would be a relief.

Someone pushed toward the bar behind me just as I stood, nudging me forward an inch or two. Logan reached to grab my arm so I wouldn't stumble.

His touch made me gasp. Concentrating on calming my nerves, I didn't notice that my blouse was wet, and most likely see-through, until my coat was off.

His eyes darted to my chest.

Yep, definitely see-through.

Without taking his eyes off me, he took my coat and shoved it beside his. We were both still standing, facing each other, very, very close. People on either side of us pushed us even closer as they wormed their way toward the bar. His eyes looked darker than I remembered, and his chest seemed to rise and fall more quickly than it did before.

"Aren't you going to drink that?" He nodded toward the shot.

My knees felt a little wobbly and I quickly sat down

before they gave out. "Yes, I think I will."

Logan handed me one of the shots. "Irish whiskey. If it doesn't warm you up, it will definitely put hair on your chest."

With a small laugh, I took the glass and his fingertips grazed mine. My body tingled, but I ignored the feeling and with a *tsk* I said, "I hope not."

He blatantly eyed the front of my blouse.

The heat of his stare was just too much and I found myself uncharacteristically downing the shot without a second thought. The liquid burned my throat, but it was worth it because my body began to warm instantly. Whether it was from the liquor or him standing so close, though, I wasn't sure. When I was done, I slammed the glass down.

His slow grin caused a sweet ache right between my thighs. As if he knew it, he inched even closer. Leaning forward, he whispered, "No hair, I hope."

Again, I sputtered out a laugh. "No, I think I'm safe," I managed around my giggle.

His eyes now on my face, he passed me the other shot.

I held my hand up. "No, that's yours."

Finally, he sat down, which put some distance between us. Not much, but some. "Two shots are guaranteed to light a fire inside you."

I was already heating up.

For a moment, we seemed to be trying to get a read on each other. After a beat, I shoved the glass back toward him and said, "Thank you, but I've had my limit."

Bemused, he asked, "Only one? That's your limit?"

The deep tenor of his voice caused my heart to pound, and I couldn't help but notice how his eyes gleamed bright when the words escaped his throat. I played along and raised a brow. "Are you trying to get me drunk?"

His low chuckle ticked my eardrum. He pushed the shot away. "Absolutely not. I wasn't going to let you drink it anyway. You're driving." He winked.

"Oh, you're an alpha male, are you?" I teased.

Logan's laugh rasped. "Absolutely not."

I tilted my head sideways in doubt.

There was a twinkle in his eyes. "You don't believe me. I'm wounded."

I found myself giggling.

"O'Shea," the bartender called from behind the bar.

The name didn't register.

"White Mercedes SUV. Flat tire," she called out louder.

Finally, it did and I raised my hand and shouted, "That's me!"

She leered at me and pointed to the door.

I turned to see a man in a blue quilted jacket. I'd completely forgotten about him. Guess with my hat off, I was lost in the crowd and he couldn't find me either. "Looks like they arrived quickly," I quipped, the corners of my mouth turning up slightly.

Logan glanced at his watch, which looked extremely expensive. "Twenty minutes—that has to be record timing," he commented, the inflection of his voice much flatter than it had been.

Rushing, I hopped off the stool a little too fast and the room started to spin, causing me to lose my balance.

Logan jumped up and grabbed me. Our bodies were aligned in such a way that we were thigh-to-thigh, belly-to-belly. It was then that I noticed just how tall he was. Six foot one was my guess. While he steadied me, he spoke and his warm breath caressed my neck. "Whoa, I see why you've got a one-drink minimum."

"I'm fine," I said, trying to find my balance.

"Where are your keys?" he asked.

I stared at him.

I didn't know him.

I shouldn't trust him.

I didn't trust anyone.

"Where are your keys?"

A command, this time voiced as a request.

Something in his eyes made it seem okay, and with a

little hesitation, I pulled the ring from my small black bag but held on to them.

With his finger pointed at me, his tone quieted. "Sit back down. I'll take care of this."

Concerned, I found myself hopelessly trying to excuse my behavior. "No, really, I'm fine. I skipped lunch and got dizzy for a second. That's all."

That stare scorched me again and for a moment I think he considered leaving me my keys.

But then I went to take a step forward and felt my equilibrium spin off kilter again.

Wow, that shot really went to my head.

Logan grabbed them and with almost a triumphant smirk, he was twirling the key ring around his finger before I even realized it. "Let me be the alpha male you think I am and take care of this."

Even though I laughed, I thought that was probably a good idea. Still, I was anything but a damsel in distress and didn't want to appear that way. I blinked a few times before conceding. "Thank you."

That smirk remained as he slid his coffee cup my way. "Here, drink this. I haven't touched it yet."

I gave in much too easily as I reached for the cup of black java. "Okay. I've already given them all my info."

The mechanic gestured toward the door and as Logan followed him outside, I watched his swagger. Concern poured through my veins. Sure, he was handsome, charming, maybe a bit brooding in the sexiest way. Still, I'd gone without physical attraction my whole life. Never really wanted to feel it. Only rarely went looking for it. Most of the time I didn't need it. But the way my body reacted to his terrified me. I couldn't fight it even if I wanted to.

Not even when I'd met my very first boyfriend right out of college had I experienced such a lustful reaction. Then again, that's what had made Charlie so right for me. We were both looking for companionship and the sex was secondary. In hindsight, look at how badly that ended. Sadness swept through me as the memory of him seeped from the place I'd stored it long ago.

"Hey love," he said the first time he laid eyes on me.

His charm got me right away.

He looked like a Charlie. Dark hair, big build, medium height, beautiful eyes. Charlie was a businessman from London with the sexiest English accent I'd ever heard. We were both working for the International Trade Center in Paris when we met. He worked in finance and had been transferred just weeks before I'd arrived. This was my first job after college and I was so nervous. It couldn't have been more perfect that I'd found him. During the day we both worked. He went to the office while I visited local exporters, purchasing the finest merchandise to sell in the States. At night and on the weekends, we explored the city together. We became best friends and since I'd never had one, I treasured him.

Over the course of my four-month stay, we did what I never thought I would do: fell in love. Unable to stand the idea of not having him to talk to every day, I made Paris my home base. ITC didn't care where I conducted business, so for the next year, I traveled to international markets, always returning to find Charlie anxiously waiting for me.

When the day came that he began to talk about marriage, I was forced to tell him what I had yet to confess. Charlie did his best to accept that hard truth but in the end, I knew he wouldn't be able to. As the weeks passed he started to pull away. I even thought about ending things before he eventually would, but I just couldn't.

He was my first love, my only love. I was young and naïve, and I mistakenly thought love conquered all.

I learned the hard way that it couldn't be farther from the truth.

"I wouldn't bother." The bartender's voice brought me back from the darkness of my past.

I swirled around on my stool to face her. "I think you have the wrong idea about us"—I paused to read her name tag—"Molly."

She dumped both of the cold coffees down the sink in front of her. "I saw the way you were looking at him and I just thought you should know he never gets attached."

If only she knew that made him all the more perfect.

"I appreciate your warning, but like I said, it's not what you think."

A hand touched my back and I felt a spark as Logan leaned forward. "What's not what you think?"

Feeling oddly shy, I barely glanced at him. "You and me. I was just telling Molly that she had the wrong idea about us."

He sat down and I felt those hazel eyes zero in on me.

Shedding the shyness that a woman my age had no business feeling, I met his gaze. I must have been crazy, seeing in his expression that he hoped she didn't have the wrong idea about us. I blinked, knowing my interpretation couldn't have been right.

Logan tapped the bar with his fingers. "Don't listen to anything Molly has to say. She grew up next door to my grandfather and thinks she knows me."

Molly hit him with the towel she had slung over her shoulder. "I do. We've known each other practically our whole lives."

He threw her a warning look I didn't understand and then shrugged. "True, but after I was fifteen, I only visited once a year at Christmas and one month every summer. So you tell me, how well can you know me?"

She frowned; obviously she didn't agree with him. "Better than most people."

He tossed her another warning look.

"Molly," an older man bellowed from a doorway behind the bar.

She rolled her eyes. "Coming, Dad."

The man lifted his chin. "Logan."

"Frank," Logan replied flatly.

"I'll see you around. I have to get back to my club. My

father prefers to be over here," Molly said with a glimmer in her eye.

"Yeah, sure." Logan's tone didn't give anything away.

"Molly," the man said sternly. "The DJ is having some technical difficulty."

With another roll of her eyes, she replied, "Coming, coming," then she turned back. "You'd think my father would know what to do when the breaker blows." With that, she hurried toward the older man and followed him through the door, which must have connected to the club-like side.

Logan swiveled on the stool and his knees touched mine. More sparks shot through me. I wondered if he felt them too. If he did, they must not have bothered him because he didn't move away. "So I've got some bad news."

I tilted my head. "Oh, no, what is it?"

"Don't shoot the messenger, but there's no spare tire and the vehicle is going to have to be towed to the station."

"Can't he just patch it?"

He shook his head. "No way. I saw it and it's beyond repair."

I looked at my watch and sighed. Michael probably already had Clementine home by now. Distressed, I said, "Are you sure there's nothing they can do? I need to get to work tonight and it's a little far to walk."

Logan became very serious. "The tire isn't repairable. He has to order a new one. Unfortunately the station doesn't stock the one that fits your SUV. He says it will be ready tomorrow afternoon. It's doubtful any garage around here stocks an expensive tire like that, but do you want to call your husband and see if he knows of someplace else you might want to try? Because there is no way you should walk anywhere this late."

"My husband?" I laughed out loud.

Logan furrowed his brows. "Yeah, O'Shea."

I laughed again. "Michael isn't my husband."

His eyes flickered in surprise. "Sorry, I just assumed."

I swore I saw a shadow of doubt so I held my left hand

out. "See, I'm not married. No ring."

Strangely, relief seemed to cross his features.

I'd already checked out Logan's hand back at Michael's office and I hadn't seen a ring, or a tan mark, or an indentation, so my assumption was the young McPherson wasn't married either. But the lipstick-stained cup meant he might have a girlfriend.

"Is the little girl your daughter?" he asked.

I shook my head. "No. Clementine is my niece. Michael is married to my sister."

Is, was. I wasn't really sure which, since she was MIA.

Logan didn't look confused, but I still thought I should probably explain. "My sister has been in rehab for the past three months, and—"

Before I could finish the well-rehearsed lie Michael had told me to tell everyone, the door opened, and with the music on pause the mechanic's voice bellowed through the bar, "O'Shea! Elizabeth O'Shea."

"That's me," I said, this time to the man in the blue quilted jacket calling my sister's name. I was Gabrielle Sterling. Long ago called Gabby, now called Elle. But after so many months, I was used to being called by my sister's name. It was the name in which the car was registered and the name on the Triple A card. It was the name on the credit cards I used. It was the name associated with everything in her life. It was the name I never got a chance to call her.

Logan looked at me questioningly.

My plan was that I would use her credit cards and car only temporarily. Until my business got up and running. Unless she returned first, then I'd be more than happy to return them both. I didn't like my situation, I didn't like relying on Michael, but if I wanted to stay stationary and be near Clementine, I didn't have much of a choice. I gave Logan a little shrug. "Michael's letting me use her car until I get my own." That was all he needed to know.

He said nothing.

I didn't like how my statement sounded and felt very

uncomfortable admitting it to him. "I should take care of this. Thank you for the drink," I said, standing and reaching for my keys.

He placed them in my palm. "Tell him to take the car. I can drive you wherever you need to go."

"No, that's not necessary. I'll just ride with him to the station and call for a rental. I'm sure they have a company they work with."

Looking nervous, he shook his head. "Not a good idea."

My eyes locked on his and all I could see were the brown flecks surrounding his green irises. They were mesmerizing. My tongue felt tied for a moment, but finally I spoke. "Why do you say that?"

"I'm not really sure—something about him seems off."

"Oh, the alpha male thing," I gave a huff of laughter. "I'll be fine."

Concerned, he said again, "I'd rather you didn't ride with him."

I wasn't sure what to think but felt I should trust his judgment. "I'll take a cab then. I can't ask you to drive me around. You know what? Maybe I should just call around and try to find someone who has the tire in stock."

He looked at his very expensive watch, then back at me. "Like I side, doubtful. The tire is too expensive for most shops to keep in stock. Besides, it's a Friday and after six. Good luck getting anyone to answer, even through Triple-A."

He had a point.

"Just let me help you," he insisted.

"I don't want to inconvenience you. Like you said, it is Friday night. Don't you have a date or somewhere else to be?"

The lipstick-stained coffee cup came to mind.

He stared at me and then ever so slightly shook his head. "The only thing you're interrupting is my planned date with the Four Seasons room service menu. But since you're going to let me take you out to dinner, I think I can forgive you for that one transgression."

Wariness crept over me. "How do I know I can trust you?"

His grin was wide. "If you don't know that by now, I can't help you answer that."

I tilted my head in contemplation.

Logan was determined, and he continued to watch me.

A fleeting, what-do-I-have-to-lose thought had me smiling at him and then when he smiled back, I thought about how long it had been since I shared a moment like this with anyone.

Why not? So what if I'm attracted to him? Dinner is dinner; it doesn't mean things between us need to go farther if I don't want them to. Even if it does, so what if we fuck? That's what two people do who are attracted to each other. My terms. My rules. I'll make that clear. One night and we could both move past this strange attraction. It could work out perfectly for the both of us. And besides, I did skip lunch and I'm hungry.

My eyes slid toward the mechanic, who appeared to be losing his patience, and without further hesitation, I nodded in agreement. "Dinner it is. Just give me a minute."

As I walked, I felt Logan's eyes on me and knew the attraction was mutual, but for some reason that knowledge didn't make me second-guess my decision. I quickly looped the oversized silver and black fob off my key ring and handed it to the mechanic. "Here's the key. Can you deliver the vehicle to where I work at 40 Charles Street tomorrow once it's ready?"

He nodded and then scribbled down the address. "The total will be four hundred and sixty dollars—that includes the delivery fee of fifty dollars."

Once upon a time, I might have winced at the amount for a single tire, but leading a life of domesticity was expensive, as I'd come to learn over the past three months. Without hesitation, I pulled out my credit card, or rather my sister's, and handed it to him.

Michael and I had an agreement: he'd cover me until my

new business got on its feet and I could pay him back. In return, while he did what was needed to make things right for what Lizzy had done, I would help him with Clementine. She had a nanny, but with her mother missing and out of the picture, she needed as many constants in her life as possible. Michael of course, did his best, but he did work a lot. Things were going to have to change soon, but since my arrival I had created a routine with her that worked wonderfully—Wednesday morning breakfasts, Friday afternoon walks, Saturday night sleepovers, and Sunday dinners.

The mechanic handed me the pink carbon beneath the yellow original.

"Have a good night," I said.

He gave me a nod. "You too."

Hmmm . . . he seemed fine. I'm not certain what Logan found to be off about him.

The music had started to blare again, this time even louder. "Ready?" Logan's warm breath was in my ear before I'd even turned around. I heard him just fine, as if my body had become attuned to his in this short period of time.

That should have worried me. But the shiver that ran down my spine erased any worries. With a slight turn of my head, I responded, "I am, but you don't even know where you're taking me. I could be asking you to drive me across town for all you know."

The crowd had seeped into this room without me even noticing and it was no longer the after-work crowd. This was the Friday night crowd. The space between the booths and the bar acted as a second dance floor. Bodies pressed together. People moved. Sweat dripped down women's bare backs and men's necks. The tempo seemed to overtake everyone and lust was in the air.

Did he feel it too?

The pounding pulse of the music had me lost for a moment. I almost considered pressing myself against Logan and wrapping my arms around his neck so we could move together in a sinful manner.

Logan, on the other hand, didn't seem to share that idea. With his jacket on, he slid beside me and handed me my hat and coat. Bringing me back to the conversation I'd almost forgotten about, his mouth was at my ear. "That's not true. I know that first we're going to eat at a much quieter place I know around the corner. After that, I'm happy to take you wherever it is you work that you considered walking to because you had to get there so badly. And later I'm taking you back to your place."

There was an edge of expectation in his voice that coming from another man might have caused me to walk away, but from him, it seemed harmlessly flirtatious.

"Lead the way," I said, needing to escape this orgy-filled place that seemed to be affecting my libido in the strangest of ways.

Leading us through the throng of bodies and out the door, he turned and asked, "Do you know what the Irish say about green eyes?"

"That they're always smiling?" I guessed.

He shook his head. "That they leave an invisible trail of magic surrounding everything they see."

I laughed sarcastically. Little did he know, nothing could be farther from the truth.

chapter

FOUR

LOGAN

"**W**HAT'S SO FUNNY?"

She averted her gaze. "Nothing."

Elle wore a sad smile that told me her laughter was anything but genuine. And for some insane reason, that only made me want to fuck the sadness right out of her—right where we stood.

Aside from the demons I could see in her eyes, she was sexy as hell, and even though I knew better than to be captivated by her, I couldn't help myself. There was just something about her. And knowing she was unattached . . . That didn't help things in the least.

With a shake of my head, I opened the door. The sky was dark, but at least the rain had let up. I looked around but didn't see anyone. Even so, I pulled out my knit cap and tugged it over my head.

If someone spotted me with her, we were both fucked.

Paranoid?

Nope.

I knew something wasn't right as soon as I saw her tire. Someone had slashed it. And there was no way it was a coincidence. Patrick must have already found out about her and I was pretty sure that mechanic's shop was on his pay-roll. "This way." I directed her to the right, veering down the closest alleyway.

Her big green eyes weren't just looking at me; they were watching me, much in the same way I had been watching her since she first turned around at O'Shea's office.

"What?" I asked.

"Where are we going?"

"To an authentic Irish pub."

Elle eyed me suspiciously.

"What?" I found myself asking again.

"You mean that wasn't one?"

"Ha, once upon a time it was, until Frank let his daughter take over. Molly rented the abandoned space next to the original structure and ever since has been slowly converting the place into a dance club."

She whipped her head toward me with an excitement in her eyes that I could have eaten up. "I knew it. I could tell the moment I walked in."

"Yep, it's obvious, but Frank refuses to give up the pub even if the club is encroaching on his space."

She was still facing me, and there was another glimmer in her eye.

"What?" I asked yet again, this time raising a brow.

She bit her lip. "Are you even old enough to drink?"

Surprised, I almost choked. "You're kidding me, right?"

"No, I'm not." She wasn't about pretense. It was a welcome change. And it was such a turn-on.

Amused, I asked, "Just how old do you think I am?" I walked ahead and turned to face her. I wanted to see her expression when she answered.

She hesitated a moment before answering, "Not quite twenty-one."

"Ahhh . . . you're killing me."

She smiled. "I'm totally serious."

I kept walking backwards. "You're a few years off. I'm twenty-seven."

Her eyes swept over me again and then narrowed in doubt.

The alleys were empty. No one was around, and I felt myself start to loosen up. No one was going to see us. I put my hand on my heart. "I'm wounded. You don't believe me?"

With a hint of smile she said, "No, I don't."

Now I found myself reaching into my back pocket and pulling out my wallet. Opening it, I handed her my driver's license. "Here you go—definitive proof."

She bit her lip as she studied it.

I wanted to bite it for her. I wanted to taste her lips on mine. I wanted to feel her skin and touch her hair. It wasn't only one thing that attracted me to her; it was everything about her. The way she smelled, the sound of her voice, the way she walked, the way she made me laugh. I shouldn't be admitting it, not even to myself.

Her grin widened. "Yes. It appears you are older than twenty-one."

"Phew. Now I can sleep tonight knowing you believe me."

She tried to contain a giggle with a hand over her mouth.

I stopped and she almost ran into me. "And you?" I countered, leaning inches from her lips.

She handed me my wallet and stepped back. "How old do you think I am?" she teased.

I took my time. I knew we should hurry off the street. I knew I was being stupid. But I didn't want to rush this moment. I was enjoying it too much. "I don't know. Come here."

She easily followed my lead.

I dragged her under the streetlight and let my eyes sweep over her. I didn't have to, though. I'd already memorized her features. She had a small nose, heart-shaped lips, smooth porcelain skin with a smattering of freckles on her nose, hair the color of cinnamon, and a body that would make any hot-blooded male look twice. I scratched my chin. "Hmmm . . . I'm not sure. My age. Maybe a year or two younger."

She threw her head back. "Just a few minutes ago you thought I was old and married."

Practically mesmerized, I watched her carefree style. She wasn't like most women. Or most of the women I came in contract with—the ones from the New York City upper echelon who prided themselves on packed social calendars and their looks. She seemed tough. Able to take care of herself. She seemed to be a fighter, like me. "First of all, I only thought you were married. You're the one putting the word *old* with married," I playfully countered.

She pulled her lip between her teeth in contemplation. "You might be right," she conceded.

Our eyes locked and I had to lick my lips as she chewed on hers again.

"What did you say?"

She rolled her eyes.

My grin couldn't be erased even if I tried.

"I turned thirty last December," she blurted out.

"An older woman." I winked.

She started walking.

When I took my place beside her, she glanced over at me and nonchalantly joked, "Just call me Mrs. Robinson."

My cock twitched at the thought of her seducing me—the game of a young college boy and an older experienced woman definitely had my attention. And although I'd already let my intentions for the evening be known, hers weren't clear and I couldn't pass up the opportunity to make sure she was on board with the fact that we were going to fuck. So I raised a brow and told her, "I'd love to."

Headlights lit up the alleyway and a car started to slow. My guard instantly went back up. My body tensed and my stance changed. The car passed and someone got out. My eyes focused, my hands ready for action, I watched as an older Chinese woman pounded on the back door of a nail salon. False alarm. Still, the moment between us was broken. Awareness took over where I had allowed playfulness to wrongly occupy my mind.

With my hands shoved in my pockets, I put my head down.

What was I doing?

Once the car passed, I looked at her. She hadn't noticed the car or my reaction. She was still lost in our Mrs. Robinson conversation and her response caught me off guard.

She was blushing.

I hadn't been expecting that.

And right then, I knew I was in trouble.

chapter
FIVE

Elle

I GLANCED UP AT the sign above the restaurant—The
Hornet's Nest.

How appropriate. I shouldn't have agreed to have dinner with Logan. After all, he was the son of the man Michael
had just told me to stay away from.

Yet I couldn't fight the sexual tension between Logan
and me. I'd never felt anything like it. And I wanted to give
in.

But I knew better. Life had taught me that lesson long
ago.

Don't get too close or you will get burned.

The restaurant was tucked away down an alley just
around the corner from Molly's. It was out of the way and
off the beaten path. I was thankful. There would be little
chance of running into anyone who knew Michael. I hadn't
decided what I'd tell him, if anything.

Logan pulled open the door and as I walked past him,
I could feel my cheeks still blazing. I had no idea what my
schoolgirl reaction was all about, but it had to come to an
immediate end. I intended to put my mind to it. But that
wasn't what happened. Instead, I stumbled to a stop when

his hand grazed my back.

Thank God he was reading a list of tonight's specials and hadn't noticed. With nonchalance, he stood beside me. Luckily, I quickly regained my composure as I observed the restaurant. Polished wood paneling and brass fixtures made the place appear slightly less bar-like. Whereas Molly's pub side looked like a hole-in-the-wall brewery, this place looked like an authentic American-style Irish pub.

"Shall we?" Logan motioned toward a booth in the back corner. He stripped off his jacket as I slipped out of my raincoat, and he tossed them both on the red leather bench. My gaze lingered over him and my pulse raced as we sat across from each other. The leather seat might have been worn, but I melted into it without a problem.

My nerves had my palms seeking the cool, smooth surface of the table separating us. My focus flicked away from Logan and landed on the menus that sat against the wall. Logan's gaze followed mine and he handed me one before I could reach for it. "It's nothing fancy but they have the best burgers around, if you like burgers."

I opened my menu. "Cheeseburgers happen to be one of my favorite foods."

He looked pleased.

Just as I started perusing the menu, the waitress approached. "What can I get you to drink?"

Still feeling the effects of the shot, I decided against alcohol. "A Coke, please."

"The same," Logan said. "And I think we'll both have the special cheeseburger and fry basket."

The waitress looked at me. "How'd you like your meat cooked?"

"Medium."

She looked at Logan. "The same," he answered.

She walked away and I glanced at him. "You're at an Irish pub and you don't order beer with your burger?"

Amused, his chin was down but his eyes lifted to mine. "No."

"Isn't that part of the whole Irish experience?"

"You know, I never thought of it that way, but I guess a Guinness does typically accompany a burger in a joint like this."

I dropped the subject. He didn't drink. It was obvious— he hadn't touched that second shot of Jameson's at Molly's. And I had a feeling there was more to it than he wanted to let on.

My thoughts started to wander.

He was a lot like Charlie.

Practical in his thinking.

Short and to the point.

Serious but also funny.

Charming.

However, there was that one difference: looking at him made me breathless. This strange sexual chemistry that existed between us hadn't been there with Charlie and me.

Aside from Michael's warning, Logan was just what I needed to help cure the restlessness I had been feeling lately.

Yes, I was in trouble.

"Here you go." The waitress delivered our Cokes and I picked up my straw to help disguise the yearning I thought must be obvious.

"So tell me about yourself, Mrs. Robinson," he asked. Logan knew what he was doing. How to set the tone and make the moment intimate.

I opened my straw and playfully blew my wrapper at him. "That's enough of the Mrs. Robinson business."

The comfort level between us was as high as the sexual tension. I'd never sat like this with a man I was attracted to and felt so at ease. Not even with Charlie. I almost felt like I was sixteen and out on my first date. Nervous in a way, but excited.

Growing up, I hadn't been allowed to date, not that I ever would have wanted to anyway. No, my childhood memories wiped any dreams of knights in shining armor and Prince Charmings right off the table. I always looked at it like this—you either became someone like your parents or stayed as far away from being anything like them as you could. My sister became the former. I became the latter.

Logan's fingers crunched the wrapper and he flashed me a flirty grin. "Let me try that again. Okay, Elle, how about you tell me about yourself?"

I fought past my emotional reaction to the question and turned the question around. "How about you tell me about yourself first, Logan."

He reached his arms out. "I'm an open book."

With my mouth barely around my straw, I mumbled, "For some reason, I doubt that."

Just like me, he was able to compose himself in a moment's notice. It was obvious; we were both good at hiding things. Which was exactly what he did.

Smirking, he said, "Fine, don't believe me. Ask me anything."

First-date questions should be easy. Like, what's your favorite color? What do you like to read? But I wasn't one for pretense. Small talk wasn't my thing. I had questions I wanted to know the answers to. And besides, we both knew this was no first date. I put my elbows on the table and tucked my hands under my chin. "Okay. Why are you driving your father around?"

Quite abruptly, he turned his head toward the door before turning back to meet my gaze and whispered, "His driver's license was revoked. One too many DUIs."

Plausible. Still, I contemplated his answer. "Then why didn't you drive him home after you left Michael's?"

Elbows on the table, he leaned forward. "Because he's a fucking hothead and he pissed me off, so I left his ass."

I tried not to laugh. I was certain the situation wasn't funny. Instead, I moved my head closer to him. "Sounds like you are too."

He shrugged. "Sometimes I am, but I try not to be."

I liked that he didn't have a filter—it made him seem

more honest.

On to question two of I didn't know how many. I had way too many questions for the man who was somehow connected to my sister and Michael. "Why are you staying at the Four Seasons if you live in Boston?"

Logan picked up his glass and sipped from it. "I don't live in Boston. I live in New York City. I've been coming here to help my father out with his practice for the last six months, but his house in Dorchester Heights is a shit hole." When he finished speaking, any amusement he once had in his hazel eyes was gone. Seriousness had replaced it all. "Anything else?"

Yes, I had a million other questions. I wanted to know who he was and what he did. What he knew about Michael's situation. Deep down, I really hoped Logan wasn't involved in what my sister had gotten herself into, but it seemed after what happened earlier, he had to be. My laundry list of questions would have to wait. I could see in his eyes that my time was running out. I leaned back in the booth. "I do have one more question."

Eyeing me wearily, he heaved a sigh. "Go ahead." But then he threw me a smile to let me know he wasn't completely annoyed—yet.

My stomach did a flip and I think he knew it. I knew I should watch my body language. I might be giving off a vibe I could never live up to. Sucking in a breath, I asked my final question. "What is it you do to help your dad out?"

My mind was coming up with all kinds of things that should have worried me.

A hit man.

A drug runner.

A bookie.

"I'm a lawyer," he said matter-of-factly.

Okay, I so wasn't expecting that. I eyed him skeptically. He wasn't dressed like Michael or even his father. Sure he had the white shirt, but that was where the similarity stopped. His white shirt molded to his toned chest like perfection, sleeves rolled up to his elbows, top two buttons undone. He wore distressed jeans that looked almost lethal on him. Add black suede sneakers and a casual black coat. Hot. Casual. Mouthwatering. Yep, other than the white shirt, he was not dressed like an attorney at all, or at least any attorney I knew.

He chuckled, and then as if reading my mind, he reassured me. "I am. I wasn't seeing clients today. But trust me, I graduated from law school two years ago and currently work for the Ryan Corporation in New York City."

Shocked, it took me a moment for his words to sink in. "The Ryan Corporation? Like in the largest international hedge fund management company in the country?"

He smiled. "That's the one."

So did I. "I'm impressed."

Nonchalantly, he lifted his gaze to mine. "Don't be. My grandfather owns the company and my position in the legal department was created solely for me. Associate counsel, Litigation and Employment. It's a bullshit job."

I was sipping my soda and almost spit it out of my mouth. "Your grandfather is . . ." I paused as it clicked.

"Logan Ryan," we said in unison.

Logan. I got it.

"You know him?" he asked, seemingly surprised.

Wrenching my eyes from his, I said, "Well, not personally, but when I worked for the International Trade Center, he was our biggest client."

Logan nodded in recognition. "Ah yes, he has a penchant for collecting exotic things."

"So what are you doing in Boston helping your dad if you have a job in New York?"

Logan's body stiffened, but he answered anyway. "When my father was arrested, I told him if he got back on the wagon, I'd come up here every Thursday and Friday and help salvage what was left of his practice. Like I said, my job at the Ryan Corporation is a joke, and to be honest, I much prefer working with my father's clients. They're people who need help."

Surprised by his candor, I asked, "Then why don't you work in Boston full-time?"

He shrugged. "That is a long story."

Well, either way, it sounded like he made an honest living. Yet something in the back of my mind still nagged me. I wondered what part of the mess my sister had created his father was a part of and, in turn, what involvement, if any, Logan had. But I wasn't about to just ask. The situation was way too delicate. And I was smarter than that. As I sat across from him, though, I had to question—was I? I wouldn't be here if I were.

"I don't understand. Why not just—" I started to ask, but he cut me off.

His expression hardened. "I think that's enough about me."

I felt myself flushing. I may have gotten a little carried away.

Expectedly, and within moments of shutting me down, he said, "Your turn."

Mentally switching gears, I tried to think about what I could tell him. I never talked about myself. I hated it, so instead I lied. "Honestly, there's not much to tell. What you see is what you get."

He eyed me dubiously. My lie was just that—a lie.

I wasn't surprised that he doubted what I'd said. I would have too.

The truth was, I often wondered if the word *damaged* wasn't inked across my forehead for any man who might be even mildly interested in me to see, because they always seemed to know something was off.

Could Logan tell I wasn't whole?

Much to my relief, he smirked and then nudged me under the table. "You're not playing fair. I just spilled my life story and you're giving me one of the oldest lines in the book? Come on."

He hadn't spilled his life story, but he did tell me more

than he had to. I'd give him that.

"Here you go." The waitress set two red plastic baskets down, each containing a huge burger and way too many fries. "Anything else?" she asked.

Logan glanced over at me just as my gaze darted to the ketchup. "I'm good."

"Me too," he said.

"Enjoy. If you need anything else, let me know." She slipped the check on the table and left us to our meal.

Logan was handing me the ketchup before I had a chance to reach for it.

I raised a curious brow.

Was he reading my mind?

He shrugged. "I saw you eyeing it."

With a quick twist, I removed the sticky white lid. "Can't have fries without it."

Logan seemed amused as I pounded the bottom of the ketchup bottle, failing miserably to make a pile in the middle of my fries. Nothing was coming out.

"Here, let me show you." Instantly, his hand was across the table and I willingly relinquished the bottle to him. When he took it, he held the glass at the neck and tipped it in such a way that the thick red liquid poured out easily.

"How?" I harrumphed.

His hazel eyes lifted seductively. "The secret is knowing where the sweet spot is."

My stomach did a full belly flop.

Oh. My. God.

Feeling heated, I knew a slight blush was coloring my cheeks. I sucked in a breath and willed all these strange feelings to go away. When I felt at ease again, I finally met his eyes. "Good to know." I tried to act as if I was unaffected by his sexual innuendoes, but I knew I was failing miserably.

"More?"

My eyes widened.

"Ketchup." He grinned.

Yeah, he knew what he did to me. I lifted the bun on my burger. "Of course," I said as cavalierly as I could.

With that insanely hot smirk on his face, he poured some on top of the cheese before he pulled back.

I busied myself by cutting my burger in half and settling my napkin on my lap, but I couldn't escape my turn for long. I was certain of that. With each passing moment, I could feel his focus on me. I took my first bite. "Mmmm," I moaned out loud, unintentionally.

Logan sucked in a breath.

I couldn't look at him.

"You like it?" he asked.

"Yes," I answered once I'd swallowed.

Nervous flutters, more like tremors, had taken up permanent residence in my belly. And when he reached across the table and dragged his finger slowly up my chin to my lips, I nearly jumped. My entire body felt alive and I swear I could feel my skin sear at his touch. He pulled his finger away, and I saw it had ketchup on it. I'd never even felt it dripping from my mouth. I licked my lips where his finger had just been. Again, he gave me a knowing smile, and then when he knew I was watching, he inserted his finger in his mouth and sucked it clean.

My pulse raced at the sight.

I felt like a horny teenager, and I'd never been a horny teenager.

My heart pounded in my chest and I decided talking was going to be way easier than whatever this was. "I grew up in the military. My father was a brigadier general."

I must have surprised him, because he paused mid-bite. "You're a military brat?"

My huff of laughter was dry. "Anything but."

That familiar smirk was back and I was beginning to think he only used it when he didn't believe me. But he didn't ask me anything else about that. Instead he asked, "Where was your father stationed?"

I dipped a fry in my ketchup. "Everywhere. My sister

and I were born in California. That was my father's home base, but he preferred international posts, and always volunteered to step in when a temporary base commander was needed. I grew up a little bit everywhere—in Germany, France, England, Italy, and Singapore. There were a few other countries, but we weren't there long enough to say we lived there."

Compassion filled his eyes. "Fuck. You moved around a lot. It must have been hard for you with the constant changing of schools and always having to make new friends. I know I used to hate just being shuffled back and forth between New York and Boston."

I gave him a practiced shrug. "My sister hated it. I saw what that did to her. She was older than me and I didn't want to be like her. But after a while, it was hard not to hate it. Every base looked like the last, but it wasn't. I never had any friends. Then, when I was a teen, I found something that I loved about the constant moving."

Curiosity gleamed in his eyes. "Oh yeah, what?"

I took a bite of one of my fries. "Instead of worrying about trying to make friends that I knew I'd have to leave, I threw myself into the countries and studied them. Their traditions. Common phrases. What each country valued. What they produced. I immersed myself in their cultures."

He raised a brow. "Wow, I'm impressed."

Already more than full, I pushed my basket away. "Don't be. It wasn't a life I'd wish on any child. I just tried to make the best of it."

"Your mother and father didn't know how much you and your sister disliked it?"

I gave him another dry laugh. "I'm not sure. I doubt it would have mattered if they did. My father only cared about himself and my mother was too concerned with making sure the General was happy."

This was more than I'd spoken about my family in years, and to be fair, my mother wanted to keep my father happy to maintain a sense of calm in our household. She was more of a victim than anything else. I felt guilty not explaining that. But that would only lead to places I didn't want to go.

"Where are your parents now?" he asked.

The question surprised me. I hadn't thought of my mother or my father as parents in so long. Again, the need to speak honestly overtook me. "My mother's dead and I haven't spoken to my father since the day I left for college. I have no idea where he is."

Something came over me. I had to get out of here before I broke down. With trembling fingers, I picked up the bill and looked at the total.

When I reached into my purse to leave some money, Logan grabbed the check from me. "I asked you out. I got this."

"Thank you. It was really good, but I need to get going. I'll grab a taxi." I suddenly felt like I should get away from him. He was making me feel things I didn't want to be feeling. Thoughts of my parents seemed to be strangling me. I quickly jumped to my feet.

Concern glimmered in his eyes and he quickly rose and pulled out his wallet, tossing two twenties on the table. "No, I'm done. I'll take you."

I wanted to argue but my mind was a jumble and before I knew it he was behind me, holding my coat out. "I'm sorry. I didn't mean to upset you." His warm breath brushed against my ear and shivers danced down my spine.

Dispelling the urge to lean into him, I pulled my hair out of the collar of my trench coat. "You didn't. I'm fine."

I clearly wasn't.

I hated my past.

I hated my father.

I hated my mother for putting up with him.

I hated my sister for leaving me.

But I hated myself even more.

chapter
SIX

LOGAN

SHE WAS ANYTHING BUT fine.

Yet I wasn't any good at consoling people. I didn't know what to say or do. Besides, I was pretty certain she wasn't looking for comfort. She was tough, and although I understood why, I also knew what she'd told me wasn't the only reason. There was more to Elle than she let on. Hey, I got it. She had some demons she didn't want to let out. And I certainly didn't want to be the one to unleash them.

I raced in front of her, taking the lead. "Come on, let's go."

She nodded but didn't say anything.

Didn't I feel like a real shit.

Melancholy seemed to swallow me whole.

Fuck.

The rain was falling harder than it had been earlier and I watched as she put that red hat on again. It was soaking wet and I was certain it wasn't helping to keep her dry, but she seemed to like it, so although I didn't say a thing, the sight made me smirk.

Once we were outside, we both kept our heads down. She followed me through the alley and back toward

Molly's. I paused for a moment at the corner and looked around before reaching in my pocket and unlocking the SUV. The taillights of my black Range Rover blinked up ahead. I had unlocked the doors at a good distance so when the rain started falling even harder, I moved faster, making sure she was right behind me. We reached my vehicle in the downpour and I opened her door. Elle didn't look at me as she got in quickly. I didn't stop to talk; I just wanted to get off the goddamn street. I ran to the other side and hopped in. When I did, I looked over at her just as she was wiping the rain from her face, or was it a tear?

Both of us were wet. Both of us were out of breath. The air in the car was cold. But the heat that rose as we looked at each other was scorching. For a second, I considered making a move on her, but then, the longer I watched her, the more I realized things between us weren't going to be that simple.

She looked vulnerable.

It wasn't something I could handle.

I just wasn't expecting it.

She was a fighter.

Or so I had thought.

I had to avert my gaze. I knew then that I couldn't see her after tonight. There were only two categories of women for me—the just fuck and the never fuck. Somehow, she didn't seem to fit in either and that was dangerous. As if the situation she was in weren't already dangerous enough, she didn't need my involvement in her life fucking her up more.

Patrick Flannigan was a heartless, greedy bastard and O'Shea was on his shit list. Add me to the mix and she was in real danger. Many years ago, my grandfather, Killian McPherson, had ordered me to keep my distance from Patrick and ordered Patrick to keep his hands off me. Since I hated Patrick, I dutifully obliged. Since my grandfather was in charge at the time, Patrick was forced to obey. But Gramps was in a home now and no longer here to act as a buffer between Patrick and me. I was on my own. For that reason and so many more, I knew better than to get too close to Patrick.

My father's well-being was one of the many reasons.

But for her, I'd have to take a risk.

I'd have to step closer.

My own consequences be damned. I was going to make sure she wasn't a part of O'Shea's issues. But I had to be smart about it. I had to figure things out first. For my father's sake.

What did she know?

I was getting ahead of myself. I had to ease into the information. I stopped thinking and started the car. "Where to?" I asked. My voice sounded low and I hated the weakness I was allowing to bleed through my words.

She, on the other hand, seemed to gather strength in the silence and spoke strongly. "A small boutique on Charles, just past Revere."

I pulled out into the traffic and turned the radio on. The Sex Pistols blared loudly. "Sorry," I said, quickly turning the volume down.

"You don't have to turn it down. I like it."

Unabashedly crude, intensely emotional, and meant to exhilarate and offend at the same time, I guess it was the perfect sound for the mood we were both in.

We rode in silence and I hummed along to the lyrics until I couldn't stand the quiet any longer. She was staring out the window and I could tell she was somewhere back in time in her mind.

I wanted to get her out of that dark place. I considered how. I thumped the steering wheel, trying to decide what to say. The car in front of me stopped and I skidded to a halt. "Sorry," I said.

The rain was falling and she was watching it, seemingly unfazed by my sudden stop, but then she looked over. "What?" she asked.

Out of nowhere, I started blurting out things about

myself I never told anyone. "When I was growing up, I hated my parents. My mother was controlling; my father was
docile, always caving in to her every whim to keep her happy. Even through all the fighting, they stayed together. I was
fifteen when they finally divorced and it was because of my
actions. That was a dose of reality and it not only forced me
to grow up fast, but it forced me to get over the hatred even
faster. Everything changed for me that year. The guilt I felt
over what I'd done, what I caused, was a bitch to handle,
and I didn't handle it well for a long time. It was so many
years later when a friend told me that everything happens
for a reason, and the more I thought about it, the more I had
to agree. My parents needed to separate. They were both so
unhappy together and so much happier apart."

"So you ended up making amends with your parents?"

My laugh was dry. "I guess you could say that. Now, I
avoid my mother. I can't stand her pretentiousness and she
can't stand my unwillingness to concede to the haughty
lifestyle she lives. So we've both agreed it's better if we limit our conversations. "

"I'm sorry."

"Don't be. It's for the best. And besides, my father and I
have a closer relationship than I ever thought we would, so
things aren't all that bad."

What the hell was wrong with me? Why was I spouting
useless information about myself to her that I was certain
made no sense?

"What happened when you were fifteen?" Her eyes
were focused and sharp when she spoke this time.

I shook my head, not willing to dare go there. "It was a
long time ago. It's not something I want to talk about."

She cleared her throat. "I get it. I want you to know, I
wasn't really honest before. I didn't really hate my mother.
I felt sorry for her but I didn't hate her. Not when she was
alive, anyway."

"What do you mean?"

She shrugged. "Like you said, it was a long time ago."

I stopped at another light and reached across the console. I thought about grabbing her hand, but that seemed too much like pity. So instead of taking her hand, I removed her hat and tossed it on the floor behind me. "It's all wet. You'll get sick if you keep it on your head."

She smirked at me. "I like that hat."

"I know," I said, smirking back.

The doubtful look on her face was so cute. "And how do you know that?"

"You keep putting it on. It's obvious you're attached to it."

"I wouldn't say I'm attached to it."

I raised a brow.

"Well, maybe a little," she said with a laugh.

The fact that I'd made her smile made me smile.

As soon as I resumed driving, I took a left onto Arlington, and she went back to staring out the window.

The brick row houses with fancy doors, decorative ironwork, brick sidewalks, narrow streets, and gas lamps told me we'd crossed into Beacon Hill. I have to say, of all the areas in Boston, I really liked this neighborhood the most. I grew up here but never spent much time here. I was always shuffling between Manhattan's Upper East Side and Dorchester Heights.

Finally, she spoke. "It's up here on the left."

I pulled into the open space just outside the boutique at the base of the hill. "The House of Sterling," I read aloud. "Is this the place?"

"Yes, it's mine. It opens tomorrow."

"It's yours?"

Her smile was bright. "It is."

"What do you sell?"

Excitement was all around her. "Imports from all the countries I've been to."

The rain was coming down in buckets. "Nice. I can't read what the window says."

Her spine seemed to straighten in pride. "It says, 'The

finest things life has to offer.'"

"Well, Elle," I glanced to the sign and back to her, "Sterling, I have to assume, show me the finest things life has to offer."

She threw me a small smile and instantly, the mood had lightened. "You assume correct, Logan McPherson."

I liked the way she said my name. I wanted to ask her to say it again and then wanted to punch myself for thinking that.

Lame.

What was I—twelve?

And a girl?

When she reached behind me and grabbed her hat, I just shook my head.

That red hat.

It was late, and everything was closed, the street empty. Still, I moved fast, but funny, she moved even faster. As soon as I'd opened her door, she bolted around the car to a small overhang just next to the sign. She fumbled for her keys and I squeezed under the overhang behind her. I was close. Really close. Close enough that I could feel the curves of her body brushing against mine.

I couldn't help but be turned on.

I peered over her shoulder like she might need help, in an attempt to move even closer. It was a dick move and even though I knew it was, I couldn't help myself. It was a case of body taking over mind. Mentally slapping myself, I glanced down and noticed her hands were shaking and that she couldn't get the key in the lock.

"Here, let me." I could be a gentleman.

Elle turned her head and her warm breath gusted across my neck. That's how close she was. She turned back but didn't hand me the key, so I reached out with my hand and covered hers as I guided her fingers toward the lock. With my hand squeezing hers, I turned the key and as I did, an overwhelming desire to take her right there overwhelmed me.

The door opened but I didn't step back.

She didn't step forward, either.

We both stood there, our bodies aligned in such a way that it would be hard to argue that we didn't want each other.

It would be harder to argue that we weren't going to fuck.

chapter
SEVEN

Elle

"IS THAT YOU, ELLE?" a voice called.

With his hard body pressed against mine, and arousal flooding me in a way it never had, her voice took a moment to register. But when it did, my eyes flew open. "Peyton, where are you?"

"I'm just coming upstairs," she called.

I was surprised she had even heard us. When anyone was downstairs it was impossible to hear anything upstairs. Peyton swore the place had been a bomb shelter at one time.

I stepped inside and the heat of Logan's body wasn't far behind. "Why are you still here? You said you were leaving with Rachel hours ago."

Her heels clacked against the wood of the steps. "More merchandise arrived just as we were locking up. I sent Rachel home but decided to stay."

"The De Bolivar soaps? I told you to call me when they arrived."

Her crown of out-of-control shiny brown curls peeked through the banister of the open staircase. "No," she laughed, "and I don't know why some soap made with

South American olive oil interests you so much, but what arrived is so much better. Check these out. I don't know which one I prefer. Maybe you can help me decide." She emerged from the stairs proudly holding a diamond ring dildo in one hand and a platinum vibrator encrusted in emeralds in the other.

My cheeks felt flush immediately. Hers turned even brighter red when she spotted Logan standing beside me. I looked at him, and the smirk on his face that said so much more than I wanted to know right now.

Surprised I wasn't alone, Peyton quickly put the dildo behind her back. "Maybe you don't need this one."

"Oh, I'm not so sure about that," Logan said half a moment later.

She pulled it back around to hold it in front of her, high in the air. Her shirt lifted and the colorful tail of a peacock peeked from under its hem. She had a few tattoos; I had thought about getting one once of a dandelion but never did.

Admiring her display, she remarked, "It is pretty big."

My mouth dropped to the floor when Peyton did a double take like she was sizing it up and comparing it to Logan.

Logan didn't miss the suggestion. "Yeah, although I'd like to say I'm bigger, I don't think I can."

We all burst out in laughter.

Shaking my head, I said, "Peyton, this is Logan. Logan, this is Peyton, my assistant."

"And best friend," she added while her eyes scanned Logan curiously.

I could tell she thought I'd been holding out, and it almost made me laugh. "Logan and I just met at Michael's office. I had a flat tire and he offered to drive me here."

Suspicion loomed deep in her eyes, but still she set the items on the nearest table and offered her hand. "Nice to meet you, Logan."

"Nice to meet you too, Peyton," he said, rather charmingly I might add.

They shook hands, and then she picked the vibrator and dildo back up. "I was just leaving. Do you want these in the case or do you want to wait for the," she paused and looked at Logan, "other items to arrive?" She was almost giggling.

Logan's smirk only grew. "Other items like?"

"The Gold Tickler from Italy and the String of Pearls from Asia." I just put it out there. I figured, why not?

"Oh, and don't forget the snakeskin handcuffs from Singapore and—"

"I think he gets the picture," I said, cutting her off.

"Oh please, keep going," Logan teased.

She actually was about to continue.

"Peyton," I admonished. "I thought you were leaving."

She handed me the items. "See you bright and early." She hugged me. "I can't believe it's finally here."

I squeezed her tightly. "I couldn't have done it without you."

I hired Peyton almost two months ago when I rented the space. She has a degree in merchandising, a skill I greatly value. Ever since I hired her, we've spent every day together sifting through the inventory from my online boutique and searching for even more extravagant items.

Peyton put on her coat. "I hope to see you again," she said to Logan.

He nodded hesitantly. "You never know."

Sounded like we had the same plan.

I took the exquisite sexual items and walked toward the center of the boutique. With each step, I could feel his eyes on me. Shivering, I scanned the room and forced myself to focus on admiring the work I'd done.

The space wasn't huge, but it was big enough. I'd refinished the ebony wood floors and purchased inexpensive wood tables, both of which complemented the simple glass fixtures and extensive shelving exquisitely. The style was shabby chic. It was eye-catching. Enticing. It was my dream come true.

"Where exactly will the sex toys be displayed?" Logan asked with a sinister purr in his voice.

Sensing I was only going to be even more turned on if I saw his face, I didn't turn to face him when I spoke. "Over here, next to the counter in this antique Chinese glass case."

I knew he was approaching me with that long, lean body of his when I smelled his delicious scent. "I have to ask. How much do the items in your hand retail for?"

Drawing in a breath, I unlocked a drawer behind the antique counter that once sold tickets for a carousel in Vienna and set the items inside it. "Each will be tagged one thousand dollars."

Logan gave a low whistle. "Nice. At least it's not as much as Beckham's gift to Posh back in their day."

Laughing, I gave in and glanced over at him. "No, I highly doubt, even with my mad selling skills, that I could sell a million-dollar item. To be honest, I'm not even certain these will go, but Peyton insisted we give them a try."

The smile he gave me felt electric. "Oh, they'll sell. In fact, you might want to order a case of those."

Discussing devices used to provide pleasure should have been awkward, yet somehow it wasn't. "Do you know something I don't?"

With folded arms, he leaned back against the counter. "About the wealthy residents of Boston, absolutely. And here's a small suggestion." He bobbed his chin toward the ornate Chinese glass cabinet beside him. "Put those items out tomorrow, and as soon as a customer asks the price, casually mention your supply is low, and I bet they buy them up."

I raised a brow. "Experienced in high-society sexual dynamics, are you?"

His grin was devilish. "You might say that. I also have a few friends back home that as soon as I mention upscale sex toys, I'm sure will be interested."

I tilted my head. "Will I have to pay you commission?" I was seriously flirting with him now.

There was just something about him.

We were facing each other and the noise he made from deep in his throat rumbled through me. "I'm sure we could work something out."

My cheeks flamed and I wasn't a blusher, or I hadn't been before I met Logan.

"Show me around." His tone was commanding again.

I couldn't understand why I liked it.

I shouldn't have.

More than happy to escape his lustful stare, I circled the counter and pointed. "To my left I have rugs from Persia, silks from China, and perfumes from France. To my right I have the finest cotton sheets from Egypt, English soaps, Wiley Wallaby gourmet licorice from Australia, Himalayan gourmet salt, and Hacienda La Esmeralda coffee beans from Panama." I continued around the space, pointing out all the finest things I'd managed to find around the world.

Logan was right next to me and I watched as he picked up a few items with keen interest, whistled at one or two, and raised an impressed brow every now and then.

When I finished, we ended up back at the vintage cash register stand and near the sex toys I'd locked away in the drawer beneath it.

He glanced into the empty cabinet meant to house them. "I'm telling you, I'd put those items out for opening day."

I tilted my head. "You would, would you?"

His gaze was bold. "Trust me."

The key was on the counter and I unlocked the drawer. "Maybe you'd like to buy one? For someone in your life, I mean."

"Wh-what?" he stuttered with a laugh.

A shyness lingered in his eyes that made me yearn for him.

He stepped closer to me and I breathed him in.

With shaky fingers, I opened the drawer.

Logan leaned even closer and whispered, "If I had someone to buy one for, I would."

I chewed my bottom lip as I hurried to transfer the items, secretly ecstatic I now knew for sure he didn't have a girlfriend. "Okay, done." I sighed with relief.

His eyes were warm as he looked around, taking everything in. "Elle, this is really incredible. And I'm not just saying that."

The compliment moved me and I searched for how to respond.

"How long did you say you've been in Boston?"

Um . . ."Three months," I answered, not certain I had mentioned that and if he'd make the connection to or knew that my sister wasn't really in rehab . . . that she was missing. That she had been . . . for three months.

Logan casually leaned back against one of the display tables, his palms flat on the wooden surface. "Where were you living before you moved here?"

Feeling more at ease, I leaned back against the counter behind me. "Nowhere."

Curiosity glittered in his eyes.

I shrugged. "I was somewhat of a nomad. A gypsy, is what Peyton calls me. I had a small place in San Francisco but I rarely ever went there. For the last five years, I've just traveled the world and sold my treasures on the Internet."

Logan picked up a silk scarf that lay on the table and ran his fingers over it. "You liked moving around so much after your childhood?"

"It was the only life I knew until I came here."

"Weren't you lonely?"

I shook my head and gave him a forced smile. "Isn't everyone in their own way?"

Forcing his own smile, he said, "Well, I think what you've done is really impressive. And I can see you really love it."

Things seemed to be getting serious between us again and I felt myself needing to push him away. "I don't want to keep you. I can walk home. It's less than a mile from here."

He stepped forward and tugged my hat off. "I said I'd see you home and I'm a man of my word." He glanced over his shoulder out the window. "And besides, this," he held my hat up before setting it on the counter, "isn't going to keep you dry. Nor is your trench coat with the winds as high as they are."

He had a point.

I laughed. I'd laughed a lot with Logan. "Okay, then would you like to help me move these boxes downstairs?"

Logan looked at the stacks of cardboard boxes, some empty, some not. "Sure, I'll get the heavy ones."

"So chauvinistic," I teased.

He pretended to be pained and placed his palm on his heart. "And here I thought I was being chivalrous."

I clapped my hand to my forehead. "What was I thinking? Of course you can carry the heavy boxes."

Logan moved closer to me still. "Are you mocking me?"

I squeezed his biceps. Electricity struck and my flirty voice fell. "No, not at all. Just testing your strength." Breaking the connection, I bent to lift a box. "I'm much stronger than I look, you know."

He raised a brow and then purposely shifted his gaze down my body. "I bet."

The heat between us was palpable and I found myself setting the box back down so that I could take my coat off, but then feared I might have looked weak. "I am. Yoga, Pilates, kickboxing, boxing, Tae Bo. You name it, I've done it."

The corners of Logan's mouth tipped up. "I don't doubt your abilities. Something tells me you have mad self-defense skills and can hit your target as well."

I tilted my head to the side. "Wing Chun and point blank."

It seemed like I was boasting as soon as the words left my mouth. "Not that I'm bragging," I added.

He ran his fingers up the sleeve of my blouse. "Not at all. I respect the fact that you know how to protect yourself."

"I didn't have much choice." My expression must have portrayed my anguish, even though I hoped it hadn't.

Immediately, Logan asked, "Why? What happened?"

With a shrug, I dislodged myself from his hold and nudged past him to the boxes. "Too long and too sad of a story to share now."

There was no way to explain my life easily. That since I was fifteen, I'd basically been on my own. And that I'd had to learn to protect myself because I didn't know what to expect. That since then, I'd only ever relied on one person—Charlie. And that didn't end well. So ever since, I'd believed the only person I should rely on is myself.

Logan seemed impervious to my mood. Either that or feelings weren't his thing.

Not that they were mine.

He removed his jacket and moved his head from side to side as if preparing for a workout before rubbing his hands together. "I think I'm ready. Where do you want the boxes?"

Okay, definitely impervious.

Our conversations were up and down. They went from brutally honest, to serious, to funny in the blink of an eye. And as I looked at him now, I had to laugh. In fact, I couldn't stop laughing. He was easy that way. He made things easy. I liked that.

"Downstairs." I pointed.

He hefted the box I'd just set down. I went for the empty ones.

Just because.

Boxes at my sides, I saw the metal tucked in his waistband as soon as he stepped in front of me. His shirt mostly covered it, but I was good at catching things like that. I didn't say anything. After all, I, too, carried protection everywhere I went—it wasn't tucked in my pants, but it was zipped inside my purse.

We made almost a dozen trips up and down the stairs. Our conversation was light. We talked about Boston, the weather, and baseball. Once all of the boxes were out of sight, he helped me break down the ones that were empty and restock the items into inventory that I didn't need up-stairs. Finally, I made one last lap around the boutique. "I think it's ready."

He followed the path I had taken. "I think you're right."

The cuckoo clock from Germany started to go off. The little bird popped its head out and as soon as the music started to play, the dancers spun with the music and the bell ringers rung their bells. Nine times this cycle continued.

Logan stared at the clock. When it finished, he looked at me. "I hope to fuck that sells right away."

I crossed my arms and tried to look insulted, but I couldn't fight the smile.

He snapped his fingers and pointed one at me. "See, you feel the same."

Knowing exactly what he meant, I moved toward him and lowered his finger. Sparks flickered when I touched him. I dropped my hold and recovered. "I refuse to speak ill of any of my treasures, but I do hope the clock finds a home quickly."

Logan smiled softly. "Speaking of homes, it's time I take you there. I'm sure you have a long day ahead of you tomorrow."

I did.

Still, I couldn't help but think about him in ways I knew I shouldn't for so many reasons. And the main reason wasn't even the gun he was carrying. I glanced out the win-dow, pondering what was going to happen when he got me home. I noticed the rain had let up, so while I put my coat on, I left my hat behind.

Logan and I had spent only four hours together, but it felt like so much longer. I felt like I knew him. Not well, but I'd gotten closer to him than I had to anyone in years. Michael and Peyton didn't count—they were people brought into my life by circumstance.

But then again, if I thought about it, I supposed he was,

too.

"Where to?" Logan asked as he got in the Range Rover.

Still pondering my last thought, I answered quietly, "Thirty-six Melrose Street."

Logan knew where he was going. He did a U-turn and headed south on Charles, then made a right on Melrose. We were in Bay Village and on the quiet tree-lined street in no time.

"It's right here on the left."

He stopped in front of the brick row houses, and I indicated the end unit with the red door and black painted steps.

"That's mine." I pointed.

Logan searched the deserted street before he got out and came around to open my door. I stepped out and started walking, assuming he would be coming in.

Again, he stopped and studied the street as if assessing the neighborhood and the building.

When I threw him a curious glance, he simply said, "It's nice."

Suddenly very nervous, I fumbled for my keys. "I like it. It's one of the only original row houses still standing in Boston. The architecture and very cheap price is what sold me. It's small and needs a lot of work, but it's more of a home than I've had in a long time."

The way he looked at me, I felt like he was staring through me. "I'd love to see it sometime."

More than ready to do this, I turned and unlocked the door, pushing it open but not stepping in. "How about now?" I whispered.

Logan focused on my mouth but didn't answer me.

I was already nervous; I didn't invite men into my personal space, and his silence was making me uncertain. I rephrased the question. "Would you like to come in for a drink?"

He shoved his hands in his pockets. "I don't drink. With two alcoholic parents, I quit long ago. Figured it gave me a better chance of not turning out like either of them."

"Then coffee? I know you drink coffee." My nerves were showing and I was babbling.

Logan pounced. He caged me within the open door, his arms gripping each side of the jamb as his mouth neared my ear.

Frightened wasn't the word to describe what I was feeling. *Aroused* fit much better, as desire shot right to my core.

Warm breath gusted down my neck as he exhaled a string of raspy words. "If I come inside, you and I both know what's going to happen."

The hush of the night sky made everything he said seem hotter. Yes, I did know what would happen, and I wanted it. "Logan," I gasped.

His mouth was practically on my ear when he spoke again. "But you have a big day tomorrow and even though I want to fuck you like I've never wanted to fuck anyone, I also respect you enough to know I shouldn't cross over your threshold. Not tonight."

Crushed, I felt my body stiffen as rejection wove its way through me. Who said no to sex when it was being offered with no strings?

Logan stepped back and lifted my chin. "Hey, that doesn't mean I don't want you. You know I do." He let his words trail off. "You know it."

Obviously my disappointment had shown in my body language. Yes, he'd said that, but I couldn't help but feel unwanted. The night had started out with expectation in his words. And now this. What had happened? Had I shown him too much of the real me?

When I didn't respond, because frankly I didn't know what to say, he stepped into me, close again, so close that there was only a breath between us. He stared at me, really stared at me, for the longest time. When I blinked, his hands shifted and he grabbed my face. Crashing his mouth to mine, he forced me to part my lips.

Electricity sparked. I felt dizzy. Even though his mouth

was moving in a harsh manner, his lips felt soft, tender even. His tongue met mine and the minute it happened, I felt a tingling travel down my body all the way to my toes.

I couldn't help the low moan that escaped my throat. Desire was taking me over, but I tried to stop it. He'd just told me he wasn't coming in.

This was just a kiss.

A good-night kiss.

But oh, what a good-night kiss.

Whether it was on purpose or simply reflex, his hand traveled down my body, sending me all kinds of mixed signals. One signal that was quite clear was that this feeling, whatever it was, had consumed him as well.

Whatever his intention, it felt good, even if it was just the slightest of touches. Unexpectedly, he found my hand and laced his fingers between mine. His lips still moved against mine with a fervor I savored. Somehow, he managed to drag our hands inside my coat and under my blouse. We were skin to skin—his knuckles against my bare stomach.

Yes, I wanted him. I wanted him like I hadn't wanted anyone before. Enough to let him take me in the doorway of my home, but then I remembered he had already said no. No, just that he wouldn't come in.

As his kisses grew harder and his grip tighter, I knew if I didn't pull away he might just try to put his cock inside me right here.

The worst part? I might have just let him. "You have to stop," I whispered against his lips.

A deep sigh escaped his throat and then he tugged at my lip one last time. My lips felt swollen, but I missed his mouth on them.

"I know, but I don't want to," he whispered back.

Masking my disappointment, I gave him a slight smile. "And we already determined I have to get to bed."

With a drop of his forehead to mine, he breathed heavily. I was doing the same. His hands, though, stayed where they were, still under my blouse. He hadn't forgotten they were there, either. Purposefully, he swiped his thumb across my abdomen and played with the waistband of my leggings.

With an ache between my legs that was anything but sweet, I gave him one last brush of my lips.

This was the hardest good night.

I craved his touch.

I wanted to feel him skin to skin.

All of him.

But I did have a big day ahead of me and needed to get some rest.

Besides, I was confused. And after that kiss, I knew if he came in, there wouldn't be any sleep. So I did what I didn't want to do. I took the one step up and broke his hold of me. "Logan McPherson, I had a really nice time with you tonight." It was all I could say.

He stepped back and shoved his hands in his pockets. "Elle Sterling, the feeling is mutual."

I smiled at him sweetly.

Logan didn't return my smile but instead turned and walked toward his Rover, getting in and driving away without ever turning back.

We didn't exchange numbers or make plans to see each other again. It was when I realized this that I figured it out—we had both known all along that it could never be.

And what I'd thought was a good-night kiss was really a goodbye kiss.

chapter
EIGHT

LOGAN

FUCK, FUCK, FUCK.
   I slammed the wheel.

I wanted her. Wanted her more than I had wanted anyone in a very long time. I had tried to turn it off. My emotions were like a chick's.

Hot.

Cold.

Up.

Down.

Where was my fucking head? I had to stay focused. I knew I needed to get to my father and find out what Patrick had planned for O'Shea, but then after that kiss, I wasn't able to pull away.

She was doing something to me that I didn't understand.

Twisting me in a way that I shouldn't have wanted to be twisted.

Thank God she had come to her senses.

It was late when I opened the door to the house that had once belonged to my grandfather. Killian McPherson had lived here for almost fifty years, and half of those years were with his wife. Sadly, my grandmother died of cancer when I was five. All I remember about her is that she took me to church and taught me how to pray. And that when we went, her white hair was always pulled tightly back and she wore the same blue dress. That woman was the love of his life and he never remarried. In fact, he never brought another woman to this house, and he lived here alone until my father moved in once he and my mother divorced.

All the lights were off. "Pop, you here?"

There wasn't any answer. I looked in his office. It was empty. I ran up the stairs to his room. He wasn't there. I came back down and opened the door to the family room. Nothing. He wasn't back yet.

I flicked on the television and sat on the couch.

I'd wait for him.

A hand on my shoulder woke me. "Logan, what are you doing here?"

I blinked and looked at my watch. It was almost one in the morning. "I came by to talk to you. Why are you home so late?"

He rubbed his hands on his pants and sat on the chair beside me. "Patrick wasn't at Lucy's when I arrived, but he told Tommy I was to wait."

Lucy's was not only the largest but also the best-known strip club in Boston. It was also the Blue Hill Gang's headquarters.

It was only one of twenty other strip joints that fronted Patrick's illegal operations run under the corporation eerily named All My Women. *Sick fuck.* The strip clubs, or gentlemen's clubs as my pop preferred to call them, were named after women all right, but the women were cartoon characters. There was Betty's, Veronica's, Wilma's, and a slew more I couldn't recall.

Tommy, the prick, was Patrick's son and just as big of a douche as his father. He and I never did see eye to eye, and while he had reason to hate me, I had reason to hate him more.

Worried, I clicked on the lamp sitting on the table and

studied my father. "Have you been drinking?"

He shook his head. "No, but I wanted to."

I narrowed my eyes at him. "Did the prick pour you one?"

He nodded. "Left the bottle on the bar in case I changed my mind."

It wasn't the first time.

Scowling, I let my anger out. "Son of a fucking bitch. That's it. You're not going there without me anymore."

My father slammed his palm on the table beside him and the lamp shook. "Logan, I can take care of myself. I told you I want you to stay out of this. And besides, you know you can't set foot inside there or anywhere near that little prick."

Knowing he was right, and feeling empathetic after my outburst, I said, "Don't you get it? Now that Gramps is gone he's trying to break you."

My father's jaw clenched. "Let him try. I'm not as weak as he thinks."

"Pop, you have to get out before you can't. Things are different now. The stakes are so much higher with Gramps gone. He's got you doing things you've never done and you know you shouldn't be doing them."

He sat back in the chair. "You don't think I know that?"

I grunted, "I'm not so sure."

His voice rose. "Well, I do. And you also know I can't get out."

Frustrated, I stood and went to glance out the window. "It's been twelve years. I think that's long enough to be Patrick's personal counsel, liaison, or whatever the fuck he calls you."

My father leaned his head back and shut his eyes. "Son, you know it doesn't work that way."

Practically growling now, I spat, "Fuck him and fuck the way he thinks things should work."

My plan had better be successful because if it isn't, I just might kill the motherfucker. Then where would I be?

"A life for a life," my father muttered.

Feeling like I might explode, I punched the wall. My hand started to throb instantly. "Fuck."

Shaking his head, my father went into the kitchen and came back with a bag of frozen peas. "You need to calm down. Put this on your hand and have a seat."

I took it and sat on the couch. In a much calmer voice, I said, "Tell me exactly why you went to O'Shea's like a madman today and what he told you when you were there."

My old man let out a heavy sigh. "I don't know, Logan. There were a few factors that played into my demeanor today, but mostly I'm just tired of people getting hurt. And if this son of a bitch thinks he's going to get a pass from Patrick because he's blaming his wife or because his old man Mickey O'Shea, Patrick, and me grew up together, he needed to know neither means shit to Patrick. I wanted to make that crystal clear right off the bat."

"Did you get his attention?"

"I don't know. I hope I made him weigh his options because if he doesn't stop thinking out of his ass, he might not even get enough time to try to right the wrong he claims his wife caused."

Sympathy?

I got it.

He didn't want any undue harm to come to anyone else.

And finally, I was learning something that mattered. "What makes you speculate O'Shea thinks he might get a pass?"

My old man steepled his hands. "It's just a feeling I got on the phone."

I treaded lightly. "Tell me more."

"It's the way he's handling this whole situation. He's not stupid. Either he thinks he can get out of this or he has an ace up his sleeve."

"What do you think the ace might be?"

"Who knows? His wife, maybe, or the source."

I gave him a questioning look.

"Some time ago, I was in a meeting with Patrick when Tommy burst in and announced he'd discovered an underground drug operation taking place on Blue Hill turf with a woman as the front man. Patrick didn't ask questions. Just told Tommy to take care of it, find the source, and squash it."

"Patrick leaves something like that for Tommy to take care of? Are you kidding me?"

"There's been so much underground drug activity going on over the last few years, Patrick is tired of dealing with it."

"But he chose to lead the gang."

"I know. But Patrick only wants to deal with the girls, the goods, the numbers, and protection. The rest is up to Tommy."

"So what happened after Patrick told Tommy to take care of it?"

"Months later, Tommy shows up out of the blue and tells Patrick he tried to find the source by playing the chick, but it didn't work out the way he thought. Patrick flipped out and told Tommy he didn't want to hear it, he just wants him to take care of it. Later I asked around. It turned out the girl not only somehow lost the drugs, but she lost the cash Tommy had paid her for them as well, and the worst part is, shortly after that, she went missing."

"Who was the chick?" I already knew the answer.

My old man closed his eyes. "O'Shea's wife."

Interesting. Maybe she wasn't in rehab like Elle had said. "Do you believe she somehow lost the drugs and money?"

He opened his eyes. "Do you?"

"It sounds like she was working with someone who double-crossed her or she stashed them both for later and then disappeared."

My old man nodded in agreement.

"Where does O'Shea think she is?"

"He says he knows as much as we do. She just up and disappeared. He claims to have known nothing about the operation she was running, and says he doesn't know where the drugs or the money are that she told Tommy she lost."

I scrubbed my jaw. "Do you believe him?"

He flung me a look. "No reason not to. He hasn't been involved in Blue Hill affairs at all—ever."

"But?"

"But, no reason to believe him, either. The whole thing is weird."

"What exactly does Patrick want from him?"

"He hasn't told me, but my guess is he wants both the money and the drugs as compensation. I overheard Tommy say he wants the girl."

"All three? That's insane."

"O'Shea's wife disappeared with Blue Hill money and what were also, technically, their drugs. Patrick wants retribution."

"And O'Shea. What was his answer when you told him his payday would be coming?"

"He didn't have one. He kept quiet."

"But he knows he needs to deliver something soon?"

"He does. I told him twice. He also knows that if he doesn't, something bad is going to happen. All I can say is, he's been warned."

"And even after you delivered the message, he was still acting calm and cool, like it was no big deal?"

My father nodded.

"Do you believe he has a huge trump card to present if he doesn't deliver all three things? Because, come on, he can't be that stupid."

His shoulders lifted. "He could be just buying time, hoping his wife turns back up before the deadline."

"Or maybe he does have something in his back pocket as you mentioned earlier, like the missing drugs and money that his wife stashed away."

He pursed his lips. "Yeah, could be either. Not sure."

"Does he have money to front if all else fails?"

My father shrugged. "I can't imagine he has the kind of money he's going to need."

I didn't know O'Shea, but I could see his arrogance a mile away and I knew if he didn't lose it, he was going to get someone killed. "What do you think Patrick will settle for?"

"It's possible O'Shea knows who the big supplier is and plans to spill it to Patrick when the time comes."

My eyes widened. "Would that be enough to satisfy Patrick?"

"In the short term, maybe. It depends on who it is and what O'Shea knows about him."

My head was spinning.

When Patrick declared O'Shea's payday, all the cards would be on the table, but until then, we could only speculate.

Putting all the unknowns aside for now, I focused on the known. "Someone slashed her tire." I didn't have to clarify who the *her* was. After what happened earlier, I was certain he knew.

"You sure?"

"Yeah, I'm sure it was slashed. I saw it."

"Logan, you don't know it was Patrick or Tommy who did it."

With a shake of my head, I admitted, "It would be a huge coincidence if it wasn't."

"Listen, son, I have to say, I don't think Patrick knows about her."

I looked up. "What did Patrick say to you when he finally showed tonight?"

"Not that much."

"Then what was the summons for?"

My father sat beside me. "Just flexing his control. Nothing out of the ordinary. He wanted to know how my visit with O'Shea went so he could plan his next move. Nothing we couldn't have taken care of over the phone."

"Did he ask about the girl?"

My old man shook his head. "Like I said, O'Shea's wife has been missing for three months. Whoever that woman is that was in his office tonight, she couldn't have been her. O'Shea wouldn't be that stupid to have her walking around in the open when he knows she's wanted by the Blue Hill Gang. That girl must have been a nanny or girlfriend."

I recoiled at the word *girlfriend* and couldn't stop the jealousy that spiked in my veins. "She's not his wife," I said flatly, trying to pull my shit together.

My father scrubbed his jaw. "That's what I thought. Like I said, he's not that stupid."

"She's not the nanny or girlfriend, either."

His eyes narrowed on me. "Logan."

"Look, she has nothing to do with this. I want her left alone."

"You don't know she's not involved."

He was right, I didn't—but my gut told me she was an innocent. I ran a frustrated hand through my hair. "If you thought she was his wife, what's to prevent Patrick from thinking the same thing?"

"Nothing."

"Yeah, that's what I thought too."

"Who is she, Logan?"

"His wife's sister. She's new in town."

"And you know this information how?"

Confessing, I answered, "I ran into her."

He narrowed his eyes once again. "You ran into her?"

"Yeah, I did."

"And you don't think she's involved?" he snapped.

For once, I stayed calm. "No, I don't think she is. What makes you think Patrick doesn't know about her?"

My father shrugged. "I stayed clear of mentioning her and Patrick didn't say jack about her. Just mentioned the missing wife. Asked if she'd been found and if O'Shea said anything about her."

Clearly, my interest had been evident. "What did you tell him?"

He drew himself up. "I told him the wife hadn't been located as far as I knew and that O'Shea was still claiming to know nothing about her disappearance. But Logan, Patrick already knew about the baby girl."

"Do you think he has someone besides you on O'Shea?"

He looked out the window. "It's possible, but baby news is easy to find out."

"If he does have someone on O'Shea, maybe he's following anyone close to him and that's who slashed her tire?"

He pulled the curtains closed. "Like I said, it's possible, or maybe some punk on the street did it and you're overreacting."

I was done with that conversation. I knew I wasn't overreacting. "Maybe. Did Patrick say anything else tonight that mattered?"

With a deep sigh, he told me, "He declared the payday."

"What? When?"

"He's giving O'Shea until next Friday. Seven days. If he doesn't have the money, the drugs, and his wife by then, I'm to deliver a message."

Troubled, I squeezed the frozen bag with my fingers. "What's the message?"

A weighted silence fell between us.

"Pop, tell me," I said softly.

Shifting his eyes toward the closed curtains seemed to make it easier for him to speak. "He'll let me know."

"Cocksucker," I muttered.

The television was still on and my father stared at it. "I want you to go back to New York and stay there. I'm fine. I can handle the client load and I can handle Patrick."

I leaned forward and put my elbows on my knees. "I can't do that."

Cautious now, he spoke softly. "Why?"

I looked up. "Because of her. I can't explain it, but I don't want her or that little girl hurt."

He drew in a breath. "They aren't your concern."

"I can't leave."

"Just say it, Logan. The woman looks like Emily."

Unable to stand the pain of the memories, I pushed up and headed for the doorway. I knew that was coming, but still, I wasn't going there.

My father's reaction was to follow me. He just wasn't going to let it go that easy. He also knew I'd never stand in the kitchen willingly and talk about it, so he had limited time to make his point.

But feeling like I owed him an explanation, I stopped just before I opened the door. "Yes, she does. But my reasons for being concerned about her aren't what you're thinking."

I could tell he didn't believe me.

"Pop, I'm not attracted to her because she looks like Emily, but I am attracted to her. And I'm afraid for her because she does look like Emily. I'm afraid of what will happen if Patrick—or worse, Tommy—notices the similarity."

"Yeah, I am too," he sighed.

That wasn't reassuring at all.

chapter
NINE

Elle

CRIES IN THE NIGHT.

That's what I remembered most from my childhood.
The root of my self-pronounced aversion to desire. With the
memories ripped open so unexpectedly, I had a hard time
sleeping.

Nightmares.

My nightmares.

They kept waking me up, forcing me to remember what
I've tried so hard to forget. My fists gripped the sheets and
I fought the panic they evoked, but it was too late—they'd
already surfaced.

"I asked you to take your clothes off," he barked.

"The doctor said we should wait at least two weeks."

"It's close enough."

"But Henry, the doctor said—"

*"Do you think I give a shit what advice some doctor is giving
you? You're my wife and I'll fuck you whenever I want to."*

"Have you been drinking, Henry?"

"This isn't about my drinking."

"But it is. I'm not sure you're thinking clearly. It hasn't been

that long since I lost the baby."

He huffed in frustration. "Susan. Not this again. It's the same thing every night. Now I've waited long enough. Take your clothes off or I'll rip them off."

My mother protested. "Henry, I'm not ready."

Under his breath he muttered, "You never are."

"That's not true. I'm just not sure I'm up to it."

"Fine, then lift your nightgown and turn around."

My mother sighed.

My father's voice was soft when he spoke again. "Come on, baby, I need to be inside you. It's been weeks. You know how crazy I get when I can't have you."

I was confused by the silence, but then a few minutes later, I heard the mattress shift.

I was six and in my bed, clutching my teddy bear. The walls were so thin. When the creaking started, my big sister crawled in beside me and hugged me. "Don't listen, Gabby. Don't listen," she whispered. She always blocked out the noises at night. I never could. I didn't like to hear my daddy angry and my mommy upset.

There was a thumping against the wall and my mother started to cry. I couldn't help but listen. I wanted to help her.

"What's he doing to her, Lizzy? Why is she crying?" I whispered.

"Shhh . . . close your eyes. Think happy thoughts. Don't listen."

I tried, but nothing could block out my father's words. "I provide for you. Why can't you just take care of my needs without all this horseshit all the time?"

"I try, Henry, I do. I can't help how I feel, though," she whimpered.

Skin slapped against skin. "You like it this way. Tell me you do."

"Henry, please," my mother cried.

Sweat covered my body. I wanted to climb through the walls and tell him to leave her alone. "We should go help her," I told my sister.

"No, never do that," my sister warned. "Do you hear me?"

I nodded.

I heard my father laugh. "That's it, beg for it."

I wondered if everything was okay now, but then I heard the thumping against the wall, and it was getting louder and coming quicker.

"Please stop," my mother cried.

He let out a huge sigh. "You've got to be fucking kidding me. Could you please just stop complaining? Every time, Susan. Every time it's something."

"It hurts."

"You know, Susan, if you can't give me what I want, then you can damn well spread your legs when I tell you to or take it this way."

"Henry, please. It's not like that."

"Fuck, can't you give me anything I ask for?"

Her sobs grew. "Please don't blame me for losing the baby."

The thumping stopped.

"Who else should I blame? You lost my son. And now that it's time to try for another, you're not ready. How will the Sterling name carry on? This is on you, Susan."

"The doctor said we should consult with her before we decide on another pregnancy. She says my diabetes is continuing to weaken my kidney function and the miscarriages are a result of that."

"Fuck that. You're a strong woman. She's just being overcautious. They're all like that."

The thumping started up again and this time my mother was crying even louder. I could tell she was in pain.

"What's he doing to her?" I asked Lizzy again.

She was still squeezing her eyes shut. "Just something a husband and wife do together when they love each other."

"But it doesn't sound like Mommy likes it."

"Sometimes you do what you have to for love, Gabby. You'll see."

The pounding ceased. "Stop your fucking crying. Just turn around and put me in your mouth," he barked.

The mattress shifted again. Then my father started moan-
ing. "That's it. That's it baby. See, you do know how to make me
happy."

My father, the well-respected General. He demanded of
his family what he expected from his men—order, disci-
pline, and obedience.

He was vile.

Evil.

Sick.

A sex addict and a control freak.

And my mother was no match for him.

Sweat covered me as I fought to block the memories, but
they wouldn't stop assaulting me.

Lizzy and I were asleep in our room.

We were in England and I was almost eight.

That day we'd run through the meadow near our house and
picked hundreds of dandelions. My mother wasn't feeling well
and we'd brought them to her. We'd also put some in vases in our
room and in the kitchen, too.

My mother had a small baby bump; she always seemed to have
one, but it never got much bigger than it was at that time. Her di-
abetes seemed to hinder each pregnancy that came after my birth.

I heard the front door open and the sound of my father's boots.
"Susan!" he bellowed. He was used to my mother waiting up for
him. She never went to bed without him.

My mother called to him. "I'm in our bedroom, Henry."

His footfalls echoed down the hall. "You went to bed?" he
sneered.

The bed squeaked. My mother sitting up, I assumed. "I'm sor-
ry. I was really tired. I left your dinner on the stove."

"I'm not hungry," he said.

Everything was quiet for a bit and then I heard our door lock. I
knew what that meant and anger welled deep within me. I ran to
it and turned the knob. "Daddy?" I called.

A minute later I heard my father. "You went to bed without me," he said again, but this time it wasn't a question.

My mother answered, "Henry, I'm sorry."

My father was eerily silent.

"Daddy?" I called again.

Lizzy grabbed me and covered my mouth. "Gabby, you have to be quiet or he'll use the belt again. You know the rules. Go to bed and don't bother him and Mommy."

I glared at her, but her eyes were squeezed shut. She was doing what she always did—blocking it out. I didn't care how many times he told me I was misbehaving for screaming out in the middle of the night or for pounding on the door, feigning I had to use the bathroom. There were times I just couldn't take it.

"Henry, please, not tonight," my mother begged.

It sounded so familiar.

My father said nothing, but soon we heard the familiar thump. It seemed to go on for hours that night. I couldn't stop crying. I cried a tear for every one that my mother shed.

I hated him.

After a long while, Lizzy opened her eyes. She grabbed one of the vases and opened a window. "Come on, Gabby. Make a wish."

I walked over to her. "We have to help Mommy."

"We can't."

"Why not?"

"Because it will make things worse. All we can do is wish we could." She handed me the vase she had in her hand. "Here, take one."

I plucked one of the dandelions from the water.

"Blow. Just blow. It will make everything better," she whispered.

I knew it wouldn't.

And it never did make anything better but after that night, every time we were locked in our room, Lizzy would open the window and pretend she was blowing on a dandelion. She was able to escape into another world that way.

I never could.

One after the other, the nightmares of my childhood

kept coming. I couldn't block them out. He was a monster who demanded more of my mother than she could give. I might have been the one who killed her, but he drained the life right out of her.

Finally, I sat up in my bed and turned the light on. My body was covered in a cold sweat and I stripped my damp clothes off.

I hated that feeling of helplessness. How I'd wanted so badly for my mother to stop crying. For my father to stop what he was doing to her. So many nights. So many times my father had locked my sister and me in our room and taken my mother in ways that let him have full control. His driving need sickened me.

Sometimes he was loud, sometimes not. My mother would beg him to be quiet, but it was his house and he'd do as he pleased. And that's just what he always did. Sometimes it was fast; sometimes it went on for hours. It was always worse after a miscarriage. To this day, I still have no idea how many miscarriages my mother had.

When I was younger, I was terrified of the cries in the night; unlike my sister, I wasn't able to block them out by pretending to make wishes on dandelions.

As I grew, though, that changed. Anger ate away at me and I found myself spending my time praying I wouldn't turn out like him. After all, my sister had. And addictive behaviors were hereditary. Funny how I'd worried I'd be a sex addict. Nothing could be farther from the truth.

In fact, it wasn't until Charlie and I broke apart that I really understood that I could repress desire. That was not healthy either, though. It bred loneliness in a way I hadn't really noticed until tonight, when Logan had lit me up from the inside and I realized just how alone I was.

Tossing and turning, I knew sleep was impossible, so I got up. Moving around, I felt uneasy and found myself crossing the room. For some reason, I peered out the window.

It was dark, but I swore I saw someone out there.

I squinted.
It wasn't just someone that I saw.
My mind had to be playing tricks on me.

chapter
TEN

LOGAN

EMILY.

Dead Emily.

Elle might bear an eerie resemblance to Emily but she was nothing like her. Unlike Emily, I could tell Elle hadn't been sheltered, coddled, or treated like a princess. She didn't think she owned the world or that it revolved around her. No. Rather, she wore a protective shell and had a fierceness about her that I knew grew out of need. A need to not only protect her physical well-being but her emotional one as well. She was strong and independent and didn't seem to rely on anyone except herself. I hoped that continued to hold true, because relying on O'Shea would be a mistake. It wasn't something I could prove. It was something I felt.

After I left my father's, I had an overwhelming need to check on her. To make sure she was okay. I just doubted the slashing of her tires was a coincidence. There was something going on, but what, I had no fucking clue.

That was going to change.

The street was void of people as I pulled down it. I was easing by her place and noticed a light was on upstairs. Slowing, I looked around. The glow of that light illuminated a dark figure in the bushes.

I jerked my SUV to the curb and flew out the door. It was darker than fuck. The streetlights didn't do shit to overpower the gloom of the weather. Whoever it was had already moved around the building before I reached the sidewalk. I was almost certain the perp was unaware of my approach. Quietly, I skimmed along the sidewall, the rain steadily falling and blurring my vision with every passing second. As I blinked the water away, I saw movement. The figure had just rounded the building. I ran and then stopped at the corner to peer around to the back. The perp stood on a small porch, two steps high. He had something in his hand. I pulled out my SIG Sauer and hugged the wall as I quietly crept along the brick. I'd jump him and find out who the hell he was and what he was doing here.

Suddenly, the back porch light flicked on and the door opened.

Elle appeared in the entry.

"Stay inside," I snapped.

The figure, covered in black from head to toe, jumped down the two steps and took off at a dead run into the small park that butted up to the back of the building.

I tore after him.

"Logan!" Elle screamed.

I turned back, my heart in my throat. "Close and lock the fucking door."

"No, Logan, don't. Leave her alone."

Her?

By the time I turned back, there was no trace of anyone having been there. Bay Village was dense with row houses, iron gates, and so many alleys. I had no idea where the perp had gone once he'd—she'd?—slipped into the park.

I tucked my SIG back inside the waistband of my jeans. "Fuck."

Elle stepped outside with a small gun in her hand pointed at me.

"Put that away," I ordered.

She stared at me. "What are you doing here?"

I stopped at the base of the stairs and surveyed the area one last time. There was nothing but the darkness. "Let's get inside."

She steadied her arms and kept her finger on the trigger. "Why did you do that?"

I wanted to get out of the fucking vast space. "Elle, let's go inside and I'll explain."

She was still pointing her .22-caliber at me.

Impatience took over and I mounted the porch stairs.

Her hands started to tremble.

I knew she wasn't going to shoot me. "Give me the gun, Elle."

She didn't move. "No. Tell me what you're doing here."

To pacify her, I raised my hands surrender style. "I went to see my pop after I left you and on my way back to my hotel, I found myself needing to make sure you were all right."

She shook her head. "Why?"

"I don't know. I can't explain it. It was a feeling. But it's the truth. I was driving by when I saw a light on upstairs and then saw someone near the front door. That's when I got out of my SUV, but they were already around the building."

"Why were you after her?"

I looked around again. "Who?"

She moved her shoulders as if the position was uncomfortable. "My sister."

I gave her a puzzled look. "You think that was your sister?"

"I'm . . . I'm not sure." Her hands were shaking even more now.

Maybe she was nervous, or maybe it was because she was barely dressed and had to be freezing. Maybe it was because I was supposed to believe her sister was in rehab. I didn't. Still, I played along . . . for now. "I'm not going to hurt you. I promise." I reached and gently took the small pistol from her hand. "Come on, let's get inside. We'll talk there."

"I'm sorry," she whispered.

"You don't have to be," I whispered back.

She was still. I couldn't tell if she was in shock or if something else was going on in her head.

I opened the screen door and placed my hand on the small of her back. I liked the feeling of it there. I shoved the wayward thought away and focused instead on ushering her inside, on keeping my movements impersonal.

The door opened into the kitchen, which was open to the family room. Once I flicked the light on, I looked at her. She was barely dressed. *Impersonal. Keep it impersonal. Don't worry about how she's dressed, or not dressed as is the case.* I spotted a blanket and made my legs move toward it. Water seeped onto the hardwood floors from my sneakers, and once I'd grabbed the blanket I wrapped it around her. Then I found a towel and cleaned up the water on the floor.

Keep busy.

A to B to C.

I couldn't let my mind wander.

I had to think with my head, and not the one that was roaring at the close proximity to the unbearably sexy woman beside me.

She seemed to be zoning out as she stared at me.

"How about I make us that coffee?"

She nodded.

Okay.

Pot. On counter. Check.

Water. Sink. Check.

Coffee.

She was watching me. Knew what I needed next. "It's in the cupboard," she said, pointing above the pot.

My eyes lingered on her bare legs. They were long and lean.

Coffee. Check. Check. Check.

She sat at the table that divided the kitchen from the

living area. She was facing me, but her head was turned toward the door.

The kitchen was somehow new but old-looking at the same time. Obviously it had been recently remodeled with new appliances, but everything else looked old, even the chandelier over the island. The white cabinets and deep-veined marble counters were a stark contrast to the dark floors and redbrick walls. Paintings and photographs of flowers blowing in the wind decorated most of the wall space. They were a mixture of modern and traditional.

I scanned the rest of the area. It was sparsely furnished but looked more than adequate. A single dark gray sofa, white carpet, red pillows, and large wooden tables filled the living room. The open staircase with its Plexiglas guard made it easy to spot the second floor.

I marked the points of entry to the single large room. A door to the south leading to the backyard from the kitchen, a few windows down the east side, a window to the north, and the front door. No other points of entry. Nothing to the west, as another townhome was conveniently located there. If only she didn't have an end unit. The points of entry would be fewer. I wanted to check upstairs but decided I'd wait a bit.

As I pivoted to see if the coffee was ready, I noticed a door just under the staircase that most likely led to the basement. It had a lock on it but it wasn't engaged, and as I moved toward the refrigerator, I casually crossed over to the lock and turned it. I eased back and opened the fridge, where I spotted a bottle of creamer. I poured two cups of coffee and brought them, along with the creamer, to the table.

"Sugar?" I asked, like it was my house. Like I knew where it was. Like I was Martha fucking Stewart. I rolled my eyes at what this girl was doing to me.

She shook her head and then covered her face with her hands.

Distress emanated from her. Without a second thought,

I sat beside her and pulled her hands away. I couldn't help but notice how soft her skin was and how much I liked the feel of it. "What's going on?"

She straightened her shoulders. "I honestly don't know. I've been sitting here trying to figure out if that was my sister or just my imagination."

Looking for answers, I asked, "What makes you think it was your sister?"

My father told me Elizabeth O'Shea was MIA. Was the intel wrong?

"Nothing. It's just . . ." She stopped and rubbed her hands together in a nervous gesture.

"Go ahead. Tell me."

She shook a little. "I'd been having dreams about her all night when I finally gave up on sleep and decided to get up, I looked out the window, and I swear I saw her. But now that I've thought about it, I'm not so sure if it was my sister or my imagination putting her face on whoever it was."

I pushed her coffee closer to her. Her face was bare of makeup and her hair wild. She looked utterly beautiful and vulnerable at the same time. The vulnerability scared the shit out of me.

Focus.

I had to focus on finding out what I could, in order to keep her safe. "How about we back up. Why would your sister be lurking around your house in the middle of the night?"

With both hands around her cup, she glared at me. "How about you tell me what you and your father have to do with Michael?"

Well, that was an abrupt about-face. I put both elbows on the table and leaned forward. "Elle, I want to help you, but I can't do that if you won't talk to me."

Lifting the cream, she poured some in her cup and handed the bottle to me. "Why should I trust you?"

I tipped the creamer and added a small amount to the

jet-black liquid. "Because I'm sitting here. Because I care about what's going on. Because I want to help."

"Tell me what you and your father were doing at Michael's office."

She was suddenly all business.

Assessing the situation, I leaned back in my chair and stretched my legs as I tried to decide the best way to go about this. I looked at her. At my cup of coffee. And back at her. "My father is legal counsel to a man involved with Michael and he came to brief Michael on a . . . situation."

Her eyes bore into mine. "You mean the drug issue?"

My nod was hesitant, but enough that she knew the score.

Elle drew in a deep breath. "How does a boy from New York get involved in a Boston drug ring?"

"If you're talking about me, I'm not involved."

She raised a doubtful brow. "Who is this man who sent your father?"

Hesitation furrowed my brows.

"Tell me."

"Patrick Flannigan," I said, not really sure why.

Nothing registered. She didn't know him.

I sipped my coffee. She really knew very little and that was how it should stay. I felt the need to clarify something. "Elle, there are some things you are better off not knowing."

She held her hand up. "I'm tired of hearing that. My sister was into something illegal and if dangerous people are involved, I have a right to know."

Ruffled, I ran a hand through my hair. "You're right. I don't disagree. At the same time, I'm here because I want to help, not hurt you. But you need to let me do that."

She gave me a slight nod. "Fair enough."

The blanket had fallen off her shoulders and tiny nipples were protruding through the thin fabric of her top. My cock hardened, and I had to shift in my seat and reset my focus. "So tell me about your sister."

She pulled the blanket up. "First tell me who you think

that was. Were they trying to hurt me?"

With a jerk forward, I had a strange urge to grab her hand. "I don't know. That's what I'm trying to figure out. And I'm finished with you firing questions at me. I want to be honest with you, but I need you to talk to me first."

Annoyed, she wouldn't let up. "I will. After you tell me who you think that was."

My temper was flaring and I took a moment to calm down. "Straight up?"

She gave me the barest hint of a nod.

Ready or not, it was time to lay it on the line. "Your tire wasn't just flat, it was slashed. I hate to say this, but I'm almost certain it was deliberate."

Elle gave me another nod, this one no more certain than the last, and she shivered at the same time. Tough shit— there was no time to sugarcoat the truth, not that I would have done so anyway.

"It just seems way too coincidental that with everything going it was some random perpetrator. Whoever it was must have been here to leave a message." As soon as I said the words, the knot I felt in my stomach prevented me from forging on. Clint Eastwood sounded great, but in reality the Dirty Harry thing was wearing thin. I didn't like to see her in this state. She looked way too vulnerable for my liking.

Frowning, she circled her finger in the air. "Go on."

Did she just give me an order?

And had I just said *vulnerable*?

Composing myself, I told her what I knew. "He came here to scare you in some way. That's about the only thing I'm one hundred percent certain about."

"Buy why?"

"More than likely to send Michael a warning through you."

Her inscrutable countenance gave little away.

Frustrated, I cast her a wary look. "Now it's your turn. Tell me why you think it might have been your sister."

Elle's bravado seemed to deflate as soon as I put the

conversation in her court. With a hand on the table, she stood up and went over to the couch, still wrapped in the blanket and carrying her cup with her. Once she settled herself, she looked over at me and I could see the gloom on her face. "My sister's missing. We don't know where she is. I lied to you earlier. She's not in rehab."

I nodded. I already knew that, but I was glad she'd come clean. "Why the lie?"

She drew in a breath. "Michael is worried that if he reports her missing and the police find her, they'll figure out she's been involved with illegal activities and arrest her."

"So, he claims to be protecting her, but what if she's in trouble? What if that was her?"

"I don't know. I have to trust Michael on this. I haven't seen my sister in fifteen years. There's a chance I might not even know her if I saw her. But talking to you earlier tonight opened up some old wounds, and she has been on my mind more than usual. Like I said, now that I've had time to think about it, I really don't believe it was her."

Feeling like an asshole for pushing, I stood and walked over to the sofa, sitting on the opposite end. "Do you have any idea where your sister is now?"

She pulled the blanket from her shoulders. "No. My only guess is that things got too tough for her to handle and she ran off."

I tried not to look at her sexier-than-fuck body, but my own body had a mind of its own and I could feel my blood coursing hot through my veins. "Tell me what you know."

Elle turned sideways to face me and pulled her legs up, covering herself with the blanket again. "Not much. Almost four months ago I got a call out of the blue from my sister. I have no idea how she got my number, though we do have a mutual acquaintance in California. Like I said, we hadn't seen each other or spoken in fifteen years. When she called, she told me that she thought she was in trouble." Elle took a deep breath.

"Go on," I prompted.

With a slightly hesitant nod, she did. "She asked me to look after her baby if anything happened to her."

A tear rolled down her cheek. I wanted to wipe it away but I didn't. "Did she say what she thought might happen to her?" I asked.

Elle folded her hands together. "No. I was in shock that she was even calling me and even more shocked by what she was telling me. I would never have guessed she'd be married, let alone that she'd have a child. Before I knew it, she was telling me she'd be in touch and then hung up before I could get any further information out of her. When I tried to reverse the number, I couldn't. I had no idea what part of the world she was in. Our friend in California couldn't give me any info. So I did nothing."

"What else could you do?" I asked.

"Something. Anything. Look for her. I don't know," she said tightly.

My mouth opened, then shut. I wasn't sure what else I could say.

"You probably think I'm heartless."

Again, I resisted the urge to reach for her hand. "I don't think that at all."

Her face went a little blank, like it had in the car. Silence filled the space between us and I let her have a moment. If she was anything like me, memories had surfaced that she didn't want to remember. Finally, she took a breath and spoke. "It's just . . ." She waved her hand in the air. "Lizzy disappeared from my life and never looked back. When things got tough, she left."

"Were you close?"

She looked a little lost. "Yes and no. For so long she'd been the big sister, the protector I needed, but then as we grew older, she rebelled against my father and just kept getting into so much trouble. She was three years older than me, but sometimes I felt like the older one. Still, we'd shared so much in our childhood that I thought we were connected forever. I was wrong, though. She knew I needed her, yet she left, and after that she never called or told me where she was. I never heard from her until that day." She paused for a moment to gather herself.

My muscles went stiff as I watched the pain she felt flash across her face.

A few seconds later, she put a finger to her lips as if trying to quiet herself down.

The gesture made my heart pound like that of a wounded animal. It killed me, but there wasn't anything I could do to ease the pain of the past. This I knew all too well. All I could offer her was my ear. "It's okay, Elle. Go on."

As if determined to brush off the feelings, she lifted her chin. "One day I got a phone call from Michael. He told me who he was and asked me if my sister had been in contact with me. I guess he'd found my number among her things. I told him she had, but nothing else. He asked if she was with me and I told him no. That's when he told me she had left the morning before and never came home. She was missing and he was worried about her. I'm not sure why, but I felt compelled to come to Boston. And once I did, once I met Clementine, I couldn't leave. It wasn't until after I decided to stay that Michael told me what she had been involved in and explained why he hadn't involved the police. It made sense, then, anyway. Now I'm not so sure."

Elle's bare toes were sticking out of the blanket and her fingers were clutched around her knees. Her nails were glossy but she wore no color. They were short but shaped. I could tell she didn't care about the shit that didn't matter. In New York, I'd spent so much time around artificial beauty—boob jobs, plumped lips, fake nails, haute couture. In Boston, I never even looked at women. She was like a breath of fresh air.

Focus, asshole.

Focus.

"What does O'Shea think happened to her?" I asked.

"We're being honest with each other, right?"

I nodded.

"According to Michael, she was running some kind of white-collar drug op. He said as far as he knew she had been clean since Clementine was born, but then started up with the coke again. Something happened and her last deal went bad. He thinks she'll come out of hiding sooner or later. Or he's hoping."

"Where was she getting the coke from?"

If I had to guess, I'd guess Tommy was involved or that there was some connection to him. My guess is that although Patrick didn't condone it, Tommy was much more involved in the drug market than his father had a fucking clue about.

"I don't know. All I know is that according to Michael, she was selling to Michael's colleagues and connections before she disappeared."

I narrowed my eyes. "Are you sure it was her and not O'Shea?"

I didn't have a fucking clue who it was. Up until the point that my gramps went into a home last year, Patrick kept my father on the easy shit—his role, as counsel, was to make sure Patrick's businesses used for money laundering looked legit, liquor licenses were granted, real estate issues were taken care of, prostitution charges were avoided, and payoffs were made. Nothing to do with the drug side. The side that Patrick liked to think didn't exist. The side that Tommy ran.

It was still no surprise Pop had been ordered to make contact with Michael, though. My father had also always been sent to deal with the more influential people of Boston. He had the finesse, my gramps used to say. So at first, when he was told to pay O'Shea a visit, I thought it was no big deal.

Hell, I even volunteered to drive him there.

My false assumption had been that either Michael had reneged on a gambling debt and needed to pay up or did some damage to one of Patrick's girls and had retribution to pay. Or who knew—it could be any other kind of bullshit that Patrick wanted to flex his ego over.

It was a common thing.

It wasn't until we were on our way to see O'Shea that my old man told me it had to do with 250 kilos of missing cocaine. Five million dollars was no small chunk of change for anyone. But a total outstanding debt of ten million—the drugs and the money used to purchase them—was obscene.

Yeah, I choked on that.

"It was her," she said, refocusing me. She was angry now. "Michael didn't know anything about it until she told him the day before she disappeared. She put their child in jeopardy."

Scrubbing my jaw, I asked, "Do you know O'Shea is out there trying to make deals?"

"Look, Logan, Michael is a really good guy. All he wants is to keep Clementine safe and make everything right, but he has kept me pretty much in the dark. All I know is Lizzy pissed the wrong person off and Michael is trying to fix it."

Doubtful, I tried not to let my suspicions bleed through my words. "How does he plan to do that, Elle?"

She shook her head. "I don't know. He won't say anything other than that he has it under control."

Wary, I stood up, wondering how far I should go. I paced over to the window and glanced out of it. O'Shea was a fucker. If he was going to tell her something, he could at least make sure she understood the severity of the situation. "You know the clock is ticking?"

She swallowed. "I figured that by your father's visit earlier tonight."

I looked at her but said nothing at first. My mind was spinning with which was the worse of two evils. Then I decided that if Patrick had someone on O'Shea, they already knew about Elle. Making myself cut the shit, I walked over to her and crouched down. "Can you stay with O'Shea for a few days?"

"Yes, I'm sure he won't mind. I stay there a lot to be with Clementine. But why? What's going on, Logan?"

The idea of her with him made me mental, but it was the better option over her being alone, or worse, her with me. "I'm not certain, but I don't think you should be alone. I'm going to stay with you tonight just in case anyone comes back."

"Why? Who do you think is going to come back?"

"I honestly just don't know, but something isn't right."

"I can take care of myself."

Tough as nails. "I'm sure you can, but for my own peace of mind, I'll stay, just in case."

She stared at me with narrowed eyes but said nothing. If she was frightened, she wasn't going to let me see it.

"Now that we've got that settled, I'll go upstairs and check things out. Then you can head up there for the night."

Her features softened. "Then what?"

"I'll need a few days to look into what's going on. Once I know for certain, I'll tell you everything. In the meantime," I picked up her baby gun and palmed it, "we need to get you something a little bigger than this."

She shrugged. "It works fine."

With a shake of my head, I put the gun down. "You know how to use it?"

"Yes."

"Okay then, it will do until we can get you something better."

She took my hand. "Why are you doing all of this for me?"

I leaned forward and brushed a piece of hair from her eyes. "This thing you're involved in is more dangerous than you know, and I don't want you to get hurt."

In that moment, I had an overwhelming urge to kiss her. To push her back and bury myself in her. To fuck her worry away. The thought struck without warning. I wanted to take care of her.

That was a dangerous thought.

I jumped to my feet. "I'll be right back."

She nodded and looked at me with those watchful eyes.

My thoughts scattered, I turned away and strode to the stairs.

On the second floor, the light was on in one of the two rooms. I peered into the first one. Nothing. It was completely empty, as in no furniture, and the closet door was open. Then I looked into the hall bathroom. Other than the frosted glass shower, there was nowhere for anyone to hide. Finally, I went to the front room. It was her room. There was a brick wall painted off-white, two large glass lamps, an oval braided throw rug that looked worn, a plain comforter, and various paintings and pieces of art with splashes of red in each of them.

It felt like her.

What I knew of her, anyway.

And I knew then that she liked the color red.

I checked the windows. They were all locked.

Opened the closet.

Went into the bathroom attached to her bedroom. It was small, with just an old-fashioned tub, a sink, and a toilet. No shower. No linen closet.

There was no one up here.

The staircase wasn't wide, nor was it narrow. I occupied my mind with facts about her place as I descended the stairs. If I didn't, I know what I'd do when I got near her again. My body hummed a tune all its own when she was close. To be more accurate, my cock had its own heartbeat.

As I took the last stair, I kept my eyes down. I'd send her up to her bed without really looking at her. That had to help. But fuck me if I'd be able to sleep. My soles hit the hardwood and I couldn't control my urge to sneak just a peek of her. When I did, I saw that she was snuggled up in a ball on the couch, fast asleep.

Okay.

With a slight change of plans, I checked all the doors. Closed the blinds. Turned the lights off.

It was three thirty. As soon as daylight hit, I'd leave.

I sat on the other end of the couch—it was that or the

kitchen chair—and slid my SIG Sauer on the end table next to me. My head fell back and I decided to close my eyes for a few minutes.

In what seemed like moments later, the couch shifted and some kind of cry filled the room. I snapped my eyes open and switched the lamp on.

It was Elle.

A tortured moan ripped from her throat and her knuckles were white as they gripped the blanket that was wrapped around her.

I reached for her. "Elle, you're having a nightmare. Wake up."

She didn't wake.

I crawled over her and shook her gently. "Elle, wake up."

She was squeezing her eyes shut. "Stop it. Stop right now."

I ran a hand down her face and tucked her hair behind her ear. "Elle."

She opened her eyes and shot up.

"You're trembling. Are you okay?" I asked in a hushed, whispered tone.

In this single moment, I wished I were better at this. Wished I knew what to say to make her feel better. But the truth was, I had no fucking clue.

She didn't say a word. She just looked at me with that vulnerability she was usually good at covering up and the only thing I could think to do was hold her.

I don't know why.

Falling to the couch, I pulled her to me. At first I felt awkward, but she was shaking so much, I just wanted to help her calm down. I stroked her back with one hand and her hair with the other.

She clung to me like I was her lifeline. I held my breath, afraid to move. When I felt her steady breathing, I finally relaxed a bit. I don't even think she ever really woke up.

I covered us both and found myself still holding her.

Wanting to make all her hurt go away. Needing to keep her safe. I didn't let go.

Her body formed to mine in the most perfect way. One of her arms wrapped around my waist and one of her legs was tucked between mine. With her against me, my body felt strange. Alive. Like it had been brought back to life.

I knew then that I'd do whatever I had to do in order to keep her safe.

I also knew that staying away from her was the best way I could do that.

I just hoped to fuck I could.

chapter
ELEVEN

Day 2

Elle

RING. RING.

The incessant ringing of the telephone jarred me from slumber.

But it was the strong arms, warm body, and rhythmic breathing enveloping me that made me jerk my eyes open.

Oh. My. God.

I ignored the intrusive sound and peered up. Logan McPherson. How had I ended up sleeping in his arms? But more importantly, why did I feel so safe?

The phone cut off and then started up again.

Oh shit. What time was it?

The thought that I might have overslept and missed the opening of my store launch had me jumping up and lunging for the phone.

I looked over at Logan, who had just sat up and was scrubbing his jaw. "Hello?"

"Elle, it's Michael. Are you okay?"

Logan was in a white T-shirt, his button-down tossed to the side of the sofa sometime during the night. "Michael, I'm fine. I was going to call you this morning to talk to you."

"If it was about the car, you don't have to. The garage already called to notify me that the window of the Mercedes had been broken and it wasn't noted at pickup. I was obviously confused, but it was quickly cleared up when they told me about the flat tire. Why didn't you call me last night?"

"The window?" I questioned.

Logan was stretching, his washboard abs peeking between the hem of his shirt and the waistband of his pants. When he heard the shock in my voice, he immediately stood and walked over. "What?" he whispered, his warm breath ghosting across my neck.

My mouth shut, my mind clouded, and my body felt aflame. God, everything about him was molten lava, hot to touch and ready to erupt.

When I didn't answer, he repositioned that long, lean body of his so that he could hear. Closer, and closer still until his hand covered mine, and he was obviously satisfied.

That didn't help at all.

Now our bodies were so close that I not only became very aware of just how little clothing I was wearing, but just how much I wanted him.

Michael was still talking. "The driver's side, evidently. The garage wants me to stop by and verify that there is no interior damage from the rain before they begin the repairs."

Shaking the fuzziness from my brain, I realized how stupid I had been. "I'm sorry. I had the garage tow it because there was no spare. It must have occurred in the process."

"Are you okay?" Michael asked again with concern.

I didn't want to discuss what had happened last night over the phone. "Yes, I'm fine. But can I come over after I close the boutique? There are some things I'd like to talk to you about."

"Yeah, sure, of course. Listen, do you want me to pick you up and take you to work?"

Muscles rippled beside me with Logan's slight

movement. "No, I can walk but thanks for asking."

"You sure?"

My eyes were on the impressive muscle tone beside me. "Yes, I could use the exercise. I'll be inside all day."

"Okay then, since Clementine is already awake, I'll head over to the garage as soon as I get her fed and changed to sign off on the estimate for the damage. They said they could still deliver the vehicle today, but it would be a bit later with the additional repairs that are needed. I told them that was fine since you were working until six anyway."

The sea of white still encompassed me. "Thanks, Michael."

"Elle," he said in a low tone.

"Yes."

"You should have called me."

Logan's body stiffened at that and he moved away from me.

"We'll talk later," was my only response. After all, he was right. I should have.

Logan was rinsing out the coffeepot, and as soon as I hung up he said, "I'll drop you off at the boutique. What time do you have to be there?"

I looked at the clock on the wall and sighed. I really had wanted to walk but time wouldn't allow for that. "About five minutes ago."

With a rumble from deep in his throat, he turned around and his hazel gaze raked my length. "You'd better hurry then."

I felt the heat in his glance and the warmth chased my chill away. "Yeah, I will."

Logan bobbed his head toward the stairs. "I'll be here waiting."

I gave him a slight smile. "Thank you ... for everything."

Our eyes connected, but eventually he turned around and busied himself scooping coffee into the filter.

Not quite a full minute later, I managed to unglue my gaze from him and make my way up the stairs to hop in the shower. Standing naked as the warm water flowed over me, I couldn't help but think of Logan. The way he moved. The way he spoke. The way he watched me. The way his body had been wrapped around mine so protectively. I remembered waking from a bad dream and him trying to console me. How I'd ended up in his arms, I didn't recall, but it didn't really matter.

No matter what he said, I knew the truth—we were on opposite sides.

And that meant there was no way we could be together.

Logan had never showed anything but concern for me. Yet, he'd come with his father to give Michael a warning. What came after the warning was what concerned me. And would Logan be involved with that?

I had no reason to believe he would. I didn't want to. But I had to push the intoxicating man from my mind and face reality. My first step toward that was to concentrate on getting ready. I wanted to look hip for my boutique opening but was in a hurry, so I had to compromise.

I pulled on a pair of black skinny jeans and found an off-white flouncy blouse to wear under my black leather jacket. I went with chunky ankle boots and quickly blew my hair dry to calm some of the wildness. I coated my lashes with mascara and dabbed on some clear lip gloss.

When I looked at myself in the mirror, I envisioned Logan putting his arms around me. Running his fingers through my hair. Kissing my glossy lips. Tucking his hands under the flare of my top.

I squeezed my eyes shut.

"Stop it," I chastised myself.

And besides, I had bigger issues to think about, such as who slashed my tire and broke my window, and who had been lurking around my house last night.

With that in mind, I stepped into my closet and pulled a tote down from the shelf and then threw a few things into it. I was going to take Logan's advice and stay at Michael's, at least for the night.

Thirty minutes had elapsed when I started down the stairs.

Not bad.

Logan was fully dressed and on his phone, quietly talking over near the door that led to the back. As soon as he saw me, he hung up. I knew better than to ask.

My .22 was on the counter. He opened the chamber to check if it was loaded. I already knew it was.

My larger purse was beside me and I reached to take the gun.

That was not what he had in mind. Instead, he emptied the chamber. "Let me show you."

"Logan, I know how—" I started to protest, but he wasn't listening.

His long, lean body was behind me in a matter of moments and his hands were on mine, raising them. "Aim and shoot." He squeezed my finger against the trigger, firing off dry rounds. "You don't hesitate. You understand?"

I nodded and concentrated on the weapon in my hand, not the powerhouse of a man practically holding me.

His strong body pressed to mine. His competent hands were showing me how to take care of myself. He didn't appear to be holding anything back—he knew what he was doing to me, to my body. The thought snapped me out of my haze. "Logan, I know how to use a gun."

Moving to the side, he reloaded it. "I'm sure you do. It's just that last night, you were aiming that gun at me but I knew you had no intention of pulling the trigger." He set the gun on the counter and stepped into me. "If I were anyone else, you'd be dead."

I bit my lip. "I . . . I wasn't ever going to shoot you."

"Why?" He didn't even blink.

Because I want you madly. Because I can't stop thinking about you. Because there's just something about you. I couldn't say any of those things. Blinking those thoughts away, I said, "Because I knew you weren't here to hurt me."

He stepped even closer. "No, you didn't."

All I could do was shake my head. I did know it. I could feel it.

"Listen, if you don't plan to pull the trigger, then you never aim. If you think even for a minute anyone is a threat to you, I want you to shoot first and think later. This isn't a game. These people don't dick around. Do you hear me?"

I nodded. I was a little freaked out, but I wasn't going to admit to that. I wasn't sure just how much danger I was in. Maybe he was a little paranoid. Either way, I needed to stay strong. "Yes."

His voice softened and his demeanor changed. "I don't mean to scare you, but these guys are professionals. They creep around in the dark, lurk around corners, hide in alleys. Don't go anywhere alone."

"Who are these people? Are they going to come into my store?"

He shook his head. "They won't do anything out in the open and they may not even be after you."

"Then why are you telling me these things?"

"I just want you to stay safe. Do you understand? Stay safe."

"I understand," I said, sounding a little breathy.

His hands gripped my hips and he pulled me to him.

I went more than willingly.

His lips hovered over mine. "You have to stay safe," he repeated.

Just then my cell phone rang. I jerked back and reached for it. It was Peyton.

"I'm on my way," I answered.

"I can't believe you're not here yet. Did you hook up with Mr. Big Dick?"

"Peyton!" I admonished. "I'm just running a bit behind. I'll be there in a few minutes."

"Okay, but when you get here I want all the details."

"'Bye," I said, trying not to smile and wishing there were details to spill.

He took my phone and hit some buttons. "Here's my

number. Call me if you need anything. If you can't reach me, I'm at the Four Seasons. I'll leave your name at the desk."

I took the phone back. As soon as I shoved it into my bigger purse, he handed me my gun. "This too."

I put that in my purse as well, and grabbed the smaller purse. I'd switch everything else later. "I'm ready."

He nodded toward the front door and grinned at me. "Come on, then, let's get you to work."

I should have been scared.

And I was.

I should have been worrying about why all of this was happening.

And I was.

But right now I just wanted to bask in how much that grin melted me.

chapter
TWELVE

LOGAN

THE CLOCK WAS TICKING.

Seven minus one. Six days left. Six fucking days until Patrick makes his move.

Time had given me clarity. Whoever had been harassing Elle was doing just that. If Patrick were trying to strike, there would be no close encounters. And if it were Tommy . . .

With a shiver, I shook that thought away.

I'd know if it were him.

Lost in my thoughts, I glided into the parking lot of the garage where Elle's car was towed last night. The place was more like a compound. There was a row of five bays on one side and five more bays directly opposite those, with an office connecting them. Once I parked, I looked toward the only open bay and saw O'Shea standing near Elle's car. He had his kid in one arm and a piece of crumpled paper in his other hand.

Fuck.

I had hoped to beat him here and scope out the inside of Elle's vehicle before he did. Whoever broke the window did so after I had seen the car—either on the way here or after it arrived. Still, my head was clearly not in the game last night. How the hell had I missed the piece of paper? Unless I hadn't. When I checked the car last night, I know I looked around, including in the backseat, where I tossed some toys aside. It couldn't have been there then.

Shoving my thoughts aside, I watched as O'Shea spoke briefly with someone near Elle's car. The guy wore a blue quilted jacket but also had a tie on, so I assumed he was the manager. O'Shea seemed twitchy. He was bouncing the baby nervously on his hip. She was playing with the large silver rattle attached to a red ribbon that I moved off the seat last night. Despite the manager edging toward the door that must have led to the office, O'Shea seemed to have no interest in following him. The mechanic reached inside and pulled out a clipboard.

O'Shea turned and I put my hat on and slid down in my seat. I probably didn't have to; my windows were pretty heavily tinted and he didn't seem to be on alert. O'Shea had stepped out of the bay when he stopped and turned back around. The manager was holding up the clipboard. O'Shea took it and scribbled something, his John Hancock more than likely, and then quickly walked out.

The manager wandered back toward the door and I watched as O'Shea shoved the paper he had been holding into his pocket and then loaded the baby in his own car. I needed to see what the hell was on that piece of paper. The way he was acting was shady at best, and instinct told me it wasn't just a receipt for his dry cleaning. I wanted to follow him, but if Patrick was already tailing O'Shea, him finding out I was stalking O'Shea wasn't going to be pretty.

His tires practically squealed as he pulled out of the compound. He was obviously in a hurry.

I couldn't help but wonder why.

My greatest obstacle was time. As I was pondering my next move, I spotted the mechanic from last night getting ready to close the bay.

Bingo.

Moving quickly, I strode over to him. "Hey dude, remember me?"

He glanced up, rope in hand. Jerking his head toward Elle's car he said, "Yeah, I talked to you about this Mercedes SUV last night."

I nodded. "I just wanted to check on it. Make sure you were able to order the tire."

He scratched his head. "Let me find out."

As soon as he started walking over toward the office door, I darted for the Mercedes. I knew I wouldn't find anything, but I wanted to have a look-see for myself. Sure enough, the window was completely busted and glass shards covered the seat and floor.

"Hey, there you are." The mechanic looked me over like I'd been the one to bust out the window.

"Yeah, sorry. Just wanted to have a better look in the daylight. What's the ten on the tire? Did you get it ordered?"

"You're all good. It should be here soon," he said, my explanation apparently not appeasing him. "Anything else I can do for you?"

"No," I said walking backwards, edging away from him before he asked too many questions or called anyone else in. "Thanks again."

"Sure, anytime."

I hopped in my Rover and hightailed it out of there. As I drove, I prayed like hell O'Shea mentioned his stop at the garage to Elle and in turn she trusted me enough to tell me about it. I needed to know what was on that piece of paper. Was it a threat? A warning? From Patrick? From Tommy?

By the time I reached my suite at the Four Seasons, I was utterly wiped. I needed to catch a few z's before heading to my father's to discuss the best way to have a face-to-face with Patrick in order to find out what he had in mind for O'Shea.

The amount of effort Patrick was putting into this whole thing told me he wanted something more than just the net out of the five mil. I knew how he operated. He sent his associates first and then shortly after failure of delivery, Tommy would show up. And nothing good could happen then. Yet, Tommy had been sitting on this for almost three months. That alone told me there was something in it for him. A connection? A product? A pipeline? I didn't know what, but I was going to find out. And if, by chance, it was about the money, I'd give Elle, who in turn would give O'Shea, what I had in my accounts; it wasn't much, but it might buy some time.

That reminded me, I had to call my grandfather Ryan and tell him I wouldn't be back in New York this week. There was no way I was leaving Boston.

I flopped on the couch and pulled out my phone to make the call, but then thought an email would be so much easier. Logan Ryan had already revoked my access to my restricted trust fund. It didn't become legally mine until I turned thirty. My maternal grandfather was cutting me off until I severed all my ties with the Blue Hill Gang. Too dangerous to access that kind of cash, he reasoned. If I told him I wouldn't be back this week, chances were good he'd put a hold on my paychecks, too.

I typed a simple email that said I had a case that could possibly detain me and hit send. It wasn't entirely a lie.

There was a mixture of guilt and resignation in my mind as I headed for the Liberace-style bathroom. I sat beneath the heat lamps as I glanced around. The large Jacuzzi tub and black marble shower with six jets and rain head were way more than I needed on a daily basis. Sure, I'd grown up surrounded by luxury, but sometimes it was a little over the top.

Many months ago, after I received the call about my father's arrest, I'd checked in here. I went for a standard room, but then Grandpa Ryan made an appearance, and before I knew it, I was upgraded to this suite. I scratched my head. How the hell had I agreed to that? *Right, you never said no to Grandpa Ryan.*

At first, he covered the hotel bill. Then last week, he

called me into his office after my weekend visit here and told me he'd been checking on my father's progress. Since he appeared to be doing well, it was time for me to leave him on his own and concentrate on my own job. He wasn't asking.

That was the first time I'd seen that side of him and I tried to bite my tongue at the audacity of that arrogant old man, but I didn't do a great job and I knew my anger bled through my response. Although I was in no way disrespectful, when I returned to Boston, the front desk asked for a new credit card, since it seemed the one on file had been declined. I didn't bother to call my grandfather; I knew it was his way of telling me he was in control. I also knew then where my mother got it. It obviously ran in the family.

Well, fuck him. I did have my own money.

Still, it was probably time to break down and move over to that shit hole my dad was living in, because the cost of this place together with my New York apartment was putting a huge dent in my funds. Although I had to say, last night my pop's house looked in better shape than I'd seen it in years. Then again, maybe last night was just the first time I looked at it differently.

No matter how clean he tried to make it, though, nothing would ever erase what had happened there or the blood that had been spilled. What Tommy had done was an act of revenge that he never wanted me to forget.

He had succeeded in that.

I cranked the water as hot as I knew I could stand it and tried to wipe my mind clean of what he'd do to Elle if he saw her and worse, much worse, what he'd do to her if he saw her with me.

Fuck.

Stripping off my clothes, I stepped into the large glass expanse and let the water flow over me, welcoming the familiar burn that was never enough to really make me feel clean.

And thought of Elle.

Beautiful.

Natural.

Smart.

Tough.

Vulnerable.

Vulnerable enough that if I couldn't have taken her when I dropped her off last night, I knew I could have when her body covered mine as she slept, or this morning when she stood next to me practically naked. Those visions of her made my cock throb so much it hurt. But I craved her for more than just a single fuck.

And that just wasn't possible.

I was already hard just thinking about her again, her long, lean legs, her perfect body, her small, tight ass. The water ran onto my hair, down my face, and fell to the drain. Before I knew it, I wasn't paying attention to the water. Instead I had my cock in one hand, my balls in the other.

It had been a while since I'd fucked anyone. This shit with my father and Patrick had my mind on other things. But damn, my body needed this. I wanted her hand to curl around me and feel how hard she made me. I wanted to tell her what she did to me. Whisper in her ear. Scream it if I had to.

That wasn't happening, though, so I settled on this.

I closed my eyes and gently rubbed first around the head, and then down my shaft. I fisted my balls in my other hand.

Fuck, that felt good.

Because I couldn't help myself, I pictured her doing it. Her in the shower with me and us free to explore each other in any way we wanted. God knew, I wanted to explore her. All of her body. I grabbed my shaft and moved up toward the tip. I wanted her hands to be the ones gripping me, not mine.

Water droplets from the shower pounded down my body and acted as lube, making it easier to move faster. I thought of her, her face, her body, how much I wanted to touch her, where I wanted to touch her.

Oh, fuck.

I imagined driving my cock into her sweet pussy and it made me want to come hard and fast.

Oh, fuck yeah.

My fist pumped at a quicker pace and I licked the water from my lips. I thought about slowing down but I was already too far gone.

My forehead fell to the shower wall and I grabbed my balls tighter, twisting my cock to feel a little pain.

Oh, fuck.

Pressure welled deep within me and a tingling radiated down my spine.

I was going to come.

I was going to come.

Oh, fuck.

As my orgasm sped higher and higher, so did the pleasure—it felt like electricity was shooting through me. That unbelievably good feeling mounted and I couldn't hold on any longer.

I clutched on tight and let myself go.

As I came, my cock twitched so fast, it felt like a spasm, but so incredibly good. I exploded at the thought of her and the intensity of my orgasm shocked me. When the feeling rose again, I couldn't believe it.

I wasn't finished.

This time I really let myself go—crossing that threshold to another world and reliving the same feeling again and again until I was spent. Just the thought of her milked me for everything I had.

Afterward, I slouched against the glass and thought that if this was all I could have of her—a hand job given by my own palm with her in my mind—I'd take it.

It felt that fucking good.

As my breathing returned to normal, so did my senses, and I chastised myself. I shouldn't be thinking of her at all, especially in that way.

With a sudden urge to want to chop my dick off, I lathered up with soap, rinsed off, and got the fuck out of there.

I didn't bother to shave.

Wrapping a towel around my waist, I wiped the steam from the mirror and stared at my reflection, the scar under my eye opening up the memory that grabbed me before I could shut it down.

"You sure your family doesn't mind if I stay at your house?" she asked.

"Fuck no, my pop's passed out somewhere by now and my gramps isn't home."

It was the summer after college graduation and I was spending it with a bunch of my friends in the Hamptons. At a party, I had met a girl named Kayla who I wanted to get to know better. It had been the first time since Emily that I had taken any real interest in any chick.

After about a month of dating, I liked her enough to ask her if she wanted to road trip it to my hometown of Boston with me. It was last minute. I was on a drug run for my friends. It was supposed to be quick. Drive to Boston, spend the night at my gramps's, pick up what I needed, and turn around and go back.

Kayla was excited to tag along and packed quickly, but then had a number of stops she wanted me to make before we actually got on the road. I was a bit annoyed but rode with it. By the time we pulled into Boston, it was late and Kayla complained that she was hungry. I remember thinking how high maintenance she was and that I wasn't sure the relationship thing was for me. Still, I took her to a local pizzeria in Dorchester to get something to eat and put those thoughts on pause for the night.

It was around eleven before we finally reached Gramps's place and I unlocked the door that led to his kitchen. Just as I stuck my key in the door, I remembered what it was I really liked about Kayla. It was her aggressiveness. She wrapped her arms around my waist and her hands drifted down. With my cock taking over my thoughts, I turned toward her and started kissing. We stumbled inside in a tangle of tongues, arms, and legs. I seriously doubted we'd make it past the kitchen.

I reached behind me to close the door but before I did, I felt another pair of hands on my shoulders and thought, what the fuck. *Out of nowhere, I was shoved forward. I whipped around to see a gang of guys bursting in. There were four of them. I tried to shield Kayla, but one grabbed her from me as the other three went after me. Lunging forward, I made it to the counter and managed to clutch a kitchen knife from the wooden butcher block. This time when the three of them tried to secure me again, I flipped around and blindly stuck the blade somewhere.*

"Fuccckkkk, he stabbed me!" one of them screamed.

Everything happened so fast after that. The knife was still in my hand. It didn't go deep enough that I couldn't withdraw it. When I tried again, somehow one of them managed to take it from me. He brought the blade right to my face. "Stop struggling," he ordered.

Heart racing, I felt like a caged animal. My breathing constricted and I was having difficulty drawing air as I fought to free myself.

The one with the knife got real close, trying to scare me. I was lost in my own rage—fear wasn't even under my radar. I just knew I had to get Kayla out of there. I didn't know who these guys were, but I knew what they wanted wasn't anything good. The scuffle continued, and then he managed to slice the blade across my face, just under my eye.

Pain singed my every nerve.

Yet Kayla's screams had me fighting even harder.

"She's next if you don't stop!" the dick yelled.

That's when I ceased my struggling.

Three guys held me in place and the fourth restrained Kayla with her hands behind her back. Once they had us where they wanted us, one of them announced, "All set."

Stumbling through the door with glassy eyes, just as I'd remembered him, came Tommy Flannigan. He grinned like a sick motherfucker at Kayla and then pointed his finger at me. "Are you a fucking moron?"

He was coked up.

Fear finally made its way up my throat and I could feel sweat beading on my forehead. I once again struggled to get free.

Tommy closed the door and took a step toward Kayla. When she started screaming again, Tommy grabbed a kitchen towel and shoved it in her mouth.

"Leave her alone," I spat.

Tommy nodded his head to the guy holding her and turned around. He swiped the bloody knife from one of the guys holding me and strode back over to her.

"Leave her alone!" I yelled again.

He ignored me and sliced open her blouse in one fluid movement.

Jerking forward, I felt my anger burning like fire as it flowed through my veins. "Fucker, look at me!" I screamed.

Tommy slowly turned around, that sadistic grin still on his face. "You must be fucking stupid to risk being seen around here with a chick."

"Leave her alone," I said again.

"You should have thought about that before you decided to stick your dick in her."

"Tommy, this is between you and me. Let her go."

His laugh was vile. "That's where you're wrong. It's between you and my sister, but she's not around anymore to handle the problem. Now is she, Logan?"

"Tommy," I seethed.

He shook his head. "I can't have you disgracing my sister's memory by being seen around town with skanks."

I kicked, I shoved, I fought against the three guys holding me but couldn't loosen their hold. Finally, I stopped and looked at him. "Tommy, I'm sorry. You're right. Emily didn't deserve that." I tried to reason with him even as the bile rose up my throat.

He glared at me.

"Tommy—"

He held his hand up, then found another kitchen towel and tossed it to one of the guys. "Plug his hole."

Blood was dripping down my face as I fought against being gagged. I needed Tommy to think of Emily if I was going to have a shot at stopping what he was about to do. But I was completely powerless once I couldn't speak.

Tommy stripped the rest of Kayla's clothes off and my heart banged in my chest when I saw the terror in her eyes. Time seemed to move slowly as her muffled noises tore at me. My anger flamed and I became a wild animal, kicking, clawing, struggling to get free.

This only seemed to spur Tommy further. I watched as he twitched and his face grew more and more excited. I knew I needed to become a blank canvas, but I just couldn't. Then Tommy licked his tongue up Kayla's throat and something inside me went ballistic. At the sight, I stopped, letting my eyes go vacant; I tried to mentally remove myself from the situation.

Tommy's entire focus was on me. Good. That was good. He was trying to figure me out. Let him try. I withdrew further and further. He narrowed his eyes, watching me. Bewildered, he approached me as if I might attack him. Ironic. But then he snapped and stepped close to Kayla and held up the knife. "Watch this, McPherson."

I squeezed my eyes shut.

"Open your fucking eyes or I'll slice her open."

My eyes slammed open.

With the knife, he carved the letter E in her stomach.

She was screaming and I was fucking helpless.

I was going to fucking kill him.

When he finished, he took her purse and pulled out her wallet, then her license. "Kayla Williams of 1115 Park Avenue, if you so much as breathe a word of what happened here tonight, we'll find you and your family and kill you before you can even dial nine."

Her eyes were round with fear. She was terrified.

Tommy then turned back to me. "You see, Logan, all of your skank whores need to be marked. To know what a vile creature they let inside them. Do you understand that, Logan?"

I didn't respond.

"Do you understand me, Logan?"

Again, I didn't respond. I was going to kill that motherfucker, but even as I thought the words, I knew I wouldn't. I may have lived in two different worlds, but some lines should never be crossed. But I'd make him pay. Somehow, some way, he was going to pay.

"Since Mr. Silver Spoon here doesn't want to answer, how about we play a little game of question and answer." He looked at the guy to the right of me. "Would you want to fuck her after he did?"

"Fuck no," the cokehead said.

"You?" he said to other guy holding me.

"No fucking way."

"You?" he asked the guy who had my head in a vise grip.

"Not if she were the last skank on earth."

Tommy turned back to the guy holding Kayla. "That leaves you, my man. You'll take one for the team, won't you?"

The bastard grinned from ear to ear. "Only if he gets to watch."

I kicked. I tried to pound my head against either of the guys holding me and then the one behind me, but nothing I did gave me the leverage to break free of all three of them.

"Hey, Logan. Too bad your parents didn't neuter you when they had the chance."

Up until this night, I had never wanted to respond to anything or anyone in such a violent manner. I never wanted to be like my grandfather. But as Tommy bent Kayla over the kitchen table, something snapped and I knew I'd never be the same.

I watched, helpless, as she struggled and he manhandled her. He tied her hands behind her back and then he spread her legs with his boots. When he took off his belt and secured one of her legs to the table, I thought I was going to be sick.

She hadn't done anything.

She didn't deserve this.

The other guy unbuttoned his pants and then grabbed her by the hair.

Tommy whirled around with a smile on his face and the knife in his hand. He bobbed his chin to the guy behind me. "Pull his pants down. I've been thinking and I don't think it's too late to neuter this dog."

This was my chance. As soon as he let go of the chokehold he had on me, I was going to annihilate every single one of these fuckers.

"On second thought, let me." Tommy grinned.

I thrashed, but the three guys tightened their grip.

"You got him?" Tommy asked.

I saw one nod.

Tommy took the knife and dragged it up the inside of my thigh, stabbing right through the fabric of my jeans. Blood seeped into the denim as he worked his way up my thigh.

Kayla was screaming loudly now. Her gag must have fallen loose. I couldn't see her. Couldn't see what that asshole was doing to her, but I could hear it.

Pain tinged the fringes of my existence and my senses started to dull. But I made myself stand straight. I was not a pussy. I was going to get out of this and regardless of what I'd thought, I was going to kill Tommy Flannigan.

Before he made it all the way up my leg with the blade, the kitchen door flung open. Frank Reilly, my grandfather's next-door neighbor and also Molly's pub owner, was standing there with a shotgun in his hand.

Thank fuck. Thank fuck. Thank fuck.

"That's enough, boys. It's time for you to leave." He pointed his rifle between Tommy and the guy who was bent over Kayla.

Blood was dripping onto the floor. From my face, from my leg, and from Kayla's stomach. The guy who had his dick out of his pants turned around, and red footprints from Kayla's blood were left behind.

Tommy looked at my gramps's neighbor. "Get out of here, Frank. It's not your business."

Frank was a tough guy. Big. No-nonsense. He didn't take shit from anyone.

He looked at Tommy and shrugged. "Just thought you should know, I called your old man. He's on his way to get you. I also called Killian. He's on his way to kill you. So you have a couple of options to choose from. No skin off my back whichever you decide."

With that he turned and walked out.

Tommy bobbed his chin for the door. "Leave him and his whore girlfriend. Let's get out of here—Declan's in the car waiting."

They let go of me and I lunged for Tommy.

He held up the knife. "Touch me and you're dead."

"Fuck you," I spat once I'd pulled the towel from my mouth.

He smile was evil. "I'd watch my back if I were you, because the next time I see you around my town with another skank disgracing my sister's name, it won't end up as pretty as this did."

My fists clenched at my sides and I started for him.

He held up the knife and pointed it toward Kayla. "I'm not fucking around with you." He limped backwards out the door, slamming it as soon as he crossed the threshold.

I wanted to go after him, but Kayla was still bound and hysterical. I untied her and immediately pulled my bloody shirt off to slide it over her trembling body. I didn't want to leave her and I didn't want to move her.

She flung her arms around me and clung to me as we both spilled the blood that Tommy had shed.

Her cuts were superficial, but the emotional damage was anything but.

To her and me.

The day that Emily died will always remain a permanent point of reference for me. My life ever since has been "after" . . . but the run-in with Tommy was a day I'll never forget, and it, too, became an "after." Both marked an alternate path my life would take. Both had an impact on me. Yet that day with Tommy made me a different person.

We hadn't called the police. Things weren't handled that way and besides, Patrick had the Dorchester cops in his pocket. Rather, he and my grandfather roughed it out. The problem was, Patrick was already unofficially running things, so the punishment didn't match the crime. My gramps had one foot out the door and didn't have much of a choice but to agree to the terms. Patrick had sanctioned what Tommy had done as due retribution. As if he wouldn't. My gramps allowed the incident to pass, but ordered no further engagement with me by either Patrick or Tommy, on any level. I also was forbidden from going anywhere near Tommy and he was forbidden from coming anywhere near me. Neither of us violated the order. We both knew better. I hadn't been in the same room with him or Patrick since that night.

But that was about to change.

The thought of him had me seeing red. I pounded my fist so hard against the bathroom mirror that it cracked down the middle. Blood seeped between my fingers. I didn't give a shit.

Tommy was going to be trouble with his second-in-command status. Sure, he was older now, but he was still a cokehead. What made it worse was that he was a cokehead with power. With troops. With eyes everywhere. And to boot, he was more ruthless than those before him had been. Women were his favorite targets. He was a motherfucker, a ticking time bomb, and a cold-hearted killer.

The truth was, now that my gramps had left the ranks, there was no way Tommy was going to stick to the treaty made years ago.

It was just a matter of time.

This situation might speed it up, but either way, he would be coming for me.

I'd be ready this time.

I looked at my scar one last time.

His time would come, but until then . . . he couldn't see me with Elle.

Ever.

Elle

"**M**CPHERSON?" SHE GASPED.

I nodded around a sip from my water bottle.

"You're certain his last name is McPherson?" she asked again, spearing the credit card receipt that the last customer had just signed.

"Yes, Peyton," I said exasperatedly and set my bottle down.

Cracking open a roll of quarters, she kept going. "As in Killian McPherson?"

I brought my voice down. "I'm not sure. Who is he that the name has you fifty shades of crazy?"

It was the first break we'd had all day. It was close to three and the boutique's grand opening had been unbelievable. Sales were more than I had ever expected for my first day and the traffic in and out was insane.

Peyton closed the cash register drawer and whipped around. "Didn't read up on Boston before you moved here?"

I blinked. "No."

Peyton grimaced. "Oh, right, your sister. Sorry."

"Focus, Peyton. Who is Killian McPherson?"

Her face resumed its normal charm. "Killian, the Killer, McPherson was the original leader of the Blue Hill Gang."

My brows popped. "Okay. Are we talking motorcycle club or street gang?"

"Neither. They're the Irish Mafia," she whispered.

"What type of material is this?" a woman holding a set of sheets in her hands asked.

My mind was spinning. The Mafia. My sister had been involved with the Mafia. Logan was related to someone who was once in charge of underworld organized crime. Was Logan part of it too? Is that why he was so concerned about what could happen?

"It's Egyptian cotton," Peyton told the customer, and I was relieved. I wasn't certain I could talk right now, my throat was so tight.

"The fabric feels so coarse," the woman commented.

"The material softens with each wash. And it resists any type of pilling. The sheets are very durable, and extremely breathable. I highly recommend them. Egyptian cotton is known for its ability to create extra-long fibers so they not only feel luxurious on your skin, but they can last for decades."

My mind was thinking back to episodes of *The Sopranos*, made men, earners. I just couldn't see Logan being a part of anything like that. He was cultured, not brutish, although he was brooding. No—still, I didn't see it. He had to be more like his other grandfather, the one from New York City that he had told me about. Yes, that made sense.

Having talked myself off of the ledge, mention of his name had me thinking about him in other ways. His rough fingers digging into my skin, his soft lips on mine, his hard body pressed to mine. Even if he was a killer's grandson, that didn't mean anything. We couldn't control who we were related to—I knew that all too well.

Voices brought me back.

What the hell was wrong with me? I should stay away from him.

Peyton glared at me while she talked. Although I was only half listening, I was still impressed. She had done her homework. "Isn't that correct, Elle?" she said, narrowing her eyes at me.

"Yes, it is," I smiled sweetly, having no idea what I was agreeing to.

"I'll take them. Do they come in lavender?" the woman asked.

Peyton glanced toward me with a little kinder expression this time. "I'm certain we can order that color for you. Right now we only have them in gray, cream, and light blue."

"Oh, I didn't see the light blue," the woman said.

Peyton rounded the table. "It's right here."

"Very nice. I'll take them." The woman was practically giddy.

I rang her up and then handed her the beautifully wrapped package, tied with our signature red ribbon and adorned with a red bow.

Once she was gone, I turned to Peyton and shoved Logan's deliciously deep voice from my mind. "What else do you know about the Blue Hill Gang?"

She shrugged her shoulders. "They swept the streets of Boston in the seventies and focused their efforts on racketeering, loan-sharking, and illegal gambling. Years later they merged with the Dorchester Heights Gang. Lots of rumors as to why, but no one knows for certain. Now some guy named Patrick Flannigan runs the gang and they own most of the strip clubs in Boston. I don't really know anything else. I'm sure you could Google them."

Google them!

I didn't have to. I felt like I knew too much already. I was worried Michael was involved with them, and the thought scared the living shit out of me.

"Hey, who knows, they might not even be related," she said, brushing past me and making a beeline to the table with the scarves. It was in disarray and her OCD must have kicked in.

Patrick. Logan mentioned him yesterday. Patrick, the head of the Irish Mob, had something to do with my sister.

I felt sick.

As Peyton folded scarves, I thought about what she'd said, but I already knew Logan had to be related to him. It was the only thing that made sense over the past twenty-four hours. I stared at the intricate golden design of the cash register as my thoughts overtook me. This was so much more dangerous than I had thought. What had my sister gotten her family into?

"Elle, it's Michael." Peyton held out the phone that was right next to me.

I hadn't even heard it ring.

I took it. "Hey, Michael, how's Clementine today?" My voice was shaky.

"She's fine."

"Oh, good. I need to—"

"Listen, Elle, there's been a slight change of plans, though. I had to drop her off at Erin's house earlier today and I'm in New York."

"New York?" I asked, leaning back on the counter.

"Client emergency. Do you mind picking her up and staying with her at the house? I should be home tomorrow afternoon, or early evening at the latest."

Feeling restless, I moved to stand behind the cash register. "Yes, sure, of course. You should have brought her here, though. You know your sister has her hands full with the new baby."

"It was so last minute that I hated to bother you. After I tried the nanny and she didn't pick up, I called Erin. I have to run. I'll be unreachable most of the night. Leave me a message if anything serious comes up."

I searched for a pen. "Sure thing. Where are you staying?"

He had already hung up.

I felt my body slump in exhaustion.

"Everything okay?" Peyton asked. She had moved from the scarf table and was now straightening the sample bottles of perfumes and lotions lined up on the glass shelves next to the empty cabinet that had displayed the sex toys. Logan was right—they'd sold quickly.

I felt like I was in a daze. "Yes. Michael had to drop Clementine off at Erin's and wants me to pick her up there."

She spritzed the air with one of the scents. "I thought you said Erin doesn't like to keep her."

I breathed in the Jo Malone white lavender scent—it was my favorite. "It's not that she doesn't like to keep her. I think it's more that she has a lot on her plate."

"Why didn't he just bring her here?" Peyton asked, sounding shocked that he hadn't.

My temper was short and snapped. "I don't know— maybe because it is our grand opening and he assumed we'd be busy with customers."

She ignored my response and pressed on. "What about the nanny? Do you think he's screwing her?"

Straightening my shoulders, I walked over to the empty cabinet beside her and locked the door. "No, I don't. He said he tried her first but she didn't answer."

She twisted her lips. "See? He *is* screwing her."

I rubbed my tired eyes. "No he's not. You're watching too much television."

"Miss, how much are the rugs?" An older gentleman held two in his hands.

"I got this," Peyton volunteered.

I pushed up from the counter and took a few deep breaths. I hadn't even gotten to tell Michael about what happened last night. And now I had the whole *have you been keeping me in the dark because the Mob is involved* thing to discuss with him.

"I'm back."

I turned to see Rachel holding a cardboard tray of caffè lattes and couldn't be happier.

"You're the best." I smiled as I took the one marked *Elle*.

Rachel was a bubbly, determined, petite blonde with a lot of spunk and sass. Almost as much as Peyton, but not quite. She was still in college, had a serious boyfriend, a 4.0 average, and was pretty funny. I hired her to work part-time after three minutes of speaking with her.

She set the tray behind the counter. "I need to sweep up the coffee beans that spilled on the floor before Peyton sees them and blows a gasket."

I laughed at that and took a welcome sip of my latte.

The store was quiet for the first time all day and I took a moment to think about everything that was happening in my life. There were so many strange things going on that the simple fact that a guy I'd just met might be involved with the Mob didn't really faze me like it should have.

The old butler bell Peyton had affixed above the door to alert us when someone was coming in chimed, and I glanced up to see a man in a blue quilted jacket walking in.

My car. I had completely forgotten about it. Thankfully, Michael must have at least gone to the garage before he had to leave to sign off on the additional repairs.

"I have an auto delivery for Elizabeth O'Shea," he said.

"That's me."

In this moment, it felt more wrong than ever pretending to be my sister. What if that was her in my yard last night? What kind of trouble was she in? Where was she? Did she need me?

"It's parked up the street," he said.

I took the keys he was handing me. "Thank you."

A crowd of women walked in as he left, and the rest of the afternoon sped by with so many customers. Peyton and I never had a chance to talk privately again.

At six thirty, Rachel, Peyton, and I finally walked outside, all complaining that our feet were killing us. Rachel's boyfriend was waiting for her in his car and as soon as she spotted him, she fled, yelling, "See you Tuesday," as she got in.

Peyton and I both stood there smiling at her.

I turned to Peyton. "Wow. What a great day."

"High five." She raised her hand.

I slapped it. "You were amazing today."

"No, you were."

Feeling smug, I lifted my chin. "I do know my shit."

She threw her arms around me and gave me a tight squeeze. "You are great at this. The soft opening was amazing. Now you have two days off—take the time and relax. You deserve it after the hours we've put in getting ready for the opening. I don't expect to see you here until we re-open on Tuesday. There is nothing for you to do until then. You need a break. You've been going nonstop for weeks. I'll come in tomorrow and restock, and then stop in on Monday to check the deliveries."

"You sure?" I asked, feeling guilty leaving her to do all the cleanup.

She nodded. "I'm sure. You got any plans?"

"No," I said emphatically.

"Not going to see Mr. Big Dick?"

I gave her a little shove. "Stop calling him that."

"Well, are you?"

"Honestly, I have no idea."

"Hey, he doesn't seem like the kind of guy to be involved with the Mafia, so I wouldn't worry about that."

I smiled at her and answered, "I'm not." I wasn't sure if that was true, but wasn't sure it wasn't, either.

Peyton had no idea what was going on with my sister. In fact, I'd told her she was in rehab for drug use, like I'd told everyone else. I felt bad lying but knew it was for the best. The fewer people involved, the better.

"Good. If he asks you out, go." Apparently, Peyton wasn't finished with the conversation about Logan.

I rolled my eyes.

"I mean it. Just ignore what I said earlier. That was stupid of me to bring it up."

"Already forgotten." I winked.

She gave me another squeeze. "Have a good night."

"You too."

Her eyes twinkled mischievously. "I plan to." She made a rather vulgar movement with her hips.

"Not *that* good," I added with another wink.

"It's our first date, and it took him a month to ask me out, so I won't get my hopes up."

I had to laugh. "You've gone on more first dates in the short time I've known you than I've gone on in my entire life."

Not that dating had ever been on my mind.

She responded with a hearty dose of laughter. "What can I say, I love men—just not the same one for long."

As we started to walk in different directions, I half turned. "Oh, and you'll call me if any good deliveries arrive?"

There was a wicked gleam in her eyes. "Yes, I'll call you if the sex toys are delivered. Are you antsy to check them out?" She winked.

"Peyton," I admonished. "No."

She shook her head. "Whatever you say. Oh, and Mr. Big Dick would be a great place to start."

No words. I had no words.

"I'm talking about the dating scene." She tossed the words over her shoulder with a giggle. "Not the sex toys. But both would work."

The thought hadn't escaped me.

But it wasn't going on a date with him that had been on my mind.

chapter
FOURTEEN

LOGAN

IT WASN'T THE SAME table.

The floor had been ripped up and replaced.

Yet the kitchen still held the ghosts of that night.

My father set his fork and knife down. "Logan. What's on your mind, son?"

I'd been silent about Elle and O'Shea since I'd arrived over an hour ago. I'd even agreed to eat dinner with him, which I never did.

Not here, anyway.

I pushed the plate of chicken and rice away and tried to pull my shit together. I needed to man up. I couldn't sit at the fucking kitchen table in my father's house and eat dinner?

I lifted my eyes to his but kept my head bowed. "That it's time for a face-to-face with Patrick."

He slid my plate back toward me. "That's not a good idea."

Man up, I reminded myself. I raised my fork to my mouth but with each bite I chewed, I felt more and more like I might explode. "Why not?"

He plowed a hand through his hair. "You know why."

My fists clenched under the table. "So what? His prick son has a hard-on for me. It's not going to change anything."

In frustration, my father shoved his chair back and pointed his finger at me. "I'm warning you, Logan: you go anywhere near Patrick or Tommy after all these years and mention O'Shea, it will set off all kinds of warning bells."

I stood up. Paced to the counter. To the refrigerator and opened it. To the sink to pour a glass of water. Fuck, he was right. Besides, he was stuck in Boston for life for what I'd done; I couldn't risk getting him into trouble either.

His eyes were on me.

Tracking me.

I could tell.

Finally, I asked, "What if I give you the money to deliver to Patrick?"

My father practically choked. "You know we're talking about ten million to settle the score?"

I leaned against the counter. "Yeah, I do."

"Even if you had that kind of cash handy, why would you give it up for someone you just met?"

I shrugged. "I can't explain it."

"Do you have that much?"

Uncertain, I shoved my hands in my pockets. "No, but I should be able to get it."

With slow strides, he crossed the kitchen and stood next to me. "Involving your grandfather Ryan will come with all kinds of strings. And even if you get the money, I don't know if it will help, son. It could backfire. We don't have a clue what O'Shea is up to or what it is Patrick is really after. I have to say, I'm almost certain Patrick is looking for something more than the cash."

Hiding my surprise that he didn't dismiss me right away, I pressed on. "But, if nothing else, you think it could be an option?"

He tapped his fingers on the counter. "It's a risky option. I have a meeting set with Patrick on Tuesday to go over operations. Let me see what I can get out of him. If it's the girl or the source he wants, there's a chance not even the full kitty will suffice to settle the score."

"You really think he won't take the ten million as settlement?"

Another shrug. "Like I said, I just don't know. In the meantime, I'll ask around to see what kind of operation O'Shea or his wife might have had going on. How big it was. What, if anything, anyone knows."

I nodded in agreement and started the pacing again.

With narrowed eyes, my father pointed his finger at me again. "But you have to stay out of it."

Every muscle in my body was taut. "I told you, I can't do that."

His jaw clenched. "I know what you said and now I'm telling you, if you want my help, you'll lay low. In fact, I think you should pay your grandfather a visit."

Playing stupid was never my game. I knew what he meant, so why I chose to answer the way I did, I have no idea other than the fact that it was on my mind. "Good idea. I think I'll go see Killian."

Exasperated, he picked up the pot of rice and started toward the sink. "I'm not talking about my father and you know it."

Still, playing stupid or not, his remark irked me. "And I'm not going to New York."

He heaved a deep sigh.

The argument was all too familiar and I had to get out of there. The more I paced the floor, the more it felt like the ghosts were closing in.

In a huff of frustration, I headed for the door. "I'll call you later."

chapter
FIFTEEN

Elle

I APPROACHED WITH CAUTION.

The car was parked right where the mechanic said it would be.

I had one hand in my purse, as it was getting late, the area was unfamiliar, and I was uncertain as to the safety of my surroundings. As soon as I got in, I locked the car and looked around the interior. I was worried about what I might find, but it looked just like it had before last night.

Once I was satisfied, I didn't waste time staying parked on the street. The sun was setting and although I'd never been afraid of the dark, tonight I felt like it was somewhere I didn't want to be.

The traffic was light and the ride to Erin's house in Weston didn't take all that long. Her neatly trimmed hedges and classic colonial home looked every bit Erin's style. She was a woman who had married her high school sweetheart and whose life had been overtaken by her children. Erin was a bona fide soccer mom who also held a position on the PTA board. She took care of four kids, a husband, and their house, and she never had time for herself. I wasn't sure if I envied her or pitied her.

It didn't matter—that would never be my life.

I rang the doorbell and immediately heard the sound of little footsteps coming my way.

The door swung open. "Put 'em up or I'll shoot," William drawled.

William was Erin's oldest and at seven, he was quite a little man.

I raised my hands. "Don't shoot."

Disappointment flickered on his face. "That was too easy, Elle. Next time you have to draw your own gun."

Little did he know, I was toting a real gun in my purse. "You mean like this?" I pretended to have a gun pointed at him.

"Whoa, you're fast," he said, his eyes like saucers.

"Elle, is that you?" Erin called from the kitchen.

"Hi, Erin. Yes, it's me."

"Come on in. Clementine is just finishing dinner," she said.

"Race you to the kitchen," I challenged William.

He promptly took off, practically mowing over Conner on the way.

"I want to play," Conner said. Conner was five and always wanted to be doing what his older brother was doing.

While they sped ahead, I walked past the family room, which was completely littered with toys, and stepped on a Lego or two in the hallway. Erin's house was always chaos, but the kids always seemed to be laughing and having fun.

Given that, I guessed, what did a little mess matter?

I passed dozens of pictures on the wall. Mostly of the kids, who obviously ruled the household. I stopped at one in particular. It was of a family of five. I knew it was Michael and Erin and their parents, but I wasn't familiar with the third child. He was an older boy, and his eyes were just as ice blue as Michael's and his mother's. I would ask Erin, but she didn't like to talk about her parents. She and her father didn't get along, and for that matter, neither did Michael and his father.

The kitchen was in the back of the house and I knew just when the boys reached it.

"I win!" William yelled.

"No, I win," Conner countered.

"I think you both won," I said from the archway.

I knew better than to look around but I still did, growing a bit uneasy at the mess. Bottles, cups, and bowls covered almost every inch of the counter. Pots and dishes filled the sink. Crayons and markers were all over the table, and I couldn't help noticing someone had decided to try his hand at sketching on the wall.

Finally, my eyes landed on a little treasure. Clementine sat in a booster chair with a tray of food and beside her in a high chair sat Braden. Braden and Clementine were practically the same age. I think Braden was a month or two older.

Erin turned around in her chair. She was wearing sweatpants and her fiery red hair was in a disheveled ponytail. She looked how I felt—exhausted. Taigh, who was six weeks old, was at her breast. I think she was still breast-feeding Braden and I wondered how that worked.

"Mama!" Clementine shrieked when she saw me.

My heart stilled and panic struck at the same time.

With uncertainty, Erin's eyes darted to mine.

"She's never called me that before," I managed to say, not sure how to respond to either Erin or Clementine.

Erin waved her free hand dismissively. "It's the only word Braden knows. They've been copying each other all day. She even wanted to drink from my breast." Erin let out a laugh. "And he wanted to drink milk from her sippy cup."

Okay then.

Perhaps that was all it was. With a smile, I crossed the room to greet the happy little girl. "Hi, sweet girl. How are you are today?" I cooed.

My heart still wasn't beating as it should and I had to fight back the urge to cry. She wasn't my daughter. She had a mother. And hopefully her mother would be returning to her soon. But all of that didn't make the moment any less special.

"I couldn't get her to eat the peas," Erin said, switching breasts.

I looked at Clementine's tray and had to laugh. Green mushy blobs were everywhere. "Yes, I can see that."

Erin blew a loose piece of hair out of her eyes. "At least she ate all her applesauce and macaroni and cheese."

Clementine's navy-blue dress showed signs of both. "Thanks for feeding her."

"Mommy, he hit me."

"No, Mommy. He hit me."

The older boys were yelling from the other room, but it didn't seem to faze Erin a bit. "John, the boys are fighting and they need a bath anyway. I'd like to go to early Mass tomorrow," she called to her husband, who must have been elsewhere in the house.

I hadn't realized he was home. John was a doctor and usually took call on the weekends. Weekend call made it easier for him to be home at night during the week, and it was important for him to see his children. He was a nice, respectable man who took care of his family with more than just money.

"I'm on it," John answered from somewhere upstairs.

His response didn't surprise me—he was always helping with the boys.

So different from how I'd grown up.

"Come on, boys," John called. A moment later I heard laughter and the boys giggling as they ran up the stairs.

"I want to go first," William said.

"No, I do," Conner whined.

With a tight grip on the sticky handles, I carefully removed Clementine's food tray.

Giving the kitchen my full attention now, I couldn't help but think about what a stark contrast this house was to the one I grew up in. Everything in our home always had to be clean, orderly, in the right place. We had to eat everything on our plate, we weren't allowed to yell or scream, and we always tidied our own messes. And my father never helped my mother with anything except for disciplinary issues.

I wanted Clementine to grow up in an environment like this. Not one where order ruled over chaos and one man reigned supreme.

"Will you take her tomorrow?" Erin asked, jostling me from my thoughts.

I lifted Clementine from her seat. "Take her where?" I asked.

"To church. I know Michael tries not to miss a Sunday."

"I don't typically attend Mass with him."

"Oh," was her only response.

I didn't add that I gave up on God a long time ago.

Clementine put her hands on my cheeks, reminding me that this wasn't my dark past. I shook off my thoughts and looked at her. "Let's get you changed, silly girl."

Erin was patting the baby's back.

"Is his reflux any better?" I asked.

Just then, projectile vomit answered my question. Erin grabbed a burp cloth and wiped the baby's mouth. "Not at all." She juggled the baby and cloth without frazzle or tears.

"Can I help?" I offered.

She shook her head. "No. Clementine's diaper bag is on the couch in the family room. There's a pair of pajamas in there and a change of clothes, but I have to warn you, she didn't take a nap. She was too busy watching the boys."

Erin was no-nonsense and had all her ducks in a row.

"Thanks for the warning." I smiled.

Clementine was pointing to the milk on the floor. "Messy," she said.

With a laugh, I leaned my forehead to her. "Speaking of messy, little miss, pajama time for you."

Erin had Taigh laid across her thighs and was patting his back again. "You're good with her, you know."

I looked at her and how good she was with her kids and then at Clementine's smiling face. "You think?"

The baby burped again, and this time Erin caught the small blob of spit-up with the cloth diaper in her hand. "No, I don't think, I know. I can see it. Elizabeth always seemed afraid around her, like she might break her. But you're different."

I shrugged. "Isn't everyone?"

She cradled Taigh in her arms. "Yes, that's true. I'm sure when Elizabeth returns she'll embrace motherhood. Any word of when that might be?"

The lies were getting to me.

I couldn't answer her because I had no idea if Lizzy would return and, if she did, what kind of shape she'd be in. I shook my head. "I'm going to get her changed now so I can pop her straight into bed if she falls asleep in the car."

Erin stood and set the baby in the bouncy seat on the counter. "Elle."

I turned back.

"I don't think I've told you how much I admire you."

"Me? Why?"

She picked up some dirty dishes from the table. "You put your life on hold and moved here to help take care of your sister's daughter. Not everyone would do that."

I swallowed the lump in my throat. "That's just it, Erin. I didn't put my life on hold." I kissed Clementine. "I started living it." I didn't explain any further. I couldn't. Some emotions were too painful to discuss.

On shaky legs, I turned and left her in the kitchen as she bent to clean up the vomit on the floor.

The family room was quiet, but I could hear water splashing upstairs and Erin talking to Braden and Taigh as she cleaned up.

Their house was messy but it was anything but a mess.

It was filled with laughter, not tears.

It made my heart warm to know Clementine was part of a family that was happy.

And that's the way every child's life should be.

chapter
SIXTEEN

LOGAN

THE PLACE SMELLED LIKE piss.

Brighton House was the top facility for elder care in Boston.

And it still smelled like piss.

I hated coming here and hated not, in equal measure.

Gramps didn't really have to be here, but after his last fall, my uncle insisted on it. Uncle Hunter is my father's older brother. He was the one who'd been able to stay away. He went to college, and then made his own way, free and clear of his Blue Hill Gang ties. My father had done the same. That is, until my stupidity drew him in. I was the only reason he was pulled into a world my grandfather didn't want him to be a part of. And I lived with that guilt every day.

Gramps didn't try to stop it, though.

He couldn't.

Rules were rules.

A life for a life—dead or alive.

I wasn't there for the conversation my father had with Killian, but I was certain it went something like *it's either him or me.*

Maybe that was why Gramps didn't try harder to fight it.

Nobody could have seen what was coming. That Patrick owning my father would bring my grandfather down. Looking back now, it seems so obvious. Once Patrick had my father, Gramps was under his thumb. With the tables turned, Patrick moved quickly, merging the smaller Dorchester Heights Gang with the infamous Blue Hill Gang. That's when he unofficially began running things. Gramps was the boss by declaration, but everyone knew Patrick made the decisions.

I stood in the doorway to Gramps's room and just watched him for a few minutes. His mind was sharper than a tack. But sadly, it was his body that was giving out. After years of fighting, I don't know how many gunshot wounds, and myriad broken bones, he had a hard time getting around.

Dark eyes glanced over.

I gave him a nod. "Hey Gramps, how's it going?"

The old man tore himself away from his crossword puzzle. "Logan, back so soon?"

I walked in and took a seat on his bed. "Yeah, I guess I missed you."

Gramps looked more than delighted to see me. "Buttering me up?"

With a shake of my head, I just grinned at him.

He shifted in his favorite chair as if he couldn't get comfortable. "No matter—that's always good for an old man to hear."

"You okay?"

He nodded. "Just been sitting too long today."

I smiled at him. Old age had a way of softening even the hardest of men. And Killian McPherson was one of the hardest.

When he was on the street, that is.

When he was with me, he was just the man who wanted to make sure I knew how to take care of myself. Since

Uncle Hunter never married and my father never remarried, I was his only grandchild, and he hated that the guys referred to me as the Silver Spoon. A few suffered broken bones as soon as those two words escaped their lips in his presence. He didn't mind my trust fund ties, but he wanted me to fit in both of the worlds I was raised in. He was all for cotillion and mixing with New York City's high society, but he also wanted me to learn the ropes of Boston, more specifically those of the Blue Hill Gang.

My parents believed they could shelter me from the latter; he knew that wasn't possible. So he took it on himself to teach me what I needed to know. He'd tell my parents he was taking me for ice cream and we'd go to watch a fight instead. He'd tell them he was bringing me to a Red Sox game and we'd sit with one of his bookies while he'd show me the ropes of illegal gambling. He'd tell my parents we were going camping and we'd spend the weekend sparring. He taught me how to shoot, to fight, and to take care of myself.

At the time, I was young and I didn't know any differently. I looked up to him. I liked to be with him. Thought of him as my hero. Looking at him now, I know he's done bad things but he's always loved me. He'd do anything to protect me.

The truth of the matter is Grandpa Ryan might have taught me to be book wise, and Gramps McPherson might have taught me to be street wise, but both are skills I've never underestimated. And honestly, both worlds are ruthless in different ways. Grandpa Ryan uses money to get what he wants, whereas Gramps McPherson used to use muscle. Psychoanalyzing their worlds wasn't going to change anything. The bottom line was that after everything I'd done in my life, and the trouble I'd caused my family, I now walked on the right side of the law and wanted to stay as close to it as I could.

Shaking off these thoughts, I rubbed my palms on my pants. "I need to talk to you."

He put the newspaper on the table and tucked the pencil behind his ear. "I've seen that look only twice before in my life."

I bunched my brows.

What the hell was he talking about?

"Once when I looked in the mirror after the first time I met my Millie, and again when your father came home from college with your mother at his side."

Okay, so maybe his mind was going.

My huff of laughter wasn't deliberate. "I'm not in love, Gramps. You know me better than that."

He eased forward with a groan. Moving around was difficult on him. "Pull that chair over here and sit closer."

The look in his eyes told me I'd better do as he said.

Once I was sitting directly in front of him, he placed his hand on my knee. "I've taught you many things, Logan, but I think I neglected to teach you that you don't decide when you fall in love. Love decides that for you."

I lowered my head and raised my eyes. "What's the matter, old man, got chicks on the brain? Don't tell me the cute blonde who gives the hand jobs while she bathes you has been standing you up?"

Gramps gave me a wicked laugh. "Think I'd still be here if that were the case? She makes her rounds, don't worry."

I couldn't help my smirk. There was the guy I was used to.

"I assume you're not here to ask me about the birds and the bees, so cut the shit and tell me what you *are* here for."

I gave him a hesitant nod.

"Go on."

"There's this girl." I cringed at the first words that left my lips.

He slapped his hand on my leg and smiled like a motherfucker.

I held my hands up. "Wait—it's not what you're thinking."

Gramps had triumph in his eyes as he eased himself

back, looking very proud. "It never is, my boy, it never is."

I scooted my chair back and rested my forearms on my thighs. "Let me start again. Patrick had my father go on a drug warning last night."

As soon as I said the words, I felt the temperature in the room drop, and it had nothing to do with the thermostat. The old man's eyes darkened as the playfulness I'd just seen evaporated into the hard man from the street. Faster than sin, he took the pencil from behind his ear and plunged it into the chair cushion. Some kind of animalistic growl left his throat, and then he brought himself to his feet. "That wasn't how we left things. Take me to see Patrick," he barked.

Looking into his dark eyes had me jumping up. "That's only going to stir shit up and you know it."

"Now!" he demanded.

"Talk to me first. Listen to what I have to say," I pleaded.

His disposition didn't change and his scowl remained.

Worried things would only get worse, I reasoned with him. "Please, this isn't about your son. I'll take care of him. He'll be fine. I'm here because I need some advice. Some insight. Or innocent people are going to end up hurt or, worse, dead."

Gramps reluctantly sat on the edge of his bed. "Go on."

I told him everything that I knew that had taken place so far between Patrick, O'Shea, and Elle, which wasn't much. Even about how much Elle looked like Emily. I kept my voice even, but it broke more than a few times. Finally, I shared my plan to bail O'Shea out if I had to.

He listened intently. When I finished, he scratched his chin and seemed to think hard for a few moments before he spoke. "Let me get this straight. Someone has been funneling cocaine through the high-society circuit and when Patrick got wind of it, he went ballistic because he doesn't own a piece of it; and then true to form, he put Tommy on it, who in turn questioned everyone, beat doors down, made threats, but whoever was running the ring remains a ghost on the street."

I nodded. "Yeah. Makes me think he's running more than just the small, wealthy circle."

"I have to agree. This source is bigger than even Patrick thinks."

I was certain he was right.

"And you think it could be this chick you mentioned?"

"Yeah, O'Shea's wife. I'm not one hundred percent on that, but that's what I'm told."

He harrumphed, since his old-school beliefs meant a chick could never pull something like that off. "I don't think so."

"Gramps," I started to say, but he cut me off.

"And O'Shea, he's that Black Irish Mickey, the florist's boy?"

I had to shake my head. No one used that term anymore but him. He had this thing about the Irish having dark hair. Some old wives' tale that they had a little bit of the devil in them. "Yeah, that's him. He's an attorney."

"Is he anything like his old man?"

"He has dark hair." I smiled.

"You know what I mean, smart-ass."

I shrugged. "I don't know either of them, but in what way do you mean?"

"Devout Catholic. Never misses a Sunday Mass or a confession. Carries a rosary with him too. In fact, if I recall correctly, he had a delinquent son he shipped off to Ireland at a young age to prepare for seminary school years ago. That's what a fanatic he was."

"To each his own I guess, but like I said, I don't know the father or the son. I do, however, think this son is a douche, but a devout Catholic, that I doubt."

Gramps raised his brows. "You say," he grinned, "this douche is claiming he isn't involved with the drug ring at all?"

"That's what he told Pop, but I'm not so sure."

Gramps shook his head. "I'm with you. Not sure I'd

believe him."

The tiredness in the back of my eyes faded at the realization I might be right. "Why do you say that?"

Shifting on the bed, he brought his large frame to the head and settled back. "I can't say, really. It's a feeling based on what I know of his old man. When Mickey O'Shea was a teenager, he was a small-timer hoping to hit it big. Always doing stupid things. I warned your father to stay away from him in school. And it was a good thing I did. At nineteen, just after he got married, Mickey did a five-year stretch for hijacking a fleet of trucks. His first big job and he gets caught right out of the gate. *Fucking idiot.* When he got out, he started up his own gang with Patrick Flannigan as his number two. Some shit went down with his wife, and after that the gang folded. Lucky for him, his mother had passed and he took over her flower shop. I have to say, I was surprised that he gave up on making his fortune on the wrong side of the law and settled for domestic life."

"So he dropped out just like that?"

He shrugged. "As far as I know. Then his wife was killed in some gang-related incident and honestly, I haven't heard much about him since. But if the young O'Shea is anything like his old man was, he's a dreamer hoping to hit it big the easy way."

I shook my head. "I don't think so, Gramps. O'Shea seems to be doing well on his own. I asked around and he's thinking of running for District Attorney next year."

"Doesn't mean it isn't him."

"He claims it was his wife who set up the drug ring with his friends."

"Well, talk to her."

"Can't. She disappeared three months ago and from what I can piece together, no one knows where she is."

"And you're in love with her?"

"No, Gramps. I told you, I haven't met his wife."

His eyes narrowed on me. "I'm old, not senile. I'm not talking about the wife and you know it. I'm talking about the one that looks like Emily."

Cringing, I paced around the room. "Gramps, I only told you that about Emily so you'd understand where my concern was coming from. I'm not in love at all. But last night someone slashed his sister-in-law's tire and then later tried to break into Elle's place."

"And how much longer are you going to pretend that look on your face isn't what I thought it was when we first started this discussion?"

I shook my head, getting a little aggravated with his misdirected focus. "Give it a rest, old man. I've already told you, there's nothing there."

He stared at me, his mood contemplative. "I'll let it go for now, but only because there are more important things to focus on. Was she hurt? Were there any messages left?"

I leaned against the wall. "No, she wasn't hurt. I'm not sure about any messages."

His wheels were spinning. "Then it wasn't Patrick or his prick son, for that matter. The one thing you can count on is that they are lowlife scum. If it had been them, there would have been no doubt it was."

I sighed. "Yeah, that's what I think. Which is why I think there's time to get Elle and her family out of this."

The hardness was back in his features. "Come over here, sit down, and listen to me."

By the time I slid the chair over and sat, I was all worked up again.

Gramps leaned forward with that scowl on his face. "I'm going to tell you right now, you give O'Shea that money and you're opening up a can of worms you won't be able to crawl out of. First, it means you're getting involved in the drug ring, and you know as soon as the DEA sees you on that radar, they'll be up your ass. And second, I know Patrick. He's not going to let that debt be settled so easily. Even if it was O'Shea's wife running things, O'Shea obviously knew about it. Patrick will use him until there's nothing left and once he's useless, Patrick will dispose of him."

Harsh words, and I didn't want to process them. "But he has a little girl. What if she gets hurt?"

My grandfather shrugged coolly. "Collateral damage never bothered Patrick."

Furious, I stood back up and began pacing. "And the wife's sister?"

Again with the cool demeanor. "More than likely, she'll be dead by association, and anyone else who he's close with."

I slammed my hand against the wall.

"Admit it, boy. She's the one?"

Annoyed, I turned to face him. "The one what?" I barked.

His face creased. "The one that has got your insides twisted all up. Whether you want to admit it to me or not, at least admit it to yourself."

Sighing, I couldn't believe I was saying this. "So what if she is?"

He drew in a deep worried breath. "Walk away, Logan," he almost pleaded.

I crossed the room and stood in front of him. "I'm not doing that."

Silence filled the space and I could see the harshness in his facial expression fading. Finally he spoke. "That's what I thought. Tell me, what's your father's involvement?"

I brought my temper down a notch as well. "Minimal. He's just the messenger. Even if Patrick wanted to involve him further, he doesn't trust him enough."

Gramps nodded. "That's good. He won't get hurt that way."

He knew I was stronger than my father. After all, he made me that way. Not only in the physical sense, but in my fortitude as well. Gramps hadn't taught my father the ways of the street. My grandmother wanted her boys to have a different life and he'd agreed. But as time passed, he learned that wasn't always possible and he worried for me, which is why he took me under his wing. He taught me what he'd neglected to teach my father. That's why my awareness and resolve was more like a soldier's, whereas my father was like a new recruit, not entirely brought in.

Unfortunately, my father also used booze as a crutch, and that was a dangerous thing. Then again, having your life turned upside down would do that to a guy. And working with Patrick had done just that to my old man. As soon as he started, my mother found out and demanded I stay in New York full-time and attend school there. It wasn't like I had much of a choice. My father made me go. I wanted him to move there too. He couldn't, though, and I knew it. So instead, he was forced to lead a life he'd never wanted.

All because of what I'd done when I was fifteen.

I looked at my grandfather and braced myself for the fallout. "I'm going to have to talk to Patrick myself."

The old man rose so fast, he had me by the shirt collar before I knew what was happening. In a beat, he pushed me back and slammed me against the wall. "You even think about going to see him and I'll kill you myself."

I stayed where I was. Shocked that he had that much fight left in him. "What else can I do?"

When he released me, he almost collapsed.

I grabbed him and helped him back to the bed.

Once he was sitting, he said, "Bring that chair over here."

I again moved the fucking chair.

With my ass on the hard wood, he pulled my face close to his. "Here's what you're going to do."

I listened intently.

Absorbing every word.

The old man knew best.

Elle

SOMETHING WASN'T RIGHT.

I pulled into the side driveway of Michael's corner lot and put my car in park. With a flick of the switch, the interior light turned on and I proceeded to search the floor. It wasn't there.

My garage door opener was missing, and for some reason the button programmed into the vehicle hadn't worked in weeks.

Feeling slightly panicky, I opened the glove compartment. It wasn't there either. Maybe I'd stuffed it in my purse. After all, I did it all the time when I'd take Clementine for walks. I reached for my bag and realized it wasn't the same purse I'd used this week. That one I'd left behind at the boutique.

Clementine had fallen asleep in her car seat and I wanted to get her in her crib and avoid the cold while doing so.

To be certain the repair shop hadn't moved it, I lifted the center console lid and rummaged through it.

Something sparkled.

My eyes dipped down and I reached inside. When I picked the charm up, my fingers trembled. Sucking in a breath, I pinched the silver and turned it around. But I didn't need to. The glistening of the small speck of a diamond was all I needed to see to know for certain. Still, I read the inscription anyway.

It was the charm from the bracelet my sister had given me for my tenth birthday. The same one I threw at her the day she left.

My heart stilled as the memory flooded me and I tried to hold back the tears.

"Happy birthday," my mother and sister sang as the candles flamed before me.

Just as I was blowing them out, the door swung open and my father strode in. I froze in mid-blow, but the candles went out anyway.

Traitors.

His eyes darted to my mother. "You couldn't wait?"

"It's almost ten, Henry, and the girls have school tomorrow."

He disarmed and left his gun on the counter where he always did. We were living in Germany at the time and since we'd just arrived, we didn't really know anyone, so we had no one to invite to my party.

Not that we ever would have invited anyone anyway.

"Let's eat the cake," he said, more jovial than he'd been in a long time.

My mother smiled at him and started cutting it.

It was strange; I felt like we were a family. That didn't happen often.

My father moved closer to the table and gave her a kiss. "Did you give Gabby her present?" he asked my mother excitedly.

She sniffed him and twisted her head. "No, not yet. Where have you been?"

His demeanor changed instantly. "I told you, I had a meeting. Now let me give Gabby her present. Where did you hide it?"

My mother looked upset. "It's in my purse. I'll get it in a moment."

As my mother was cutting the cake, my father disappeared

into the mudroom, where my mother always hung her purse.

Everything had a place in our house.

My mother gave me the first piece and then turned around to hand my father a slice, but he hadn't returned yet. I guess she never realized he'd left the room. "Henry?"

"He went to get my present, Mommy," I said excitedly.

There was a growl-like sound from the mudroom. "Susan!"

My mother paled right before us.

A thud had us all jumping.

"What's the matter, Mommy?" Lizzy asked.

She set the cake down. "Go to your room, girls."

"But Mommy, I haven't finished my cake or opened my present."

Lizzy stood and tugged on my nightgown. "Come on, Gabby."

I shook my head.

My father appeared in the doorway holding a round, pink compact in his hand. His eyes were dark and his demeanor was now terrifying.

"Go, girls," my mother said, beckoning us. "Now."

Lizzy pulled me along and I went, but my eyes never left his.

"Susan," he said again, even more sternly.

"I can explain, Henry."

Before I was out of the kitchen doorway, I saw him take the handle of his gun and start pounding on the compact. Small pills were being crushed. I watched him, and then he glanced up and saw me. "You are supposed to be in your room," he barked, and took a step toward me with his hands on his belt.

"No, Henry. No!" my mother yelled.

My sister pulled me harder and I followed her. With each step I could hear my father behind me.

As soon as she closed our door, he locked it.

He locked us in.

"Susan!" he yelled.

I heard her patter down the hallway. "Henry, we need to talk about this."

"How long?"

There wasn't an answer.

"How long have you been taking birth control pills?"

"Not as long as it took you to find another whore," she spat.

His laugh was wicked. *"I wouldn't have to seek pussy elsewhere if you'd let me inside you when I need you. But that's about to change right now, Susan. No more options for you. Now tell me, how long?"*

My mother was whispering and I couldn't hear her.

"My house. My rules. Get to our room, now!"

"Henry, we need to talk."

"There's nothing to talk about. I'm going to have to punish you. I can't let this go. You're deliberately keeping something from me that I really want. What kind of wife does that to her husband?"

Even my sister had sat on her bed and was listening. We were both scared. We'd been punished with his belt a few times. Would he do that to our mother?

Their door shut.

"Give me your wrist," he said. "Give it to me, Susan."

"You don't have to tie me up, Henry. You can have me."

"I can have you? I can have you! You're mine. I don't have to have your permission. I've let you get away with your 'I have a headache, I don't feel well, the girls are awake, I'm really sick today' excuses long enough. From now on, when I want you, you're mine. Do you understand me?"

"Yes," she said calmly. She wasn't as upset as she usually was.

"I thought we had an understanding, Susan."

"So did I."

He laughed. *"What? You're upset because I'm putting my dick in someone who wants me?"*

"Yes. You promised me you wouldn't do that again."

"I have needs that you can't meet. When you can, I won't have to seek alternate outlets. But Susan, you're distracting me from the issue. The problem isn't me or who I have to fuck because you can't satisfy my needs. It's what you've been doing behind my back. I provide for this family and you grow it. That was our deal. I'm doing my part but you're not doing yours. Do I have to stop providing for you to understand? Leave you and girls on your

own? With nothing. Would you like that?"

She didn't answer.

"Do I?" He yelled louder.

"No," she cried.

I knew she was scared to be on her own. I'd heard her talking to someone about it once.

"I didn't think so. Now give me your ankle."

I left my bed and went to sit next to my sister. "What's he doing?"

"I think he's tying her up."

"Why?" I gasped.

She shook her head. "Because she doesn't want to have any more babies."

That thumping started again, but there were no cries from my mother and no yelling from my father.

It was scarier than when there were.

My sister ran to the window and opened it. "Come over here, Gabby."

I did.

She opened her dresser, which was beside the window, and handed me a small box with a red ribbon around it. "Here, happy birthday. This is from me. Mommy let me buy it with my babysitting money."

I looked at her.

"Open it."

I did. Inside was a delicate silver chain with a silver disc on it. On one side was a tiny diamond chip. On the other the words, "Blow, just blow," were engraved.

"Blow, just blow, Gabby. Everything will be okay."

I turned the charm around and pretended the diamond chip was a dandelion and blew.

We heard the thumping off and on all night. I'm not sure if we fell asleep or not, but around seven the next morning, our door unlocked.

"Get yourselves ready for school, girls, and make some breakfast. The bus will be here in thirty minutes," my father commanded.

My mother always had our breakfast ready and walked us to the bus stop. I opened the door and saw my father walking into the kitchen. I tiptoed to my parents' bedroom door and knocked, but my father was back before I opened the door. "Your mother isn't feeling well. Now go on and get moving. You don't want to miss the bus."

I did as he said.

My sister had to babysit after school for our neighbor and when I came home, my father was there. He didn't have a shirt on and he was dressed in the same pants he had been wearing this morning. Beer bottles cluttered the table. I knew he hadn't gone to work.

He looked up from the papers he was reading. "You got homework?"

I nodded. "Yes, sir."

"Go to your room and do it. And Gabrielle," he said.

My body started to tremble.

"When Elizabeth gets home, have her make you some dinner and go straight to bed. Your mother will get you off to school in the morning."

His words were slightly slurred, but I understood we were not to disturb him.

I nodded again and walked down the hallway. Instead of going to my room, though, I went to my parents' room. I didn't knock. I just opened the door. My mother was lying on the bed, not moving. I was petrified.

Until she glanced up.

She must have been sleeping.

"Go, Gabby, go. Please," she pleaded.

Her tearstained face was all I could see and I hated that she'd been crying.

"Go, before you sees you in here."

Terrified, I looked around the room. The rug had been moved to the foot of the bed and rope was tied around the posts, but everything else seemed in place. Not understanding what was really going on, I shut the door and ran to my room. A few minutes later I heard the lock of my door.

That thumping that drove me mad started right afterward. This time my father was louder, groaning and talking to my mother. "I'm sorry, Susan. I don't want to hurt you, but I need to be inside you."

"I'm fine," she said, no inflection in her voice.

"You're not. I can tell."

"I want to see the girls."

"Tomorrow. This is for your own good."

"How is keeping me away from my children for my own good."

"It's the only way I can think of to make you understand I have needs, too."

What am I not giving you?"

"Besides a son to carry on my name, your attention."

"You are always at work," she muttered.

"Yes, Susan, I'm at work and my work is stressful. I can't afford to be so tightly wound. There are times I need you to help relieve my stress and you just refuse me. If you want me to be able to continue to provide for this family, you have to be available to me more than you are."

She muttered something.

"Don't be mad."

She didn't respond to his form of apology.

"Don't be mad, baby."

Still, no response.

He said it again. Over and over, until I couldn't stand the sound of his voice.

When I thought I might scream, I ran to the window and held up my bracelet. Blowing on it, all I wished for was that the incessant thumping end.

Something had happened that day. Some kind of switch had turned off for my mother. She was never the same after that. She didn't cry anymore at night. Sure, I heard the thumping, and my father's words, "I need to be inside you," but that was all I ever heard again. Her cries in the night were gone.

Clementine started to cry and jolted me from the space

in my head.

Had my sister been in the car, or had the charm been there the entire three months I'd been driving it?

I wasn't sure, and I wasn't sure if I would ever know.

Clementine's cries continued, and I pulled her juice cup from my bag and handed it to her. She smiled. Happy and content once again, she leaned against the seat and drank from her cup.

Locked out of the garage, I backed down the side driveway, rounded the corner, and pulled up to the curb in front of Michael's regal-looking brick home. There were no front lights on, and that made me nervous. They were on a timer, so they should have been on.

Was I being paranoid?

I contemplated for several seconds what to do before deciding what was best. I'd hurry up the walk to unlock the house and turn the lights on before I brought Clementine in.

She'd be safe. I wouldn't be far away and I wouldn't be long. I looked back at Clementine. She was chewing on the cup now. "I'll be right back, silly girl."

With a quick turn, I removed the keys from the ignition. My hands were shaking as I took the gun from my purse. Locking the car doors, I hurried up the walk.

That's when I saw a shadow flicker across the only room in the house that had a light on. It was Michael's office and he often forgot to turn it off, but the movement was what frightened me.

I gripped the gun tighter.

Logan had said, "Shoot to kill," and that's what I planned to do.

Was it my imagination, though?

Tree branches from the wind maybe?

A red light seemed to be blinking in the study.

I stared through the window, trying to figure out what it was. I couldn't. Was I really seeing something? Was it my imagination? When I saw the same shadow again, I knew what I was seeing had to be real.

I scanned the dark street and my entire body started to tremble. Without a doubt, I had seen movement in Michael's office. I was now certain that someone was inside.

I glanced back at the car and the thought of Clementine being alone terrified me. I started to run to get to her, but I tripped on a step on the pathway, which landed me on my back.

Pain tore through me and I wasn't certain I hadn't sprained something, but my fear was greater than the pain. Forcing myself to move, I got up and somehow managed to stumble to the car. When it was within reach, I used it for leverage to help guide me around to my door.

Once inside, I pressed my foot on the gas hard. I had to get out of there. About ten minutes later, when I reached a busy intersection and the adrenaline that had been pumping through my veins slowed, I slumped forward. Feeling the weight of everything going on, the only thing I knew for certain was that I couldn't take the chance of anything happening to Clementine.

And that's why I was going where I was going.

It was the only place I could feel safe.

chapter
EIGHTEEN

LOGAN

LIFTED THE LID to my laptop and fired it up.

My fingers hovered over the keys.

I typed two words, four syllables, *Michael O'Shea*, and then hit the delete key over and over.

I made another attempt, retyping the same words.

There was a knock on my hotel room door and without overthinking it, I pressed send. I shut the lid to my computer and then grabbed my SIG. I approached the door with caution and stood to the side. "Who's there?"

"Logan, it's me, Elle."

My heart thundered in my chest.

I knew her voice before she even said her name.

What was wrong?

What had happened?

I tucked the gun behind my back and swung the door open as fast as I could.

She stood there with one of those folding strollers that cradled a sleeping Clementine in it, a bag on each shoulder and her purse right at her hand.

Good girl.

My heart clenched as I allowed myself a quick look at

her before scanning the hall.

She looked terrified. "I'm sorry. I didn't know where else to go. The front desk had my name and sent me up. I hope you don't mind."

My eyes came back to her and our gazes collided. Again, I allowed myself just a quick glance. She looked to be physically unharmed. Without hesitation, I quickly stepped into the hall. Holding the door open with my bare foot, I looked to the right and then the left. I didn't see anyone. "Elle," I said, taking her bags from her and urging her forward. "It's fine. But why aren't you at O'Shea's?"

Had my assumption been wrong? Was he incapable of caring for Elle and his daughter?

With urgency, she pushed the stroller inside. "He's not there."

"Where the fuck is he?" I asked way too loud.

Elle turned to face me.

That goddamn vulnerability was all I could see. I had to drop my gaze just to keep my distance. I felt an odd need to get close. See her even closer. Make sure she was really, truly okay.

"I didn't know where else to go," she said again, this time even more shakily.

The fear in her voice rattled me, and I stepped closer to her and grabbed her arms. As soon as my fingers wrapped around them, I felt a flame light from within me that hadn't stirred in years. After that, I couldn't stop the flood of feelings that were coursing through me. Seriously, what the hell was going on with me?

Control.

I was all about it.

I had to regain it.

I drew in a deep breath and let it wrap around me. With my armor in place, I slowly looked her up and down one more time. She didn't appear to be hurt. "What happened?" I asked, making certain my voice was at an even keel.

Tension eased from her and she let out a relieved sigh.

"Can I put Clementine somewhere and then we can talk?"

Keenly aware that the two of us being alone in a hotel room probably wasn't the best idea, I shoved the remaining strange feelings I had deep down within me. Just a slight chink in my armor. Nothing to worry about. But the protectiveness that was surging under my skin might be. Needing to ensure her and the baby's safety, I reached behind and turned the lock. The entire time I never let my gaze leave hers.

Forcing myself to be mechanical, a moment later I said, "Yeah, of course. Do you want to lay her on my bed?"

Elle looked at me with uncertainty.

I nodded at her. I wasn't going to let anything happen to her. If she didn't know that, I'd show her. I twisted to put the chain on the door and when I turned back, I looked at her again. She was still looking at me. That look was putting more dents in my armor. Mentally punching them out, I crossed the room and set her bags on the table in the corner. With a flick of my eyes, I saw she was still looking at me. She was weary, worried. I felt compelled to reassure her. "It's okay, Elle, she'll be safe in there. I promise."

Elle was exhausted, I could tell. The circles under her eyes weren't the only sign. I could see it not only in the way she looked but the way she moved. Possibly realizing I was assessing her state of duress, she dropped her gaze and attempted to push the stroller across the plush carpet. When she couldn't, she gingerly bent down to pick up Clementine, but just as she was about to scoop her up she stiffened and winced, her hand reaching for her back.

She was hurt.

Fuck me.

Not being able to stand the thought of her in pain, my feet moved like lightning to where she was standing. "Here, let me," I said, and without really thinking it through, I picked up the sleeping baby girl. But once she was in my arms, I started to panic. I'd never held a baby before. I wasn't sure what to do. She was lighter than I would have thought. And so much more fragile than anyone should be.

My uncertainty was rising.

And like an idiot, I just stood here.

"Is that the bedroom?" Elle pointed.

"Yeah," I breathed, trying to keep my shit together.

What had happened to her?

Elle walked into the room and turned the lamp on.

My feet moving on their own, I followed her.

Standing stiffly, she pulled back the covers and placed pillows on each side, leaving an opening in the middle.

"Here?" I bobbed with my head toward the gap.

"Yes, this way she won't roll off."

Roll off!

Fuck.

I carefully set the sleeping baby where I was instructed. I sighed in relief once she was safely out of my arms, but I couldn't stop staring at her. She was a beautiful little thing.

Elle pulled the covers over her and made sure the pillows were secure. "Let me just get her blanket and see if I can find Rosie."

I followed her out of the bedroom and watched her rummage through one of the bags. "Rosie?"

She glanced up. "It's a large silver rattle shaped like an elephant's face that dangles from a red ribbon. For some reason she's attached to it."

With that, I turned back to what had been eating at me. "What happened to your back?" I asked, unable to wait one minute longer to find out.

I had all kinds of things running through my mind.

She pulled a few items out of her bag. "I tripped on a step. I'm fine, really."

Irritated at her cavalier attitude, I snapped, "When did this happen?" I wasn't sure she was telling me the truth.

"Just before I came here," she told me.

My eyes scanned the length of her body, looking for further injuries. I was forced to stop when she found what she needed, because she turned and headed back into the bedroom and out of my sight.

Not knowing what to do, I picked up the phone and dialed room service.

"How can I help you tonight?" the voice answered.

"Can I get a bucket of ice, some bottles of water, and a burger and fries?"

Elle came out of the room and pulled the door partially closed.

"How would you like the burger cooked, sir?" the operator asked.

"Medium."

I wasn't sure if she'd eaten, but I knew she needed ice.

"We'll send it up," the operator said.

"Oh, and can you send a few cartons of milk?" Babies drink milk, or most do, I thought. I hung up, then looked over at Elle, who was searching her bag. "Does Clementine drink milk?"

She gave me a small smile. "Yes, she does. But she should be out for the night."

"I'll put it in the refrigerator then, just in case."

She nodded and went back in the bedroom. I felt like she was gone for hours before she emerged and carefully took a seat on the sofa.

I wasted no time. "How about you tell me what's going on?" I tried to keep my voice down.

"It's probably nothing," she answered.

I sat on the sofa—not too close, but not that far away. "Tell me what happened. Where is O'Shea?"

She took a pillow and placed it behind her back. "Michael called me late this afternoon. He got called to New York City. Something last minute. It's not unusual."

"The fucker left you alone with the baby?" I seethed.

She reached over and placed her hand on me. "Logan, he still doesn't know anything about what happened yesterday. I hadn't gotten a chance to tell him yet."

The heat of her fingers on my thigh caused my pulse to race. I looked at where her hand was. My blood was roaring as the lust I was feeling coursed through my veins. She was trying to calm me down and instead I was getting aroused.

I shifted awkwardly in my seat. I couldn't think while she was touching me. Needing to lose the connection, I shuffled to my feet.

I was such an asshole.

Elle quickly folded her hands together in her lap and I swear I saw a thankful look on her face. Had she done that without thinking? Did she feel what I felt?

Still way too close, the flames from the stoking fire were roaring. I glanced at her and hoped they would die soon. With a slight shake of my head and a step back, I refocused on what was important. "That's bullshit. He shouldn't be leaving you alone with his kid."

What was his game? I'd seen him at the garage. What was on that paper? Did the fucker run?

She just stared at me like I was the crazy motherfucker.

Okay, so I was being a dick. I needed to let her finish. I drew in a breath. "Sorry, go on."

She still looked at me.

I put a hand up. "I'm cool."

"You sure?"

"Yes, Elle." I tried to keep my voice tight.

"I might just be unnecessarily acting paranoid."

"Tell me," I urged.

"Well, after I picked up Clementine and we got to Michael's house, my garage door opener was missing from the car."

"And then what?" I asked her, impatient to get to it.

"I drove around to the front and noticed the lights were off. That's unusual. They're on a timer. I got out to check the house before I brought Clementine in and that's when I saw someone inside. Or I think I did. I saw shadows moving in Michael's office. I didn't stick around to make sure. I just turned and ran. That's when I fell."

My heart in my throat, I hated to even ask this. "Was someone chasing you?"

She shook her head vehemently. "No, I didn't see any-one. I didn't go any farther than the walkway, though. As soon as I was certain I saw movement, I ran to my car and drove here. I'm sorry, Logan. I didn't know what else to do."

She was more scared than she was letting on. I went and sat beside her, closer this time. "Hey, don't be sorry."

"I didn't know what else to do," she repeated again.

Nothing mattered but making sure she knew she'd done the right thing. I took her face in my hands. "You did the right thing."

We looked at each other.

Her lips parted. My breathing was heavy.

Was I really considering kissing her?

The knock on the door had me pulling my hands away. It saved me from making a dumb-ass move.

Elle, however, jumped.

"Hey . . . it's okay, it's just room service. I told you, you're safe here," I reassured her. I wasn't being entirely honest. Yes, she was safe here, but she wasn't safe with me. And somehow I had to tell her that.

The guy in white stood there with a tray. I didn't let him past me. I searched the hallway, saw no one else, signed the slip, and then I wheeled the cart in myself. "Thanks," I told him.

"Have a good night," he replied.

With the door closed and locked up tight again, the first thing I did was grab a towel and pour some ice in it. Tying it up, I handed it to her. "Here, put this on your back."

She took it and slid it behind her to rest on the pillow and then leaned on it. "Thank you."

"Did you eat?" I asked, keeping my distance.

Close was bad. I couldn't seem to control my libido.

"No, but I'm not hungry," she answered.

Ignoring her comment, I took the plate of food and set it on her lap. "You should eat."

She lifted the lid. "I'll share it with you."

My whole body tightened. Share. I could do that. Put the food between us. Keep my thoughts on what mattered. Back to mechanical steps, I put the milk in the refrigerator and brought two bottles of water over. I set them on the coffee table and sat down. Trying unsuccessfully to not really look at Elle, I grabbed the ketchup bottle and poured some out on the plate, then grabbed a fry. "Your turn."

She pinched a fry and dipped it in the ketchup. She seemed calmer, more relaxed, and I was glad. "Can I ask you something?" she said after a few bites of the burger.

I leaned back on the couch and saw her eyes travel the length of me. My blood started pumping again. "Yeah, sure." I shifted in my seat.

After chewing, she asked, "Are you related to Killian McPherson?"

I should have hesitated. I should have hated dirtying her with the knowledge. But I didn't. It was a gateway into what I had to tell her anyway. And hopefully, once she knew, it would make her want to avoid any sexual involvement with me. She needed to stay close to me, though, until I knew she would be safe. I dropped my head but raised my eyes. "Yeah, he's my grandfather."

Stunned, she set the plate down. "Logan, are you in the Mafia?"

That was direct.

My head snapped up. "Fuck no."

She didn't look convinced.

Somehow, I found myself leaning toward her. It was like I was a magnet, drawn to her, no matter how much distance I put between us. "First of all, the Mafia is Italian. The Mob is Irish. Not that it matters. But anyway, my grandfather and my father worked really hard to make sure I kept my distance. I'm not a part of that organization. And my father is just what I told you, Patrick's legal counsel. Nothing more."

She pulled the towel filled with ice from behind her back. The cubes started falling out. "Then why were you with him last night?"

I took the towel from her and scooped the cubes up. "Here, let me fix it."

She shook her head. "It's fine." She was staring at me, waiting for me to explain.

There was no denying the way we'd crossed paths. "Things have changed recently for my old man, and I've been going with him on 'calls' whenever I can." I tried to tell her as much as I could without telling her more than she needed to know.

She rubbed her fingers around her eyes. "Look, Logan, I already know my sister must have been involved with something really bad or Michael wouldn't be jumping through hoops to try to fix it. And by doing so, I can only guess that now Michael is involved in something equally as dangerous. The question is, should I be worried for myself and Clementine?"

The towel was dripping on my pants, so I set it in on the table, and then I stupidly moved closer. "I'm not going to lie to you or try to make you feel better. I'm going to be honest. Yes, you should."

"Now you're really scaring me."

"I don't want to, but you need to understand how dangerous this situation is. What do you know about the drug ring?"

She pulled her legs up. "Nothing. I don't know anything."

My eyes met hers. Was she lying? I had no idea, but I chose to believe her and tell her what I could. "Patrick Flannigan, the guy who runs the organization my father works for, is the one that told my pop to pay O'Shea a visit. It was a warning, not a social call. Patrick is a dangerous man and his son, even more so. O'Shea might not realize it, but he is in over his head. You have to believe me about this, Elle."

She sat still, as if absorbing my every word.

"What's he doing? What's his plan?"

My question jarred her. She twitched a bit and then reached for a bottle of water. "I don't know."

I narrowed my eyes at her.

"I don't. He doesn't tell me anything."

That only made the guy a bigger ass in my eyes. I took a deep breath. "Any chance you can take Clementine and get out of town for a week or so?"

She took a swallow of water and seemed to move subconsciously closer to me.

My body reacted to her close proximity. My eyes were focused on her. I couldn't help but watch the path that the liquid took as it moved down her throat. Every minute I spent with her, I found myself wanting her more and more.

I couldn't stop it.

I wanted to ease her pain.

But it was my cock that was really feeling the pain of it. It was rock hard. And tough shit, there was no relief coming anytime soon.

It took her a second, but she looked at me and I cleared my lustful thoughts. "No, I can't. I just opened the boutique. I couldn't possibly leave. I only have Peyton and Rachel to help me with it, and besides, I have nowhere to go even if Michael lets me take her."

"Okay, I get it. But you have to think of yourself. I want to help you, but I can't if I don't know what he has planned. You need to sit down with O'Shea and make him tell you what's in his head." I had to be straight. There was no dancing around it. He didn't have time to fuck around.

She nodded. "I'll try."

"You have to tell me what he tells you."

She looked hesitant.

"That's the only way I can help you."

"Logan, I just don't know. I'm risking a lot by being here, but something inside me tells me I'm safer here than anywhere else. What I don't get, though, is . . . why do you want to help me? Aren't we supposed to be on opposite sides?"

I shook my head. "No, we're not on opposite sides. We're on the same side. I promise."

"How do I know I can trust you?"

I brushed some hair from her face. I knew I shouldn't be touching her but I had to. "Because all I want is to keep you and that precious little girl sleeping in the other room safe."

She leaned into my touch and I felt it everywhere in my body. "I don't understand. Why? Why would you help us?"

There was no way I couldn't be honest. Not when she was this close to me. Not when her voice was pleading with me to tell her. "Because, Elle, you remind me of someone I should have helped but didn't. Someone I failed."

Our eyes locked. I swear her lips parted. I know I felt my own mouth open and I couldn't stop my tongue from sneaking out and licking my bottom lip. In my mind, I was imagining how much better she'd feel about all of this if I could drive my cock deep inside her. What a fucked-up thought. I shook it away.

Finally, I cleared my throat. "I want you to stay here tonight. And then tomorrow, when O'Shea gets back, you'll talk to him. I can't help you if I don't know what he's planning to do. But Elle, you can't tell him you're talking to me. Not yet."

She nodded in silent agreement as if she didn't want him to know either.

Interesting.

"You take the bedroom. I'll sleep out here."

She nodded again. "Do you mind if I take a shower? It's been a long day."

"No, go ahead."

Oh fuck, the things I was already picturing.

Elle stood up and I watched her as she grabbed her bags and went back into the bedroom. She paused at the door. "Thanks, Logan. For everything."

"You don't have to thank me," I said.

If she knew what I was thinking, she wouldn't.

She disappeared into the darkness and I refocused. My

dirty mind aside, I couldn't help but think to myself, *Please trust me.*

Trust in what I told you.

Trust me when I tell you how dangerous this is.

Because if you don't—we'll both be dead.

chapter
NINETEEN

Elle

N AUSEA TWISTED MY GUT.
     If what Logan had told me was true, and Michael was in over his head, he wasn't wrong—we were in trouble.

And something told me there were no lies in Logan's words.

Michael had told me just enough, hinting at the danger but making it sound like everything would be okay. Was he being overly optimistic or was Logan being paranoid?

I just had no idea.

Stepping inside the large space, I left the door open a crack from the bathroom to the bedroom in case Clementine woke up. I dimmed the bathroom lights and looked around. Marble covered almost every surface and the heat lamps in the ceiling were supposed to warm me, but the chill I was feeling wasn't one that could be cured by supplied heat.

My clothes felt like they weighed a hundred pounds as I stripped out of them and let them fall to the floor. When I turned on the shower faucet, the water sprayed from jets in every direction. I stood outside the shower and decided to allow my skin the luxury of being warmed by the steam as the water got hotter.

When I felt ready, I stepped inside. A bar of soap sat in a small alcove built into the shower along with bottles of shampoo, conditioner, and body wash. The soap and shampoo had been used, but not the other two. I cracked open the body wash and the scent of lavender filled the large space.

The liquid seemed to caress my body as I smoothed it on, almost as if it might help wash away the danger that lay ahead. The water beat down on me from all directions and I enfolded myself in it. In this sanctuary, I could let myself be afraid. I could cry because I was scared. I didn't have to be strong.

The emotions I was holding in gave away, as did my wall of strength. Like a rag doll, I limply slid down the wall of the shower. After a few moments, I cradled my head in my hands and let the tears flow. I cried for as long as I could and when I knew I had no tears left, I resolved to cry no more. It was time to be strong, if not for me, then for that innocent little girl sleeping soundly in the next room.

Fortitude was a virtue I knew well and, as I forced myself to rise to my feet, I reminded myself of that. Finding the shampoo, I scrubbed and rinsed my head. When I looked at my fingers, they were wrinkled, and I wondered just how long I'd been in the shower. Running my hands through my silky smooth strands, I scrubbed some more and then rinsed again, finally adding the conditioner and rinsing one last time.

My mind felt freer by the time I turned the shower off. Logan assured me we'd be safe, and for a reason I didn't want to examine too closely, I believed him. Logan—what was it about him? What were these feelings that were whooshing through my belly just thinking about him? Was I genuinely attracted to him, or was my reaction simply a by-product of the fear I was feeling? The answer could easily have been yes to both questions.

Steam filled the air in the room. Something came over me in the haze—lustful visions that I couldn't control.

When I stepped out of the shower, I tried to block the image I had in my head of Logan's parted lips—soft, sensual. As soon as the cooler air hit me, my nipples peaked. I ignored the desire that was blooming within me and reached for the fluffy white towels that were just beside the counter.

First, I wrapped my head in one and then my body. The terry cloth absorbed the water instantly but I still rubbed one corner over my skin to dry it thoroughly. The arousal I had been feeling blossomed beneath the surface of each place I rubbed and I made sure to leave no place untouched.

The air was still hazy and the mirror was coated in steam. That was fine; I didn't need to see myself. I knew the state of affairs. My skin was pink from the heat, my body was clean, and my mind was on the man who would be sleeping in the next room tonight.

Squeezing my eyes closed, I bent forward and gripped the counter. I had to think clearly. I couldn't allow anything or anyone to cloud my judgment.

"Are you okay?" His voice was low, rumbly, and my insides came even more alive at the sound.

Surprised, I stood straight and turned around. My heart leapt into my throat when I saw him occupying the doorway. In the midst of all this chaos, he was a welcome breath of fresh air.

"Yes, I'm fine. Sorry if I'm taking too long. I'll hurry."

He leaned against the doorframe and his long, lean body was all I could see. "No, that's not why I'm here. I knocked lightly but you didn't hear me."

I drank him in from head to toe, not sure how to stop what was coming over me. "It's okay. What did you need?"

"I didn't want to disturb you, but I saw you were out of the shower and thought you might freak out if you didn't see Clementine in the bed."

I stepped forward, freaking out more than a bit.

Logan spoke, though, before I could express my concern. "Nothing to worry about. I wanted to let you know," he jerked his head toward the bedroom, "I had housekeeping set up a crib and I moved Clementine into it. I hope you don't mind."

My vision became blurry from all the steam, or maybe it was the gratitude I felt from his constant vigilance over Clementine and me. "Thank you."

"Are you sure you're okay?" he asked again.

As my body reacted to his presence, warmth overtook me, and my desire heightened with each passing second that his eyes were on me. I didn't try to hide it. I didn't want to. "I was just thinking about you, actually."

He grinned at me, and something that seemed like shyness glimmered in his expression. "About me, in what way?"

Pure male was all I heard in his words.

I didn't answer.

I didn't have to.

After studying him, I surmised it was hesitation I saw, not shyness. While his face appeared to remain reserved, his body told a different story.

I traced the lines of it. He wore a long-sleeved black T-shirt that clung to his broad shoulders and flat stomach. His black cargo pants hugged his lean waist, and the bulge in those pants let me know how much he wanted me. His thighs may have been lost beneath the fabric, but I had to bet they were equally as exquisite.

When my gaze returned to his, he slid his focus painfully slowly down my body.

It was as if I could feel the heat of those hazel eyes with each inch they traveled downward, and I wanted to feel more of it. The longer they lingered, the more my body reacted. When his eyes returned to mine, I felt this strange pull that I couldn't explain if I had to, but all I knew was that I had to have him.

Recognizing I might never get the chance again, I acted without another thought.

I wasn't going to hold back.

I was prepared to go all the way.

Focused on just that, I took the towel from my hair and shook my head so that wet strands of ginger locks covered my shoulders. Then I tugged on the fabric that wrapped my torso and let it fall to the ground.

Logan drew in a ragged breath and slowly stepped over the threshold and into the bathroom.

I waited, breathing hard, heart pounding, as he carefully closed the door and turned the fan on. A whirring sound encompassed the space at the same time it drew the humidity from the room.

His long strides had him in front of me in a matter of seconds.

In a state of delirium, my hands grabbed for his waistband and I wildly pulled the snap open. I couldn't stop myself even if I tried. I wanted to see him naked. I wanted to see every square inch of his body and then I wanted to feel it against mine.

"Elle, this isn't a good—"

I put my finger on his lush lips. "Shhh . . . no talking. Not now. We've done enough talking."

Uncertain perhaps, he met my eyes questioningly.

Even though I was completely naked, I was unabashed. Certain.

I wanted him.

He wanted me.

I'd never felt this kind of want before and I needed to see it through.

I prayed he wouldn't say another word. I didn't want anything to jar me from the euphoric state I had somehow entered.

This close to him, I could see the exact shape of the scar beneath his eye. I could also see the brown flecks in his green eyes, so many they transformed the color to hazel. They glistened in the dim light and mesmerized me.

In this moment, we weren't on opposite sides, we weren't strangers, and we weren't denying the oddly intense attraction that had been there from the start. We were just two consenting adults who wanted to fuck.

Logan seemed to feel the same. He dropped his gaze and didn't speak a word as he molded himself to me. His touches were like sparks of electricity that tingled all of my nerve endings. I felt them everywhere.

One hand went to my back and the other curled behind my neck as he pulled me to him. Still contending with the magical feel of his hands, the contact made by his mouth was unexpected. It was on mine so fast that I started to sway in a dizzying combination of lust and want. The soft, tender feel of his lips was delicious. Our mouths moved in tandem and our tongues met as we devoured each other with the hunger we both felt.

I tried to ignore the fact that I'd never felt this way.

I needed to get out of my own head.

And I did. I let thoughts of him sweep me away. Strange thoughts. Like how I wanted to taste him from his lips to his feet, how I wanted to drag my tongue down his body and lick every bit of him.

My fingers fumbled with his zipper and I faltered when his hands shot right between my thighs.

Raging doses of hormones were in the air. Bucking wildly, his hips pressed against mine, and his cock felt like steel against my lower belly. We'd both been overtaken with the need to fuck, and he urged me back until my ass was flush against the countertop.

"Let me take care of you." His voice was rough like gravel.

I squeezed my eyes shut.

I didn't want any talking.

Thank God, there were not more words. The only thing that followed was touching. By the time I could think again, his fingertips were already stroking my pussy and it felt way too good to think about stopping.

With skill, he rubbed small circles around my opening, getting closer with each one. "Fuck, you're so wet," he groaned.

No talking during sex was always my rule. Normally, I would have dictated the terms up front and left by now due to their violation. Yet instead of backing away, I found myself moaning, what, I'm not even sure. Before I could figure out what I was saying, he pushed a finger inside me. He wasn't in a hurry as he plunged deeper and drew it back up all way to my clit. He repeated this over and over, and I responded to every delicious movement he made.

I was thankful for the whirring of the fan because I couldn't stop the noises I was making. I wasn't sure if it was the way he moved or the fact that a man hadn't had his hands on me in so long, but the feeling was intoxicating.

I felt lost to my body.

To him.

To what was inevitable.

When he inserted a second finger inside me, I gasped, but when he moved his hand in the same way that he had before, I cried out.

My lips were still on his, and our breathing was becoming heavier and heavier.

As his hand continued to pleasure me, I tried to reach for his zipper again, but then he inserted a third finger and started circling my clit with his other hand and I lost my mind.

He was fucking me with his hand, and the sensations were building and building. I abandoned any thought of touching his cock and held onto his shoulders to keep myself upright.

When I bit down on his lip to stop myself from screaming, his kisses turned rougher. His lips traveled from my mouth, along my jaw, and down to one of my breasts, and his teeth skimmed along the way as well. The sting felt good as he licked it away.

Pleasure began to course through me in a way I'd never felt. Sparks of sensations lapped at my core over and over. Perhaps it was what happened when danger, terror, lust, want, and need all mixed together, or maybe it was just him. But when those tiny sparks came faster and faster, I felt my pussy tighten around his fingers. The pleasure was unbelievable, and I came with such intensity that each spasm was like a shudder that rolled into the next but at a higher level, and I had to bite my lip so hard to stop from screaming that I could taste blood.

As my orgasm slowed, I let go of my hold on his arms and reached for his zipper again. "I want to see you naked," I said breathlessly.

I couldn't believe I said that.

But I did.

He dropped his forehead to the crook of my neck. "You don't know what you're doing. What this means."

I leaned back to look at him. He wouldn't raise his eyes, but I could see that his face was almost pained. "I don't care about any of that right now."

He shook his head. "Elle, there's so much you don't know about me."

I took his face in my hands. "And there's so much you don't know about me. But right now none of that matters." I eased my lips back to his and started licking around them. As I dragged my tongue down his jaw, I slid my hands under his shirt, and I swore I felt him shudder.

Logan stepped back, and I wasn't sure if he was still torn or had decided to leave. He wouldn't look at me.

All I could see was his heart beating wildly. "Logan, it's okay. It's just you and me in this small room."

It was obvious he was waging a war with his own demons. I'd waged enough of those in my time to know one when I saw one.

He nodded, and then he pulled his shirt over his head.

I stared at the smoothness of his skin and couldn't wait to touch it. I admired the twin dark circles on his chest and wanted to taste them. I counted the rips in his abs—six. I sketched with my eyes the lines of his hip bones that jutted into his pants and reached to trace them.

Logan slid his pants and boxers down at the same time

and let them fall to the ground. My fingers didn't waver as they continued to glide down the path I had started upon. I stayed on task and dropped to my knees so as not to get off course. What was it I'd thought in the back of my mind when I first saw him? He was a man who could bring a woman to her knees. I wasn't wrong.

I licked my lips at his naked form. He had another scar on the inside of his thigh, very close to his private parts, and I wondered what had happened. But it didn't matter, because he was still beautiful. A very faint, thin line of hair led down to his cock, which was jutting out in the most magnificent way. He was big, really big, and the thought of tasting him made my mouth water.

With my tongue, I traced the line I had just drawn with my finger. When I reached the inside of his thigh, he pulled me back up.

His gaze was so intense, it was practically smoldering, and then he buried his hands in my hair and kissed me with those lush lips. As our mouths moved, our bodies drew closer and closer still.

After a few minutes, he lifted me and as I automatically wrapped my legs around his waist, I felt movement swirl in my stomach. It was a feeling I hadn't felt in a very long time and for one single moment, I thought about stopping this.

When he reached for the counter and grabbed a condom, I pushed the past back where it belonged, in the past.

He stepped toward the shower and opened the glass door, turning the water on and adjusting the knobs so just the showerhead sprayed.

Although I was certain Clementine couldn't hear us, I was thankful for the added buffer of the water.

I'd never let her hear anyone having sex.

Two long strides and my back was against the wall.

"Hold on to me," he commanded.

Without even flinching, I snaked my arms around his neck and watched as he ripped the condom open with his teeth. He tried to roll it on while still holding me at his waist, but it was an impossible feat.

"Dammit," he said in a low voice.

I pulled back and looked at him. My mouth and throat went dry. He was all hard lines, chiseled abs, such a strong, lean body.

I shivered at the sight.

While the water lapped us, his hair fell forward. He looked incredibly sexy—unshaven, naked, and soon to be mine.

I couldn't believe I was even thinking this way.

With the oddest urgent need, I dropped to my knees again and whispered, "Let me."

His face was the epitome of seriousness as he handed me the condom.

My fingers were shaky when I took it, but I still managed to slowly roll it over his silky smooth shaft.

Once the condom was on, I couldn't resist touching him. I closed my fist around his big cock and could feel it throbbing. With deliberately slow movements, I stroked up and back down.

He bit down on his lip and watched me. I was careful to keep one hand at his base and keep the condom in place.

Something erupted inside me when he thrust his hip forward. I was doing this to him. Turning him on. Making him feel good.

Oddly, I'd never really cared about anything like this before.

Feeling needy, I increased my pace.

He tipped his head back, thrusting his cock into my fist and letting out a muffled noise that made my body quake.

His hair in his face, the stubble on his jaw, the look in his eyes—it was all too much. My clit started to throb again and I wondered if I was going to orgasm without any manipulation.

I squeezed my eyes closed, unable to curb the overwhelming sensations washing through me.

"Hey," he lifted my chin. "Are you okay?"

I nodded, unable to speak. I couldn't find my breath.

He must have sensed I was on the edge or maybe he was, because he pulled me to my feet, took my hands in his, and raised them over my head. He held them in place with one hand and then guided his cock into me with the other.

Oh. My. God.

While his lips found mine, his mouth devoured me and his cock began to fill me.

A peaceful blissfulness washed over me. I was thirty years old and I had never felt this kind of passion. I honestly didn't think it existed.

He pushed inside me slowly. A little at a time.

In.

Out.

In.

Out.

Heaven.

"Oh, fuck, you're so tight," he moaned.

At first, alarm rose in my belly, but somehow I managed to push it away. My gaze flickered over his jaw, his hair, and landed on his smoldering eyes. Needy, I jerked my hips forward, urging for more, and suppressed the fact that he was talking.

He laughed and groaned at the same time. The one sound I knew I'd never forget. He pushed deeper and then again slowly withdrew.

My hands were bound and I wanted them free so I could reach behind him and push him all the way into me.

He was breathing hard and so was I, but we still kissed, opened mouthed, tongues touching, teeth clashing.

Logan dropped his hold.

Curious as to why, I peeked up at him.

He blinked the water from his eyes. "Wrap your arms around my neck."

The deep sound of his voice.

The way he spoke.

It didn't bother me . . . and I didn't hesitate.

As soon as my body surrounded his, he lifted me again and . . . oh God . . . he sank deep inside me. I snaked my legs around his back and this way, in this position, his cock fit in my cunt in the most perfect way.

His thrusts were quick.

They felt so good.

His kisses rough.

They felt so good.

His grip tight.

It felt so good.

Moving together, we fucked hard and fast. And all the while, incredible bursts of pleasure crested through me, making my entire body shake.

My orgasm struck fast and shut my mind down. Tiny explosions behind my eyelids took over, and in that moment there was nothing else that mattered but him and me and the way our bodies responded to each other.

Logan started to come in the midst of my orgasm. I could feel his body still and felt that one, last deep penetration before he called out my name.

My name.

I loved how it sounded groaned in ecstasy.

It was the perfect ending to an incredible union.

With my clit pulsing around his cock and my body wrapped around his, I wanted to stay like that forever.

It was strange, but in the moment, I didn't care about what could never be, or what might be.

This feeling was what I had been searching for.

My experience with Charlie had taught me many things, but most of all it taught me love would never be a part of my life. I was fine with that. It's not like I ever thought it would. He was unexpected. At the risk of sounding cold, he was a nice distraction from my struggle to figure the whole sex thing out. Sex with him hadn't been the focus of our relationship, which was what had been most appealing about him.

After him, though, I felt compelled to continue with my quest. Although a self-repressed sexual being by nature, I spent years chasing after what my father needed so desperately from sex that he bled the life out of my mother to get it. I tried everything I could but never found it. I slept with men for the sole purpose of finding it. Once, I even slept with two at the same time. I had a cock in my mouth and one in my cunt. And still nothing. I used vibrators, cock rings, and a drawer full of toys chasing that high that was supposed to come with sex. I had begun to think that it wasn't for me to experience. And then, with a man I'd just met, a man who by circumstance should have been my enemy, I found it.

And the worst part was that it took me experiencing it to know for certain that my years of searching were futile—that in no way was that feeling the reason my father fucked my mother to death. Because what I just experienced was entirely mutual. It was as much about what I gave as what I took. And that is what made it so incredible. In my parents' case, that was in no way what was going on between them.

Some things in life will just never make sense.

chapter
TWENTY

LOGAN

I HADN'T SMOKED IN years, but I needed a cigarette.

I didn't want to move, and it appeared Elle didn't either.

With my cock buried deep inside her, I felt invincible.

But as my breathing started to recover and the high of my orgasm faded, reality came crashing down.

I was a fucking idiot.

I was anything but invincible.

She was anything but safe.

And I'd just done the one thing that was certain to cause her harm.

It didn't matter when I fucked around in New York City. The Blue Hill Gang didn't extend their reach that far and besides, it's not like I went looking for pussy. I let it come to me. Hell, most of the time I didn't even know their names. They were women looking for a break from the boring social circles we traveled in, and for some reason I was their guy. It worked for me. They'd call my name as I fucked their brains out trying to drown out the memory of Kayla's screams. I never took numbers, never made promises to see them again, and I never went back for seconds.

But with Elle something was different, and it scared the shit out of me. Now, even after I was completely sated and spent, I knew once wasn't enough with her. I had known it all along, though. It wasn't just that I wanted more; I needed it. She had lit a small flame inside me that I thought had died long ago, and I wanted her to keep that fire alive.

I wasn't ready for this to end, so I slid a hand to the back of her neck and drove my fingers into her damp hair, and then I took her mouth eagerly once again. I kissed her passionately, furiously, drawing every ounce of pleasure I could from her—I kissed her the same as I had when I'd been fucking her.

Like it was the first and last time.

Because it was.

She moaned, and I ate up the satisfaction I knew she was feeling.

It felt good to make someone happy.

After more than a few beats, I stopped kissing her. I didn't want to, but I had to. I was out of breath and so was she. But mostly I stopped because reality kept creeping into my head. My highs and lows were becoming more unstable, the endorphins waning the longer the time span from my orgasm.

Elle used it as her cue to pull away. "We can't stay like this."

The high building again from the sound of her voice alone, I looked down. I didn't see why not. It was the only time we could. The thought of one more time had my cock stirring in her pussy again. Keeping the mood light, casual even, I shrugged and offered, "I'm up to it if you are."

Why beat around the bush?

She gave me an amused laugh, and it was the most beautiful sound, a sound I knew I'd never forget. "Is that a challenge?"

I raised a brow, and having a feeling she didn't back away from challenges, I teased, "It can be."

"Your legs must be tired," she said with the sexiest,

raspy tone that I don't think was on purpose.

I nipped at her neck. "Nope."

She tossed her head back. "Your arms?"

I couldn't remember the last time I was playful with a woman.

If ever.

Then I remembered. "Oh fuck, your back."

"I'm fine," she said, but I could tell by the way she was twisting that it was bothering her.

I gently set her down and reached between us to hold the condom in place as I pulled out of her. I missed the warmth instantly and I could tell she did too.

As soon as I opened the shower door to dispose of the condom, my eyes landed directly in front of me and I froze.

I was a dumb fuck.

How the hell had I let my wall down?

I couldn't do that.

I knew better.

I tried my best to put it back up. Staring longer at the sight of the crack down the mirror I had made earlier certainly helped. It served to remind me who I was, and what I shouldn't be doing. I was the grandson of the once head of the Irish Mob who had made an enemy of the now head and I knew I couldn't be seen with any girl around this town, especially not this girl. Somehow, some way, Tommy would find out, and I didn't want to think about what that meant.

His day would come.

"Hey, are you okay?" Elle asked.

I dared to look at her.

I shouldn't have.

When our eyes met, all I saw was the smile slip from her face.

I really was an asshole.

Dropping my gaze, I grabbed a towel and handed it to her. Completely pissed at myself, I avoided looking at her and answered, "Yeah, I'm fine."

The chill in the air said I wasn't.

She wrapped the towel around herself and then opened one of the bags she must have set on the floor earlier. "I should get dressed," she said quietly.

I could tell she was putting up her own wall.

The tension in the room left me feeling guilty. I dried off and pulled my pants on, then turned to her and lamely said, "I have some things to take care of. I'll be out in the other room if you need me."

Her mouth thinned and I could see her armor go all the way up. "Yes, sure, of course."

I was being a dick and I knew it.

The awareness of my actions cut like a knife.

Odd.

It had never bothered me before. I did what I did because I had to, and I'd grown used to it. Numb to any reaction. I shook off the strange feeling and looked at my watch. "Almost ten."

Elle nodded. "I think I'll just go to bed."

I turned around to walk out the door and didn't even look back before I left. I felt like I was bleeding. I wanted to kiss her. To say good night. But I couldn't, because I knew if I looked into her green eyes and watched them fill up with some unknown emotion, I'd scoop her up and pull her in my arms and tell her I was sorry for being an asshole. The cold routine was for her own good, though.

That I wanted her but couldn't have her didn't matter.

I feared that if I spent another minute with her, I'd tell her why.

And then what would she think of me?

The closed door between the living area and the bedroom acted as a buffer between us, which was good because I needed to think clearly about the situation. And not the one that had just occurred. The one we were both in with Patrick, and Tommy, too, of course.

Someone stalking Elle made no sense. It wasn't Patrick's style. I started to wonder if maybe she was being paranoid.

The shadows she saw could very easily have been caused by the wind. But where the fuck was the garage door opener? Had whoever broken into her car taken it? I'd have her check for that first.

It was the logical step.

I pulled my body onto the couch and threw my head back on the small pillow. Exhaustion eased its way into my bones and I allowed myself to close my eyes.

Screaming woke me up.

Elle's voice.

My heart slammed like a rock against my chest and terror raced through me. I bolted up, grabbed my SIG, and ran for the bedroom door. I wanted to kick it down but thought better of it and eased it open instead. Light spilled into the dark room from the living area and I shot a 360-degree glance around. The baby girl was sleeping soundly in the crib, but Elle was thrashing in the sheets again.

No one was in there with her.

Thank God.

After I realized she was having another nightmare, I rushed over to the bed and set my gun down on the night table, where the digital clock read 2:31 in the morning.

"Get out. Get out. I never want to see you again!" she yelled.

I might have thought it was me she was yelling at if she hadn't had a nightmare just last night. The thought it could be me was like a heavy weight on my shoulders and I instantly regretted my retreat just a few hours ago. I stared down at her and kept my voice quiet. "Elle, wake up. It's just a dream."

Her fingers were gripping the sheets so tightly that I could see the material pulling. I placed a hand on her shoulder. "Elle, wake up," I whispered.

She sat up.

Confused.

Exhausted.

Vulnerable.

My head spun a little bit and I realized I'd been holding my breath. *Dumb ass.* What the fuck was wrong with me? I had to man up.

She looked at me and seemed to blink everything into focus. Then her eyes darted to Clementine.

"She's fine," I whispered reassuringly.

Elle was shaking, her body still experiencing the trauma of the nightmare even though she was fully awake. "What's going on? Why are you in here?" she asked frantically.

The covers were tangled and tossed to the side. I pulled them up and sat beside her. "Elle, talk to me. What were you dreaming about?"

She shook her head.

"Who do you want to go away? Did someone hurt you?" My voice was unbelievably calm considering the thumping of my pulse in my throat.

Her eyes bore into mine, searching.

Something inside me said, *Fuck reason.* She needed someone. It wasn't her fault it was me that was here. That's when I did it. I moved closer to her. But that wasn't enough to relax the taut muscles and scared look on her face. To try to help, I pushed her hair from her eyes so she could see me. "It's okay. Tell me," I said, my voice low.

Elle took a deep breath and blew it out. "She left me alone with him. She knew what he was like and she left me alone with him. That's why I hated her."

My brain started to spasm at what exactly that meant. "Who, Elle?"

"Lizzy. My sister. She left me alone with him. Right after my mother died, my sister came to my hospital room and told me she had to leave."

I already knew who she was talking about, so I clarified, "She left you alone with your father."

She nodded.

I struggled to speak as my stomach knotted. It felt like I had balls of rubber bands in there and they were bouncing from side to side. "Did he hurt you? Is that why you were in the hospital?"

Elle shook her head. "I begged her to stay. When I knew she wasn't going to, I blamed her for what had happened. I knew it wasn't her fault. But then she told me she'd send for me when she got her life settled and I lost it. I told her not to bother. I never wanted to see her again, and then I took off the bracelet she had given me and threw it at her like it never mattered. It mattered. It did matter. I told her if she walked out that door, never to contact me. Why would I do that?"

I pulled her to me and tried to soothe her. "Shhh . . . Elle, we all say and do things sometimes that we regret. I'm sure your sister knows that."

Her tears were spilling down my bare chest as she shook her head. "No, she didn't. If she did, why did she wait until she was in trouble to contact me?"

I had no response for her, but I was compelled to lie down and pull her to me. Stroking her back, I kissed her head and tried to ease her pain. I didn't know exactly what had happened but whatever it was, it had impacted her life. And I felt somewhat to blame for invoking those memories. I shouldn't have questioned her about her parents last night when the vibe was clear from the start that her relationship with them was fragile.

Her breathing started to settle and she flung her arm across my chest and held on to me.

A panic started to rise in me and I considered jumping up.

That would be the biggest asshole move I could ever make.

At least I knew that.

I talked myself off the ledge. It was okay. She needed me. I could be there for her. It didn't have to mean anything else.

Did it?

Fuck.

I had to admit it.

The truth was, no matter how much I tried to distance myself from her, physically or emotionally, she was already in me.

It was too late.

No amount of space was going to stop what I was feeling.

I was fucked.

chapter
TWENTY-ONE

DAY 3

Elle

CLEMENTINE COOED IN THE early morning light.
I panicked, wondering if Logan was still in bed with me.

Uncertain, I opened my eyes and peeked.

He wasn't.

I should have been relieved, but I wasn't sure I was. Logan was messing with my mind. I'd never met anyone like him. He radiated sex appeal but could turn it off in the blink of an eye. I shouldn't have cared—but I did. He'd opened something in my mind that had me thinking that way. He turned me on. He'd awakened something in my body that had me wanting him. That worried me.

Clementine was still babbling and I rolled over to see her cute little face staring at me through the rails of her crib. She was a good sleeper, but as soon as the sun came up, so did she.

Forcing myself out of bed, I took the few steps toward her. "Good morning, silly girl. You ready to get up?"

"Up," she said, the strange environment not bothering her in the least.

I smiled at her. She was so easygoing. She was also

parroting back more and more words. When I reached for her, she let out a loud cackle.

"She's happy in the morning." His voice was smooth like honey and made me shiver.

I turned with her in my arms to see Logan leaning against the doorframe with a cup of coffee in each hand. My pulse quickened at the mere sight of him. He was showered and dressed in another pair of black cargo pants and a long-sleeved white T-shirt. He looked rakishly rogue. My hands itched to glide under his clothes and touch his naked body. Such an odd feeling. His hair was still slightly damp and I remembered how soft it felt under my fingertips. I wanted to feel it again. He'd shaved, but I'd never forget how good his stubble felt against my skin. Really good.

Clementine reached for him and my heart fluttered.

She found him irresistible too.

Shaking the feeling off, I gave a slight laugh and told him, "I think she likes you."

Logan strode my way with the swagger back in his step that had been missing last night when he left me in the bathroom. "You think?"

I reached for the cup of coffee he offered me. "You're afraid of her." It wasn't a question. "You don't have to be."

He sipped from his cup. "I wouldn't say I was afraid. It's just that I've never been around babies."

"I see." I looked up and right into his eyes.

Out of nowhere, his lips pressed to mine.

The kiss he gave me was unexpected. It was sweet. I liked it. Clementine seemed to like it too, because she grabbed for his lips.

Shock tore through him and I had to laugh again as she twisted her fingers in his mouth.

Logan gently pulled them away. "She probably shouldn't do that." He wrinkled his nose. "You know, germs and all."

I chewed on my lip to stop from laughing. There were two ways to look at it, after all, and I didn't want to tell him but I was certain worse things had been in her hands.

He pointed his finger at me. "Don't say it," he said, grinning.

With a shrug, I set my coffee down and walked into the bathroom to grab the diaper bag.

"Does Clementine eat regular food?" he asked. "I ordered eggs, pancakes, and toast."

I glanced over my shoulder. "Yes, she does. Let me change her and we'll be right out."

He nodded. "There's a whole pot of hot coffee, too."

I smiled at him. He smiled back. When I turned around with Clementine on my hip, he had just reached the door.

His smile widened when we appeared back in the bedroom and he gave a slight wave before walking out. It might have been for Clementine, but I returned it.

I don't know why.

He slid his tongue around his lips in a heated response.

And my heart skipped a beat.

Logan disappeared into the next room and I set the baby down, all the while my pulse aflutter. Before I changed her, I took a few deep breaths and then sipped on my coffee to try to calm it down.

What was this thing between us?

I wasn't about to overanalyze it, but I knew we needed to eventually talk about it. Something was causing him to war with his emotions, and he should know that he didn't have to worry about me.

I wasn't looking to attach myself to him.

I wasn't looking to attach myself to anyone.

Once I'd changed Clementine, I decided to at least brush my teeth, but then I looked at myself and thought a comb would be a good idea too.

The mirror had a crack down the center and I wondered what had happened, but not for long as Clementine led the way into the living room. I had her bag, which contained her sippy cup, the fail-safe Cheerios, and her toys, so she was all set.

Logan was sitting on the couch with what I could only

call "old school" Vans up on the table, reading something on his phone. A cart of overflowing food was next to him, along with one of the small cartons of milk he had ordered last night.

He peered up at me.

With his eyes on me, I poured the milk into the cup and made Clementine a plate. I didn't have a high chair, so I set everything on the coffee table and let her pick at her food while she played. I knew it wasn't ideal, but it worked and it made her happy.

Once she was settled, I poured myself a hot cup of coffee and added some cream, then took a piece of toast and went to sit on the chair.

Logan patted the seat next to him. "Sit here."

I shrugged casually, surprised but not. Hot and cold seemed to be the beat in which he breathed. "Okay."

After I sat, he pulled his feet from the table and leaned forward, turning his head to see me. "So here's the thing, I'm not really good at anything when it comes to women except fucking."

I practically spit my coffee out. "That was . . . honest."

His eyes caught mine and trapped me. Hazel irises that looked more green than brown today had so much more to say than what he had just said.

There was something in them, something that made him the way he was.

I wasn't one to judge.

The napkin was close and I wiped my mouth. "Logan, I'm attracted to you, and I think I can safely say you're attracted to me."

I heard the smile in his voice. "That's an accurate assumption."

My words came out very matter-of-factly. "We fucked. If we fuck again, I wouldn't mind it and if we don't, that's life."

Logan's gaze darted toward Clementine. "Should we be saying *fuck*?" He'd lowered his voice to a whisper.

I looked at her happily busying herself transferring the pancake squares I'd put on her plate to the table and then whispered, "Probably not."

He leaned close to me. "You didn't let me finish."

Was he dismissing what I'd just said?

"There's more to it than that," he continued.

I put my finger on his lips. "There always is. Thank you for comforting me last night. I'm sorry I lost it on you. There's just so much going on right now, I'm having a hard time keeping my emotions in check."

He opened his mouth and licked my finger. "You haven't mentioned the shower."

Heat crept up my cheeks from his words.

I was really getting tired of my schoolgirl reaction.

Logan glanced over at Clementine, who was now sitting on the floor with her toys, not paying any attention to us, and crashed his lips to mine. The kiss was short this time but it was rough, sensual, and took my breath away.

I gasped, as that strange feeling coursed its way through me.

"In case you needed reminding," he added.

I took a few deep breaths and cursed the desire that was running through my veins. No, I certainly didn't need reminding. I needed more. And now was so not the time to get all hot and bothered. The question was—would there be another? I looked at him. "Has anyone ever told you, Logan McPherson, you're a contradiction of emotions?"

His expression fell. "More than once."

Confused by not only my own emotions, but also his, I nodded. "Well, at least we're on the same page," I said, and then I stood up. "Do you mind if I take a shower?"

His eyes darted to mine and the heat that I saw in them was almost volcanic. "Yeah, sure," he managed to say through a voice full of gravel.

His mind was right where mine was—somewhere it couldn't be right now.

With one hand on my back, I bent to scoop up

Clementine.

"You can leave her here. She seems perfectly content playing in between bites of food."

I looked at him. "You sure?"

"We'll be fine." He looked up at me. "And there's some Advil in my bag on the bathroom vanity if you need one."

I headed for the bedroom. "Okay. I'll be quick."

"Hey," he called.

I glanced over my shoulder.

"It will happen again."

For a moment, I was confused.

But then what he meant clicked at the same time he mouthed, "The fucking."

Shivers ran up my spine as arousal flooded me even more. If the words were meant to be a promise, I found myself looking forward to it. This man was complex and yet I felt I understood him. I didn't know what drove him, but I knew the multitude of emotions behind his reactions were complicated for a reason. Defense mechanisms of some sort was my guess. I think I got him because he was a lot like me.

As soon as I entered the bathroom, memories from last night, his hands on me, his cock inside me, the way he moved, were everywhere. Once the water was hot and steamy, I stepped in and palmed the bar of soap I knew he had rubbed over his skin. I did it until it lathered and then I smoothed it all over me.

It was odd.

I was certain that we would fuck again, too, but everything else in my life held a chilling uncertainty. The words I had spoken to him were true, though. I wanted to be with him again, but that was all there was to it. I was damaged goods. My father so much as told me that the first time he saw me in the hospital after the surgeries. He had said, "I told you not to do this, Gabrielle. No man will want you now." I think he might have even had a tear in his eye. It was the only one I ever saw him shed, although I did hear him crying many nights after my mother's death.

In his own way, he truly believed what he had told me to be true. At the time, I hadn't believed him, but years later his words rang true with Charlie.

The water cascaded over me and I turned my face into the spray. Once I rinsed all the soap away, I quickly toweled dry and dressed in the running clothes I had thrown in my bag yesterday when I thought I'd be staying at Michael's. My plan was to get up early and run in the park, but that was before I knew I'd have Clementine with me.

I brushed my hair and pulled it back in a ponytail, then decided the Advil was probably a good idea.

The black toiletry bag sat on the vanity and I opened it. The bottle of Advil was right beside a partially empty box of condoms. An odd wave of jealousy hit me from out of nowhere. That was one emotion I'd never had to deal with.

Where was this coming from?

Logan's words whispered in my head—"I'm not really good at anything when it comes to women except fucking"—and my fists clenched at my sides. The thought of him with someone else was something I couldn't think about, whether it was before or after me.

Those kinds of feelings weren't healthy. Not for me. Not for him. Not for us.

I swallowed the pill in one gulp and turned the bathroom light off. *Out of sight, out of mind.*

Sunlight gleamed through the bedroom window in abundance. Maybe spring was making an appearance today. I grabbed my phone to check the weather and saw I had a text from Michael telling me he'd be back late afternoon and that he would be stuck in mediation all day. I texted back that Clementine was fine and we'd see him later, and then pulled up the weather app. With the prediction of a sunny, 60-degree-high day, I decided it was a perfect day for a walk in the park.

The living room was quiet and as soon as I walked in, I knew why.

Logan was hovering near Clementine with his shirt pulled up to his nose, exposing those washboard abs I had run my fingers over last night.

I wet my lips at the sight.

It took me a moment to find her, but Clementine was hiding behind one of the chairs, making the noises that I knew only too well.

A soft giggle escaped my throat and caused him to glance up from his vigilance over her.

The look on his face was one of sheer horror. "I don't understand it. How does something so small smell that vile?"

Laughter rolled through me as I waved him away from her. "She likes to poop in private."

He raised his hands in defeat. "No problem by me."

Leaving her alone to let her finish, I started to gather our things.

"What are you doing?" he asked.

"Packing up. It's time for us to go."

"Elle."

My gaze shot to him at the sound of my name. I liked the way he said it.

"O'Shea back?"

"No, he texted me that he'd be home late afternoon."

Logan crossed the room. "I don't want you going back to his house until he returns."

Goose bumps rose on my arms under my fleece. "Logan, this has to stop. All of this talk is making me paranoid."

The most serious hazel eyes stared back at me. "It's not paranoid if you are in trouble. Your sister, and now Michael, got into bed with the Mob and didn't deliver. Patrick doesn't tolerate fuck-ups for any reason. I don't know the specifics, but there's a reason O'Shea is still alive, and the only reason I can think of is that it has to do with a shitload of cash flow. And once Patrick secures that pipeline, who the fuck knows what he's going to do."

I looked automatically toward Clementine, suddenly fearing for her safety. "Patrick is the Mob boss?" I couldn't

of that room. Away from Logan. Behind the closed door of the bedroom, I set Clementine down and found myself crumpling to the bed.

What had my sister done?

Where was she?

Did she know her child was in danger?

Anger flared up inside me, and it was what I needed to pull myself together.

I had to make sure Clementine would be safe.

I didn't need a man messing with my head.

I'd avoided it too long to let it happen now.

chapter
TWENTY-TWO

LOGAN

TERRIFIC, I THOUGHT.

When she slammed the door, I couldn't breathe. I felt as if I'd stabbed myself in the heart.

Guns, I could handle. The torture of high-society galas—a piece of cake. Fuck, even the threat of physical pain didn't faze me anymore. But women—I didn't know a damn thing about how to cope with their feelings. Just the word *feelings* had my stomach in knots.

I let out a forced breath. At least I'd told her just how serious things were. She needed to know. Thinking about it now, I felt a surge of relief. And something else—a strange feeling I couldn't quite describe.

Fucking feelings.

Toughening up, I looked at the situation realistically. Elle could be angry with me if she wanted, but she wasn't going out alone. I winced that I'd told her she should leave. Like I'd let her. There was no fucking way that was happening. I needed to learn to tame my temper around her because I could tell she wasn't going to make excuses for me.

Time to get ready. I grabbed my sweatshirt, hat, and sunglasses that were thrown on the chair from the other day, and then I slipped my gun into my back holster where I always carried it.

While I waited, I glanced out the window. The Charles River was glassy with the sun reflecting off it. Spring was close and the dead of winter was gone. I stared out at the Boston skyline and the in-between stage the city was in. Most of trees were bare, but some were starting to bloom. Within the next month, the Public Garden would be filled with blooming cherry blossoms and the swan boat would be in full gear. Busying my thoughts with random facts about the city helped distract me from what was blooming within myself. That was one thing I didn't want to come to life.

I won't say she snuck up on me, but let's just say I didn't hear the pitter-patter of Clementine's tiny feet, until I felt someone tugging on my pants.

"Up," she demanded.

With a glance down, I froze like a deer in headlights.

She tugged again. "Up," she repeated.

She wanted me to pick her up?

With uncertainty, I glanced toward the doorway just as Elle entered the room. "Come on, Clementine—we'll go outside where you can see the ducks better," she said.

When I looked back out the window, I noticed the flock of ducks. Funny, I hadn't before. "You want to see them?" I asked Clementine, pointing out the window.

The cute little thing nodded with glee.

Unable to deny her, I picked her up under her arms and put her on my hip like I'd seen Elle do.

She leaned toward the glass until her forehead was touching it and started saying, "Duck, duck, quack-quack."

Her excitement was contagious and with a genuine smile on my face, I turned toward Elle to say something but paused for a moment just to look at her. Her hair was pulled back, but still it appeared untamed.

Beautiful.

Like her.

The thought of taming her or better yet, never taming her, had my blood pumping. Her ginger locks still bounced, even tied back, as she wheeled the empty stroller to the door. They were mesmerizing. I watched her until I realized she was gathering her bags and getting ready to leave. And then my heart felt like it was swinging at a ball and missing the contact with each try. Like I just couldn't win no matter how hard I tried, but this time, I really wanted to.

With a gruff voice, I said, "Hey, leave that stuff. We'll figure out what to do with it after we take a walk through the Public Garden."

It was my way of apologizing.

"We?" she said with a tense, forced smile.

"Yes, I'm coming." My eyes lingered on hers and I figured I should add, "If that's okay."

Elle shrugged coolly. "I guess so. If you want to."

I was going whether she said yes or no. Still, I was glad she hadn't said no. However, the frosty response didn't feel so great. I don't know what I expected, though. I'd been a real ass. I had some amends to make—obviously. Yet the only way I knew how to handle awkward situations with the ladies was through humor, so I smirked and said, "By the way, we call it the Garden, not the park."

Her return smile was genuine. "Right. The Boston Public Garden or the Boston Common. I usually run along the paths on the shores of the river and I haven't ventured into either yet."

"You're a runner?"

She nodded. "Yes. Since I got here, I've been training for the Boston Marathon. I didn't know I'd be here, so I didn't register for it this year. But next year, I plan to run in it."

I glanced down when a little sneaker kicked my thigh. I'd forgotten I was holding Clementine. "No shi—" I stopped myself from cursing. "No joke, I haven't missed one in years. What's your qualifying time?"

She pulled her lip to the side with her teeth as if thinking. "I've been consistently running three hours, fifteen minutes."

"That's fantastic."

With a shrug, Elle settled her things and took a hesitant step toward me. Her body language told me she didn't want to be close.

Was it anger or fighting the want?

I needed to know.

"What is the qualifying standard for women over thirty?" It was an innocent enough question. One that I knew would ease the stifling atmosphere in the room in case it was anger.

She narrowed her eyes at me and snarled, "There is no bracket for women over thirty and by the way, I'm just barely over thirty."

I studied her face in the soft light. Even with her features bunched up, she was stunning. Beautiful. Natural. My body started to ache for her to be nearer. With nonchalance, I lifted a shoulder and a brow. "That's right. We're in the same age bracket."

"Stop with the Mrs. Robinson jokes. There's only three years between us. That in no way makes me that much older than you."

Good. The tension was eased.

I gave her a slight smile. "I guess you're right."

She walked over to me and extended her arms to take Clementine. She was careful to leave enough space between us. It didn't matter. I was drawn to her the moment she entered the room and with paper-thin spaces between us, I couldn't stop myself from making that physical connection with her that somehow I craved.

"Elle." I drew out the single syllable and dragged on the tail of it, turning her name into a plea.

"No, Logan." Elle shook her head and without taking Clementine, took a step back.

My hand grabbed her wrist and tugged her closer. Clementine was oblivious as she stared out the window with both hands on the glass now. With a need I couldn't explain, I kissed her.

Maybe sensing it was coming, Elle didn't open her mouth for me. It didn't stop me from kissing her. My lips parted and I gusted hot breaths over her mouth. I urged her closer with the hand that held her in place. She didn't struggle to get away. With the tip of my wet tongue, I probed between her lips until she couldn't fight it and opened her mouth to let me in.

The kiss was harder than it should have been, and when my tongue swept inside her mouth she moved even closer.

I almost felt as if she was shaking.

Elle suddenly jerked her wrist from my grip but didn't move away. "No, Logan, we can't," she said softly, our mouths still so close they almost touched with each word she spoke.

I pulled my head back a little so I could see her. "Why not?"

I knew why I shouldn't be with her, but not why she thought she shouldn't be with me—that's what I needed to know.

Her eyes closed for half a heartbeat. "Because I can't think straight when we're this close."

I wanted to respond with something witty like *I can think for the both of us,* but I knew humor wasn't the answer. I reached inside myself to figure out what was, but before I could determine that, I was interrupted.

Little hands reached out. "Momma."

With a proud look, Elle took Clementine.

I stared open-mouthed at what she'd just called Elle.

Elle fidgeted a little and said, "She was with her cousins yesterday and is in a phase where she repeats everything she hears. They called for their mother all day, so now she's doing it. It will pass."

I nodded, not so sure about that. Not that I knew anything about kids, but Clementine looked at Elle like she was her mother and Elle looked at Clementine as though she liked it. I felt a sharp pang of hurt when I thought about what would happen when Elle's sister returned.

"Ready to go?" Elle asked, strapping Clementine into the stroller.

She'd put as much distance between us as she could as fast as she could.

I zipped up my sweatshirt, pulled my hat on, and slid on my sunglasses. "Yeah, let me push that," I said, indicating the folding contraption she had set Clementine in.

Every muscle in my body flexed as soon as we hit the sidewalk. It was one thing to be alone with Elle; it was entirely another to be out in public. I could feel the thudding in my chest. My fingers were white knuckled wrapped around the handles of the stroller. When a gust of wind blew across my neck, I stiffened even more. With a glance from side to side, I quickly pushed across the street and toward the entrance to the Garden. Making sure Elle could keep up, I stopped and took her hand, placing it with mine on the stroller handle, and she didn't pull away.

I liked the warmth of her skin near mine.

As soon as we hit one of the entrances and entered the Public Garden, I felt a wave of relief. We looked like every other couple out for a Sunday morning walk to enjoy the breaking weather and admire the early buds of the magnolia trees.

Slowing the pace, I stopped at the first monument we came across.

"William Ellery Channing," Elle read and glanced at me.

"He was one of our country's foremost Unitarian ministers."

She raised a quizzical brow.

I pushed forward. "Hey, I had to come here every year on school field trips. Whether I cared to know or not, I had to learn the name of every monument and why they're here."

She laughed.

I liked the sound.

We strolled a bit and stopped at the 9/11 memorial.

Knowing that needed no explanation, I let her glance at it for a moment and I looked too. When she was ready, she urged me forward.

I noticed something about Elle: if we pretended to be two people getting to know one another and let go of all the shit that was really going on, she was relaxed. Sure, the sexual tension was still there, but I knew that wasn't going anywhere no matter what we did unless what we were doing was fucking, which we weren't. Even now, the way my skin felt heated where her hand was touching mine, I knew she felt it as much as I did.

She leaned in closer when I veered toward the footbridge. I pointed. "Look, Clementine, the ducks."

The excitement in my voice had Elle's head snapping toward me in surprise.

I shrugged. "What? I can't be excited about ducks?"

She laughed. "I like this side of you."

I looked at her with an eyebrow slightly tilted. Quizzical. "There's no other side of me."

She let her thumb slip around mine, and I felt the intimacy of this minor connection almost as if she'd wrapped her arms around me. "If you say so, but just so you know, I think it's cute."

Just yards from the base of the bridge, I stopped and gave her a chaste kiss. It was as if I was compelled. I couldn't help myself. When we started walking again, I watched the rise and fall of her shoulders as she tried to catch her breath. We affected each other in the most intense way. I, too, had to intentionally relax my breathing.

The three of us stood in the middle of the footbridge and gazed over the railing for the longest time. The joy Clementine radiated at seeing the ducks was contagious, and something inside me had me pulling Elle closer as the little girl stood between us.

Not wanting the moment to end, I led us to a place I thought they would both like—the Duckling Sculpture. And I was right. Excitement gleamed in both their faces and Clementine squealed in delight. The statue was made of bronze and featured nine ducks: Mrs. Mallard and her eight ducklings.

The fact that I remembered that from my childhood blew me away.

But what blew me away even more was that no matter how wrong this thing was between us, right now it had never felt more right.

chapter
TWENTY-THREE

Elle

I STARED AT THAT mouth. Those lips . . .

Oh my God.

My heart was beating so fast.

My breathing felt erratic.

He was so masculine. So sexy. So attractive.

Did he know it?

I didn't think he did.

It wasn't just the way he walked, or talked, or looked. It was his body language. His mannerisms. The ease in which he moved. It was everything.

We were strolling back to the hotel and talking about the Boston Red Sox. Mid-sentence, he looked over at me through the fringe of his lashes and smiled. It was devastating. Charming. "Don't you agree?" He asked.

I was melting. That look warmed me all the way to my toes. I had to swallow hard to fight off the lustful feelings flowing through my veins.

Logan bumped my shoulder and said, "Should I be worried that I'm boring you?"

"No, not at all." My voice had dipped low and husky. It was a voice I'd never heard before. "I do think the Sox will turn it around this year."

A slow, lazy smile spread across his face. "You were listening."

It was confirmed—he absolutely had no idea what effect he was having on me.

We reached the hotel before I knew it. As we strode through the lobby my mind was on him. On his smile. His scent. His low-slung pants. It wasn't like I was thinking about some unreachable fantasy. I was thinking about him. And me. And fucking.

As we got into the elevator and it started to move, I became all too aware that my body was humming, buzzing with need. In the confined space, it was taking all of my strength to fight against the lustful desire that was trying to make its way deep inside me. I'd told myself to push him out of my thoughts, but how could I do that when he was right beside me, exuding whatever it was that kept drawing me to him?

Logan glanced over at me and I knew the moment he became aware of my lustful trance. I felt the blood rush to my face, and I swallowed hard. My parted lips and heavy breathing were a dead giveaway. Not to mention my nipples felt like diamonds, and there was a steady pulsing between my legs that was beginning to ache.

He leaned closer.

He knew now what he was doing to me.

My clit was throbbing.

Space.

I needed space.

Thank God, the elevator doors opened and I used that as my cue to put some distance between us. With long strides, I stepped out ahead of him and but then turned back to see how Clementine was doing. Her eyes were closed and her head tilted to the side of the stroller. She'd fallen asleep on the walk back to the hotel.

Why I let it happen I don't know, but my gaze rose, and again I found myself staring at those lips. Those lips that had to send women everywhere reeling—I knew they did. With a dry throat, I managed, "Looks like she decided it was nap time."

Logan dropped his own gaze. "Will she wake up when I move her?"

I smiled. "No, she's a good sleeper. She'll sleep a solid two to three hours."

He looked at his watch and seemed to be calculating something, as if time was of the essence. "How about you stay here with her and I'll head over to the boutique and see if the garage door opener is in your bag?"

I contemplated the suggestion for a moment but found nothing wrong with it. "Sure, but I'm almost certain it must be."

The more time that went by, the more I began to think I was overreacting.

Logan stopped in front of his hotel room door and pulled his key card out. Intently, I watched him. I couldn't seem to drag my eyes away from him. Once we were inside, he pushed the stroller to his bedroom. I watched as he transferred Clementine to the crib. He was getting more comfortable with her, although he still looked worried that he might break her.

I couldn't help but laugh at that thought.

He turned around and peered curiously at me.

With a lift of my brows and a rise of one shoulder, I shrugged it off and then reached for the blanket that was at the end of the bed. As I covered her, I met his eyes and whispered, "Thank you."

Feeling warm, I unzipped my fleece and tossed it where the blanket had been. His eyes turned hungry as I circled the bed and a shiver danced down my spine. This attraction between us was too much. I didn't know how to deal with it.

Dropping my gaze, I waved him out of the room. My purse was on the table and I went for it. It was best if he left. Digging inside, I found my keys and pulled them out.

I took the key for the boutique off the loop and handed it to him. "Here you go. The boutique is closed on Sunday and Monday, but Peyton might be there. Just in case she's not, the pass code for the alarm is . . ." I faltered.

He was standing right beside me. Excitement stirred in the air. He was so close that I could smell his heavenly scent. He smelled of the soap in the shower and he smelled like pure man. For some insane reason, I wanted to bury my nose in his neck and sniff him.

Shoving the key in his direction, I finished, "two-five-six-nine. If you forget it, just spell *blow*."

Instead of taking the key and leaving like I thought he would, Logan swirled it around his own key chain and set it on the table. Then he stepped even closer. So close our bodies were almost touching.

I wanted them to be.

Then they were.

Like magnets, we were drawn together.

He had leaned forward just a bit and then his fingers were on my face, tucking a stray piece of hair behind my ear.

Feeling electrified, my body jerked as his flesh came in direct contact with mine, and my breath caught at the intensity of the physical connection.

"I want you," he whispered at the same time he lightly nipped at my bottom lip. "Right now."

I nodded, silently telling him I wanted him too—and right now.

The feeling of his lean, muscular body pressed against mine only served to further ignite my desire. With a desperation I didn't understand, I pulled myself closer. Close enough that my hard nipples pushed against his unyielding chest.

Logan made a sound of approval deep in his throat.

I wanted to close my eyes but couldn't. I had to see him. I looked up into his eyes, those light and dark eyes, and lost myself in him.

He looked at me like nothing else mattered but having me.

I shivered from that look alone.

It wasn't long before his hands were running up my sides and when he lifted me, I wanted this like I'd never wanted anything. Responding in the only way that made sense, I wrapped both my arms and legs around him and then did just what I had wanted to do—buried my face in his neck. With my lips touching his skin and his scent invading me, my senses came alive. The edges of his hair tickled wonderfully against my cheek. The feel of his hands, now firmly grasping my hips, seared me as if he were branding me. His heavy breathing was all I could hear.

What came next happened so fast. We were moving. He was setting me down on the sofa. His hands were dragging up my body to the hem of my shirt. He lifted it over my head, leaving me almost bare. Putting his hands all over me.

My body hummed with pleasure. My belly tightened, thighs trembled, and my clit pulsed. With shaky fingers I unzipped his sweatshirt and he helped me take it off. Then I grabbed the hem of his T-shirt and his chest was bare too. Now, both our hands were all over each other.

With a lick of my lips, I allowed my eyes to graze over him—he was the most handsome man I had ever laid eyes on. No, *handsome* didn't convey how devastatingly good-looking he really was. Maybe *ruggedly beautiful* better described him. I'd have to come up with the perfect phrase. He was soft and hard at the same time, muscular but not overly so. The line of his jaw, the shape of his nose—they were hard, but his features were softened by those incredible hazel eyes outlined in dark, thick lashes.

My gaze slid down. Seeing the lines in his muscles made my heart beat fast, watching the flexing of his biceps had me biting down on my lower lip, and the way his abs rippled down into the waistband of his pants caused my body to clench with a need that I'd never felt.

Logan dropped his gaze. I noticed yesterday in the shower that he didn't look into my eyes when he was fucking me. Today, I was coming to the conclusion that was also true when it came to foreplay.

It was fine. I didn't want to talk. He preferred not to look into my eyes.

We both had hang-ups.

I understood that.

I accepted that.

But right now, they just didn't matter.

He made up for his avoidance of eye contact by moving in a way that told me he was determined to have me. He pulled off my sneakers and tossed them to the ground and then he took off his shoes. In silence, he lowered himself onto me, and there was no denying how much he wanted me.

Heat flared in my belly.

I forced myself to believe we weren't on opposite sides and I focused on his movements.

Everything became this man.

Everything he did was all I could think about, including the way he slid his hands to the back of my neck and pulled the ponytail holder from my hair. I even thought about how although he wasn't gentle, he wasn't rough. I especially liked the way his fingers tangled in my locks and tipped my head back, exposing my throat.

Oh God.

Then he slid those soft lips down my skin and his fingers followed.

I felt each beat of his breath and mine.

Logan didn't stop until he reached my bra, and when he did, his tongue licked the lacy edges of the fabric and then his fingers pushed one of the cups to the side.

Excitement danced in my belly.

My nipples were tight, like hard steel tips. No, they were hard, aching steel tips. When Logan skimmed his thumb over one, I sucked in a breath and nearly gasped. But when his mouth closed around it, and I felt tongue, teeth, and lips all at the same time, I practically whimpered.

It felt so good—warm and wicked.

Eventually, my squirming must have given away how much more I needed, because Logan stopped his ministrations to my breasts and worked his way back up to my throat. That torture was equally sweet as he sucked the sensitive skin between his teeth along the way. The bites didn't hurt, but they did send sensations ripping through me.

We were on the sofa and room was limited, but still I bucked beneath him with writhing need. Like a lioness out of her cage, I felt wild. My hands found the back of his head and I threaded my fingers in his hair. Tugging it, I pulled him to my mouth where I wanted those lips on me.

He groaned, and that was when his hands slid down from my breasts to my hips to inside the waistband of my pants. He didn't take them off right away and although I wanted him to, I didn't want his mouth to leave mine either.

Luckily, it didn't have to.

He somehow knew what I needed and his palm pressed against my clit on the outside of my panties. Again, I writhed beneath him. I'd never felt this sexually charged. I was thirty years old, a self-proclaimed sexually repressed adult, and I was melting beneath this man like a sex-starved teenager.

Soon, I was reduced to nothing but a body of tingling nerve endings. The way his fingers slid inside my panties and found my slick heat electrified me from head to toe. He knew what he was doing, though; he took his time, teasing me, gliding up to caress my clit and back down.

Over and over.

He remained quiet except for the sounds of sucking in a breath and a few groans.

I'm not sure if he read my signs or didn't want to talk because he feared waking Clementine, but either way, I was glad for it.

This was far too enjoyable to end. In truth, I'm not sure

I could end it.

Breathless, I moved my hands to his bare shoulders and slid my tongue down his throat, and just like he had, I pulled his skin between my teeth. I might have been rougher, he might have a mark—I wasn't sure. I just couldn't control myself.

His responding groan told me he was burning just like I was, and his body language told me not to stop, so I didn't. Not until I had to. Not until I couldn't focus on anything but his fingers dipping inside me. The way it felt when he slid them in and out. The circling of his thumb, the movement of his hand, the wetness I could feel dripping onto my panties.

I couldn't believe it but I was going to come—like this—beneath him, with our pants on and his hands inside my panties. Oh, yes, I was going to come, right now. I didn't do this. I hardly ever came from a man's touch alone. It took moving mountains, hours of men trying, to make me come. Yet I was already tipping over the edge.

Sensation after delicious sensation was all I could feel. And they were coming one after the other, fast and furious. So much so that my fingernails dug into his skin as dizzying amounts of pleasure surrounded me. Logan didn't stop. He kept the pace up and I rode his hand.

And then I completely shattered, biting my lip to stifle my cries as my clit spasmed over and over, each spark of pleasure causing me to cry out.

Logan kissed my neck and slowed his fingers as my body shuddered beneath him. When my grip on him let up, he cupped me as he had in the beginning, his palm pressed tight to my sex.

My body was limp and sated. I felt amazing, but then I made the mistake of thinking how I'd never enjoyed a man making me come like I just had. The thought caused me to freak out a little.

Was I now going to be a sex addict like my father?

I tried to catch my breath but couldn't at first. When

Logan went to kiss me, I turned my head and his mouth landed on my cheek. Mine landed in the crook of his neck. Since his eyes were closed, I'm certain he thought it was just mechanics.

With a deep inhale, I caught his scent and immediately started breathing more steadily. He calmed me without even knowing it and wanting more of him, I moved my mouth to find his. I wanted to lose myself in him again.

Even though my body was limp and languid, his lips on mine were all I needed to restoke that fire that was already burning within me. Not only did I want to feel more of what I'd just felt, I wanted Logan to feel the exact same thing. The idea of give and take was what stopped me from thinking what my mind had just been skating around.

With desperate urgency, I found his pants and unzipped them. He helped me out again by shoving them down. When he stood before me in only his black boxer briefs, my arousal escalated to an alarming level.

I needed to touch him.

There.

My fingers grazed along the outside of the soft fabric and he was long and full. I just had to see him. With a prowess I had only ever made myself exhibit in the past, I eased off those Calvin Kleins. I was doing this willingly. My sexual interest in Logan was anything but forced. In fact, I had to take a moment to admire him. The leanness of his body didn't reflect the fullness of his cock. I wanted him.

Sex was next on the table. It was a fact. Since my limbs were no longer in a Jell-O-like state, I reached for him and stroked him up and down. He was silky soft and really hard. Logan made a noise and I looked up. As soon as our eyes collided, he dropped his mouth to my ear. His voice was tight, low, and thick with need when he whispered, "Let's get your pants off."

I couldn't have wanted anything more.

He said nothing more—I was glad. I wasn't sure what I'd have done if he had. That's not true. I would have stayed, because that one glimpse into his eyes told me everything I needed to know. It was an odd mix of emotions I saw there—fear and lust, maybe. Whatever it was, it was enough to make me want to understand him.

Without hesitation, as soon as I stood, he moved behind me and slid my pants down. I shuddered the entire time his hands glided over my hips and down my thighs. When my pants and panties were off, he blew a warm breath in my ear and kissed my neck. I shuddered again. Something about the intimacy of the way he kissed my neck had my stomach fluttering. If I were romantic, which I am not, I'd say that although he was bold with his body, to the point of being unfaltering, he was almost tender, sweet even, with his mouth. It was that whole hot/cold, hard/soft thing I'd pegged him with last night.

Logan glanced around the room. "Follow me." His voice was just as soft as it had been a few moments ago.

It didn't bother me that he'd told me what to do; in a way his words had almost been posed as a question, as if he knew I wouldn't take being ordered around well.

The space was vast but surfaces to fuck on were not. We had the couch, which could work, but it was rather narrow; we had the wall, or . . . I spotted it right away . . . we had the table, and condom in hand, that's where he was taking me.

Both of us completely bare in the middle of a Sunday afternoon, he led me to the corner table with no hesitation. My breath grew louder with each step. When we reached our destination, I bent myself over the slick surface without daring to look at Logan. It was the position that made the most sense and I really just wanted him to fuck me already.

The heat of his body radiated behind me and I could hear his own ragged breaths. They mimicked mine. I waited for him to touch me with an anticipation that surprised me. With the sounds of our mingled breaths the only noise in the room, I placed my palms flat on the cool surface. Time seemed to take forever to pass. What was he doing? I wanted to look but didn't at the same time.

Finally, I heard the tearing of paper, the manipulation of latex, and then his hands were on my hips, followed quickly by the warmth of his chest all over my back. The feeling rocketed though me and I felt every muscle in my body clench in need. He felt amazing on my skin. The kind of blanket I never wanted to shed.

"Are you sure you're okay with this?" His mouth was warm and at my ear again.

I squeezed my eyes shut and waited for the freak-out I was certain my brain would have, but it never came. I was okay with this—with him talking to me during sex. Well, technically we weren't having sex yet, so maybe that was why.

Gripping the edge of the table, I nodded and spread my legs wider, pressing my naked body farther back against his very ready one.

His exultant groan echoed in my ear, but then his mouth was gone. Luckily, it hadn't gone far. His teeth began grazing my shoulder and his fingers found my clit at the same time. Twin bursts of pleasure sizzled under his touch. I bit my lip to stop from crying out.

He played with me—his fingers outlined my clit and his tongue moved across my back in slick, steady waves.

"Please." The faintly spoken word slipped out. I'd never begged for someone to take me, but I was begging him now.

I wasn't certain he'd heard me, but then the hand that was on my hip was gone and moments later I felt the thickness of his cock between my legs. He pushed into me painfully slowly. I contemplated taking control and slamming myself back, but his hands were on my hips, holding me in place.

With steady movements he eased in and then out again. In, then out. Giving me a little bit more. Going deeper each time. When he was completely inside me, I thrust my head back. "Please," I repeated, "I need more."

His low groan was at the sweet spot he'd found behind my ear and as if he wanted to make sure I got just what I wanted, he stood straight and with his hands tightly gripping my hips, he slammed into me. Hard. Slow and easy was gone. Fast and furious took over.

Again, I had to bite my lip to stop from crying out.

It felt so good.

I wanted great.

His fingers gripped me, pinched me almost, as he slammed into me. Still, it wasn't enough. I wanted more. I wanted him deeper. I wanted him faster. I wanted all of him. He was holding back, I could tell. I needed to feel this. Wanted it so badly, I could taste it like I could taste the blood from my bitten lip as I licked it away.

Feeling unleashed, I fought against his hold on my hips and pushed my ass back. Everything exploded from there. He pulled back and thrust. His cock slid so deep inside me, deep into places I was certain no one had been, and I felt like I was soaring.

My toes curled into the carpet at such an angle they were cramping. My hands gripped the edge of the table so hard that it was cutting into my skin. His fingers were pressed into my hip bones so deep I was certain I'd bruise.

I didn't care about any of that.

This was the first time I'd ever let myself go. The first time in the twelve years since I'd lost my virginity that I'd even wanted to. That night was a night I'll never forget, but it was anything but unforgettable. I had two months until high school graduation, until I was free of my father, and still I acted stupidly. I let all the strength I'd built up to guard myself crumble without a fight and gave in to his sadistic way of life.

My father was up to his typical fuckery, but that night the sounds were louder than usual. He was fucking some whore in our living room. He never took his women into his own room. No, they always stayed in the main parts of the house and it was always late at night. I didn't understand it. We'd moved back to California by then and his room wasn't the same room he'd shared with my mother. Maybe it was the bed, or the memories. I didn't know. All I knew was that I was used to the endless women, but since my mother's death he hadn't been overly vocal, and I'd grown used to that too.

That didn't mean I didn't know what he was doing. The occasional "Oh yes" was hard not to hear, and the "That's it, don't stop" told me more than I needed to know. Sure, I heard him often enough, but nothing like I'd endured during my childhood. And to be honest, I didn't care about those women or what he did to them.

Up until that night, the very idea of having sex made me physically ill.

But that night, his grunts and groans turned me into someone else. He was calling this woman Susan. He was begging her to take her clothes off. It was his and my mother's wedding anniversary and I thought he'd really lost it. What kind of game was he playing with this woman? Her name couldn't possibly be Susan.

When he said, "But baby, I need to be inside you," I lost it. I couldn't take it anymore. Although I knew better than to leave my room, I did it anyway. I was seventeen now. What was he going to do? Whip me with his belt? I doubted it. Kick me out of the house? I could only be so lucky.

With my heart pounding in my chest, I stormed right out my door and right into the living room. I didn't think about what I'd be walking into. Or maybe I didn't care. Who knows?

My father was strewn on the sofa with his uniform pants at his ankles and those black tied shoes that echoed throughout the house whenever he walked were still on. A naked woman sat on top of him, facing those damn shiny shoes. He had a nearly empty whiskey bottle in one hand and the woman's ponytail in the other.

The sight sickened me.

She was riding him but stopped when she saw me in the entryway. "You want to join us?" she purred.

My father jerked her ponytail. "Did I tell you to stop?"

"No, sir," she answered. She was young, not much older than

me.

"Did I tell you to talk?" he said, even harsher.

Had he been like that with my mother?

God, I hoped not.

The thought sickened me and I swallowed the lump in my throat. I dropped my gaze and looked away. Wanting to escape, I moved toward the front door on shaky legs. I had to get out of there.

I was almost free when he snapped, "Gabrielle."

I froze. Even as a near graduate, he still frightened me.

"Don't be so weak," he muttered.

"I'm not weak," I shot back.

He looked at me like he had when I was younger and disobeyed him, like when he'd whipped me with his belt—the same belt that was now at his ankles—and in that moment I was weak. However, his words were nothing like the "you will be obedient" speech I'd received with each lashing. No, his slurred words cut deeper than that belt ever had. "You might want to stay and watch to learn a few things from a pro. Being good at sex is the only thing you're going to have to offer a man."

Sex. His whole being seemed to be about sex. I hated him. I hated my sister for being weak and leaving me with him. And in that moment, I hated my mother for letting it go on so long. Why wasn't she stronger?

And what was it about sex that turned him into the monster he was?

With nowhere to go, I ran to one of the gyms on base where I'd been training with a number of new recruits. In the years since my mother's death, I was determined to be strong. Stronger than my sister or my mother ever were.

Strength wasn't only physical—I knew that. But I also knew it would protect me. And I needed something to protect me.

The place was open twenty-four/seven and I knew someone would be there who'd want me. That night I picked a man and gave myself to him. It hurt, physically and emotionally, but it was quick. When it was done, I felt more lost than I had before—it meant nothing. I felt nothing. Sex really was meaningless.

Logan's breath blew warm across my shoulder, and I made myself push that dark and tainted memory from my mind. With him everything felt different. Maybe I had been wrong. Maybe, just maybe, sex could be meaningful. Maybe I had been going at it the wrong way this whole time. I had been looking for what it was that turned my father into the man he was instead of allowing myself to figure out what I needed from the act itself.

And with Logan I knew what it was. I wanted to give myself to him and in turn to feel what it was like for someone to give himself to me. We might have just met, we might only be fucking, but we were both pouring ourselves into what we were doing.

Together, we moved with wild abandon; we gave freely to each other. It was the give and take that mattered the most and I loved every minute of it.

Beating hearts with pulling and pushing bodies and ragged breathing was what we were, and I relished in it.

His desire-laced voice whispered, "Let go."

By the time those two words traveled and his breath blew hot against my skin as his mouth sought out my ear, I was already tipping, ready to free-fall into the pleasure that was building within me. My pulse pounded. My heart beat rapidly. His words pushed me over the edge rather than forcing me to retreat. I even had to bite my lip to stop the passionate cry I felt in my throat.

In an unexpected move, his bare chest met my bare back and he reached for my hands, intertwining our fingers and pulling our connected hands toward our connected bodies. The tenderness of the moment was too much and I couldn't stop the strangled cry I'd been holding back.

With my eyes squeezed tightly shut, my body took over and I could do nothing but feel. With all thoughts destroyed, I absorbed the delicious fullness of having him inside me. Without warning, an unexpected sensation overtook me. And it didn't pass. Each joyous beat of my climax drove that glorious feeling of having him inside me higher and higher until I was soaring in ecstasy.

Logan's thrusts slowed as soon as my pussy began to tighten around his cock. His fingers squeezed mine when his body stilled. His grunting sigh echoed beautifully in my ear as he, too, experienced what we both obviously needed—a release.

He dropped his head into the crook of my neck and for a few minutes, we stayed that way—me cocooned in his warm body bent over the table. I wasn't sure what would happen when I turned around. Would he run like he had last night?

Once I caught my breath and my legs stopped shaking, I shifted my stance. I didn't want this moment to end, but I knew it had to. Logan pulled out of me and I turned around. Perhaps conveniently, perhaps not, he twisted to take care of the condom.

I leaned against the table and watched him. I thought about gathering my clothes. I should have been embarrassed standing there naked, but I wasn't.

He wrapped the very used condom in a napkin and tossed it in the trash can near the bar. Focusing on the task at hand, he slipped into his boxers and started to gather the rest of our clothes. I should have helped him, but something kept me glued to where I stood. I thought now that the act of intimacy was complete and the tension between us eased, he'd just toss me mine.

Imagine my surprise when he crossed the room. That tension that I thought was gone was stronger than ever. We both felt it. I know we did. The draw to touch other, the need to feel each other, to somehow know each other, was stronger than ever. Denying it would be futile.

With the same tenderness I'd felt from him earlier, Logan tucked a piece of hair behind my ear and then shocked me by looking into my eyes. I didn't know what I saw in this, but I wanted to know.

I opened my mouth to say something. What, I had no idea. Before I could, he broke our intense connection by lowering his lips to mine in a soft kiss. His lips lightly moved against mine. There was no tongue, no clashing of teeth, and still it made me shudder.

When he broke away, he handed me my clothes and started dressing himself. "I need to get to the boutique. I don't want you to leave and go to O'Shea's until I'm back. Okay?"

The room smelled of sex; we smelled of sex. We weren't even fully dressed and he was leaving? I wasn't needy by any means, but I felt a little disappointed. I stared at him as he shoved his legs through his pant legs. "Yes, of course. We'll wait for you to get back."

Pulling his shirt over his head, he paused before tugging it all the way down. "Are you all right?"

I snapped out of my daze and started dressing. Not really. I didn't know what I was, but what else could I say? "Yes. I just feel ridiculous about this whole missing-ga-rage-door-opener thing. I doubt it's in my other purse. You're probably wasting your time."

He zipped up his sweatshirt and picked up his keys and mine. I thought he'd head toward the door, but instead he strode over to me. When he was standing right in front of me he said, "No, I'm not. Just because a few hours quiet-ly passed doesn't mean anything has changed. O'Shea is in a load of shit and there will be consequences if things don't go the way Patrick wants them to go. That's why we need to get ahead of this." He put his hands on my upper arms. "You need to find out what O'Shea has promised to deliver."

I nodded. "I'll talk to him tonight."

Seemingly satisfied with my response, his expression changed. Logan was now looking at me in a new and dif-ferent way. It was that way men look at women when they know they have a hold on them—half boyish charm, half devilish mischief. "Then we'll talk even later tonight."

I got the look then.

And I was more than up to a late-night "chat."

"I'd better go," he said.

I nodded. "Wait," I called.

He froze at the door.

Not certain what he thought I wanted, I tossed out, "Don't you want your hat and sunglasses?"

"No, I'm good."

And then he was gone—out the door without a single glance back.

Again, I felt disappointed.

What did I want from him?

Nothing, I told myself.

But I knew it was a lie.

sometimes family sucks."

"He fell in love with one of his students the first year we moved here and left my mother and me."

"Like I said, sometimes family sucks."

Wasn't it the truth?

We paused at the corner to wait for the light. I was carrying around forty pounds, so it wasn't that the boxes were heavy, but seeing over them wasn't easy. I had to peer around the sides, and there were more and more people on the sidewalk the farther north we went. I turned my head. "I thought you said it was right up the street."

She shrugged. "Sorry. I've never actually walked. When I drive it is, but we're almost there, promise."

I didn't complain but wondered why we just didn't drive.

"It's right there," she said, pointing across the street.

My heart started to pound in my chest. "When did Mulligan's Cup move from Dorchester to Beacon Hill?" I asked, taking a deep, nervous breath.

Mulligan's Cup was a family-owned coffee shop that, once upon a time, had been Mulligan's Bakery. In the eighties, when coffee shops became the thing, they changed names and direction. That wasn't what was causing alarm bells to go off in my head, though. It was the fact that the owner's son ran with Tommy's crowd. It was the fact that he was the one who'd waited in the car while Tommy attacked Kayla and me that night more than five years ago. And it was the fact that he was a punk I never wanted to see again.

"I don't think they moved. I think they expanded," she said, interrupting my dark thoughts.

I took a minute to calm myself down as we waited for the light to turn. Expansion, that was a good thing, and it didn't mean Declan would be there. Either way, I went on instant alert.

When we walked in, I quickly glanced around for a place to set down these fucking boxes. I wanted to get the hell out of there. It looked like the coffee bar was the only open space. The place was extremely crowded, and I had difficulty navigating through the tables and chairs to get to it.

Peyton was in front of me. "Declan," she called. "These are for you—they were delivered to the boutique by accident."

Fuck! Fuck! Fuck! Nearly out of my mind, I considered dropping the boxes right where I stood, but that would only make a scene.

Someone lifted the top one from my grasp. Not just someone. Declan Mulligan. He still looked like the punk he was. Even at twenty-seven, his jeans were still baggy and cinched with a black leather belt complete with small spikes. He wore a short-sleeved T-shirt, and I could see all the new ink he'd gotten since I'd last seen him not long enough ago. He had the same multiple piercings in his ears and lip, and it looked like in his nipples now, too.

Shock registered on his face and he looked anxious. "Logan," he gasped in a voice that spoke of way too many cigarettes.

I might have sneered at him. I really don't know.

He looked down at the box in his arms.

He *should* be fucking anxious. He was lucky I never went after him. He was lucky I didn't kill him the day I ran into him a few years ago when I saw him with his old man at a funeral. He was lucky word on the street said he was no longer involved with Tommy.

Panic and fear in his eyes, he twisted toward Peyton. "You could have just called down here and I would have sent someone to get the boxes."

She waved her hand in a flirtatious way. "I've been in and out all day and I wanted to make sure you had them in case you needed them."

She'd used me in a ploy to see him.

She'd fucking used me.

The bastard actually smiled at her. "That was nice of

you."

I dropped the box I was holding on top of the one in his arms and then turned to Peyton. "Come on, let's go."

My voice was tight and she gave me an odd look. "Go ahead." Her tone clearly said I was an asshole.

Great.

She hurried to Declan's aid but he didn't accept her help. "I got it, Peyton. Look, it's really busy in here—let's talk later."

I closed my eyes and pinched the bridge of my nose, willing patience. Then I took a deep breath and opened my eyes. "Peyton," I said.

She turned toward me with a scowl on her face.

"I need to get back inside the boutique and get that black bag."

Her eyes went back to Declan and she was clearly distracted. "Right, El—"

I cut her off. "I'm sorry, but I'm in a hurry," I said as calmly as I could considering I felt like my skin was about to bust open with the hatred that rushed through me. I also didn't want her to even breathe Elle's name near Declan.

It wasn't until Declan was in the backroom that she finally started for the door.

I really didn't have time for this shit.

Hustling, I caught up with her. "Sorry about that, but I really am in a hurry."

Angered, she stopped and turned to look at me. "I had the wrong idea about you. I thought you were someone nice."

Ouch.

Feeling like I had to somehow explain, I said, "Declan Mulligan and I have a history. And not a good one." A pang nudged my ribs. What if Declan told Peyton everything and she in turn, told Elle? I didn't want Elle to know that side of me. To pity me. Or hate me. To look at me differently. However, I was pretty certain he wouldn't tell anyone about that night. It didn't make him look good. Deciding to cling to that argument made me feel only slightly better.

She started walking again. "Well, whatever. I just hope you're not an asshole to Elle, because she deserves someone nice."

Speeding up, I turned to walk backwards and face her. "I promise you I'm not, but I don't think Elle would stick around anyone who was."

The red in her face began to fade. "I'm going to choose to believe you because my first instincts never fail me. But I have to tell you, I'm not so certain that Elle's instincts are always spot on."

My own instincts started to buzz. What did she mean? There were too many people on the sidewalk and I kept bumping into them, so I turned back to walk beside her and blatantly said, "You mean Michael."

Her eyes dropped and she gave me a slight nod. "In the three months I've known Elle, you're the first guy I've seen her with. Well, besides Michael, and I'm sorry, but I think he's a creeper."

My pace picked up as if every second counted now. "Tell me why you think that."

"He just reminds me of my father. His wife's in rehab and I'm pretty certain he's fucking the nanny, although Elle tells me no. And I know he wants to fuck Elle."

My muscles stiffened; that last part had me seeing red.

Peyton waved her hand. "I shouldn't have said that. Just forget I did."

I gave her a forced nod and lost myself in my thoughts.

We walked the rest of the way back to the boutique in silence. I grabbed Elle's purse and looked toward Peyton. I wanted to tell her to stay clear of Declan, but I knew she wouldn't listen to me without an explanation and there was no way I could give her one, so instead I said, "Lock the door behind me. You shouldn't leave it open when you're in here alone."

She responded with something that sounded like "point taken," or maybe that was just in my mind and she'd actually said goodbye.

I waited until I drove away to pull over and look inside Elle's purse. It was small, and the only things in there were a comb, a tube of lip gloss, and a hair tie. I dumped it upside down on the passenger seat just to be sure.

Nothing else.

Fuck! No garage door opener.

That meant whoever broke into Elle's car did so with the intention of gaining easy access into Michael's house.

The question was—why?

What was in there?

chapter
TWENTY-FIVE

Elle

I KNEW ALMOST EVERY defensive maneuver in the book.

When to duck.

Where to weave.

How to dodge.

I'd studied so many different techniques over the past fifteen years, I was confident in my ability to defend myself. I also knew how to take the offense if needed. How to throw a punch—where to deliver a blow that would incapacitate a guy and let me get away. Firearms were nothing I was afraid of. I'd been taught to fire a weapon—how to stand steady and level my arms before squeezing the trigger.

In addition, I was a fast runner. I was confident I could outrun almost anyone.

My only deficiency? My size. And there was nothing I could do about that.

None of that mattered, though, when it came to guarding my heart.

It was utterly defenseless when it came to Logan McPherson.

That worried me.

The smile that bled across my lips as I parked my car in front of my townhouse was one I couldn't hold back. Logan was sitting on my steps, waiting for me, and I felt my body go liquid when I opened the door.

Something was happening between us.

My stomach was a tangle of nerves as soon as I rounded the corner, and I swear my insides were slushing the closer I got to those ever-changing eyes.

What was wrong with me?

The response I received told me I wasn't the only one feeling a little giddy. As soon as his eyes lifted, his smile quirked higher on one side, as if he was trying to charm me.

He didn't have to.

He was doing something to me no man had ever done. Breaking me down. Reducing me to nothing but hormones. I wasn't sure if that was good or bad, but right now my mind wasn't in charge. My body was. And it wasn't leaving me options, so I had to let my feelings take their own course.

It wasn't like I had a choice.

His gaze flickered over me. Hot. Intense. Mesmerizing.

I melted a little more and I swear my toes curled in my sneakers.

Once Logan had come back to the hotel with the news that my garage opener was not in my purse, we talked a little about what that meant. It frightened me, but at the same time I felt safe with him. I just knew he'd make certain Clementine and I wouldn't be hurt. I could see it in his determined eyes and I could hear it in the way he spoke.

Michael had called just before five to tell me he was home. He was anxious to see his daughter and I was anxious to talk to him. He hadn't mentioned anything to indicate that someone might have been in the house, which must have meant nothing had been disturbed.

When I arrived at Michael's, he was out of sorts. I was surprised. He was unshaven, looked exhausted, and it was more than clear that he didn't want to talk about anything to do with Lizzy.

After I told him about last night, that I thought someone was in the house and that my garage door opener was missing, he shrugged it off to paranoia. When I told him Clementine and I spent the night in a hotel, leaving Logan completely out of the conversation, he told me how ridiculous that was.

He had me believing it, too.

He reminded me that his house was equipped with state-of-the-art security. And it was. He had alarms on every window and door. Call buttons scattered every ten feet or so that were wired directly to the security service. He even had a panic room.

He was right—there was no way someone was in his house, garage door opener missing or not. It was sealed up tighter than Fort Knox.

I'd let that conversation fall and waited until after Clementine's bath to broach the subject of Lizzy's ties to the Blue Hill Gang.

"Where'd you hear that?" Michael snapped.

I swallowed and told him Peyton had mentioned to me in passing conversation about Killian McPherson, and that I had drawn my own conclusions from there.

It wasn't a lie.

It just wasn't the whole truth.

Michael turned to me with an icy expression on his face. "I told you to stay out of it and I meant it. You know all you need to know."

That was the end of our conversation.

Frustrated, I left shortly afterward, letting Logan know I was heading home.

"Everything okay?" Logan asked as I approached him.

His voice reassured me. Michael might think I was being paranoid, but I knew Logan believed me. Things weren't adding up. Something more was going on.

His smile faded. "Elle?"

I realized I hadn't answered. "Everything's fine. It's just that Michael wouldn't tell me anything and he assured me no one was in his house." With a frustrated sigh, I added, "I couldn't find anything out."

Logan was calm. "It's okay. I honestly wasn't expecting much. I'll figure it out. I don't need him."

I gave a frustrated sigh.

Logan's mouth was on mine so fast I wasn't ready for the kiss and it made my knees wobble. Our tongues met. We were hungry for each other. His hands anchored my hips and mine gripped his shoulders as our kiss sizzled in the chill of the night.

His lips—soft and smooth.

His tongue—wet and wild.

I kept pace with the frantic way he consumed me, or maybe he was responding to the frantic way I was consuming him. I wasn't sure. But soon it wasn't enough. Needing more of him, my fingers traveled up to his neck and I twisted them in the softness of his hair. Playing with it, tugging it, making him groan.

I felt alive in his arms.

He needed more too. With what I think might have been a growl, his mouth left mine to trail along my jaw, down my neck.

It felt so good.

I loved it when he did that.

I wondered if he knew I did.

Giving myself to him, I tossed my head back to allow him full access. His teeth were sharp as he dragged them down my throat, but the moisture of his tongue soothed away any lingering sting.

In the faint distance, I heard my neighbor's door open. I ignored it. But the sound of it slamming closed was impossible to ignore and I was forced to pull away. It was then that I realized I'd been so lost in Logan I'd forgotten we were still outside. In public.

Logan had told me he wanted to make sure I was safe

inside my house, but we hadn't made further plans for the night. Feeling bold, knowing what I wanted, I extended my hand. "Come on, let's go inside."

Logan kissed me again, almost as if in defiance of being made to behave in public. "That's probably a good idea," he mumbled against my mouth.

I laughed into his kiss. "I think we have an audience."

The moment I spoke the words, Logan's body stiffened and he pulled away, scanning the area left and right, front and back. "Let's go," he said in a serious tone, all playfulness gone.

Moving fast, he led me to my door. I unlocked it and as soon as we were inside, he closed and locked it. Fast as sin, I was pressed up against the door and his lips were on mine again, devouring me. Our mouths were glued together in a sensual, consuming kiss and I felt all of him. From his mouth on mine, to his hips holding me in place, to his thigh pressing between mine.

Something was bouncing in my belly and I shooed away the idea that it was butterflies. I was a grown woman, for God's sake.

Grown woman or not, the heated moment had me breathing hard. I broke away, pushing lightly on his shoulder to give me some space to move. "Follow me."

He did.

Up the stairs, down the hallway, to my bedroom.

Like two magnets, we were together as soon as the door creaked closed.

My bedroom was a reflection of me, much like my boutique. Nothing too frilly. Various paintings hung on the walls that I had collected from all the favorite places I'd been and loved. They were my treasures. In addition to the paintings, throughout my home I had sculptures, pottery, and various items I'd collected in my travels as well. In this room was also the last piece of my childhood I'd brought with me—the oval braided vintage rug that had belonged to my mother. My father had wanted to throw it away after she died, but I couldn't bear to see it discarded. I'm not sure why I kept it, but I did.

Whereas my home was a reflection of who I was, my bedroom was even more of a reflection of my inner being. On the walls were the places that I'd searched for myself and found peace. Sharing this part of me with Logan seemed appropriate.

Logan tugged my shirt off. I pulled his over his head. I wanted to feel his smooth skin against mine, to touch and caress it.

Our lips crashed together again before our clothes even hit the floor. My head was spinning from the delicious taste of him alone, but the sensual feel of his hands on my bare skin made me even dizzier.

As our teeth clashed, he moved me backwards until the back of my knees hit the bed and I tumbled onto it. He didn't let me fall, though—he was right there to catch me. For the first time with him, my back was against a mattress and his body molded to mine exquisitely.

We were all hands as we kissed some more. His were on my breasts. Mine were digging into his back, pressing against each muscle as it flexed.

I was so ready for this.

So was he.

I was surprised when he rose on his elbows and broke our mouths apart. I even tried to pull him back down to me, but I stopped when I saw him gazing into my eyes.

Warmth spread through me like fire.

His expression was so intense.

Without so much as a blink, I took the time to study him. His eyes appeared so vibrant, green rimmed in chocolate brown. Mesmerizing. I reached up and smoothed my fingertips over the arches of his brows. I could feel words sticking in my throat. I felt this urgency to speak. Something about the pain I saw in the depth of those pools. It was so strange. I'd never, ever wanted to talk to a man while he was hovering above me.

Garnering all of my courage, I urged myself to ask him about what I saw. It was now or never.

Before I could make my lips move, he tenderly pushed some hair from my face. The soft touch was unexpected, and I closed my eyes and let the feeling absorb into my whole being.

"I need to be inside you," he murmured.

My eyes flew open. I became disoriented. Fuzzy. Unclear. Flickering emotions cascaded through me as a whirlwind of terrible memories sliced through my soul. Shocked, panicked, unable to breathe, I shoved him off me and bolted off the bed. "You need to leave."

"Elle?" he asked, clearly concerned.

Gasping for air, I didn't answer him. I didn't look at him. Instead, I grabbed my top and ran down the stairs as the first fifteen years of my life assaulted me. My father. My mother. The words I heard spoken through the thin walls. The crying. The yelling. The grunts and groans. It was too much.

"Elle," he called again, right on my heels.

It was dark and my mind started to spin. I turned, backing myself up against the door. Frightened. Afraid. I just wanted him to stop.

The silhouette came closer. I put my hands out. "Please, leave me alone. I won't do it again," I cried.

"Elle, what's going on?"

The voice had no shape.

White knuckled, I dug my fingers into the doorframe. "Please," I begged. "Please leave me alone."

"Not until you talk to me."

The voice amplified. It sounded angry. His eyes flashed. He was a tough guy. Too tough to let a woman tell him no. Too tough to let a little girl try to stop him.

Every muscle in my body was taut. I stayed still. Very still. I didn't move. I didn't breathe. Maybe if I were quiet enough he'd just leave me alone. Leave her alone.

"Elle, it's me. Logan. What's going on? Where are you?"

I blinked as that soft voice broke through to me. "Logan?"

With tentative steps he approached me. His voice now soothing. "Elle, yes, it's me. I'm not going to hurt you."

My eyes began to readjust as I broke from the horror I dreamt about every day after my mother died and my sister left. "Logan," I said again, needing to be sure it was him and not my father.

His fingers were on my face, stroking away my tears. "Yes, it's me. Yes, it's me. It's me." His voice broke as he repeated himself over and over.

I swallowed hard and tried to look away. He wouldn't let me. He held my face in place. Shame and embarrassment were all I could feel. My heart pounded in my chest. What had I done? Why had I overreacted?

His fingers caught my chin as I managed to drop it. He wasn't going to let me evade him. His touch soft and gentle, he lifted it and looked into my eyes.

I was begging myself not to burst into tears. I didn't know if it was working, so I slammed by eyes shut. I couldn't let him see me like this. This was the broken me. Not the one I had glued back together. Not the tough girl who didn't let anyone in. I needed to get that girl back.

No one saw me like this.

No one.

Before I knew it, I was engulfed in his arms and my face was against his chest. "It's okay, Elle. I'm here. You can talk to me."

I pretended the water leaking from my eyes wasn't tears. I pretended I was stronger than this person who needed this powerful man to hold her up. I pretended and pretended as he continued to soothe me, but then something happened—I felt safe.

And I let my barriers down.

When his constant soothing became too much to bear, I stopped pretending and collapsed in his arms, a sobbing mess.

Somehow we ended up on the sofa and I was curled in a ball against him.

"Elle," he whispered after a long while.

I wanted to fade into the leather of the sofa and disappear. I couldn't look at him. I was weak and pathetic. My father would be laughing at me if he could see me now.

When I didn't respond, Logan lifted my head to look at him. His hands trapped my face and his eyes searched mine in a way they never had. "Tell me what happened. Did your father—" His voice cracked on the words, but I knew what he wanted to ask.

My throat was dry. "No, he never touched me, not sexually," I croaked.

The sigh he made was more than audible. "Then tell me what happened to you. What did I do that triggered this? I need to know."

With a deep inhale, I forced myself to be honest. Aside from Charlie, I'd never talked about this to anyone. I wanted to tell Logan. I sat up straight and looked at him. I wanted to at least appear strong when I told the sordid details of my past. "My memories start at age six. My father always worked late and my sister and I were usually in bed when he came home. Still, every night he'd lock our door, and the sound of the lock turning would wake me up. And then I'd hear him begging my mother to have sex with him. It didn't matter if she said no; he wouldn't take that for an answer. He was a sex addict. He needed it. She was the complete opposite and never wanted to give it. What I remember the most is . . ." I paused.

"Tell me," he urged.

"Is him telling her that he needed to be inside her."

Logan cringed and his face paled. "Oh God, Elle, I'm so sorry."

I shook my head. "You didn't know. It's not your fault. You see, I've had this rule when it came to sex—no talking. I've always made it very clear. But I didn't tell you. To be honest, I didn't want to tell you."

His brows furrowed in confusion. "Why?"

Bracing myself, I pulled back and wiped the twin streams of water from my cheeks. "You were different."

He hesitated but still asked, "In what way?"

I was barely breathing, I was so nervous. I was always petrified of telling anyone anything about myself. I wouldn't blame him if he had run. The perversity of my situation wasn't easy to swallow. But he hadn't run, not yet. He was still beside me, waiting for what else I had yet to say. It shouldn't have mattered to me so much that he was, but it did.

What would happen after I confessed my strange reaction to him? I had no idea. But Logan wasn't mine and if he chose to leave, I wouldn't blame him. What was coming sounded beyond bizarre, even to me. "You're going to think I'm crazy."

His gaze gently flickered across my face. It was the first time he'd looked at me that way—like he saw me, not the person I reminded him of. It was like he was looking at me, not avoiding her. "No, Elle. No I won't. Tell me."

Ironically, I had to avert my own eyes before I could say it. When I was looking anywhere but into his eyes, I finally spoke. "Since the very first time I had sex, I thought I was like my mother."

"What do you mean?"

I shrugged. "*Asexual* isn't really the right word, but it's close. Not really into sex. I had sex but I felt very little, nothing really. For years I was relieved, because at least I knew I wasn't a sex addict like my father. One day I met a guy and he became my boyfriend. We were compatible in so many ways, especially in the way that sex was secondary. It wasn't what drove our relationship. Our friendship did. But then we broke up and I fluttered again from man to man."

Logan bristled slightly and I lifted my gaze. He was staring at me. I couldn't tell what he was thinking. "Why did you break up?" he asked.

I wasn't ready to share that part of me—the most broken part—so I shook my head. "Things just didn't work out," was all I said. I wanted to finish this, to tell him what I was feeling for him, but he had to understand me first. "After Charlie was out of my life, I started searching for what it was about sex that could turn someone into the monster my father was. My sister was afraid of my father and even though she always warned me to be quiet on those nights I'd woken up, there were times I couldn't stand to hear my mother cry or to hear my father's demanding voice. And during those times, I'd scream and scream and scream until my father marched in the room and whipped me with his belt. I didn't care, though, because after he was done with me, he'd also leave my mother alone."

Logan drew in a breath before he pulled me to him. I wanted to shrug him off, but not as much as I wanted to feel the safety in his arms. He kissed my forehead. "I'm so sorry, baby. I'm so sorry."

Baby?

No one had ever called me by that term of endearment. The strength I had gathered was starting to weaken and I jumped out of his hold and to my feet. "I want to finish."

Although he paled, he nodded in understanding.

I walked to the kitchen and made a pot of coffee. I could feel his eyes on me the entire time, but I never looked back. Busying myself in the kitchen, I was allowing my strength to build. Once the coffee was done and I'd poured us each a cup, I felt much stronger. Turning back toward him, I could see that his eyes were filled with sympathy and something else.

I didn't want that.

He took the cup I offered him and then I sat down next to him, with my own cup in hand. My hands were shaking, but I ignored it and took a sip of my coffee.

Clearing my throat, I finally continued. "Up until I moved here three months ago, that was who I was. A single woman who didn't really care that much about sex but was searching for answers, so I pursued it from time to time."

Logan tried to remain undaunted, but I could see the muscle in his jaw clench.

I set my cup down. "I'm only telling you this so that you can understand me."

He nodded in understanding and then he opened his mouth, "Elle, I should—" He stopped, paused, drew in a breath, and then took a sip from his cup. "Never mind, go on."

I did. "Last night when I was with you, that changed. For the first time ever, I felt alive. Involved. Not removed. I wanted to feel everything. I didn't have to go through the motions. And even when you spoke, I was okay with it. At times, I liked it."

Logan looked stunned. Uncertain.

I knew I should clarify. Let him know I wasn't declaring my love or laying claim to him. "Please, don't worry. It doesn't mean anything more other than I really enjoyed having sex with you."

The corners of his mouth tipped up.

A shiver slowly danced down my spine at the same time a wave of embarrassment crashed over me. Heat worked its way up my body, flaming all the way to my fingers and toes, until I couldn't take another minute of his focus and covered and my eyes. "See, I'm crazy."

Through my fingers, I saw him set his cup next to mine. Standing, he emptied his pockets and removed his gun, and then I felt him move closer to me. The air was thick and laced with so much of whatever it was that traveled between us. But he didn't make the moment sexual. Instead, he pulled my fingers from my face and entwined them in his. When he spoke, his voice was soft, calm. "You're not crazy. I feel this thing too. I don't know what it is, but please don't tell me I fucked it up."

I shook my head. "Why would you still want to be with someone like me? I'm weak and pathetic."

His fingers squeezed mine. Not roughly. More like

passionately. "Don't ever say that. Don't even think it. You're a strong woman who has been through a lot."

My tears started again. "But I'm not. I'm broken and I can't be fixed." I almost told him the rest of my story, but I just couldn't. Not now. Not today.

Logan's lips found mine and he kissed me lightly. "You're not broken," he whispered.

I nodded, letting him know I was.

He kissed me again. "You're not."

He did it over and over, and eventually I started to believe him.

Maybe if I pushed that one part of me aside, I could be whole.

Even if it was only for a little while, I'd take it.

chapter
TWENTY-SIX

Day 4

LOGAN

HEADLIGHTS SHINED IN THE window.

My eyes scanned the two circles of white that dissolved into the darkness. Stuck somewhere between alertness and grogginess, it took me a moment to figure out where I was.

Elle's.

Fuck!

Instantly, I snapped awake.

Drenched in a cold sweat and breathing hard, I managed to heave myself out of bed and over to the window without waking Elle. Taillights blinked down the road. I fucking hated that she lived on a corner.

The digital clock read 2:40 and I decided to slide back into bed for another hour. I should have already left. We'd redressed when I was planning on it earlier but then she'd asked me to stay. Now, I couldn't. I wanted to tell her I was leaving before I actually did and I didn't want to wake her yet.

I walked the line between right and wrong.

Sometimes towed it.

But tried really hard not to cross it.

Yet, her father was a man I might just kill with my bare hands if I ever laid eyes on him. To do what he'd done to his wife and children was unforgivable, and in his case I'd take the role of judge, jury, and executioner if I had to. I didn't know him. Didn't know his background. I didn't have to—he, like Tommy, was a coward of a man who preyed on women to make himself feel more like a man, and like Tommy, he was a man I'd love to bring to his knees.

Tommy, though, was forbidden territory—her father was not.

My brain started swimming with everything going on in my life, but then her body found mine and we melded together like two puzzle pieces. I found a strange peace in the feel of her skin against mine. Giving in to it, I closed my eyes and let the calmness suck me in.

I jolted awake.

Fuck, it was dawn.

I'd only meant to sleep another hour. I shouldn't have stayed here all night with my SUV parked right in front of her place.

I knew better.

I fucking knew better.

I did.

Needing a moment, I didn't move. I stayed where I was, with my heart racing and my breathing as heavy as though I'd been running.

A few calming breaths had me thinking more clearly. Regardless of how reckless I felt right now, I wouldn't have changed anything. There was no way I could have left.

She needed me.

Elle needed me and I had to be there for her.

With that very thought in my mind, I opened my eyes to look at her. She was in my arms and although I knew it was wrong, it still felt so right.

Last night we crossed a line we shouldn't have. A line that brought us closer, and considering my current situation, that was unfair. She told me things about herself that were difficult, not only for her to say but for me to hear. She didn't know what she was involving herself in with me. I was an asshole for not confessing my sins right then. She spilled her heart and I couldn't even tell her what being with me meant to her safety. I wanted to. I tried to. I just couldn't. I knew if I did, she'd make me go, and I wasn't ready to say goodbye.

Not yet.

I had to hold on until Friday for her sake, and mine.

I had to keep her safe or I'd lose my mind.

That was the bottom line.

I drew a deep breath and exhaled.

When I did, a hand reached up and touched the side of my face. It was a delicate touch. A soft one.

One that I really liked.

One I should push away.

One I knew I wouldn't.

I wanted to feel it.

I wanted to do more than feel it.

I wanted to own it.

The thought made me sit up.

Dangerous.

My heart was still pounding and it wasn't slowing down.

I'd made some stupid decisions in my life and some not-so-stupid ones. The one to stay away from anyone who might get hurt because of me was one of the smarter ones. And I'd been doing that. Doing great at it. It had become my way of life. But it had seemed so much easier before her. Was she a "before" and "after" marker in my life? Was I destined to have an after Emily, a before Kayla, and now a before and after Elle?

Fuck!

The thought had my head spinning.

"Good morning," she said into my ear in a low, slightly purring voice.

That was all I needed. I would take care of whatever I

had to take care of, but right now, I needed her in my life. I'd never felt anything like what I was feeling for her with anyone else. I couldn't let her go—not yet.

She was behind me, on her knees, with her arms wrapped around my waist. I had already been revved up from her earlier touch, and now I was instantly hard. Around her, it didn't take much. If she thought I made her feel good, I wished she could feel how I felt with just the sensation of her fingertips.

Alive.

Electric.

Owned.

I twisted my body so I was facing her and then I lowered her down onto the mattress. I wanted to make her feel good and I was going to as long as she'd let me.

She blinked a little as if adjusting to the postdawn light, and when she looked at me with that seductive gaze, I knew she wanted me. Without hesitation I lowered my mouth to kiss her.

Her lips were soft.

Her mouth welcoming as she opened it to let me in.

Our tongues collided and all thoughts of anything but her left my mind. Needing her, I rolled on top of her. She felt so good. I wanted to tell her. I wanted her to know what she was doing to me right now. But I didn't. I was careful to keep my thoughts to myself. Still, I wanted to let her know how much I wanted her. That my need to drive inside her was so deep, I couldn't think of anything else.

That her crazy thoughts were my same crazy thoughts.

I might not be able to tell her with words, but I could definitely show her how I was feeling.

Control left me as that thought lingered in my mind. Devouring her mouth in gulping, sweeping movements, I had to have every part of her.

My pulse raced as my hands drifted up her body. From her slender hips, to that taut stomach, up to those perfectly shaped breasts. This was the first time that we'd be fucking when her niece wasn't nearby and I hoped I drove Elle so far over the edge, she screamed my name when I made her come—over and over.

I wanted to give her that.

At least that.

We were dressed, and the first place to start was getting naked. I lifted my shirt over my head and her eyes watched me. I swear I saw her lick her lips. It was her turn and I pulled her top off, making sure to skim her skin with my fingers. She shivered a bit and I grinned at how her body reacted to my touch.

Refocusing, I looked at her. Her bra was black and lacy, and I sucked in a breath when it came into full focus. I think my fingers were trembling when I ran them around the fabric to her back to unclasp it.

With a simple toss, the bra hit her floor and her perfect breasts were all I saw. Overcome with the need to touch them, squeeze them, suck her nipples into small peaks, I had my mouth and hands on them in less than a heartbeat, but then I remembered to slow down.

I could take my time with her today and wring every ounce of pleasure out of her—make sure she knew how much she turned me on.

My fingers skated over her smooth skin and her body responded instantly. In a way I'd never watched a woman before, I watched her. This was as much for her as for me. I was captivated not only by her actions, not only by her beauty, but by her body language—she was telling me she wanted me in the only way she knew how.

Message received.

Holding each breast, I didn't let my gaze wander as I lightly massaged them, pinching her nipples between my fingers when I did. Her eyes were hooded and I knew she was enjoying this.

The eye contact was too much, I felt a little too exposed, so I lowered my mouth, trailing my tongue down her neck, using my teeth to guide me.

She trembled with each inch downward and I knew just how much she liked it.

I kept going until I reached my hands. Keeping one in place, I let the other drift lower as my mouth took over its actions. With my tongue, I licked around her nipple over and over. She writhed beneath me and I went further, tugging it with my teeth and then pulling it into my mouth to suck on it.

Her skin tasted so good.

She arched her back when my free hand slid under the elastic of her sweatpants. My pulse was racing in anticipation of tasting her pussy. And I was tasting her pussy today.

Her body was responsive and the more I touched her, the more untamed she became.

She was letting go.

I loved it.

I couldn't wait to do more, but I was taking this slow. Letting her decide if something was too much.

My mouth drifted to her other breast and I repeated my actions.

Lick.

Tug.

Suck.

At the same time my mouth moved, my fingers dipped inside her panties. She was so wet. So wet I couldn't resist slipping a finger inside her right away.

She moaned when I did, so I added another. She moaned even louder this time and her hips bucked, so I added just one more. Stretching her, fucking her with my fingers, my own body felt explosive. I was worried I might come before I was even inside her.

She was still moaning and I lifted my head to see her again. I had to see her. Her body started to shake and her fingers gripped the sheets so tightly, her knuckles were turning white.

She was wild.

I bit my lip to stop from telling her to let go.

My fingers slid in and out. She was tight, wet, and ready. Her eyes closed and a blissful look overtook her. "Oh, God," Elle cried out in pleasure.

Not yet, I thought. *Not yet.*

I removed my fingers. I wanted to replace them with my mouth. I wanted her to come with my tongue inside her, not my fingers.

Her eyes were wide now—questioning why I'd stopped. I answered quickly by letting my lips trail down her body. Taking my time no longer an option, I pulled her pants off at the same time.

She lifted her hips and assisted me. She was just as ready for this as I was. Her hands gripped my shoulders tightly and I swear she was urging me to move faster down to her pussy.

I obliged.

It thrilled me how much she wanted this.

Sweetness was on the tip of my tongue as soon as it circled her clit. She tasted unlike anyone; she tasted like something I wanted to taste more than once. I knew I was in serious trouble. Once was never going to be enough. I didn't know if I could ever have enough of this.

"Logan!" she cried out when I found her clit with first my lips then my tongue.

My insides clenched, thrilled that she was vocally expressing how she felt. My hands wrapped around to her tight little ass and I pulled her closer to me. I didn't just want to eat her . . . I wanted to devour her. Her body trembled and she called out my name louder and louder with each passing second.

I knew she had come, but once wasn't enough. I went back, first slowly tasting her but only for a bite or two. Then I hungrily devoured her like I knew I had to.

She tried to push her body into the mattress as if she couldn't take anymore.

I wanted to tell her to just feel it, but I didn't.

I didn't have to.

Her grip tightened in my hair and she cried out, "I need more of you."

Those words had my cock throbbing to be inside her. Torn between finishing what I'd started and giving her what she wanted, I managed to pull myself away from her sweetness and stood up. Like a bolt of lightning, I shoved my pants off and stood fully ready in front of her.

She reached for me across the bed. Her fingers wrapped around my hard cock and I found myself starting to tremble.

Again, I had to take a few moments to admire her. Her smooth, pale skin, her seductive, stormy eyes, the cute sprinkling of freckles across her nose, her lush lips, and those perfect breasts—all her, all things I feared I would never stop wanting.

Finding my way back beside her, I let her set the pace. It was so unlike me to give anyone control, but I knew she needed to have it. Lying beside her, I collapsed on my back.

Her hand was still wrapped around me, stroking me, up then down, slow then faster, just the way I liked it. My eyes drifted closed and I let myself feel her. I think you could say I gave myself up to her. I was hers to do with what she wanted.

Oh. Fuck.

Her mouth was on me.

My cock was inside it.

The tip hit the back of her throat.

Her teeth grazed my shaft.

My balls started to tighten. I was going to come. I had to stop her. I needed to come inside her.

I moved fast.

Sitting back on my knees, I pulled her onto my lap. We were aligned perfectly, my cock nudged the flesh of her opening. Her hands gripped my shoulders and she lifted herself. Anticipation had my heart pumping. I'd never wanted to be inside someone so badly.

"Condom," I whispered with a wince. Hating to have to

speak. Hoping like hell I hadn't just put an end to this.

In a raspy voice she made me look at her. "Logan," she said.

I found her eyes.

She was fine, smiling even. She glanced toward her night table where my gun lay. "Is your wallet downstairs?"

With a nod, I dropped my head to her shoulder. *No. No. No.* Way to ruin the moment.

"I'm clean and safe," she said.

I lifted my head and met her gaze. "I am too."

I felt her fingers dig down into the bone of my shoulder at the same time her lower body rose and then eased down . . . right onto my cock.

Oh fuck.

Warm.

Wet.

Tight.

Enveloping.

Sensation after sensation paraded through me. I'd never been inside a woman without a latex barrier. The feeling was incredible.

I had to take control. I needed to be all the way inside her—from tip to base. I wanted to feel her around my entire cock. My hands gripped her hips and I eased her farther down on me.

More.

More.

It still wasn't enough.

I needed more.

I could tell she did too.

This angle prevented me from slipping all the way inside her. Sliding my hands up her back, I eased her to the mattress and hovered over her. As soon as I plunged inside her, her legs wrapped around me.

That was it.

I was all the way in.

She was moaning.

I knew she felt what I was feeling.

I knew I was groaning, but I had to. I felt like a teenage boy. A horny teenage boy. I couldn't control myself. I found her mouth to stifle the noise I was making but I was pretty certain her noises were louder, drowning me out.

"Look at me," she commanded.

Her demand slowed my relenting pace but only for a moment, because as soon as I did look at her, lust and desire were all I saw.

I couldn't hold back anymore. Thrust for thrust, she met each and every one. My cock pulsed and I pumped my hips into her. I lowered to my elbows, straining to keep control. She gripped my shoulders, holding on so tightly her fingernails dug into my skin and I could feel cool pricks of blood pooling around them.

I didn't care.

Trying to push deeper, wanting to be as far inside her as I could, I kept my pace fast but even—quick thrusts that allowed me the luxury of not leaving her warmth for long. Everything about her was so sweet. The feeling of being buried deep inside her was one I never wanted to lose. A loud growl-like groan stuttered out of me as I tried to hold on for her, but I couldn't. Letting go, I watched her face and hoped the bliss I saw on it meant she was coming too.

She was.

She moaned, "Oh God," and I could feel her walls tightening around my cock.

The feeling pushed me off kilter.

It was unlike anything I had ever felt.

Absorbing it, taking it, owning it, I let myself feel it without fear.

She gasped, and I could tell her orgasm was rocketing through her like the magnitude of the one that owned me right now.

Then everything went quiet.

All I wanted to do was hold on to her for dear life, because I was pretty sure I was going to die in the unbelievable pleasure I was basking in. We came in unison, our eyes glued to each other. Looking at her, I knew she had no doubt as to who I was and how I was making her feel.

Fuck, it felt so good—seeing the ecstasy on her face, hearing it in the sounds she was making. After a beat, I let myself go. When I did, I couldn't hear anything. It was the loudest silence I'd ever heard in my life. Out of nowhere, my vision went a little hazy, and there was a gentle ache that radiated around all parts of my cock—all reminders of the intensity we were sharing.

When I was spent, I dropped down and buried my face in her neck. After a few minutes I was able to move, and I rolled over and pulled her to my chest. She smiled against my neck and rested her head on my shoulder. I had to say something, so I murmured in her hair, "That felt so good."

She lifted her head and her beautiful eyes danced in the light. "More than good."

With a grin, I nodded in concurrence.

More than good, the truest words ever spoken.

chapter
TWENTY-SEVEN

Elle

WHAT HAD I BEEN missing?

If this was it, I had a lot of making up to do.

In the midst of all the chaos in my life right now, Logan was a welcome distraction. The post-sex glow I was feeling had to be plastered across my face like a neon sign. True to both our natures, we didn't stay wrapped in each other's arms for long. Cuddling, snuggling, nestling, or whatever you want to call it didn't appear to be either of our things. We were lying next to each other, but neither of us was speaking.

Maybe we were both thinking about what had just taken place?

My phone rang and we separated from each other. I rolled onto my back. Logan shifted to his feet before me.

Distracted by him, I didn't reach to answer it. The mere sight of him made my eyelashes flutter, my throat burn, and my heart pound. He hadn't shaved and his hair fell forward as he moved, making him look impossibly sexy. The hint of stubble I was staring at had just rubbed against the sensitive skin of my face, my stomach, and everywhere else, but the yearning I felt for him was still raging—I couldn't believe it but I wanted more.

Wasting no time, he pulled up his pants and zipped them. Standing before me bare-chested, he looked hotter than sin.

His eyes, as usual, weren't on mine. Yet he must have felt my gaze because soon enough those lustful hazel pools were looking at me. He reached for his shirt but before he pulled it on, he leaned down and kissed me. "I've got to go into work this morning. I'm going to run back to my hotel and shower. Will you be okay here until later?"

I bit my lip. "Yes, of course."

He eyed me and I wasn't certain what he was looking for.

Did he want me to say I'd miss him?

At that, I laughed a little and jokingly quipped, "Don't get too caught up in me."

"It's a little late for that," he said with a wink.

My heart felt like it might explode a thousand times over. It was my turn to look away. He was too much to look at and I averted my gaze back to his body. I'd allow myself the luxury of this sexual affair. I deserved it. I also knew not to read any more into it than what it was about. Plain and simple, it was about the fucking.

My eyes drifted. I licked my lips at the sight of the way his pants hung low on his hips, and I took in the perfection of his chest, the muscles in his arms, the line of his collarbone up to his neck. The jaw I was desperate to kiss, to taste.

I could almost feel my hands sliding inside those pants and I sucked in a deep breath as I imagined the feel of his warm, thick cock—the one I'd just felt. My pulse was racing at the thought and when I finally raised my eyes back to his beautiful face, he was watching me curiously.

"Elle, your phone is ringing again. Maybe you should answer it. Whoever it is has called twice now."

I was on the other side of the bed and as I rolled toward it, he grinned and reached for it.

He glanced down and handed it to me. "Here, it's Peyton."

I blinked out of my trance and tapped my screen. "Hello," I answered, and let that warm tingle I was still feeling continue to caress its way through my veins while I forced myself to look at the clock. It was early even for Peyton to be calling.

Logan tucked his gun in his waistband and was walking toward the door.

"Elle, I hope I didn't wake you. I know it's early, but I'm in the hospital and wanted you to know I won't be able to make it in to work today," Peyton said warily.

My heart stopped and I quickly sat up. "Hospital? What happened? Are you okay?"

Machines beeping in the background told me she couldn't be, yet she sounded like she always did—fine. "Yes, or I will be. Some jerk attacked me last night after I left the boutique. A few cuts here and there, but nothing major and certainly nothing to worry about. You know me—I'm tough."

My pulse was literally in my ears. "You were attacked?" I gasped in question, unable to believe it.

Logan was stepping out of my room when his spine straightened and he jerked around. His body language had me concerned about more than just Peyton.

"Yeah. Some asshole looking to get his jollies jumped me and pulled me into an alley when I was walking to my car."

Covering my mouth, trying to find my pulse, and feeling awful for her, I didn't know what to say or what to ask. "But you're not hurt?" was my only concern.

Stupid question. She was in the hospital.

Her voice was firm. "No, not really. He just scared the shit out of me."

"What did the police say?"

She laughed. I swore she laughed. "They aren't certain yet. I can't ID him, so there isn't much to go on. The creeper wore a ski mask and I didn't get a good look at his build at all. It was just too dark. But I think I hurt him because when he took off, he limped away. The police think it was an attempted mugging gone wrong."

I gasped again. "Did he take your purse?"

"No. Weird, right?"

"Muggers don't usually attack you and then leave your purse behind. Why would they think that?"

"Who knows? If you ask me, the guy had an agenda."

Still trying to process all of this, I asked, "What do you mean, he had an agenda?"

"I don't know. Like it was a dare or a gang initiation. He grabbed me, pulled me into the alley, and with his knife, sliced through my clothing right to my stomach to start carving the letter *E* on it. *Freak.* Somehow, I managed to free the chopstick I had holding my hair up and then I plunged it into his thigh. He screamed, and someone started shouting at him. That's when he ran. The person shouting was a homeless man. He hurried over to me and I gave him my phone to call 911. The ambulance arrived quickly and I was kept overnight for a dose of IV antibiotics, but I'm being released this morning."

"Peyton, oh my God, a knife!" I cried. "But you're okay? You're certain?"

Logan was next to me now, looking really pale. "What exactly happened?" he asked, expelling all the air from his lungs.

Covering the microphone with my hand, I whispered what she'd just told me.

He bristled and looked like he wanted to jump out of his skin or maybe lose his stomach. "Ask her if he said anything," Logan said.

Peyton was talking. "That man was really nice. I have to find him."

Perplexed, I gave Logan a curious look. "Peyton," I interrupted her.

"Right. I'm droning. Honestly, Elle, I'll be fine."

"Did the guy who attacked you say anything?" I asked

her, wondering why Logan wanted to know that.

There were voices in the background. "Yeah, he told me to tell that dog he'd been warned."

"Dog? That makes no sense."

A noise escaped Logan's throat. His hands were clenched into fists and he looked like he was a loaded gun and ready to shoot himself through the wall.

"Yes. I know. He was a crazy tweaker if you ask me."

My mind became a maze of impossibility. "I'm so sorry. What hospital are you at? I'll be there as soon as I can."

The voices grew louder. "No, Elle, that's not necessary. My mother is here to take me to her house. I'm so sorry, but I'll have to miss a few days of work."

Tears welled in my eyes. "Don't you worry about work. What can I do for you?"

She inhaled a breath. "Nothing. Listen, I have to go—the doctor just walked in. I got everything restocked yesterday. There's nothing for you to do today. Any deliveries made will be redelivered tomorrow, so you don't have to go in. Tomorrow will be crazy enough for you."

"Peyton, stop. Don't worry—I'll take care of everything."

"I know. I know. I'll call you when I get to my mother's house."

"Take care," I said, and hung up.

"Tell me again, and don't leave anything out—what exactly happened to Peyton?" Logan asked in a rush.

My voice became one giant exhalation as I told him everything, from the letter *E* on her stomach to what her attacker had said.

"He said the word *dog*. You're sure?"

"Yes, why?"

"We have to go." Logan's voice was low and shaky.

Something tight twisted in my gut.

Concern.

Fear.

The unknown.

I felt myself start to tremble and pulled the sheets up to

cover my naked body. "What are you talking about?"

With unrepressed determination, Logan was picking up my clothes and tossing them on the bed. My bra. My shirt. My panties. My sweatpants. "Get dressed now. We have to leave."

Apprehension rang through me. "What's going on?"

He stood tall, his shoulders broad, but wariness was all I could see. "Elle, please get dressed, pack a bag, and meet me downstairs. I'll explain everything when I get you back to my hotel."

I stood up, taking the sheet with me. "Logan, you're scaring me. Do you think Peyton's attack had something to do with Michael and Lizzy?"

With quick strides, he came over to me and put his hands on my shoulders. "No. Peyton was attacked because she was seen with *me*. Now do as I said and I'll explain everything when we get to my place."

Fear seized me. I didn't know what he was talking about, but I knew he was telling the truth. The question was . . . should I stay with him or should I run?

"Elle, listen to me. We need to leave. And you have to come with me. I can keep you safe."

Safe.

Could he keep me safe?

"What about Michael and Clementine?"

"They aren't in any danger right now. Hurry, and I promise I'll explain."

Drawing in a breath, I looked at him again and knew I had to trust him. "Give me ten minutes."

With a heavy sigh, he nodded and left the room.

The air felt thinner with him gone but not necessarily any easier to breathe.

Logan eyed the cars stacked ahead as if trying to determine how he could maneuver around them. All I saw were their red taillights in a flashing line of stop and go that was never going to end. No alternate was available in the morning traffic and five miles or fifty didn't matter—it was going to take an eternity to get to his hotel.

The day was overcast and colder than yesterday. Staring out the window, I watched the birds as they flew by, moving at a much faster speed than we were. I was feeling twitchy. I needed to know what was going on. "Talk to me."

I could see his jaw clench. He was waging a battle from within.

"It's okay, Logan, just tell me.

His chest rose as he inhaled a breath. "What I'm going to tell you isn't going to paint me in a good light. I was young, and stupid. I thought I knew what I was doing, but you have to know how much I regret what happened."

"What you did when you were younger won't make me think any differently about you, if that's what you're worried about."

He let out a huff. "Trust me, it will."

"Logan, please, tell me what you think happened to Peyton."

He shifted in his seat and his eyes scanned every inch of me. The slow motion of his stare made my heart race even faster. He opened his mouth and it was as if a chill cascaded around us in the confined space. His tone was distant, direct, matter-of-fact. "It's not what I think. It's what happened."

For as strong as I was, for as courageous as I wanted to be, I was suddenly very afraid. I pressed my lips together and stared out of the glass to wait for what came next.

It wasn't what I expected.

His hand was on me.

Fingertips softly searching to lock between mine.

That scared me even more.

Ready to burst, I turned toward him. "Just tell me."

Those hazel pools looked murky as they flashed at me one more time before he looked away and finally, he began to speak. "When I fifteen," he started, "I met this girl. Her name was Emily."

Something inside me felt like it might explode. I wasn't sure what was coming, but I knew it wasn't going to be anything good—it was in his tone.

"My mother was spending more and more time in New York City and my father and I were staying at my grandfather's house a lot back then. Anyway, Emily was interested in me."

I interrupted him. "Emily, is she the girl I remind you of?" I wasn't sure why I thought that, but his tone was reminiscent of the tone in which he'd told me I reminded him of someone he'd once known.

He gave me a slight nod.

I wondered why I'd bothered to ask that question. I already knew she was. "Sorry, go on."

He pulled his arm away and gripped the steering wheel with both hands. "I had a lot going on in my life with, my parents on the verge of divorce and my grandfather trying to introduce me to a world my parents wanted me to stay away from. I was a rebellious teen looking for an outlet. Looking to have a good time. Then I saw her. It was summertime and we were all hanging out in the park at the top of Savin Hill. She was there with her friends and the only one not wearing a bikini. I asked around. Who was she? Where did she live? Turned out Emily was not only the sister of a dude I hated, but she was forbidden. And if that didn't make me want her all the more."

"What do you mean, forbidden?"

"Everyone knew she was off-limits. She was from the other side of Dorchester Avenue. A Catholic girl who went to a Catholic school. She practically wore a chastity belt. What I didn't know at the time was that she also happened to have lunatics for her father and brother. I liked the challenge, the danger of it all. It took some time, but eventually she latched onto me,"

I tried not to parallel Logan, the teen, with Logan, the

man, but it difficult. Was that what I was to him—a challenge? The thrill of danger?

God, I hoped not.

"I know what you're thinking. And no, that's not what this is." He motioned between the two of us. "I'm not that same lost kid anymore who thought he could rule the world with money and power."

I pushed my doubts aside. This wasn't about me—it was about him. "I'm fine. Go on."

He assessed me for a long time.

I gave him a slight nod to let him know I was okay.

"For a while, I thought I loved her, but then I realized that was my friend James talking, making me think that. Don't get me wrong; I liked hanging out with her. It made me forget everything else I had going on. But I wasn't looking for all the shit that would come with telling her father or my grandfather, and she was cool with that until one day when she wasn't. Out of the blue, she told me she wanted to tell them."

I could see the confusion in his face, like he just didn't get women and their changing their minds.

"After that, I started to get nervous. She said she'd keep us quiet, but I wasn't so sure. Then she started to get more and more serious about us and she was throwing around words like *love*, *marriage*, and *forever*. The day she told me she loved me and she wanted to run away together, I broke it off."

The words were spoken with such absolute distaste, the sound made me cringe.

He shook his head. "I mean for fuck's sake, we weren't even sixteen."

"I take it she didn't take the breakup well?"

He shook his head again. "No, she couldn't accept that we were over. For almost two months, she kept coming over, calling me, crying to me that she wanted me back. She was like a stalker. I did my best to ignore her, but then she threatened to tell her father about us."

"Did she?"

"Fuck no, I knew she wouldn't. She was smarter than that."

I was almost afraid to ask. "Logan, who was her father?"

In a mumbled voice he answered, "Patrick Flannigan."

Two words that put everything in perspective.

I drew in a sharp breath, not liking where this was going at all. The car was stop and go but I felt like we were flying down the road, ready to crash into anything that got into our way. "Patrick Flannigan," I gulped.

A slow nod.

"Was that when he was part of the Dorchester Heights Gang?" I asked, starting to wonder if Emily had anything to do with the merging of two gangs.

Another slow nod.

His knuckles were white around the steering wheel. "To say he was an overprotective father would be downplaying it. When he found out, I knew he'd cut my balls off. But I had to call her bluff, so I told her I didn't really care who she told. As callous as it sounds, I was done with her. By then I'd learned just how selfish and self-centered she was and I couldn't stand to be near her. Anything I had felt for her was gone. I just wanted her out of my life."

Trembling, I knew something bad must have taken place. I turned my body toward him and with my voice nothing more than a squeak, I asked, "What happened?"

Logan wouldn't look at me. "It was a Saturday and the Red Sox were on. I was at my grandfather's house watching the game. I was the only one home when she came over. I didn't want to let her in, but she left me no choice when she wouldn't stop ringing the fucking doorbell. I remember it like it was yesterday. I flung the door open and left her there while I walked into the family room and flopped on the couch with my arms behind my head. She came in and handed me a piece of paper with all these different numbers on it. When I asked what I was supposed to do with it, she told me it was confirmation of her pregnancy."

The flashing lights in front of us seemed to be getting closer and my eyes darted to the sneakers on his feet and the slamming of his right foot on the brake. His arm jerked in front of me as if he could hold me in place. We were inches from the car, but there was no impact.

He finally looked at me. "Are you okay?"

"I'm fine."

We were close to the hotel and I wanted to know what happened. "Logan, please just tell me what all of this is about? And why you're telling me this story."

He scrubbed his jaw and resumed driving. "I crumpled up the paper and threw it to the ground. I told her it couldn't have been mine. We hadn't fucked in months and I'd always used a condom. She told me she was three months along. That I should know condoms aren't always effective. When I didn't blink an eye, she insisted it was mine. I still didn't believe her. Not that she was pregnant, and not that it was mine. I lost it then. I told her I'd had enough of her lies and to stop harassing me. I didn't hold back. I told her what I thought of her and that I couldn't believe she'd stoop to the oldest trick in the book to try to be with me. I couldn't stand her—why would she even want to be with me? She cried that her father was going to kill her. Send her away to live with the nuns. I didn't listen; instead I told her to leave and never come back. She ran into the bathroom and I didn't bother with her. I wasn't about to play her game. An hour later, I didn't know if she was still there, but I got up to check anyway. That's when I saw the blood pooling from under the door. I busted it open and she was lying there. Blood had arced up in splashes on the wall, the ceiling, and the side of the toilet. It was everywhere. It took me a moment to figure out where it was coming from. Then I saw it. She'd cut her wrists open—she'd killed herself, and it was too late to save her. I was too late to save her."

There was no color. No light. No words. Nothing I could say.

The inflection in his voice told me of the pain he felt. Who was I to judge? And I still didn't understand how he knew Peyton's attack was because he'd been seen with her.

I reached over to him as he pulled up to the hotel valet. "Logan, you were a kid. How were you to know what she'd do?"

Ignoring me, he grabbed my bag from the back and got out without a word. My door opened and he stood there waiting for me. We stayed silent until we got to his room. I sat on the couch. He paced the room.

Finally, I spoke. "I don't understand what this has to do with Peyton."

He ran his hands through his hair. "I didn't know what to do when I found her, so I called my old man. When he got to my grandfather's, he called someone to come get me and told me he didn't want me anywhere near there. I had no idea what he was doing, but found out later that he took the blame for her death."

"What do you mean, took the blame? She killed herself."

"In our house," he muttered.

"But it wasn't anyone's fault." I insisted.

"You don't understand. A powerful man's child doesn't just die. They don't just get shot, and certainly don't just kill themselves. There has to be a reason. Always a reason. My father took that blame."

My heart leapt. "How could he?"

"After he called 911, he called Patrick and told him what had happened. His version anyway. He told him Emily stopped by to see me but he didn't know why. He knew it was going to get out that Emily and I had been together anyway, and he wanted to be the one to put it out there. He went on and told Patrick that when he told her I didn't want to see her anymore, she started to cry, and then asked to use the restroom. He finished the story by telling him she'd been in there a while, so he'd gone to check on her, and that's when he found her with her wrists slit, but it was too late. She was already dead."

"I still don't understand."

"In Patrick's eyes my father caused her distress. He was the reason she killed herself. And code mandates a life for a life. He thought Patrick would kill him but instead Patrick took his life in a different way. That day my father sold his soul to Patrick to save me."

I was shaking my head. "But you didn't do anything. It wasn't your fault."

"But it was—and my father knew Patrick would see it that way. I had gotten her pregnant. I was the one who didn't believe her. I was the one who left her bleeding out in that bathroom."

"Logan, she took her own life."

He sat in a chair. Clasped and unclasped his hands before rubbing the back of his neck. "Don't you get it? It was because of me."

"Logan." I said his name only. I could see the pain he was feeling, but I didn't think worse of him because of this. He was a young teen. It wasn't his fault. No one makes another person do something like that—people do it to themselves.

It was enough to make him glance up. "I'm getting off track. After everything happened, my parents divorced and I moved to New York with my mother. Patrick never spoke about the pregnancy and to this day, I'm not certain he ever found out, but Tommy and his sister were close, and he knew."

"Tommy never told his father?" I asked.

"No. I don't why. Probably because he knew Patrick would beat the living shit out of him for letting something like that happen to his sister, or maybe because he knew Patrick would kill me and he wanted to punish me in his own fucked-up way. Who knows why? Anyway, a few years passed and I began to distance myself from that painful day, from what I'd done, and get on with my life. One summer, I came back here with a girl, and Tommy saw me with her. He followed me back to my grandfather's with four other guys and they attacked us."

"Oh my God, Logan."

Logan ignored my compassion. He was in a trance, talking with no feeling whatsoever, just citing the facts. "Tommy had a knife and he carved the letter *E* in the girl's . . . in Kayla's stomach. He told me if I was ever seen around town again with any other girl, he'd do the same, or worse."

Shuddering, I sat here absorbing what he'd told me. "Are you certain he attacked Peyton?"

He ran his hand over his stubble. "I'm sure, Elle. He called me a dog that night. I'm sure. Peyton had me go with her to Mulligan's Cup yesterday and the guy who works there was with Tommy that night so long ago. He must have told him."

"Declan?"

He narrowed his eyes at me. "You know him?"

"Yes, he's a really nice guy. And he likes Peyton. I can't believe he'd do anything to hurt her."

Logan stood. "Stay away from him."

I nodded. I finally understood what he was worried about. Why he wore the hat, the sunglasses, whenever he went out. Why he looked around everywhere we went as if scouting the area. It was because he was. But I also knew I could take care of myself. "Logan," I said before he walked into the bedroom.

He stopped.

"I can take care of myself."

At that he turned around and reached into his back pocket, pulling out his wallet. He thumbed through the card slots and removed what looked like a tattered newspaper clipping. It was in color; maybe it was a magazine clipping. He handed it to me. On it was a picture of a girl who bore an eerie resemblance to me when I was younger. The headline read, "Young teen kills herself."

My hand flew to my mouth. The similarity I bore to her initially seemed uncanny, but a closer look showed that while we shared the same ginger-colored hair and a smidgen of freckles across the nose, that's where the likeness ended.

Logan gave me an intense look. "Tommy's a sick fuck. I'm not as worried about what he'll do to you because you're with me. I'm worried about what he'll do to you if he sees the resemblance."

"Logan, we don't look that much alike."

"I know that. But from a distance there are similarities."

My eyes closed in a subconscious effort to block out the fear in his voice. Out of nowhere, a thought struck. My eyes popped open. "Do you think he did something to my sister?"

An audible intake of breath was his response.

Like it was on fire, and burning me, I shoved the newspaper clipping as far away from me as I possibly could. "This isn't your fault. I'm involved in this because of my sister, not you. This started before we ever met."

He dropped his gaze.

"Logan," I said softly.

His eyes surprised me. "I'll find out where your sister is, Elle. I have a plan."

Surprised, my brows raised in question. "What's the plan?"

Not wasting any time, he stood and started back toward the bedroom. "I can't tell you right now, but you have to trust me. I will keep you and that little girl safe."

"And Michael?" I asked.

He just stared at me.

"Logan?"

Without another word, without an answer, he closed the door.

chapter
TWENTY-EIGHT

LOGAN

REALITY SLAPPED ME IN the face.

Even after a shower, my skin still felt like it was bathed in a cold sweat. My fingers continued to tremble with the disgust I felt for what I'd done all those years ago.

I hated that I'd had to tell Elle about it, but she had to know.

As I walked into my father's law office, my legs were rods holding me up with each step, but I couldn't feel them. I was on autopilot. I was gunning first for Declan, and then finally Tommy.

Tommy was close, but I had to believe he didn't know about Elle because if he did . . . I couldn't even think what that would mean.

Sure, I had a plan.

One that would protect her.

But my plan was shaky at best.

I had to put the pieces in motion.

Stacks of newspapers were piled on my father's desk. The lights were dim and the gray clouds outside didn't make the room any brighter. We'd had one wonderful day before March storms kicked up again. He was at his computer, reading glasses on, studying some documents on the screen.

"Anything?" I asked, not certain he was working on anything to do with Patrick or Tommy.

He slid his glasses down his nose to peer at me. "Actually, yes, I think so."

Like a bat out of hell, I dashed around his desk and looked over his shoulder at the computer screen. "What?"

He twisted in his chair. "I met with Patrick's accountant this morning and told him I needed bank statements for All My Women for the past two years."

Exasperated, I said, "Why would you do that? He's going to want to know why."

"Relax, Logan. This isn't my first rodeo. I fed him a bullshit story that the Financial Action Task Force is cracking down on certain types of wire transfers, looking for terrorist cells. I explained to him that I needed to see for myself exactly where Patrick was moving the money so I could advise him on what he should and shouldn't be doing to avoid being targeted, or worse, being pinned as a terrorist."

Chuckling, I shook my head. "You must have had Hal shaking in his shoes."

His eyebrows popped in amusement. "More like shitting his pants. He emailed me the statements as soon as he got back to his office."

"Sounds like you found something interesting."

"I did. And not just the fact that the five million used to make the drug buy that went bad wiped out Patrick's operating fund."

"Completely?"

"Just about. That's why he's freaking out."

"What else?"

My father turned back around and used his mouse to highlight something on the screen. "Look at this."

I leaned closer and twisted my lips. "It's a withdrawal."

He highlighted a deposit. Then a withdrawal. Then another one of each. And then another.

"Okay, Pop, so someone is withdrawing a lot of money."

He zoomed in on the withdrawal slip. "Not just someone. Tommy. The dumb shit has been depositing money and withdrawing more than the deposit on the next day for some time now."

"Would explain the lack of money in the operating."

"Yes, it does."

I shook my head. "What? Is it Tommy's idea of laundering?"

His brows rose. "Who knows, but he knows it's forbidden in the organization. These are unsanctioned cash withdrawals and although they occur often during most of the statements I have, they started ramping up even more about six months ago."

"How do you know Patrick is unaware of this?"

"Trust me, he is. Tommy is going to the bank and making the small deposits and larger withdrawals himself. Patrick would never allow that. Too risky. The dirty money has to be cleaned first—always. That's Patrick's rule. Patrick also doesn't allow cash withdrawals. Funny thing is, Tommy stopped this activity three months ago."

With a slow shake of my head, I said, "When O'Shea's wife disappeared?"

My father turned back around. "Yes. But I'm not sure the two are connected."

"But possibly?"

He shrugged. "The only thing I'm sure of is that something was going on behind Patrick's back."

"More drug buys?"

"Could be. Tommy knows Patrick doesn't want Blue Hill relying on the drug trade to earn."

"Do you think he'd be that stupid to defy his father?"

"I don't know, Logan, but I've been thinking about this whole situation. Tommy first brought Patrick's attention to the drug ring for a reason."

"Because he needed the funds?"

"Yes, but why wait so long after the deal went bad to tell

Patrick?"

"He tried to handle it himself?"

"There's something else."

"What?"

"I wish I knew. At this point Patrick wants his money back, but I'm almost certain he's looking to eliminate whoever is running the renegade op. It's like that person is some kind of threat to him or something."

I leaned back on his desk and crossed my arms. "Okay, so how does this help us move forward with a solution?"

"It doesn't. But if we can find out who O'Shea's wife was working for and/or who she was getting the drugs from, we should be able to follow the trail up to the source, which will more than likely be the person in charge of the renegade operation. And if we deliver that person or persons by Friday, that girl you're so concerned about should be safe."

That girl.

She wasn't just *that* girl anymore.

She was *my* girl.

Admitting it would be futile, though. What mattered was that I keep her safe. And that I would do, no matter what. "I know where to start," I said.

My father looked at me skeptically.

I shoved off the desk. "Something happened last night."

It took me fifteen minutes to tell him what happened to Peyton. He had so many questions—why was I there, what was I thinking, I shouldn't even be near Elle. When the lecture started, I started for the door.

"Where are you going?" he asked.

"To see Declan Mulligan. I'll call you later."

His eyes narrowed. "Don't do anything stupid."

I indicated my appearance. "I'm in a suit—what am I going to do?"

My father said, "That doesn't mean anything."

"I'll be smart."

"Dinner?"

"Can't tonight, but tomorrow night I'll be there,"

I responded as I left his office. I had no idea what today might bring. Plans weren't anything I needed to have.

His heavy sigh could be heard down the hall.

My heavy sigh, though—that was what Declan should be worried about.

Tie pulled loose, suit jacket off, and sleeves rolled up, I found a place to park on ever busy Charles Street.

Mulligan's Cup was open for business and full of patrons when I walked through the door. And Declan himself was working the espresso machine like he was born to brew lattes.

"I need to talk to you," I said, bending over the counter.

"Yeah, give me a minute," he responded without glancing up.

"In less than a minute, this fancy machine of yours is going to be on the floor."

That got him to look up and when he saw my unhappy face, he paled, and then cranked a knob or two on the Italian masterpiece in front of him that had to cost at least thirty thousand. "Logan, look, I don't want any trouble."

"I said, I need to talk to you." I was seething. My fingers gripped the back of the machine so tightly it shook. I would shove it to the ground if I had to—if it was the only way to get his attention.

He swallowed nothing in his throat and gave me a nod. "Charlene, can you finish this order?" he asked the girl behind the register.

"No problem," she answered, eyeing me with distaste.

Declan took off his apron and bobbed his head toward the door leading to the backroom.

As soon as we were through it, I slammed him into the wall. "Why would you do that?" I said with disgust.

Sputtering, gasping for breath, he choked out, "I didn't do anything."

"Wrong answer." I punched him in the gut.

Declan curled around my fist as all the air went out of his body. "Logan, I didn't do anything. I don't even know what you're talking about."

I pulled him up by the shirt collar. "You're trying to tell me you didn't put Peyton in the hospital?"

"No! What do you mean? What happened to her?" He coughed the words out, his concern clear in his tone.

Shoving him back against the wall, I looked him in the eye. "Someone saw me with her yesterday and last night she was attacked—by Tommy."

He blinked rapidly as if trying to process what I'd just said. "Is she okay?"

I stepped back so I could better assess if he was lying to me. He looked genuinely upset. With narrowed eyes I hissed, "You'd better not be fucking with me."

He raised his palms surrender style. "I swear, man, I haven't seen Tommy in years. I'm staying clean and trying to run an honest business."

I clenched my fists, trying to beat back the urge to knock him around a bit and see if he really was telling me the truth.

"What happened to Peyton?"

Calming myself, I leaned back against the counter. "She was attacked and left with an *E* on her stomach as a warning . . . to me."

He ran a hand through his hair. "Fuck, no."

Declan reached behind him, but I was on him too fast. My face was right up in his. "Don't even think about it."

"I'm not carrying. I was reaching for my phone. I want to call Peyton."

Unsure, I patted him down.

"Logan, I told you, I'm not in that life anymore. And besides, I like Peyton—I'd never do anything that might hurt her."

Images flickered in my mind of the long walk up the hill yesterday, of the dozens and dozens of people we must have passed. Was Tommy one of them? Was he combing the streets looking for the same thing his father demanded be delivered by Friday?

Drugs.

Money.

The connection.

What the fuck was it?

I found myself staring at Declan. "What do you know about Tommy and dealing drugs?"

He shook his head. "I told you, I'm out of that life."

Air pushed from my mouth. "Come on man, I'm not stupid."

"I am."

"Tommy let you out?"

"Patrick did. He knew my old man needed help with his business and for some reason, he let me go. Said it was for the good of the neighborhood."

Possible, but not probable. "Come on, Declan, don't lie."

"I'm not lying."

"Then what's the real reason you're out and still alive?"

He sighed. "Tommy got shot a few years back and the guys he was with left him on the ground bleeding. I saved him and in return, Patrick let me out. But it really was to work my old man's business."

For some reason, I believed him. "Even out, I know you have to hear things. Peyton is an innocent girl who got caught up in Tommy's shit. If you care about her, you'll help me out."

An unlikely ally, I was surprised when he said, "I heard he was dealing and had been seen over at the waterfront with a redhead a lot, but that was months ago."

"Can you find out where exactly?"

"I can ask around, but I'll need some time. I can't just bring it up. I have to run into the right people."

My mouth twisted. "Something is going down soon and we don't have much time."

His eyes told me he understood. "I'll hit the neighborhood tonight."

The room was organized and I reached behind him for a clipboard hung on wall. Tearing a corner from a sheet of paper, I wrote down my number. "Call me as soon as you hear anything. I don't care what time it is."

I was out the door when I turned back. "Hey—"

He was already on his phone.

For a minute, I wondered again if he'd played me and was calling Tommy.

As if knowing my thoughts, he held his phone. *Calling Peyton* flashed on the screen.

"Sorry about the misunderstanding."

He gave me a nod and then turned his attention to his call. "Peyton, it's Declan . . ."

The door closed and I reached in my wallet and stuffed a twenty in the tip jar. Charlene was still eyeing me, but at least she added a smile.

Once I was back in my car, I sent Elle a text.

Me: What color hair does your sister have?

Elle: Red, why? Do you think you found her?

Red.

Could Tommy have been in business with Lizzy? Was O'Shea on the up-and-up when he said he had nothing to do with what went down?

I texted Elle back.

Me: No, I haven't. Do you have a picture of her you could send me?

Elle: I don't have any recent photos, but I know there are some on Michael's FB account. Hang on.

Elle sent me a link.

Me: Thanks. I'll be back soon.

Elle: I'm at the boutique. I took a cab. I'm waiting for the deliveries and then I'll meet you back at the hotel.

Me: I told you to stay put.

Elle: I've been here for months. It's safe.

She had a point. As long as I didn't go there and she wasn't seen with me, she was safe—for now. My fingers hovered over my screen. I wanted to say something to her to let her know I was thinking about her. My feelings confused even me. I'd known her what, four days, and I wanted to know more of her. I'd told her about the darkest part of me, and she didn't think I was a monster. Something was happening between us, but I wasn't sure either of us knew what it was.

Me: Looking forward to seeing you.

Elle: J

A smiley face? What the hell did that mean? I shoved my phone into my pocket before I sent her back a matching one or worse yet, a wink, or who the hell knew, maybe an *xoxo.* If I didn't get my thoughts under control, I might just be texting her a heart before I even realized it. My groan was loud enough for everyone in the vicinity to hear. I wanted to plug my own ears.

Pulling out, I focused on the traffic, the cloudy day, the people on the street. Anything to take my mind off the girl I was becoming way too attached to.

I spent the afternoon at the waterfront. What I thought I'd find there, I had no idea. I roamed Seaport Boulevard. I saw nothing out of the ordinary. I ventured into the hotel lobbies. I found shit. Wandered the waterfront. The only things there were boats and seafood.

By five o'clock, I'd had enough.

It was time to get back to the hotel.

And I wanted to see Elle.

chapter
TWENTY-NINE

Elle

I CLOSED MY EYES and leaned back against the couch.

My laptop was on my knees, my inventory pad beside me, and my cell close at hand. I felt drained and done with work. The crackle of the logs caused me to open my eyes. Setting my things aside, I looked around.

Logan's suite was swanky. That was the best word to describe it. Modern black sofas, crystal chandeliers, fine abstract art, and beautiful side pieces to accompany it all.

The vanilla curtains blew in the breeze and the fireplace warmed me. I'd decided on opening the terrace door and turning on the gas fireplace. My nerves had my temperature fluctuating. One minute I was hot, the next I was cold.

Peyton had said she was absolutely fine, but I forbade her from coming to work until Saturday. She needed to take a few days off. If what Logan said was true, and I was certain it was, I wanted her far away from anything until after Friday passed.

Friday.

D-day.

I hoped Michael knew what he was doing.

He'd stopped by the boutique with Clementine and

Sarah, the nanny, at lunch. Peyton had me seeing things that weren't there, I was sure, but Michael did look pretty at ease with the nanny. He also seemed to be back to normal. He acted like nothing out of the ordinary was taking place in our life. He also acted like his wife hadn't been missing for three months. I think he'd convinced himself that she really was in rehab. Both behaviors bothered me.

Cracking open a bottle of water, I checked the time—five fifteen. My stomach was growling, so I reached over to the pile of snacks I had brought from my stash at the boutique. The coffee table was littered with fruit roll-ups, granola bars, pretzel bags, and a few Snickers.

My fingers glided over each one before I decided on pretzels. They were the flat kind with salt-and-pepper flavoring. My favorite.

I pulled my laptop back onto my lap and in the search bar, feeling oddly curious, I typed in two words: *sex addict.* Not that I thought I was one. It's just that for so long I'd thought of myself as almost asexual and now, after meeting Logan, that clearly was not the case. Still, naturally, I had to wonder if it was possible to move to the other side of the spectrum.

An article in *Psychology Today* magazine caught my attention. It was titled, "How to Tell If You Are a Sex Addict." The article contained many stories of people who had thought they might be. I read them all but couldn't relate to any of them. Still, I read on. I stopped when I came to a quiz with a series of questions:

1. Do you find yourself unable to concentrate because you're thinking about sex?
2. Do you pay for sex? (Porn or prostitution.)
3. Has your sexual activity ever caused problems for your family?
4. Even when you're in a relationship, do you still masturbate two or three times a day?

There were dozens and dozens more questions, but I stopped there. I was confident that I was most definitely not a sex addict. Who knows? Maybe I was just a normal woman with healthy sexual urges.

Munching on my pretzels, I liked that thought. Curiosity drove me to keep searching, and this time I Googled *sex drive*. The first article I read stated that the majority of Americans in their late twenties and early thirties have sex with their partner two to three times per week. There were tons more articles, all stating the same thing. Interesting. I was pretty sure Logan and I might have sex two to three times per *day* if we could.

That put a huge smile on my face.

I was biting down on another pretzel in fascination when I heard the lock. The sound caused my heartbeat to step up.

Slowly, the door opened.

My eyes were glued to it and then glued to him the minute he stepped through it. He paused in the doorway. Right away the air felt thick—just the way I seemed to like it as of late.

I licked the salt off my lips and stared at him. When he flew out of the bedroom this morning, he left so fast, all I saw was a flash of gray. Now, I could see him, really see him, and he looked edible in the designer suit he had on. And the tie loose around his neck with the first few buttons of his white shirt open only made him look even sexier.

I was becoming obsessed with this man.

Was obsession one of the questions in any of the quizzes I'd looked at, I wondered?

If so, I didn't care. I wanted this man. And that had to be a normal, healthy, and happy reaction.

Logan looked over at me—his eyes on me like they had never been. "Hey." His voice was smooth like honey.

Something fluttered in my belly—butterflies? No. I was a grown woman. I didn't get butterflies. Yet they felt an awful lot like them. "Hi," I said back. "How was work?"

"I spent the day at the waterfront," he said, striding toward me, tugging his tie off as he walked.

My pulse raced. "Why were you at the waterfront?"

I breathed him in. I hadn't realized it, but I think I might have missed him.

Logan moved my computer aside and bent to brush his lips against mine. "I'll tell you later."

I accepted his answer—for now.

His mouth felt warm above mine, and I closed my eyes, reminding myself this was only supposed to be about the fucking. And it was normal.

He pulled away and smiled at me. The way he was look-ing at me made my skin tingle.

That was when I knew I was lying to myself—this was about more than just the fucking.

I was falling for him.

"What are you reading?" He nodded his head toward my computer.

I quickly moved to slam the screen down, but he was faster. He grabbed it and sat beside me. With a wiggle of his brows he read the name of the article I had been reading: "Sex Drive: How Do Men and Women Compare?"

"Give me that," I said, reaching for the laptop.

With a boyish grin that melted me, he shook his head. "You're looking at porn."

"Please," I said rather haughtily. "I am not looking at porn. I'm doing research."

"Number one," he said. "Men think about sex more. Number two," he went on. "Two-thirds of men admit to masturbating three to four times a week." He chuckled at that.

The thought of watching him do it seemed highly erotic. "Do you?"

He sat back and ran his fingers through his hair and grinned. "Well, yeah, sometimes."

"The answers to that question are either 'yes' or 'no,' not 'sometimes.'"

His coyness was adorable. "I don't really count how many times. Do you . . . masturbate three to four times a week?"

"Next question," I said, feeling oddly embarrassed by that one. It wasn't that I was immature; it was just that my reasons for masturbating in the past weren't the same as Logan's, and admitting that wasn't something I was proud of.

His laugh was low. "It's okay if you do. In fact, I wouldn't mind watching you sometime."

Suddenly it felt like 1,000 degrees in the room. The thought of that turned me on as much as the thought of watching him pleasure himself.

He laughed again, and it was low, and growly, and deep. "Number three." He cleared his throat as if trying to ward off the laughter. "Sex drive increases with exploration." There were a couple of clicks and then he turned the screen toward me. "Wow, look at that."

My hands moved instinctively to cover my face. I wasn't really feeling embarrassed, though, so I peeked through my fingers and saw he had clicked a link to demonstrate various unusual sexual positions. Dropping my cover, I commented, "Kinky."

His grin widened and he pointed to a picture. "We've done this," he scrolled down, "and this," he scrolled some more, "and I think this. Oh, we should try this one."

Rising on my knees, I leaned over and snatched the computer, closed the top, and set it on the table. I was really close to him. Really, really close.

He breathed in deeply and when he turned his head, his lips grazed my throat.

Heat flooded me.

"You smell so good." Logan's voice was hoarser than it had just been, the playfulness replaced with something more lustful.

"It's lavender," I told him, my voice husky too.

He breathed me in again. "I really like it," he said, and dragged his tongue up my throat to my mouth. His lips felt so soft against my skin, his tongue so wet. He was easing me closer now and I was putty in his hands.

The fabric of my simple white blouse seemed to come alive as soon as his body covered mine. My nipples tightened and strained against it. The denim of my jeans also seemed to give way as my knees got weak with his legs between mine.

As soon as I felt his erection straining through the fine fabric of his pants, instant arousal spread through me like a wildfire out of control.

His tongue flicked my lips. "You taste good, too."

"Pretzels," I said, a little breathy.

Our mouths parted and the onslaught of needing to be closer, needing to consume each other, took over.

His tongue stroked mine.

I stroked his back.

Wet, wild, pleasure. That's what I felt with his mouth on mine.

The kiss broke and left us both breathing hard.

He lifted a little to look down at me. "I know you have a lot going on in that mind of yours, but Elle, you don't need to try to categorize yourself as asexual, sexual, or anything else."

"You don't understand," I said and then leaned forward, my mouth seeking his. When I reached it, I found it closed to me. I felt a little disappointed.

Did seeing me reading that article worry him?

Logan's eyes glittered green with small flecks of brown. "Let me finish."

I blinked my stupid fears away and smiled at him. "Go on."

He sat up.

I gathered myself together and sat up too.

He looked at me. "I don't care what you were or thought you were. All that matters is what we are—together. And that is pretty great."

"Do you really think so?'

He tilted his head to the side. "I'm pretty certain you

know I do."

We looked into each other's eyes for a long silent moment.

"I don't know why it matters to me. My whole life I've tried to figure myself out and just when I thought I had, whatever this is between us happened and I feel like I have to go back to the drawing board and figure myself out all over again."

"Then let me help you."

I gave him a huff of laughter. "I think I am."

He wasn't laughing. "You said this thing between us was just about the fucking. What if I told you I thought it was more?"

There was a feeling of ease with Logan. One where the truth was the only thing that needed to be spoken. No games. No beating around the bush. "I'd say I think it is too."

"So can we agree to figure out what we are—together? Because I have to admit, this is all new to me too."

I felt a weight lift off my shoulders. Maybe he had a point. I didn't have to be asexual or sexually repressed or whatever it was I thought I was. It didn't mean I was a sex addict either. Maybe, just maybe, I hadn't turned out like either of my parents. "Yes," I answered, and launched myself at him.

Just as my lips found his, my stomach roared with the loudest hunger cry I'd ever heard.

Our mouths connected, we both laughed.

"I need to feed you," he said.

I sat up again. "I skipped lunch and I am a little hungry."

As he rose to his feet, his full form took my vision—the width of his shoulders, the length of his torso, the narrow hips. I was hungry all right, hungry for him.

"Elle," he said.

I bit my lip. "What?"

"I asked what you feel like eating."

Okay, so I wanted to say *you*. "It doesn't matter.

Anything."

The room service menu was on the desk and he glanced down at it. "Fish, steak, or pasta?" he asked.

I twisted my lip. "Pasta, I think."

"Good choice. I think I'll have that too. Spaghetti, linguini, or penne?"

"Spaghetti, please."

"Carbonara, Arabiatta, Bolognese, tomato, *aglio olio*, or lemon capers."

I laughed. "Too many choices. I'll go with the traditional tomato sauce and a meatball."

His eyes twinkled. "You're easy."

"I prefer *simple*," I said saucily.

He shrugged and picked up the phone. "Easy." He winked.

"I'd like to place an order," Logan said into the phone.

I liked what this was between us. It seemed with our secrets confessed everything was lighter, easier, and dare I say fun.

His harsh tone drew my attention. He was still on the phone. "I'll take care of it tomorrow, I said, for now, just deliver my order. I'll pay with cash." Logan's voice was gruff and laced with anger as he slammed the phone down.

"What's the matter?" I asked him.

He stalked toward the bedroom. "Nothing. I'm going to take a shower before the food arrives."

Whoa.

Mood change much?

"Logan," I said, my voice harsh.

He stopped.

"What we just talked about—the figuring out what we are, you talking to me is part of it."

Even before I finished speaking, he had turned around. He drew in a breath. "I'm sorry. You're right. My grandfather wants me back in New York and to get me there, he's frozen my accounts. The front desk told me my company credit card was declined earlier today, and now they won't allow me to charge to my account."

Not expecting anything like that, I offered, "I have some money if you need it."

His laugh was dry. "I'll take care of it. I might have to move to my pop's until I can talk to my grandfather, but trust me, I've got enough not to worry about paying this bill."

Logan was out of the room before I could respond.

Why is it everything in life comes with a price? I thought.

Logan didn't need me to point out which one was Lizzy.

Her red hair gave her away.

While we were eating, he had filled me in about what the day had brought. Like him, I was certain the woman Declan had mentioned had to be my sister. I just wished I knew more.

"It was the only picture I could find," I told him. I was on my phone searching for other photos of my sister on Michael's Facebook page—Lizzy didn't seem to have one—and as far back as I went, I still found only that one picture of her in some group shot with a bunch of people. I had no idea who they were. I found it really odd and it was bothering me.

"The one you sent me was fine—don't worry about finding another. If Declan finds anything out, he can just point to her in the group photo."

I didn't like it. I wanted a picture of just her. I zoomed in on her face and cropped the picture and then texted it to Logan. "There. Just her."

It made me feel better to be reassured Declan would be able to show Lizzy's picture. It made her more identifiable.

Satisfied, I swallowed one last bite of deliciousness before I pushed my plate away and watched Logan across the table.

"What?" he asked, catching my gaze.

"So help me out—you did or you did not grow up with a silver spoon in your mouth?"

His laugh sounded anything but genuine. "Hell, no. I did not. The Ryan name has so many strings attached to it. Even my mother avoided it for as long as she could."

"What do you mean?"

"My old man says she was different when they were younger. She didn't care about what her father thought or the money or the differences in lifestyle."

"What changed her?"

"Life, I guess. Growing up. Marriage. Having to pick what mattered more. Who knows? Don't get me wrong: as a child I never wanted for anything, but between my gramps and my father, they made sure I understood money—and Ryan money in particular—wasn't all there was."

"I guess that means I can't call you Richie Rich?" I joked.

Logan rose and prowled over to me. He put a finger to my chin and lifted it. "You can call me anything you want—when you're naked."

My body jerked when his skin came into direct contact with mine and my heart leapt at the desire in his eyes.

We'd both come so far in such a short period of time—I didn't cringe or shut down when he talked to me in that sensual tone of his, and he was now able to look at me during sex. I didn't know what that meant; all I knew was that I wanted to find out.

My gaze swallowed him whole. He was wearing a pair of nylon track pants and a beat-up old T-shirt, and to me he looked just as yummy as he had in his suit.

I wanted to eat him up, and this time I planned to.

Goal clear in my head, I stood up.

Without thought, we automatically drew closer. His hands slid beneath my arms to rest at my waist and his fingers splayed around my slight curves. His cock pressed hard against my belly.

Heat that had nothing to do with the fire roaring beside us flamed within me.

"Take me to bed," I told him.

He didn't hesitate. In one fell swoop he scooped me off my feet and tossed me over his shoulder.

My laughter was loud as he strode across the room. "Not like that."

He was laughing too as he kicked the door shut behind him. "This was faster than carrying you any other way."

No doubt about that. I was already on the mattress and lying on my back.

He positioned himself on top of me, propped up on his arms.

I reached up and tangled my fingers in his hair. "But not very romantic," I whispered.

Lowering himself slightly, he just barely covered me with his body so he could kiss me on the mouth. "I'll work on that," he murmured, his voice sounding so damn sexy he could have said anything and I would have been fine with his answer.

It wasn't like I was really looking for romance—I was only kidding.

Moments passed, seconds, maybe minutes, I wasn't sure. I felt like I could have kissed him forever. My hands were running along his body. Searching. Exploring. My fingers traced the edges of his shoulder blades, felt the way his muscles flexed under my touch, cupped his ass.

In a way I didn't understand, we just fit together so well. He was hard where I was soft. Tough where I was weak. Straight where I was curved.

My hands still on his ass, I urged him to sink farther between my legs. He gasped out a curse and the sound didn't bother me in the least. If I thought about it, I rather liked it. His muttered curses told me just how much he liked what was happening between us. This was consensual. We both wanted to feel the pleasure that was only just starting to take root. The electricity that was sparking in small fissures and promised to turn into bolts.

When he obliged, I could feel his hard cock throbbing

even through the fabric of our clothing. Seeking more, my hips tilted upward, and that's when he practically tore my clothes off.

I attacked his clothing with the same energy.

We were both naked within minutes.

Skin to skin.

And his was smooth.

So smooth.

His body was beautiful. Maybe even perfect. If I could have spoken, I would have told him so. I tried a few times to say something as his mouth began to slide down my body, but I couldn't.

When he took my nipple between his lips, I gave up. I let myself go. He was what I needed. When we were like this, we were in a bubble, and all the troubles of the outside world faded away.

The thought struck and I couldn't push it aside. Was I a distraction for Logan? If I was, did it matter? Or maybe, just maybe, it was the reverse and he was a distraction for me. Again, it didn't really matter. We'd agreed to take the ride, but neither of us had agreed to stay on and neither had agreed to get off.

I should have told him the rest of my secrets, but I'd told him enough for now.

I inhaled sharply as a tingling radiated from my core.

Soft, velvety smooth strokes lapped around my clit.

Oh God, that mouth.

That tongue.

The feeling was so intense, my fists clenched the sheets and I moaned from the sheer pleasure that was slowly sweeping through my body.

Wanting to see him, I glanced down. The dark fringe of his lashes brushed his skin just before his eyes lifted to mine.

They were so dark in the light of this room, the rims of brown so much more noticeable. It was as if his eyes were dilated with passion. I'd never seen eyes like his, ever changing based on his mood. They were a dead giveaway to his feelings, a weakness I wondered if he even realized.

I let go of the fistful of sheets in my hands. We all had our weaknesses after all, and he was slowly becoming another one of mine. I slid my fingers into his hair to tangle them around his locks. His hair was the perfect length to thread my fingers through.

Lowering his head, he parted my legs and dove inside me with thrusts of his tongue that made me feel like he couldn't get deep enough.

The sound he made when my hands gripped his hair even tighter was almost primal. He slid a finger inside me, then another, and worked his tongue in conjunction with his fingers.

My body tensed as tiny flames of pleasure flickered from my core. My senses intensified.

His touch was hot.

His breathing sounded ragged.

And his lips were deliciously wet.

I started to pulsate everywhere.

Wait. I wanted to be the one doing this to him. That was my plan. How had he taken the lead? Remembering one of the positions from my computer screen earlier, I rose on my elbows. "Logan," I said, my voice hoarse, uncertain. "I want you in my mouth when I come."

Simple words to describe the act, but still they felt like they weighed a thousand pounds as they expelled from my mouth.

He looked up at me with the same uncertainty that had bled through in my words.

But I was certain. Telling him was the difficult part. I gave him a reassuring nod that let him know—yes, I wanted this.

Without hesitation, he shifted his body.

His warm breath was gone and I mourned the loss on my flesh, but soon enough his knees were at my ears. He took his cock in his hand and I gasped at the eroticism of it. I craned my neck up to catch it with my mouth, but he lifted higher.

"Just watch me."

"I want to taste you."

"No, I want you to come," he said. His voice was so hoarse I could tell he must have been fighting against his own release.

I stared up at him in awe as his fist closed around his cock and he started pumping it. I was fixated on the movement. Spellbound at the simple beauty of his cock as he glided his hand up and down it. But then his tongue was inside me again and from a different angle, it was so much more intense. Probing and searching for my pleasure was what I felt he was doing. And he was doing it so well. It felt so good and even though I wanted to, I couldn't hold on any longer. I had to let myself go. My head tipped and I arched my back as I started to ride the wave of my orgasm.

Logan didn't stop, though—he pumped his cock while he continued to lick, suck, and kiss all of me until another orgasm hit immediately after the first. This time, my toes curled as an exquisite sensation overcame me, rocking me unlike anything I'd ever felt before. And in that single moment of ecstasy, my body trembled as it came alive under his touch and I cried out louder than I ever had with what could only be described as pure, undiluted pleasure.

Logan had let go of his cock to use both of his hands and I took the opportunity to reach up with the tip of my tongue and lick him.

"Oh, fuck." The sound roared through the room.

In a roll that I'm not sure if he initiated or I did, I was on top looking down at him.

He grabbed my hips and tried to pull me toward his mouth.

That wasn't what I had in mind.

My head fell and I started slow, swirling my tongue around his tip before sucking on it. At the taste, I realized how hungry I was for him. I licked every inch of him.

When I sealed my mouth over him, he groaned and bucked up. Sure, I'd done this before, but never in this position. Always the guy's hands were on my head to guide me.

I didn't need that with Logan.

His body's response was enough to guide me.

Each time I moved, I took him as deep as I could and each time he hit the back of my throat, he groaned. My mouth sucked, my fingers stroked, and my lips moved in all the ways I could tell he liked.

"Oh fuck. Just like that. Just like that," he muttered and it didn't scare me, it thrilled me to hear the pleasure in his voice. His muscles started to shake when my tongue revisited his tip. As I traced a path around the moistness already beaded there, he shuddered and tugged on my hips, quickly rearranging my body and pulling me up to him.

He was back on top of me, his eyes searching mine.

I was okay. I swallowed, my throat tight, my heart still beating madly. He was silently telling me that he wanted to be inside me. I could see it in his eyes.

I wanted that too.

Logan didn't say anything, though. He just reached between us and brought the tip of his cock to my entrance. We wanted each other so much. We were insatiable, and each time seemed to be better than the last.

Oh, God.

My fingers curled around his biceps and as he slid farther inside me, the blunt tips of my nails dug into his skin.

He thrust into me without resistance.

I looked at him as he looked at me, and he slammed inside me so hard, I cried out in ecstasy.

We fucked like that more than once in the next few hours. I had a fleeting thought that he was marking me, claiming me, making me his. This was something new. No one had ever wanted me like he did. The intensity of the gestures themselves gave me butterflies. And I knew they were butterflies.

With that thought in mind, I was equal parts scared and

thrilled.

I was scared because I knew things were happening too fast. Too much was going on in our lives for us to get wrapped up in each other. Yet, at the same time, I was thrilled because I had never felt so worshipped.

It had to be close to midnight before we were lying on the bed facing each other.

"You okay?" he asked with a grin.

I swear I blushed. "I think you know I am."

I'd cried out in pleasure so many times, there was no way he didn't know how sated I felt right now.

"You've only ever had one boyfriend?" he asked.

The question caught me off guard but didn't throw me. "Yes. Just the one. Charlie."

His body stiffened and I wondered if he was jealous. He had no reason to be.

"Charlie and I were best friends. We talked about everything. Liked the same things. Did everything together. But sex wasn't what our relationship was about. It was a passing act and that's why, at the time, I thought he was perfect for me."

Logan seemed to be thinking.

"And you, how many girlfriends have you had?"

Still lost in his thoughts, he mindlessly answered, "Just the two. But I'm not sure you could call them that. I never put a label on either relationship. I preferred not to."

Interesting. Relationships were never his thing either.

I ran my finger up the scar that marred the inside of his thigh and then over the one under his eye. "These are from him. Both of them, aren't they?"

He nodded.

Neither scar stole away from the beauty I saw in Logan, but I knew they must have been constant reminders to him. My fingers found his and I squeezed them tightly. "Logan, nothing is going to happen to me."

He drew in a sharp breath as if he wasn't so certain.

"Why can't the police take care of Tommy? You could

go to them and tell them what happened to you years ago. Couldn't they use that for Peyton's case and maybe arrest him?"

He bristled. "It doesn't work like that. Not in our world. There is too much corruption in the BPD, and too many bad guys on the streets. Too often, innocent people end up getting hurt."

It was all a little surreal.

Logan's real world was like a TV drama.

The thought saddened me. I kissed the scar under his eye. It was a part of him. Who he was. And no matter the healing, the scar left behind, the depth of the wound was deep. I knew that now.

It was late when his phone rang. Without hesitation he reached for it. "Yeah," he answered.

Silence.

"I'll leave now."

Logan tossed his phone aside and kissed me sweetly. "I have to go out for a bit."

I grabbed for his wrist before he was fully out of bed. "Who was that?"

Opening a drawer, he pulled out a pair of jeans and answered while slipping them on. "Declan. He has a possible lead on your sister."

I hopped out of bed and started to dress too.

Logan eyed me carefully as he pulled a long-sleeved shirt over his head. "What are you doing?"

Fastening my bra, I told him, "Getting dressed."

Sitting on the bed, he shoved on a pair of Converse sneakers that had seen better days and asked, "Why?"

"I'm coming with you."

Tying his second sneaker, he stood up.

I had my white shirt on now and was looking for my panties.

"Elle." He was right in front of me, crouching down to meet my eyes. "No, you're not."

"She's my sister." My voice pulsed with anger.

"And I'll tell you what I find out as soon as I know anything. This is a fishing expedition. I have no idea if the girl Tommy was seen with was even your sister. And I have no idea who is hanging around waiting for her. I don't want anyone to suspect you are even looking for her. As far as the world knows, you believe she's in rehab. Leave it that way."

Not that he didn't have a point, because he did. I just didn't like it. "You'll call me as soon as you know anything."

He kissed me in that sweet way he had a few times now. "Yes," he whispered, and then he tugged me toward him by the front seam of my shirt. "And keep this on. You look sexy as hell in it."

My blood ran warm like a shot of tequila going down after the third one.

Opening a drawer, he pulled some money out, then grabbed his phone and started for the doorway. I followed him into the suite and watched as he checked his gun before tucking it behind him.

Logan looked at me one last time and then he was out the door.

I glanced around at the vanilla-colored walls and heard a pelting of sorts. When I turned my head toward the massive bank of windows, I noticed the doors were still open and I could see hail as it hit the terrace. My sister always said when it hailed that God was shooting bullets from the sky.

I hoped that wasn't a sign.

chapter
THIRTY

Day 5

LOGAN

THE LEGEND OF KILLIAN "the Killer" McPherson was like a shadow over me.

Mostly it was dark and looming, but sometimes it was a blessing in disguise.

Everywhere I went, if people knew me, they moved out of my way. If I asked a question, they answered. If I needed something, they gave it to me.

Tonight wouldn't be any different.

I was certain of that.

Still, there was a taut awareness in every muscle of my body. I felt confident. Ready to do what I had to in order to find out what the fuck was going on.

Declan was sitting in the lobby of the Seaport Hotel. He couldn't look more out of place in the regal yet stuffy hotel that screamed aristocratic affiliations. Not that I looked like I fit in much more tonight.

"What's going on?" I asked him, slipping into the plush beige club chair beside him.

He wiped his hands on his worn jeans. "Miles Murphy, my buddy who works security, said he's seen someone matching Tommy's description coming in and out of here with a redhead as little as three or four days ago."

My brows rose in confusion. "Days or months?" I asked in clarification.

Declan's silver hoop earrings glinted off the light of the chandeliers that flanked the room.

It made me a little jumpy.

"Days."

Something keen to excitement whirled in my gut. "Does he know what he's been doing here?"

Declan shrugged. "I asked if he saw anything suspicious, but he said no. He's pulling security tapes for me to look at."

I was impressed. "When will he have them?"

"His supervisor goes on break at one thirty. He said he'll slip me into the security office then to take a look."

I glanced at my watch. In sixty minutes I might finally get some answers.

Declan shifted in his chair. "So, I saw Peyton."

"How was she?"

"She said she's fine. She told me what happened, and there's no doubt it was Tommy."

I nodded in agreement. I didn't have to ask him if he'd kept his mouth shut. I knew he had.

"She told me you'd walked her from the boutique to the coffee shop and back. Someone must have spotted you with her and then watched her."

An unease was in the air. Or maybe it was my guilt. "Yeah, I know."

Tension lined his face. "The flowers that you sent were nice."

I nodded. I owed her so much more.

"You know, that night was the night I decided to get out."

My skin prickled at the mention.

"What they did to that girl you were with, it made no sense."

Something attacked me. Guilt. So fierce and raw and

hard that I couldn't breathe. I clutched at the fabric under my fingertips and couldn't contain my snarl. "No, it didn't."

He didn't say anything else. He didn't have to. I saw what he was thinking in his eyes. He wanted to ask me why the fuck I would be seen on a popular Boston street with a girl after that night.

I'd been asking myself the same question, and stupidity was still my only answer. My head was so far up my ass worrying about Elle, no one else was on my radar. I couldn't justify my mistake.

Time passed so fucking slow. For the rest of the time we sat in silence. Declan kept his eyes down, while mine scanned the area for any signs of Tommy or a drug trade operation. I saw neither.

"Hey, man, you ready?"

I jerked my head practically all the way around to find a guy in black security duds, built like a tank, rubbing his hands. He was definitely ex-military. From his haircut, to the frown on his face, to the type of boots on his feet.

Declan and I stood at the same time. "Yeah, let's do this."

The security guard's eyes shifted to me and his nervousness was more than apparent. I was surprised, given his size, but maybe his worry was more about his job than me. "You didn't tell me you were bringing someone along."

Yes, definitely his job.

Declan cleared his throat. "Yeah, right. This is Logan McPherson. He's the one looking for the dude I described."

Implication—he's Killer's grandson.

I could tell the security guard was uneasy and I had two ways to go with this—intimidate the shit out of him or ease his fears. I wasn't sure I could do the former and I preferred not to anyway.

It was late and the lobby was empty of visitors. I leaned over. "Show me what you got and there's a grand in it for you."

His shoulders straightened. "Follow me."

We walked down a corridor, through a door marked employees only, and then down a flight of stairs. For a nice hotel, the offices were a shit hole.

Miles unlocked a door at the end of the hall and led us into an eight-by-eight room. There were a few monitors, a couple of computers, and large stacks of papers covering every inch of desk space.

"Over here," he said. He sat in a rickety brown leather chair in the corner that creaked and punched a few buttons on the keypad in front of him. "Here—this is the footage from the last time I remember seeing him."

On the screen, a black-and-white image just outside the entrance to the hotel presented itself. The date/time stamp informed me that this clip was taped this past Saturday at three ten A.M. My skin went a little clammy when I saw the prick. Tommy was the renegade supplier Patrick was looking for? Could it be? His limp was the first dead giveaway, followed by his short stature. Born with some disease that stunted his growth, he was always trying to make up for his physical impairments with his fists. Sure, he was tough, but that's not what kept him alive. Everyone was afraid of what would happen if they dared touch him.

A few had over the years and it wasn't them that suffered, it was their families—their sisters were raped, their fathers beaten, their mothers both.

I still didn't know if it was Patrick or Tommy commissioning the warnings surrounding Elle, but I knew better than to attack Tommy in a physical way. I wasn't afraid of what he'd do to me, but I feared what he'd do those around me. Especially Elle, if he found out about us.

Refocusing on the screen, I bit back the bile rushing up my throat. He hadn't changed—dark hair bleached blond with roots the color of midnight, black bushy eyebrows, and beady eyes.

He was standing casually in the arrival area with a leg propped up against the limestone wall and a cigarette between his lips.

A cab pulled up and he dropped his cigarette and toed it out. A smile came across his lips as he started walking. A woman got out of the cab and he approached her. She was dressed in black, all black, but the red hair told me who she probably was.

Lizzy.

The angle of the camera only allowed me to see the back of her, though, so I couldn't be certain. Tommy paid the cab driver and it was then that I noticed she had nothing on her—not a coat, not a purse—but she was holding something in her hand.

My mind rewound to the first night I met Elle. The perp in the bushes dressed in black with what I thought was a gun in his hand. Elle thought that the he was a she. Was she right?

"Can you pause it and zoom in on her hand?" I asked.

"Yeah, sure," he said.

The image was blurry at best, but the metal clip and rectangular shape peeking through her fingers looked an awful lot like a garage door opener.

Everything started to make sense. That night it wasn't Tommy or Patrick after Elle, it was her sister. And more than likely it was her sister in O'Shea's house the following night. My mind seemed so much freer knowing Elle wasn't on Tommy's radar.

On the screen, the two walked into the hotel, and the image kept playing with little activity at that late hour.

"Okay, what else do you have?"

"I have some cuts from them entering the lobby, but that's all I had time to find. I've seen him here quite a bit over the past months, but not her. It will take longer than a few hours for me to locate any more footage."

"Show me the lobby."

He hit a few keys and clicked his mouse. "This is a short clip."

A different angle, a new camera. Tommy and the girl walking into the lobby and over to the desk. That's all there was. A short view, five seconds at most. "Can you zoom in on her face?"

He rewound the footage and stopped when they first walked in. The image was clear. He was good. He zoomed in and I pulled my phone out and brought up the picture Elle sent me. I compared the two. It was her. No doubt about it.

"Do you know what room they're staying in?"

"I asked the girl that worked reception that night. Since it was so late, it was easy for her to pull up the records of the encounter at the desk. Turns out he was checking out."

Fuck!

"There's a clip of them leaving and another of them getting into a cab. It shows nothing different from the other two. I can show you, but not now. I have to get you two out of here."

I nodded in understanding. I didn't want him to lose his job. "Thanks, man—that's what I needed." I pulled out my wallet and peeled off twenty one-hundred-dollar bills. Luckily, I had withdrawn ten thousand dollars before my grandfather sealed my access to my trust fund.

Miles was watching me with a cold sweat breaking across his forehead.

I handed it to him.

"That's more than you promised."

I picked up a pen and tore off a corner of one of the papers littered on the desk. I wrote my number down and my email. "The extra is for a phone call the minute you see either of them again. And if you don't mind, email me whatever clips you can find."

"Yeah, sure. Now, I need to get you guys out of here."

We exited the same way we'd entered. He left us to walk down the corridor and into the lobby on our own. Exiting the hotel doors, I handed the valet my ticket.

Declan did the same.

The air was cold and the rain was coming down in sheets. I leaned back against the wall to wait.

"I want to help you with whatever you're doing," Declan said.

Exhausted, I turned to look at him. "You have and thanks. I can take it from here."

He stepped closer. "Tell me what's going on."

I considered it for a moment. "I can't do that."

"I'm not afraid of him and I want to make sure what happened to Peyton doesn't happen again—to her or to anyone else."

It's not that I didn't understand where he was coming from, because I did. I just didn't think it was the best idea to involve anyone else. "Watch over Peyton and I'll call you if I need anything else."

"I can help you. You know I can."

The valet pulled up with my car. "I'll call you after I get the videos."

He nodded.

I slipped behind the wheel and took off. In the dark of the night, all I could see was Tommy's face in my mind. I could hear his voice, "Watch this, McPherson."

The level of fury building within me wasn't going to help anything. I needed to stay focused, and waking the angry demon that lived inside me wasn't going to help the situation.

I dug my fingers into the steering wheel as I sped back to the hotel. I knew what I had to do. Elle needed to go back to her life—without me. I closed my eyes, hating myself for the things I'd done that had put me where I was today.

But until I could take care of Tommy, she wasn't safe with me. She might not be 100 percent safe with O'Shea, but I knew she was a hell of a lot safer with him than me.

Something felt off as I drove.

Was someone tailing me?

I took a swift turn and then another.

Looked again.

No one.

What the fuck was up with my imagination?

I had to cool it.

Concentrate.

Focus.

The lobby of the hotel was empty and I strode up to the desk, paid my bill with the cash in my pocket, and told them I'd be checking out in the morning.

When I opened the door to my suite, a chill ran through me. The terrace door was open, the curtains flapping against the wall. It was eerily quiet, and panic like I'd never experienced struck all at once.

My heart sped, my pulse raced, and a cold sweat broke out covering my forehead. "Elle!" I shouted.

No answer.

An image of Elle lying naked on the floor with an *E* carved into her stomach came unbidden. I ran to the bedroom. She wasn't in bed. My gut twisted into a knot. I drew my gun and approached the slightly ajar bathroom door.

The light was warm and Elle was standing in her white shirt, just about to turn the shower on.

She was fine.

I had to say it more than once to convince myself.

Paranoia was a dangerous thing.

She was a dangerous thing.

She'd gotten under my skin, worked her way into my veins, and was now somehow making her way to my cold heart.

"Logan." She jumped. "You scared me."

Setting my gun on the counter, I inhaled a deep breath and rushed toward her.

She'd scared me too.

"Why are the doors open?"

She shrugged. "It was really warm in here and I wanted some air."

Without a word, I backed her up to the counter and took her in my arms. I held her for the longest time before I pulled away. With trembling fingers, I unbuttoned her shirt and stripped it off her body. She was naked before me and so beautiful. As my eyes shifted, I could see myself in the cracked mirror over her shoulder.

I closed my eyes, unable to look. I didn't want that constant reminder that burdened my skin to be anywhere in my thoughts.

"Hey, are you okay?" she asked.

My mouth was greedy on her neck. That sweet spot I knew she liked me to kiss was the first place I attacked. My hands roamed her body, never lingering, just needing to feel her everywhere.

Her head was thrown back and her words came out low. "Logan, did you find out anything about my sister?"

Breaking contact with her was a struggle, but I managed to lean back. "I did, but right now, I need you." I couldn't hold my words back. I hoped she understood.

She looked at me, and then as if she knew just how desperate I was for her, she started to unzip my pants. We moved together with the rhythm we had created and together we stripped my clothes off.

I was about to set her free, but I couldn't suppress this need inside me to put my mouth all over her—to lick every part of her, to claim her, to mark her, to make her mine.

A noise escaped that beautiful throat of hers, something hoarse and raw, something akin to the way I was feeling—primitive.

My desire to fuck her was so fierce, I wasn't sure my legs could hold us. Something was bursting inside my chest. Whatever it was, it was bold and unrelenting.

We were kissing and kissing and before I knew it, I had her up on the counter and her legs were wrapped around me. My cock was right where it needed to be. All I had to do was slide it inside her.

She swiveled her hips in a way that said, *Fuck me, fuck me hard, and fuck me now.*

I kept kissing her. Her mouth, her chin, her jaw, her throat.

My name slipped out of her lips in a sigh. "Logan."

With my hands on each side of her face, I blinked a few times until she came into focus. When she was all I could see, what came out of my mouth was a surprise even to myself. "I want," I said slowly, "to make love . . . to you . . . on the bed."

The words were dry coming out of my throat and I had to swallow a few times before I could finish the sentence.

I wanted to say so much more, but for now, I settled for that.

She found my mouth again for one more kiss. "I'd like that too," she said, a little breathless.

My arms were under her back and behind her knees. I was carrying her into the bedroom, in a gallant way, taking my time, looking down at her with each step. Her eyes met mine and I wondered if she was feeling anything close to what I was.

The look on her face when I lowered her down onto the great, big bed with the clean white sheets told me she did, and her actions reaffirmed it. She brushed the hair from my forehead and drew a line down my scar. Her touch was soft and gentle and as she pulled her fingers away, she lifted herself to kiss me there, right there, the spot that reminded me what I'd done every time I looked in the mirror.

However, when she looked at me, she didn't see the monster I saw. Her eyes told me she saw something different, and it felt like another layer of the ice around my heart had melted.

"Make love to me," she whispered.

I did.

We stayed in the missionary position with my body covering hers. I shivered a little with my first thrust and she did too.

I took my time. I didn't rush things. I wanted what remained of the night to last forever. We moved together, slowly, making love over and over, until daylight flooded the room.

"Elle," I murmured when I rolled off her.

She turned to her side to face me. She was beautiful in the morning light. I wanted to tell her what I saw when I looked at her. That even though we barely knew each other, I felt something for her I couldn't explain. How she somehow lit me up from within. How the sound of her breathing was something I looked forward to hearing. And how her scent was one I couldn't live without. But that wasn't what I told her. Instead, I told her what I'd learned that night. That it was her sister the other night. That I thought it was her sister in O'Shea's house, too. That if Lizzy was still close, so was Tommy. We talked about what her sister could have been after, but she didn't have a clue. And finally, I told her that for her and Clementine's sake, we needed to stay away from each other.

Gently, she stroked my hair and kissed my mouth. And then she killed me. "I know," she said in a strained voice.

But neither of us spoke of when or how we'd do that.

In the early morning light, I pulled her close and stroked her back, softly lulling her to sleep.

When her breathing was even, I eased out of bed, tucked a few things in a duffle bag, and slipped out the door.

In the elevator, I brought up Declan's number.

"Hello," he answered.

"Hey man, I was wondering if you could do me a favor?"

"Yeah, sure."

"Elle is in my suite at the Four Seasons. Can you head over there and take her to the boutique? Tell her to stay at O'Shea's house and call me if she needs me." Although I hated the idea, I knew his house was like Fort Knox and she'd be safer there than at her place.

"Yeah, no problem. Charlene is here and can cover for me."

"Don't forget to make sure she knows who you are."

"I'm not completely stupid."

The elevator door opened. "Yeah, right. Sorry, man. I'll leave the key at the desk in your name."

"Okay, I'll head over now."

"And Declan, I'll be at my father's. Stop by tonight. If you're still willing, I could use your help."

"Sure, man. I'll be there."

"Grab Miles, too, if you don't mind. I want both of you to connect with my old man."

"Yeah, sure, no problem."

A quick stop at the desk to leave the key and tell them I'd be back for my things and then I was walking out the door.

A sudden sadness hit me.

And I couldn't help but hope I wasn't walking out of Elle's life too.

chapter
THIRTY-ONE

DAY 6

Elle

I WASN'T DOING WELL.

It had been almost two days since I'd seen Logan.

Aside from a couple of text messages, we hadn't been in contact. One message asked me if Michael had mentioned anything about Friday. My response was what it always was: no. And the other came just before I left work. It was informative only. He still hadn't found my sister.

I wanted to hear his voice, to talk to him, to tell him the things I was feeling. But he had left me alone yesterday morning without so much as a note or a goodbye, and although I knew it was the best way for us to part, it still stung.

My fantasies that the truths I had yet to tell him would be accepted were just that, fantasies. And the space he had put between us helped to put that in perspective.

Using my key, I let myself into Michael's house. I had decided to take Logan's advice and stay at Michael's for a few days to be closer to Clementine. I wasn't certain what could happen with Michael or Logan and wanted to be near her.

It was after nine and I knew Clementine would be

asleep. With Peyton recovering and Rachel working only part-time, I was working from opening to close. I set my keys on the foyer table next to the fresh vase of flowers. Michael must have gone to see his father again today at the florist's shop. He'd gone almost every day this week and I wondered if his father was ill.

Next to the flowers was a picture of Michael's deceased mother. She was beautiful, posed like an old-time actress in the photo, wearing a strapless sundress and sitting on picnic table with her legs crossed in her high heels. There were pictures of her throughout the house. Oddly, there were no pictures of him and Lizzy together in the house, though.

"You're home late." Michael, his rumpled suit, was sitting in a chair in the family room. He had a thick stack of papers in one hand and a glass of amber-colored liquid in the other. There was a yellow legal pad on the table beside him with notes or one of his lists written on it. Soft music played and the lamp beside him shined down only to give enough light for him to see whatever it was he was reading.

We exchanged glances. I hadn't told him anything about Logan and I. I just knew he wouldn't be happy about it and I couldn't jeopardize my relationship with Clementine.

"What are those?" I asked for lack of anything else to say.

"Résumés for a new nanny."

"Why? What happened to Sarah?" I asked, shocked at this news.

He swirled his drink in his hand. "She gave me her notice today. She'll stay until I find a replacement, at least."

The news made me wonder—first his secretary, now the nanny. Was there something I didn't know?

"Maybe Lizzy will come home before then." I didn't know why I said it. I shouldn't have. Logan had told me not to say anything. I knew Logan suspected foul play on Michael's part, but he didn't know Michael like I did. Still, even though I trusted him, something inside me told me to keep my mouth shut, so I did.

He sipped his drink and looked at me with suspicion. "Have you heard from Elizabeth?"

I shook my head. "No, it's just I'm sure she misses Clementine."

Michael set the stack of résumés on the table beside him and stood with his glass in hand. He strode over to the bar and picked up the crystal decanter. "Can I pour you one?"

"No, thank you. It's been a long day. I'm going to change and make something to eat and then go to bed."

With his glass full, he turned around. "I picked you up that shaved garden salad you like and a lobster roll with fries. They're in the fridge."

"B&G's," I said with a smile.

He nodded. "I knew you'd be tired and that you probably wouldn't have eaten."

"Thanks, that was really nice of you," I told him and headed upstairs.

Clementine was fast asleep and safe in her room. I stared at her for the longest time. She was an innocent caught up in a mess, but I wasn't going to let anything happen to her, nor was I going to let anything impact her blissful state. She was too precious. I swiped at my tears and kissed her softly. "I love you so much," I whispered.

In my room, I slipped out of my clothes and into a pair of comfortable sweatpants. When I slipped on the white, oversized button-down that smelled of Logan, I held it to my nose. His scent was fading but it was still there. I wanted to see him. To talk to him. To be with him.

I shook off the feeling.

Pulling my hair on top of my head, I made myself think of other things. I needed to head back to my place tomorrow to get some clean clothes. I needed to do inventory. I needed to review sales.

Socks on my feet, I went downstairs. The family room was empty. Maybe Michael went to bed. My stomach was growling and I headed for the kitchen. I poured a glass of orange juice and sucked it down before I poured another.

Then I opened the containers. I didn't even bother to sit down. Instead, I stood at the counter and nibbled on the lobster roll in between forkfuls of salad.

Ummm, Boston's seafood was so delicious.

"Is it good?" Unexpectedly, Michael was behind me and even more unexpectedly, his chin was almost resting on my shoulder as he looked down at my food.

Every part of me tensed and I quickly turned around. "Yes, I was starving. Do you want some?"

Out of character, he moved closer, caging me in. With the smell of alcohol on his breath, he said, "Are you offering?"

My heart was thumping, and not in the way it did when Logan was near me. I wasn't afraid of Michael. I knew I could take him down with a swift knee to the balls. I didn't want to have to do that. In the confined space he'd cornered me in, I casually reached back and picked up one of the containers. "Yes, here you go. I'm stuffed."

He stepped back and took the food.

We both knew that wasn't what he meant, but at least he pretended it was.

"I'm exhausted. I think I'll check on Clementine and go to bed."

"If you don't mind, I need to discuss something with you."

Anxiety tightened in my chest, but somehow I managed a smile. "Sure, what is it?"

"There are a few things, actually. Mind if we go in the other room and sit down?"

Panicked, I blurted out, "Is this about Lizzy?"

His expression went blank for a moment. "No, not directly. Are you sure you haven't seen her or heard from her?"

I straightened my shoulders, drew in a breath, and forced myself to give him a slight smile. "No, I haven't."

With a bob of his head, we were both walking toward the family room. He stopped at the bar and poured himself another scotch. "You sure you won't have just one?"

Sitting down, I found myself feeling awkward. "No, I'm good."

His liquor glass was more than halfway filled without ice and I began to wonder how much he'd had to drink tonight. Michael turned and leaned against the bar. "There's a very likely possibility Elizabeth won't ever return."

"You don't know that."

He sipped on his drink and studied me. I felt like he knew I knew something. "No, I don't, but I have Clementine to worry about. I need to start thinking about my will. Who will take care of her if something happens to me?"

I looked at him, feeling pricks of tears in my eyes. "Michael, what's changed? I don't understand why we're talking about this now."

Michael's gaze remained steady. "I think I made a mistake not going to the police. I thought I could find her and keep her out of prison for what she'd done. But now I've exhausted all of my available avenues and we still haven't been able to find her. The private investigator has found nothing, her cell has no activity, and her bank accounts haven't been touched. She's gone, Elle. Gone."

Knowing I couldn't blurt out, "No, she's not. She was seen last Saturday," I bit my tongue instead and whispered, "She still might show up."

He shook his head and the liquor swirled in his glass. "I can't wait any longer. I'm going to go to the police on Monday and report her missing. I should have done it a long time ago. I can't keep shielding her from her own destructive behaviors. It's time I start worrying about my daughter and myself, and that means legally divorcing her so I can appoint someone as Clementine's guardian."

Whoa.

My shock must have shown. He'd never talked about my sister like this. Like someone he didn't even like. Like someone he didn't have any compassion for. I was finding it hard to take in.

"Elle, I think that person should be—" He paused to

look at me. "Erin."

What?

Hurt, I had nothing to say. He knew how much I love that little girl. How much I think of her as my own. Why would he want her to live with his sister, who already has four children and her hands full?

"Of course I'll make provisions to make certain you have visitation, should something happen to me."

My patience wearing thin, I fired, "Why are you telling me this? Shouldn't you be discussing it with your sister?"

His voice as calm as an unruffled breeze, he answered, "I thought you might disagree."

Blinking at him, I couldn't help but wonder if he was somehow looking to blackmail me in some way. I hoped it was the liquor he was consuming that was sending the wrong vibe my way. Rising to my feet, I strode closer to him. "If you're asking me if I want to be named Clementine's guardian, you already know I do."

There was a darkness in his eyes I'd never seen. "That's what I thought, Elle. Now, there's something I need your help with."

Even though we were alone in the house, he turned the music up, and whispered.

I listened, nodded, and after much thought, hesitantly said, "I'll think about it and let you know tomorrow."

With his simple request on the table, he set his glass down and headed for the stairs. When he was halfway, he turned and said, "Good night, Elle."

Pulse racing, once I knew he was in his room I scurried up the stairs and into the room I'd been staying in. I'd slept here many nights, but for the first time since I'd arrived in Boston more than three months ago, I locked my door.

After brushing my teeth and washing my face, I got into bed and held my phone close. When I couldn't take it anymore, I called Logan. I had to talk to him.

It only rang once. "Elle, everything okay?"

I sunk further down onto my pillow. "I needed to hear

your voice."

There was a lot of noise in the background. He was out somewhere. "Are you sure you're okay? You don't sound right. Did something happen?"

In a whisper, I told him, "I need to tell you something."

"Elle, I can't hear you," Logan said.

I opened my mouth to speak again.

"Sorry I'm late." It was a female voice I didn't recognize.

"Hey, can I call you back?" Logan asked clearly into the phone. Clearly to me.

Crushed, I answered with barely audible words. "No, you don't have to."

"Elle." He said my name as if it pained him.

"I shouldn't have called," I said louder and hung up.

I remembered wondering that first night at Molly's if he had a girlfriend, or a girl, or someone in his life. Was that the voice I'd just heard?

Deep.

Husky.

Sexy.

Was that the real reason he'd left me alone in his hotel room?

Tears were streaming down my face.

I felt like I'd been stabbed in the chest, right through my heart.

But really, what had I expected? That he'd tell me he loved me after knowing me for only five days?

I covered my face with my hands and relived the day my mother died, the day my kidney failed her, the day I was declared unable to ever give life, the day my father declared me useless.

Somehow, amidst my sorrow, I fell asleep.

Clementine was the only joy I had in my life now. I wouldn't lose her.

Sometime later during the night I heard my phone ring.

I didn't answer.

He left a message that if I needed anything, I should

contact Declan at Mulligan's Cup or Frank at Molly's.

Obviously, that was his way of telling me to leave him alone.

Wish granted.

chapter

THIRTY-TWO

Day 7

LOGAN

I KNOTTED MY TIE and looked in the mirror.

In my black Dolce & Gabbana suit, the Martini stretch wool one that my grandfather insisted I buy five of, a crisp white shirt, and a red tie, I was the epitome of high-society class.

Just the way my grandfather liked.

Although he preferred everyone who worked for him to wear gray, it was never my nature to truly conform, and if I did that today he'd know something was up.

I had, however, gotten a haircut and given myself a close shave.

He liked the clean-cut look.

A test smile showed that I'd brushed my teeth properly. They were white and gleaming.

I looked good enough.

Good enough to charm Grandpa Ryan, I hoped.

All he would see tonight was Logan Killian Ryan McPherson—the golden boy he had high hopes for. The man he hoped to groom to take over his empire.

That was never going to happen.

Under the appearance I wore so well, I wasn't the man

he wanted me to be. I'd never be that man. I had too much of Killian, the Killer, McPherson in my blood. And I'd never felt more like him than today. I had fire in my belly and steel in my spine.

I was determined.

Tomorrow was Friday, and I had yet to figure out why Michael wasn't shitting his pants by now. A call placed to him from my father earlier today only confirmed that he was planning on delivering.

What—he didn't say.

And we had no idea.

The information we'd gathered on Tommy had led us nowhere so far. I needed a backup plan. The details of how I was going to get the money to Michael were sketchy, but I'd work that out tomorrow once I had the funds secured. No matter what Patrick wanted, I knew if what Michael had wasn't enough, offering more money would at least buy time.

Not much, but it was still time.

Disappearing with Elle was my only other option, and I knew she'd never go for it. So this had to work. Either way, it had to.

Declan had been able to track down a lead on at least one drug deal that went down at the hotel. He found the buyer, but getting him to talk, getting the details, was a different story. He was working on it.

With nothing else to go on, I had to visit my maternal grandfather in New York City. Tell him everything he wanted to hear so that he'd release his hold on my trust fund. Loosen the strings attached to it. I'd have to deliver on my promises, of course. But it didn't matter. Selling my soul to him to get the money would give Elle the reprieve I needed to bring Patrick and Tommy down.

It would be worth it.

My grandfather would never see the blood in my eyes or the hatred in my veins. He was oblivious to anything but conformation. And besides, he thought it was for my own good for me to be like him.

How could he not see that I never would be?

What he also failed to see was that what he was doing to me was just as binding as my ties to the Blue Hill Gang.

Sighing, I buttoned my designer suit jacket.

Trust fund baby.

Blue blood.

Silver spoon

Heir to a fortune.

I was more than that but today, I would pretend I wasn't.

Shoes on.

Watch on.

One last look and I was good to go.

Game time.

On a mission, I hopped in my SUV.

I-90 was a bitch.

I waited as long as I could to leave, but I needed turn-around time. It didn't seem to matter if it was seven A.M. or seven P.M., as was the case, because the pavement was always jam-packed.

Exhaustion had crept into my bones and it wasn't going anywhere, so another night of only a few hours' sleep didn't really matter.

It took over an hour to reach the I-84 exit.

Just as I was about to take the ramp, my cell rang. My dash lit up with a number I didn't want to see. "Yeah," I answered.

"We have a lead," Agent Meg Blanchet said.

"What kind of lead?" I asked, extremely curious.

"We got that warrant to tap O'Shea's office landlines early this morning. He got a call a few hours ago from a female, we're guessing his wife, telling him his delivery had arrived."

Like a crazy man, I swerved all the way into the right lane and zoomed off the interstate to turn around. "What were his instructions?"

The woman I knew as the she-devil cleared her throat.

"He didn't. He hung up without a word, like he knew his phone lines were being monitored."

"Odd."

"Yes, I agree. I think he switched to his cell and we don't have the go-ahead to monitor that yet. Do you think you can contact his wife's sister and see if she knows anything about this supposed delivery? We have a unit outside his house, and either O'Shea has slipped out of the house without us knowing or he went to bed and he's not planning on going anywhere. The place is dark and we can't see any movement inside."

"He's got a young kid—he wouldn't leave her alone. Did you notice if Lizzy's sister was with him?" I hated referring to Elle in that way, but the less the devil herself, Agent Meg Blanchet of the Drug Enforcement Administration, knew about what had transpired between Elle and me, the better.

Her laugh was abrupt, cold even. "He dropped the kid off at his sister's earlier. But Logan, I would have thought you'd know the answer to the whereabouts of *Lizzy's sister* before me." She stressed Lizzy's sister.

That's when I knew I was fucked.

"I know you're having a relationship with the missing woman's sister. I'm not stupid. I just hope you're not."

With everything in me I wanted to tell her to fuck off, but then my father would end up in jail on the trumped-up RICO charges she was ready to pounce on. It was the ball she dangled over my head. The reason I was doing this in the first place. It was the reason she had me picked up four months ago. She'd hoped my bleeding heart over my father would persuade me to help her—and she was right.

The Racketeer Influenced and Corrupt Organizations Act allowed the DEA to gather enough circumstantial information on my father for him to be formally charged for crimes not committed by him but linked to him through his assistance. The only way he would be spared from being charged was if I agreed to cooperate with the DEA and get them all the information they wanted.

God help me, Agent Meg Blanchet, the she-devil with her red hair, red shoes, and matching red lips, has been yanking my chain for way too long, and I'd just about had enough. But then I thought about my old man behind bars and knew I had to keep going. I'd done everything she asked of me in terms of cooperation—met with her at Molly's every week to give her updates on my father's "calls" for Patrick, or at any time she deemed appropriate. She wanted Killian, or more accurately the Mob-linked crime information that existed only in his head, to further her case against the Flannigan family.

With much hesitation, soon after the night she brought me in, I talked to my gramps. I told him she wanted names, dates, and facts—information he'd never want to give. "To be a rat!" he'd screamed.

I left there that night convinced he wasn't going to do it, but in the end, he, like me, couldn't stand to see my father go to prison. We both knew he'd never come out still breathing. He was weak and he'd be eaten alive on the inside. Because of this, and this only, Killian agreed to meet with the DEA and we both agreed to keep this task I'd been strapped with from my old man. He didn't need any more bullshit to deal with.

The final provision of my agreement with the DEA, the one that would free my father, the one that I couldn't wait to deliver, was the information on the next cocaine shipment. They wanted to witness the exchange between buyer and seller. With that, there would be enough solid proof that Patrick and Tommy Flannigan were running the biggest drug ring to hit the Boston streets in years.

The only reason I'd been doing this bullshit for the past four months now was because with Patrick and Tommy behind bars, both my father and I would be free. And now so would Elle and Gramps.

I couldn't wait.

"Let me see what I can find out. I'll call when I know anything."

She tsk-tsked. "I'll be waiting."

The line disconnected and my foot slammed down on the gas. At ninety miles an hour, I was back in the limits of Boston by eight forty-five. I tried Elle's cell but she didn't pick up.

Taking a chance, I decided to hit up the boutique first. She was still staying with O'Shea, so if she wasn't there, she had to be at work.

Whether or not she knew anything, I'd already decided I would have to come clean and tell her what was going on. She had to get to O'Shea and find out where the product had been delivered. The drop point was key in the investigation, and the place and people would be used as the link to O'Shea, and in turn to Patrick and Tommy.

O'Shea would be collateral damage.

I knew Elle wouldn't want anything to happen to him, but if he were smart, he'd make a deal with Blanchet. That wasn't my concern—my concern was my father, and now Elle.

Where Lizzy fit in, I had no idea.

The pieces were sketchy.

She was somehow involved with Tommy, but whether it was with O'Shea's knowledge or not, I didn't know.

My cell rang again when I was about a block from the boutique. It was my old man.

"Yeah, Pop."

"Hey, I have Declan and Miles with me. Miles did some recon and found out that before Elizabeth Sterling O'Shea got married—less than two years ago, I might add—she had been arrested a slew of times, for drugs, disorderly conduct, and the last time, a prostitution charge. And guess where she was last employed before marrying O'Shea?"

"I don't know, Pop. Where?" My nerves were shot and I didn't have time for twenty questions.

"Lucy's."

"That's how she knows Tommy," I guessed.

"Yeah, and I'm going to go through payroll and see how

long she worked there."

I dragged a hand down my face. "Might help."

"There's something else—I pulled up the records and you're never going to believe who was the pro bono attorney assigned to her case."

I slammed the steering wheel. "Son of a bitch."

"Yep. Turns out O'Shea got her off and gave her a job as his secretary. Soon after they married, and seven months after that, she gave birth."

"Seven months?"

"Yep."

"So she was pregnant before she got married. That's not a crime."

"No, but her priors show years of arrests, usually drug-related charges. Then nothing after the baby. Seems she cleaned up fast."

Maybe a little too fast.

Or maybe not at all.

"Thanks. I have some things to take care of, but I'll be in touch."

"Everything okay, son? I thought you'd be jumping at this information."

I parked my SUV. "Yeah, it's fine. I gotta run. I'll call you later."

I disconnected and walked toward the boutique. There was so much going on, I was finding it hard to focus on anyone—anyone but her.

The lights were on, but I didn't see her. After I knocked, I figured she must be downstairs. I still had the key she'd given me on my key chain and decided to use it.

I knew I'd scare the ever-living shit out of her, but I needed to talk to her. I also needed to see her.

It had been three days.

Three days too many.

I hated what had happened when she'd called me the other night, but Blanchet had come into Molly's and I—well, obviously I'd done a shitty job of covering us up.

Besides, I'd vowed to stay away from Elle until Friday.

But now, Friday was only one day away and if things went according to plan, we could soon be together without worry.

Together forever if we wanted.

Did I want that?

My mind was such a fucked-up mess. Still, I knew wanting her wasn't some fleeting feeling. It was an ache getting worse with each passing moment that I didn't have her. I felt like I could love this woman that I'd only just met. Was that even possible?

First the old butler bell chimed, which didn't alert anyone to shit, and then the alarm started to chime, which at least she'd activated. I typed in the code B-L-O-W.

"Elle," I called.

She didn't answer.

Her red felt hat sat behind the counter, and seeing it made me smile.

Feeling oddly happy, I took the stairs two at a time as I descended them. Excitement stirred within me. My world had changed. Not only was it upside down but inside out. I wasn't the same man who walked the streets of Boston alone. I never wanted to be that man again. Tommy would soon be locked away forever and then Elle would be beside me. Where she belonged.

Random, strange, somewhat foreign thoughts entered my head and unknown feelings swirled within me. She'd gotten under my skin, into my bones, and somehow had become a part of my soul. It could only mean one thing. Yes, I did love Elle and I was going to tell her so—right now.

The steps seemed like way too many. We were so close and still way too far apart. I turned the corner and—

My hands grabbed my head.

No!

No!

No!

My world started spinning on an entirely new axis.

There she was, on the floor, with a number of opened and unopened white plastic bags surrounding her.

Fuck!

I froze.

I couldn't breathe.

I gasped and choked.

No. No. No.

I looked at her again.

Fuck!

Sometimes you know something's coming.

You feel it. In the air. In your gut.

You don't sleep at night. The voice in your head is warning you, but there's nothing you can do to stop it.

That's how I'd felt since the day I met Elle.

The problem was—my warning bells were all wrong.

"Elle?" I'm not even sure how I managed to say her name.

Alarmed, she jumped and realizing someone was downstairs, she scurried to close the bags.

"Elle," I repeated.

Slowly, she turned. "Logan, what are you doing here?"

My heart stopped. My pulse faded. Shock was all I felt. "You knew?" My words came out in stuttered syllables. "You were part of it all along?" My voice held disbelief.

Elle shook her head. "No. It's not what you think."

The small bags of cocaine were all around her and the floor was covered in some kind of white crystals.

What did she mean it wasn't what I thought?

I wasn't fucking blind.

The cocaine had been transported in an endless amount of some kind of white crystals—into her boutique, and opened by her hands.

She was so fucked.

Suddenly, my head roared with the pain and anger of her deceit. I looked at her, my heart now as hard as steel.

"Shit!" I yelled. "Fuck!" I yelled louder.

"Logan, let me explain." She was crying, stepping

toward me.

I put my hand out. "Don't come near me." The pitch of my voice rose with each word.

There was no way I could stand to have her touch me.

Looking frantic, she kept walking. "You have to listen to me."

Anger ripped through me. I kicked a chair and it sailed across the basement floor.

She came to a halt.

This was all too much.

I walked up the stairs. I walked back down. I walked back up again before settling on the down. Anger and rage and a terrible fear that I couldn't help her now consumed me.

She was standing there like a deer in headlights.

Did she have any idea what being here right now meant?

I knew she didn't. She didn't know that right now, right this moment, she was in jeopardy of being put away for the rest of her life. And sure as shit, she didn't know I would be the one to do it.

I squeezed my eyes shut.

I couldn't look at her or those green eyes.

Where was the invisible trail of magic?

What were *we* to her?

Nothing?

In the darkness, every emotion I'd ever felt for Elle settled in the pit of my stomach, and like the sun's rays, it lit me up from the inside and radiated throughout my entire body.

"Logan, listen to me. Let me explain."

Disbelief beat in my heart. I couldn't listen to her. I couldn't even hear her voice. I couldn't stand her or myself right now. I had to get out of here.

In a sudden burst, I opened my eyes and ran up the stairs.

"Wait," she called, chasing after me.

Her voice made me turn but I didn't stop. I saw the

crushed look in her eyes, the one that matched mine, but still I kept going. With a harsh pull, I yanked the door open and flew right out of it. My feet hit the pavement. My ragged breathing was sucking in the cool air. The sky was dark, but I felt darker.

What the fuck had just happened?

Unable to contain my emotions, I screamed into the night, "Fuckkkk!" and thrust my hands toward the boutique window. When my eyes landed on it, she was there—standing in the window, watching me with fear—no, not fear, terror—in her eyes.

My cell started to ring and I pulled it from my pocket. The screen flashed, *Blanchet*.

This couldn't be happening.

But it was.

When life gets you by the balls, it really gets you.

Five seconds.

I had a choice to make—my father or Elle.

And I had five seconds to do it.

Now how fucking fair was that?

Our eyes locked.

For an endless moment I thought this wasn't happening. A shroud of dishonesty didn't surround her. I hadn't opened myself up to her only to be crushed. But then her guilt presented itself. Sparked through the window. Burned my skin. Sunk its way into my bones. Corroded everything we'd had.

As if she felt it too, she covered her mouth and her nose with her hands pressed together. I was too far away to see for certain, but I was pretty sure she was trembling.

Neither of us looked away.

My gut twisted into a thousand knots.

She had me.

She had me like no one ever had.

She had me hanging on every word.

She had me jumping through hoops.

She could have had me any way she wanted me.

Did she even know what she was doing to me right now? The way she was breaking me down, making me re-think everything?

In her eyes, I could see the panic, hear the pleading, smell the fear.

My resolve was being held together by a tattered string about ready to snap. Unable to look at her for fear it would, I turned around, and with a sharp intake of breath, I an-swered the call.

After all, I'd only ever had one choice.

chapter
THIRTY-THREE

Elle

MY HEART.
   My racing heart dropped into my stomach.
My heart.

It was here and then it was gone.

I could still see it, though. Slick muscle tissue that pounded faster and faster while held in the palms of his hands.

He had the ability to crush it right here and now.

Crush me.

Did he even realize that?

My fingers splayed across the window. My eyes pleaded. My body begged. Words were leaving my lips, but I knew he couldn't hear them.

Still, I spoke them.

"Logan, I love you. I would never hurt you. I didn't know what Michael had planned. I just found out two days ago. I wanted to tell you. I reached out to you to tell you what Michael asked me to do. But you didn't want me. Why are you here? Why are you acting like this? Why won't you listen to me? Why?"

I was babbling.

Spilling everything I could. Begging him to listen with every ounce of my being.

He placed his hands on his lean hips.

Dropped his head.

Lifted his chin.

Looked at me.

Looked away.

I was still babbling.

Then, as if he could hear me through the glass, he tucked his phone in his pocket and took a step toward me. Then another. And another still. He didn't stop until his hands splayed against the window right where mine were.

Mirror images of each other.

His stare locked on mine and we spoke to each other in a way we never had.

Deep.

Heartfelt.

True.

Not words.

Emotions.

Emotions that seemed to seep out of his eyes and into mine. Emotions that, if I was reading him right, mimicked my own.

Could that be?

After a moment, or two, or maybe three, he slowly removed his hands from the glass and the connection was lost. When he started to walk away, I knew I had read him wrong.

Like a rag doll, I collapsed to the floor on my knees. Burying my face in my hands, I cried for everything in my life I'd lost, for what I was doing, for who I was—the weak, pathetic girl my father had always known me to be.

"I am listening," he said in that low, husky voice that did something to my insides.

Snapping my gaze, I looked over toward the door, the sound, him. His arms were crossed over his chest and he was standing in the open doorway, the door itself locked in the open position. He looked dauntless.

Had he heard me?

For the first time since we met, he seemed intimidating. Like a powerhouse. Strong. Fearless. Unyielding. Tougher than his beautiful face and body let on. "Talk to me. What was the plan? We don't have much time."

On shaky legs, I rose to my feet. "Much time for what?"

Logan stepped inside and pushed against the mechanism that kept the door open. Once it closed, he locked it and looked at me. His eyes were distant, his expression blunted by fear or maybe hatred.

I hoped not hatred.

Something pulsed beneath my skin—despair, sorrow, love, agony? Maybe all of those feelings rolled into one.

With quick strides, he closed the distance between us and I felt like we weren't lost in this sea of a world where neither of us belonged. Yet, I knew we were. His hands on my shoulders sent that familiar energy zapping through my body and I knew that despite everything, he didn't hate me. "Elle, I need to know the plan."

My thoughts were humming inside my brain. "Logan, it's not what you think. I didn't know. All I knew up until a couple of days ago was that Michael said he'd handle it. I thought he meant legally, or—no that's not true, I don't know what I thought, but it wasn't this. I had no idea what his actual plan was. If I had, I would have told you."

"I believe you. I do. Now, please, tell me what he asked you to do."

My breath was coming fast, but my words came even faster. "He told me that the coke would be delivered tonight or tomorrow morning."

"From where? From who?" Logan cut in before I could finish.

"I don't know. He never said and I never asked."

"Where's the delivery slip?"

I pointed to the counter.

He darted over to it and picked up the pink piece of

paper, and then shook his head. "It was COD?"

I nodded. "Michael told me to pay with one of my company checks."

He shook his head. "The only portion completed is the 'ship to' information. Any idea who sent it?"

Nerves rattled me. "No. The plastic bags were on a pallet and it was wrapped in cellophane. The driver cut open the sealed pallet and carried the bags in."

Logan's expression was raw. "What did O'Shea want you to do with them?"

"I was to break the bags down and bring the—" I couldn't even say the word.

He leaned closer. "Coke," he said for me.

I nodded. I swallowed. I was finding it hard to breathe. I'd never, ever, done anything like this. "Product home in the Mercedes and park in the garage. He was going to store it in the panic room."

Logan's eyes were intense as he stared down at me. "And then what?"

I squeezed my eyes shut. "Then he'd give it to Patrick and Clementine would be safe from danger, from the kidnapping threats he'd received."

"Kidnapping threats?" Logan's brows popped.

"Yes. Michael told me that your father called him a few days ago and threatened that if he didn't deliver the drugs Lizzy had stolen, there was a very good chance his little girl would be taken and held for ransom."

That one simple fact brought it all back into perspective. I turned on my heels and headed for the stairs. I had to get the product to Michael.

To keep Clementine safe, I'd do *anything*.

Logan captured my hands and held my wrists to keep me from walking away. "That's not true."

Frowning, I glared at him. "Do you think I'm lying?"

We were both breathing fast. "No, I think O'Shea is. My father would never do anything like that. He's lying to you, Elle. Don't you see? He's been playing you. It was his plan all along to do this, to include you at the end. It had to be."

I lifted my chin, defiant, determined. Thoughts were churning in my mind and the more I thought about it, the less my bravado held strong. "No, Logan. He's doing what he has to in order to protect his daughter."

"Then where'd the coke come from?"

I looked at him. I'd already told him I didn't know.

"He had to have had it stashed somewhere. Don't you see—he's been putting your life and Clementine's in harm's way."

"Why would he do that?"

"Who the fuck knows? Waiting to see what he could get away with."

I didn't want to believe it, but where *did* all the coke come from?

"Listen to me, Elle. I've been working with the DEA for more than four months to help bring down the Flannigan family."

Shock ripped through me. "Working, how? Why?"

"They threatened to arrest my father if I didn't cooperate, and tonight is the night they are looking to bring it all home. They want the drugs, the location, the people involved, and they want me to furnish it."

Crippling horror shook my entire body. I stifled my scream. My urgency to run was never greater. How could I take care of Clementine behind bars? How could I leave her? "No, Logan. No," I cried hysterically.

My wrists were still imprisoned in his grasp, but his grip became loose and his hands spread, searching for my fingers. He was holding my hands. He was leaning his body against mine. He was whispering in my ear. I was an utter mess. Hysterical. Unresponsive. Terrified.

"I'm not going to let anything happen to you. I care about you."

His words punched the air out of me. They were an echo. They were on repeat. He was saying them over and over until finally I heard him.

My gaze flickered up to his. "You care about me?"

He nodded but didn't repeat it. "And you have to trust me. I will make this right."

My world was shattering into a thousand pieces. "How? How can this ever be right?"

He pulled me closer still. His mouth was now hovering over my ear. "I'm going to take the cocaine and plant it at a strip club that Tommy and Patrick own. Then I'm going to call the DEA and tell them you overheard Michael talking on the phone and mentioned an exchange at Lucy's. While I'm moving the coke, you are going to go to O'Shea and tell him you were mistaken and it wasn't his shipment that arrived. It was something else for the boutique. Tell him you called the company and it had been subbed out to a third party, and that it is scheduled for delivery first thing in the morning. Don't mention me. Don't say anything else. I want you out of this. The DEA are watching the house, so if anything happens, look for the unmarked cars on the street."

"What if Michael doesn't believe me?"

"Don't give him the chance to question you. He knows Peyton was hurt, right?"

I nodded.

"Tell him she called you and she didn't sound good. Tell him you think you should go stay with her for the night and that you'll be at work first thing in the morning. Then pack your bag and leave."

"Can't I just call him?"

He shook his head. "I want the DEA to see you go there so they can confirm you gave me the information after talking to O'Shea. Call me as soon as you talk to O'Shea. Then I'll know I can call the DEA. Got it?"

My heart was beating so fast. My pulse was racing. This was beyond lying. This was deception. This was a high-stakes game I had no business being involved in. "Yes," I managed.

He gave me a knowing nod and then released his grip

on me. "Clementine isn't home, right?"

"No, she's not—she's at Erin's."

Just then, as if it knew we needed a reminder of how we'd started out, that damn cuckoo clock from Germany started to sing.

In the midst of all the madness, he still gave me a grin.

I wanted to kiss him but wasn't certain that was anything he'd want.

As if reading my mind, Logan kissed me, hesitantly. Lightly.

"Kiss me harder," I said against his mouth.

He did.

And we kissed and kissed and kissed.

Rough. Teeth clashing. Chins bumping. Lips biting.

Breathless, we both pulled apart.

"What do I do after I pack a bag?" I asked.

Logan yanked out his wallet and opened it, handing me ten crisp one-hundred-dollar bills. "You go to the Mandarin on Boylston Street, at the intersection—"

"I know where it is," I interrupted.

"Check in and use cash under the last name Smith. Leave a key for me. I'll be there as soon as I'm done. And you said Peyton was coming back to work tomorrow?"

I nodded.

"See if you can get her to open up the boutique. By then the bust should be all over the news and Michael won't be looking to make any deliveries to Patrick. Still, just in case, I'd rather you be unreachable until I can figure out what's next."

I nodded again. "What do I tell him after he learns the cocaine is in Tommy's possession?"

Logan was silent for a few moments. "Tell him you don't have a clue. He'll have to assume the delivery was intercepted."

I wanted to cry, my eyes desperate, terrified, darting toward the stairs where down below lay my future. If anything went wrong, I could easily be locked away forever.

Oh, God.

Did I say that out loud? I didn't mean to.

"Elle, it's going to be okay. You and Clementine will be safe. Now go—I got this. I'll clean it all up."

In a daze, I went to the counter to gather my things.

Safe?

Was that ever going to be possible?

I just didn't think so.

chapter
THIRTY-FOUR

LOGAN

M Y HANDS WERE SHAKING as I pressed the up
arrow.

My stomach turning.

It was after midnight.

And I'd just committed a felony.

A Class B felony, punishable by prison time.

A shit-ton of prison time.

I was an attorney who'd sworn to uphold the law and
I'd just not only moved one hundred bricks of cocaine, but
also interfered with a major DEA investigation.

Also on my mind, I'd moved one hundred of the two
hundred and fifty missing kilos.

Was this really a new shipment?

Was it part of the missing deal gone bad?

If so, where was the rest?

I had no fucking clue.

Still, a major bust.

Enough to take down the Flannigan family?

I hoped so.

I'd done just what I told Elle I would. Packed up the
coke, cleaned up the salt crystals, and then driven to

Lucy's. I had a stop to make along the way. I needed empty liquor boxes. I called Frank. Told him what I needed. No questions asked. He'd been an informant on the DEA's payroll since the Tommy incident. He was also a messenger to Blanchet when I needed him to be. I knew I could trust him. The only thing he asked in return was that I stay as far away from Molly as I could. That was the least I could do.

It was well after midnight and the alley behind the strip joint was dark. Perfect. I was just starting to unload the coke into the boxes when that fucking phone call finally came. It seemed to take forever, and I was beginning to think I was going to have to abandon my plan and drive over to O'Shea's to make sure Elle was in one piece. And more than likely kill O'Shea if he'd touched a hair on her head.

All went well, though, and she was safely on her way to the hotel. Moving quickly, I restacked the boxes outside the back door and took off.

Not the safest plan.

Not the smartest plan.

If anyone came around looking in the trash, I was screwed. But my hope was that the she-devil would make her move quickly. I made the call, kept it short, and hung up on Blanchet while she was yelling at me for not being able to witness the exchange, since the product was already at the drop.

Shaking it off, happy it was almost done but knowing it wasn't over by a long shot, I used the key Elle had left for her "husband" at the desk and stepped inside.

In that moment, just as the door closed behind me, I felt an overwhelming sense of arousal. The room was small, just a giant bed, a closet, a bathroom that I knew she'd just showered in, and her, safe, and larger than life. The arousal I felt when I laid eyes on her wasn't the kind of juvenile jolt a Victoria's Secret catalog or *Sports Illustrated* swimsuit issue would have stirred up when I was fourteen. No, it was . . . I didn't know . . . like my whole mind, not just my body, was suddenly overcome by everything she was.

She was wearing the hotel's white robe and she was fidgeting with the terry-cloth belt. "Are you okay?" she breathed with a sigh a relief.

My gaze flickered hot over her.

She stopped her fussing. "I know you're upset with me. I'm sorry."

My whole life has felt like I've been suppressing my emotions and right now, I just couldn't do it any longer. I needed a release. I needed something real. I needed . . . I needed her. I stabbed my finger in the air. "Stop that shit right now. I understand why you did what you did, but you should have told me about it first."

She looked guilty. "I know. I'm not sure what came over me, but I heard that woman's voice over the phone line and shut down."

We stared at each other without blinking. "That was the DEA agent. You have to know I don't want anyone but you. How could you not know that?" My voice was raised, rougher and tougher than I wanted it to be. But there was so much bottled up inside me, I couldn't contain my anger and frustration. It was just leaking out.

Elle took a step toward me, her own anger now blazing in her eyes. "You should have told me what you were doing all along. You lied to me!"

My strides were quick. "No. I didn't. I just didn't tell you. I couldn't! There was too much at stake."

We were toe to toe like fighters in a ring. "You didn't tell me. I didn't tell you. What a pair!" Her voice was sardonic, laced with bitterness.

I looked into those green eyes. "We are a pair."

She raised her arms out and gave a sarcastic laugh. "So, as a pair, where does this leave us?"

I gripped her upper arms, bringing them down. "Together!" I shouted.

"Together?" her voice was questioning but still filled with anger.

I licked my lips. I tasted salt. "You're pissed at me

because I was at a bar with a woman I hate?"

"No, I'm not pissed at all."

My arms slid down her sides to her hips. "Then what are you?"

Her brave façade melted away instantly. "Relieved. Thankful. Grateful."

"Then show me. Tell me. Or let me show you. Let me tell you how I feel. I need to be able to communicate with you, and conversations aren't always the best way for me to do that."

In a flash, she untied her robe and I stepped back so I could watch as she shrugged it off. "Fuck me. Tell me how you feel. Show me," she whispered.

She was naked and my entire body was on overload. Amped on adrenaline, or love, or fear—I didn't know which. I didn't care. I just stepped toward her. "You sure?"

She swallowed, and this time the sound that left her throat was more like a purr. "Yes. I've never been more sure of anything in my life."

Quickly, very quickly, I dropped to my knees in front of her and buried my face between her legs. "Because I need to taste you," I told her with my nose at her clit, my tongue jetting in and out of her pussy right off the bat. Her sweetness was just too much. I couldn't get enough. My hands skimmed the back of her thighs and I brought her closer.

Her hands went to my hair, lightly at first, barely skimming it. She said something. I wasn't certain what, but it sounded like, "That feels so good."

"I need to feel how wet I make you."

She moaned so loud, I felt it down to my core and with that, I began to eat her up. Devour her. All along letting her know just how sweet she tasted.

Her fingers sunk further into my hair, tugging at it. She cried out and it was rough and raw. My hands were on her ass, holding her close, and I licked every inch of her pussy. Her moans were electrifying, and I hooked one of her legs over my shoulder so I could really get inside her. The flicks of my tongue were quick at first and then sliding it down, I buried it deep inside her with alternating sucks, licks, and flicks.

She was close. I could tell. "Come for me, Elle," I commanded.

As if on cue, she cried out. "Oh, God, Logan, I am. I'm coming. I'm coming. I'm coming for you. Don't stop. Don't stop."

Words spoken in the heat of the moment . . .

Music to my ears.

I couldn't deny that this was real anymore.

It was all too real.

Both sated and breathless, I drew in a shuddering breath and then pulled her closer so I could look at her. I swam for a minute in her gaze. She was flushed, her lips and cheeks pink. Beautiful.

She wrapped her arms around me and we held each other, kissed a little more, rolled around on the bed, and ended up a tangle of limbs. She was between my legs, curled against me with her body pressed snug against my chest, and my arms were wrapped around her protectively.

I gazed down at her. Opened my mouth. Closed it. How was I supposed to have a talk with her about us when I couldn't even bring myself to start the conversation? It's not as if I didn't understand the value of talking. I did. Communication, whether in or out of bed, was going to be key if we were going to survive as a couple when the fallout came from what we'd done.

And sure as shit, it was going to come.

When it did, we were going to have to stand strong, and stand together, and hopefully conquer more than just the world we lived in.

Perhaps, if we were lucky, we'd conquer each other.

Her fingers caressed the bare skin of my chest. "So what

happens when we don't have to hide anymore?"

My laughter was loud.

She tipped her head to look at me. "Why are you laughing? I'm serious."

My fingers wove into her hair and stroked it. "I'm not laughing at you. I'm laughing at my lame-ass self. I've been lying here trying to figure out the best way to start that very conversation and the words just flow effortlessly out of your mouth. Go figure."

She breathed in. She breathed out.

It was my cue to talk and my turn to draw in a deep breath. "We said we'd figure this thing out between us together and I think we are. But in all honesty, I've never had a relationship with a woman for longer than a month. With you I don't see an end. I see something between us that could last a long time and I want to give us a chance. I hope after everything, you feel the same way."

Wow, I'd said it.

Her hand ran up to my face and she caressed my cheek. "Logan McPherson, if you're asking me to be your Mrs. Robinson, I accept."

I laughed. "No, definitely not. I'd much rather be the teacher."

She rolled her eyes.

"But, Elle Sterling, how about you agree to be my girlfriend instead?"

She laughed. "Aren't we a little old for that?"

I raised a suggestive brow. "*Lover* sound better?"

She wrinkled her nose. "That makes us sound too old."

Feeling bold, I countered with, "Master?"

Her laugh was wicked. "I'll pass on that one."

Shifting my mouth, I kissed her fingers. "I have a few more, but I don't think you'll like them. That takes us back to *girlfriend.* Besides, there are men at my gramps's nursing home who have girlfriends."

She laughed.

Clutching her hand in mind, I asked again, "So, Elle

Sterling, would you like to be my girlfriend?"

She stared at me.

"Don't make me beg because I will."

Elle grew serious. "I'd like that, Logan. Very much."

I think I heard her whisper, "My protector," and my chest puffed in pride. Then I kissed the corner of her mouth and spoke with honesty. "I know we skipped over all the preliminaries, but maybe it was better that way."

She nodded in agreement. "First everythings are so blasé."

"Not all first everythings," I reminded her.

We both laughed and then allowed a comfortable silence to fill the room. We breathed together and for a few short minutes, the only sound besides the rhythm of our breaths was that of our beating hearts. For once, I could hear the outside traffic beeping and blaring but didn't want to get up and check it out. We were together now, safe, and looking forward to what the future held.

"You hungry?" I asked.

She tipped her head to put her lips on my throat. "Very."

I was pretty certain it wasn't food she was referring to, but I was also pretty certain neither of us had eaten. And since I wasn't anywhere near finished with having her, a shower and some food first would probably be a good idea. "Burgers?" I asked with a grin.

"With fries and ketchup." She smiled up at me.

"Like there's any other way."

Rolling off the bed, I stepped back and looked her over, head to toe. I knew my smile was wicked and I also knew what it did to her. Shivers rocked her body and usually her lids would fall in the most seductive way. I gave her one last knowing glance before I picked up the phone and ordered room service.

She rolled over onto her back with a satisfied sigh. The sheet had slipped and she was naked under it. I thought about taking her again, but first I needed to take a shower. I leaned over to push her hair away from her face. "You're so gorgeous, you know that?"

She propped herself up on her elbows and blew a wayward strand of hair from her face and then made a self-deprecating sound.

I laughed and pulled her mouth to mine. "You are. Now, I'm going to hop in the shower and come back and show you just how much I think so."

This time her response was much more enthusiastic.

"I won't be long," I promised her and headed for the bathroom.

"Logan," she called.

I turned.

"I love you," she whispered.

My body seized up. I hadn't spoken those words to a woman, ever. I might have said them to Emily when I was trying to get her in the sack, but they hadn't been real; it wasn't true love. It wasn't this burn I felt in my chest when I looked at Elle. It wasn't the fear I wore beneath my skin that something would happen to her. No, that wasn't love. This, however, was.

Still, the words stuck in my throat. Burned, settled halfway. I was scared. Scared that if I said them, something bad would happen. And how ridiculous was that? Finally, I sucked in a breath. "I love you too, Elle," I said, and turned back around with my pulse pounding and my heart beating wildly.

Some kind of bad feeling had rolled over me again. I shook it off and hit the hot water.

A towel around my waist and one at my shoulders, I came out of the bathroom ten minutes later, feeling much better. Elle was sitting on the bed with the robe wrapped around her and the Channel 7 news on.

"Breaking news," the TV correspondent announced.

My head snapped to the screen. "Members of the powerful Flannigan crime family are among at least twenty-four people arrested tonight in a major drug raid. Details are sketchy, but a confirmed two million dollars in cocaine has been seized. We'll bring you the latest as it unfolds."

"It's over?" Elle asked.

With a grin, I answered, "It's over."

Just then there was a knock on the door. "Coming," I answered, slipping my pants on and pulling out my wallet.

Feeling on top of the world, I opened the door. A man was standing there with the cart of food and a single rose in a vase. I signed the receipt and gave him a fifty. My thoughts were drifting as I closed the door. Feeling like an idiot, I took the rose from the vase and handed it to Elle. "For you," I said with a bow.

Her smile was wide. "Thank you, my prince."

"King," I corrected her with a laugh.

She raised a brow.

I shrugged. "*King* sounds much more manly."

She pulled me in for a kiss that I could easily have gotten lost in, but I didn't want our food to get cold and we had the rest of the night, and who knows, maybe the rest of our lives to do to each other whatever we wanted.

Nipping at her lip, I pulled away and rolled the cart closer to the bed where she sat. Feeling like the king of my own castle, I took her covered plate, presented it to her in a royal fashion, and then removed the lid. "For you, my queen."

Giggling, she asked, "What's this?"

My eyes darted to the plate.

She lifted a slip of paper that lay folded on it.

That feeling of fear came back full blown.

With a clunk, I dropped the lid to the ground and quickly swiped the note from her hand.

I didn't want to alarm her, but something just didn't feel right.

With trembling fingers, I unfolded the paper.

It read, "That E wasn't meant for Emily."

And just like that, my kingdom collapsed.

Don't miss
Crush

Pre-order Crush *Now*
(Book Two in the Tainted Love Duet)
Releasing November 16th 2015

ACKNOWLEDGMENTS

To Amy. Thank you for always believing in me.

To all the amazing bloggers that have dedicated their time to reading my books and sharing their experience with reviews. Please know that without your voice, it would be difficult to spread the word and to find new readers.

To all my readers. Thank you for allowing me to tell you my stories. It is truly a gift and an honor to occupy your mind for a few hours. I love your messages, emails, and reviews, so please keep them coming.

To those who have helped me tirelessly with this book. You know who are and thank you!

Much love,
Kim

OTHER BOOKS
BY KIM KARR

TOXIC

Meet Jeremy McQueen, a sexy, intense, brooding entrepreneur who goes after what he wants, and Phoebe St. Claire, a socialite-turned-CEO who's been drifting through life searching for something she thought she'd never find again—the right man to share her future.

Phoebe St. Claire has devoted herself to saving her family's hotel empire—but her best efforts have not been good enough. With her whole world in turmoil, the tenacious go-getter turns to the once love of her life. Far from innocent, Jeremy McQueen was a guy from the wrong side of the tracks, and her parents would never have approved. Their years apart have only made the sexy bad boy more irresistible than ever—and their reunion is explosive.

When she asks Jeremy to help her salvage her family business, he agrees immediately, with only one condition—he wants her in his bed.

But soon surprising circumstances leave Phoebe reeling. Was this fairy-tale romance just too good to be true? Will Jeremy's secrets pull them apart all over again?

NO CLIFFHANGER. STANDALONE ROMANCE.

THE 27 CLUB

Janis Joplin. Kurt Cobain. Amy Winehouse. Zachary Flowers. I always knew my brilliant brother would one day be listed among the great artistic minds of our time. I just didn't know he would join the list of exceptional talents who left us too young, too soon.

I was always the calm one, the perfect foil to his free-wheeling wild spirit. But since his death shortly after his 27th birthday, I'd found myself adrift and directionless.

I knew it was time to face my destiny, and I was ready to yield. But then I met Nate, Zachary's best friend. Only he could help me put the pieces together, fill in the blanks that Zachary left behind. I needed him to answer my questions—and I wanted him for more. He awakened in me a sensuality that had never been explored, never satisfied. Nate's presence controlled me, his touch seared me, and it was up to me to convince him that he was brought into my life for a reason. . . .

NO CLIFFHANGER ENDING.

THIS IS A STANDALONE ROMANCE.

THE CONNECTIONS SERIES

Connected
Torn
Dazed
Mended
Blurred
Frayed

KIM KARR IS A *New York Times* and *USA Today* bestselling author.

She grew up in Rochester, New York, and now lives in Florida with her husband and four kids. She's always had a love for reading books and writing. Being an English major in college, she wanted to teach at the college level, but that was not to be. She went on to receive an MBA and became a project manager until quitting to raise her family. Kim currently works part-time with her husband and recently decided to embrace one of her biggest passions—writing.

Kim wears a lot of hats: writer, book-lover, wife, soccer mom, taxi driver, and the all-around go-to person of her family. However, she always finds time to read. One of her favorite family outings when her kids were little was taking them to the bookstore or the library. Today, Kim's oldest child is seventeen and no longer goes with her on these now rare and infrequent outings. She finds that she doesn't need to go on them anymore because she has the greatest device ever invented—a Kindle.

Kim likes to believe in soul mates, kindred spirits, true friends, and happily-ever-afters. She loves to drink champagne and listen to music, and hopes to always stay young at heart.

CONNECT WITH KIM
Twitter @AuthorKimKarr
Facebook *www.facebook.com/AuthorKimKarr*
Website *www.authorkimkarr.com*
Instagram https://instagram.com/authorkimkarr/

FOR THE READER

Thank you for purchasing and reading this book. If you enjoyed it, please leave a short review on the site where you purchased it, or on any other book-related sites such as Goodreads or your favorite review forum. Readers rely on reviews, as do authors.

AND NOW: A FIRST LOOK INSIDE

CHAPTER 1

DAY 8 CONTINUED

LOGAN

SAY YOU WANTED SOMEONE eliminated . . .
Killed.

It doesn't matter who—your mother, your lover, your enemy.

There are guys out there who will do it for you.

It's a fact.

Not someone from the Mob.

Not someone connected to the Mob.

Not anyone you know.

A hit man.

I've heard of ways to contact one. Someone who knows someone who knows someone.

Someone from the old neighborhood. Someone with

prison tats. Someone who maybe wears a do-rag. Who the fuck cares—he could look like Motely Crue. Hell, on the other hand, he could be a business man wearing a two thousand dollar suit.

I really don't give a shit.

What he looks like is irrelevant. It's what he does that matters.

Sure, there's a steep monetary price attached to the deed. That's not what worries me.

I'd give every cent I had if it meant she'd be safe.

It's what it would really cost me—how big a piece of my soul it would take—that keeps me from making that call.

I reread the note, "That E wasn't meant for Emily."

One thing was clear . . .

He knows about Elle and me.

Tommy Flannigan, my enemy, my foe, the mob boss's son, the one I have been forbidden to make contact with, knows I have someone in my life that I care about. He might even know I love her. And she's not his sister. She's not Emily. Because I defied him, because I dared to move on, I know he'll taunt me, try to break me, try to drive me out of my mind.

For over a decade he's loomed over me.

He threatened me, mutilated a girl I'd dated, and just last week harmed one he thought was Elle. He was into drugs as a user as well as a cutthroat player in the Blue Hill Gang. He was always crazy, but lately he'd been breaking all the rules. Nothing was safe from him anymore—it was like he had nothing left to lose these days.

Breaking the treaty wasn't a surprise.

The thing he doesn't get is I'm no longer fearful. As of right this minute, the rules of the street no longer apply to me. There is too much at stake for me to think about what could happen if I went up against the Blue Hill Gang. I have to think about what has to happen in order to keep her safe. And that's one thing, and one thing only.

Tommy's threat has to be eliminated.

Somehow.

Someway.

But murder for hire would have to wait.

I looked over into Elle's eyes.

Paralyzed.

Frozen in place.

Wide.

Scared.

Still beautiful.

I haven't even known her for two weeks, but she's a part of me. I can't—no, I won't—let anything happen to her.

"Logan," she whispered quietly.

Escaping from my thoughts, I wanted to say something. Something profound. Something that would make sense. Something that would make everything okay. But there was nothing.

My eyes searched her face. As soon as they did, I saw the once glimmering green in her eyes was now dull, and her lips were quivering.

It made my chest tighten.

But it was when I saw the apprehension in her body language, the hairs on her arm rise, the unsteady rise and fall of her breathing—the fear she didn't want me to see, the fear she was trying to hide from me—that I knew what I had to do.

I had to find him.

Now.

I was going to settle the score with Tommy Flannigan once and for all.

Whatever the outcome.

The note crumpled in my fist and I let it drop to the floor. Tugging my shirt on, I once again looked over at her. "Stay here, lock the door, and don't let anyone in. I mean it, not anyone except me. I don't care who they say they are."

"Where are you going?" Fear laced her voice.

"To find Tommy."

"But the news, they said members of the Flannigan

family had been arrested. Maybe he's already in custody."

I looked down at the note on the floor. I had a gut feeling he wasn't. This wasn't something he'd send someone else to do. This was something he'd take too much pleasure in doing himself. "Maybe he is," I said to help calm her nerves, "But someone arranged to deliver that note to this room, and I'm going to find who it was."

"Logan, no." She reached for me as I slid my feet into my shoes.

I had to shrug away from her.

I had to do this.

On my way to the door, I stopped for just a single moment to look at her. In that moment there was nothing more I wanted than to feel her arms around me, press my body to hers, look into her eyes and tell her we were going to be just fine.

But that would be a lie.

And I wasn't going to lie to her.

Not about this.

"Logan," she pleaded.

I heard the pain in her voice and my heart stopped. Still, I kept moving. I had to do this—for her. The door closed behind me and I heard the latch.

She'd be safe in there until I returned or . . .

My despair was immediately replaced with rage as my eyes fell on the white jacket of the guy who had delivered the note. Unable to control myself, I rushed for him, but came to an abrupt stop when I got a little closer. He was standing in the hallway with his back to me, kissing a girl, also in uniform. I waited. She giggled, gave him a wave, and then walked down the hall. As soon as he entered the waiting elevator it started to close, and I darted for it.

My hands jammed between the panels and the doors flew open.

There he stood.

Lipstick on his lips.

Smiling.

Like he didn't have a care in the fucking world.

He couldn't have been more wrong.

I lunged for him.

Had his lipstick-stained collar in my hands so fast, I could barely see the fear in his eyes. "Who put that note on the food cart?" I hissed.

He was shaking. "I don't know what you're talking about."

With a tug, my grip tightened. "I'm not going to ask you twice. Who put the note on the food cart?"

There was a dripping sound on the elevator floor. I think he pissed his pants. "Some dude paid me fifty bucks to slip it onto your tray. He said it was a joke between you and him."

I slammed him against the wall. "What did he look like?"

Mumbling, words barely coherent, he answered, "Short, brown hair, piercings, and he had a limp."

Tommy.

"Where is he now?"

"I don't know."

"Where is he?" I said through gritted teeth.

The guy was crying. "I don't know."

I loosened my grip. "Where did you leave him?"

He crumbled against the wall. "Outside the kitchen door."

I hit the service level. "Scan your card. Show me."

Shaking, he nodded. "Look, mister, I didn't mean to cause any trouble. He said it was a joke. I believed him."

My body went rigid.

A joke!

When I slipped my hand in my pocket, he raised his palms. "Don't hurt me. I didn't mean anything by it."

Ignoring him, I pulled out my money and handed him a fifty. "Just show me where you saw him last. I'm not going to hurt you."

Visibly relaxing, he scanned his card and the elevator

glided down toward the service level.

Within minutes we were just outside the kitchen.

With a shaky finger he pointed. "He was standing right there when he approached me, but once he gave me the note, he headed for the stairs."

"Where do they lead?"

"To the lobby."

I gave him a nod. "Thanks, man. I didn't mean to scare you."

His laugh was more like a cry. "Nah, I wasn't really worried," he said.

That was a lie.

Taking the stairs two at a time, I pushed open the door and hit the service hallway. Once inside the Mandarin lobby, I scanned it and then the lounge. *Nothing.* No sign of him. I searched the bar. The restrooms. The offices. *Nothing.* I climbed the grand staircase and then combed the exterior of the building. *Nothing.* He was nowhere in sight.

That didn't mean shit.

CHAPTER 2

Elle

EMOTION RUSHED THROUGH ME.
I wasn't going to cry.

My clothes were scattered and I busied myself dressing.

Seconds passed.

Minutes passed.

Pacing, counting steps, back and forth from the door to the window, I wore a path into the carpet.

Finally, I couldn't take the monotony and flopped on the bed. Unsure of what to do, my thoughts started to wander.

My defense mechanisms weakened with each additional tick of the clock and soon I found myself swallowing against the knot that was lodged in my throat, but I could do nothing about the sting of tears behind my closed eyes.

Logan and I had come so far, so fast.

Neither of us had expected to meet in my brother-in-law's law office less than eight days ago, neither had expected to run into each other at Molly's Pub later that night, and certainly neither of us meant to have this intense connection.

It was all so surreal.

Somehow we'd become entangled in a drug war brewing amid the Irish mob here in Boston, and we weren't the only ones.

There was my missing sister. I had no idea how innocent or guilty she actually was. Then there was Logan's father, who had been skirting the edges of the law with the Blue Hill Gang for years. There was also Michael, my brother-in-law, who was acting suspiciously. And on top of all of that, Logan was working undercover with the DEA but also trying to protect me from everyone.

And me? I just wanted to keep my niece, Clementine, safe. And if things went well, have Logan be a part of my life.

The odds were against us.

Was this a sign? Was this fate telling me I should have known better than to think I could belong to him?

I refused to let my thoughts go down that road.

Logan was different.

This was going to work out.

Pushing my issues and insecurities aside, I had to believe that with me by his side, Logan would be strong enough to fight his demons. It was just a note. It didn't scare me. It really didn't. And I was certain it wouldn't scare him. Besides, by all accounts, if the news was correct, Tommy was in jail and no longer a threat to us, *or me.*

I pressed my lips together, keenly aware of the passage of time.

My attention went to the TV, where the Channel 7 news was still on. They were replaying the arrest. I turned the volume up. This time names were flashing across the bottom of the screen.

"More breaking news," the TV correspondent announced. "Members of the powerful Flannigan crime family are among at least twenty-four people arrested tonight in a major drug raid. Details are sketchy, but a confirmed two million dollars in cocaine has been seized. Among those arrested tonight, the alleged head of the Irish Blue Hill Gang, Patrick Flannigan. Sources confirm some members of the family are still at large but all efforts are being made to bring them in. If you have seen any of these men, call our hotline."

I crossed my arms, fighting off the chill that had seeped into my bones. There, before my eyes, was a picture of Tommy Flannigan. I hadn't known his face before now, but I knew I'd never forget it. Those cold brown eyes, the lifeless expression, the evil that was written all over him.

Knock. Knock.

I jumped, startled out of my own skin.

My heart started to race.

My pulse thundered.

Fear set in.

It wasn't like me to be afraid.

I was strong.

I was resilient.

I'd been through a lot in my life and I'd come out on the other side.

Hardened.

Determined.

Immune.

What had changed?

"Elle, it's me—open up." His voice was husky, commanding.

Relief washed through me. "Logan!" I rushed to the door and threw it open.

In a flash, he was inside and locking the door behind him. He slouched against it and his eyes moved over me like he wasn't certain I was really standing here before him, alive, unharmed, in one piece.

With a determined step, I pressed myself against him and stroked my fingers through his beautiful hair. It was rumpled and sticking up everywhere but still, he was breathtaking. "Did you find him?"

He let out a long sigh. "No, not yet."

The words *not yet* made me shiver. I pushed my fingers through his hair again. "His picture is on TV. They said he hasn't been picked up yet."

Logan's eyes closed as if in pain, and then he leaned in and let his forehead rest against mine. "Get your things to-gether—we have to go."

Pausing, I breathed him in—my friend, my lover, the man I loved. I didn't argue. I knew we had to leave. I just wished we didn't. "Give me a minute."

He nodded.

In the bathroom, my reflection confronted me. My hair was a mess. My eyes were red, my face blotchy. My clothes in disarray. Could Logan see that I was scared?

I hoped not.

With a deep breath, I shook off my own fear.

It was just a note.

It didn't mean anything.

What really frightened me wasn't what might happen to me, but what might happen to him.

I heard his voice. He was on the phone. "Fuck you. You said you'd get him. You reassured me he, of all people, would be brought in."

Silence.

"Don't tell me what I can and can't do. I'm going to find him."

Silence again.

"I can't guarantee that."

There was a crash, a thud.

Then silence.

More silence.

I waited to open the door.

He was going to go after Tommy, and there was nothing I could do to stop him.

I was scared. I was scared for him. Sure, he was competent, strong, capable, and dauntless even, but Tommy was a part of the Mob, and the Mob wasn't just one person, not just one set of eyes, or hands, or legs, or barrels of guns ready to hunt him down—it was tens, potentially hundreds.

When I opened the door, Logan was composed and dressed in the same clothes he'd arrived in only hours ago. But it seemed like a lifetime ago.

"Who were you talking to?" I asked.

"Agent Blanchet of the DEA."

Ironically, knowing he was working with them helped soothe my nerves. "What did she say?"

He shrugged. "Nothing. Absolutely nothing. They don't

know where Tommy is. Come on, we have to go."

"Where are we going?"

He indicated I should walk toward him. "I'm going to take you to my father's house."

My steps were slow. "What about you?"

With an extended hand, he urged me to move faster. "I'm going to find Tommy."

Hearing him say it again didn't make the blow any easier. I stopped. "Logan, please don't do this. The police are looking for him. Let them find him."

His head shake was determined. "They'll never find him. He might not be very bright, but he's not stupid."

My fingertips reached for him. "I don't want you to get hurt."

There, I said it.

He took my hand and tugged me toward him. He didn't answer me. Didn't give me false hope. Instead, he kissed me like I was his world. I could feel him, I could taste him, I *was* him. His hands clutched my face tightly as his lips moved against mine. My hands rested on his chest but then moved up to wrap around his neck. I needed to be closer. His moved back and started grabbing fistfuls of my hair. He wanted to be closer too. He held me tight, as if it were the last time we'd be like this. I wanted to fight for control with him, tell him not to kiss me like this, but our lips and our bodies were moving in such perfect sync, I couldn't. It was as if our minds were branding this feeling into our souls, and I didn't want the moment to end until the full image was captured.

When he pulled back, I looked at him. I wanted to beg him to stay with me. Not to go out into the night alone. Yet, I knew there was no arguing with him. He was determined to protect me no matter the cost. Besides, he had already made up his mind, and the way he was staring at me told me what I already feared—if he didn't succeed in finding and stopping Tommy, he was going to leave me in order to save me.

And crush my heart.